THE DARK HORSEMAN

Marianne
Harvey

A DELL BOOK

Published by
Dell Publishing Co., Inc.
1 Dag Hammarskjold Plaza
New York, New York 10017

This work was originally published in Great Britain
by Futura Publications Ltd., London

Copyright © 1978 by Marianne Harvey

All rights reserved. No part of this book may be reproduced
or transmitted in any form or by any means, electronic or
mechanical, including photocopying, recording or by any
information storage and retrieval system, without the written
permission of the Publisher, except where permitted by law.

Dell ® TM 681510, Dell Publishing Co., Inc.

ISBN: 0-440-11758-5

Printed in the United States of America

Previous U.S.A. edition
One printing
New U.S.A. edition
First printing—April 1981

CHAPTER ONE

She gazed with relief at her reflection. The mirror showed a pale self-contained looking woman with dark hair drawn from a center parting under a small perched-up flowery hat. The neck of her tightly cut green velvet bodice reached to the level of her chin, and provided, as she had hoped it would, an air of dignity. Her waist was slim, and appeared even smaller than it was under the gently swelling breasts, where a froth of lace was pinned with the cameo brooch that had been her mother's. The skirt, though simply designed to emphasize her natural grace of movement, was full enough to be fastened from sides to back in the suggestion of a bustle, though without the unnatural horsehair cushion or cage that was fashionable in sophisticated society in that year of 1880.

It was her best dress, and she was thankful that she'd had the sense to keep it fresh and new-looking. It might almost have been designed for the occasion that lay before her now: the distasteful ordeal of her meeting with Nicholas Trevarvas. The fact that just then she looked considerably older than her twenty years gave her further confidence. Trevarvas was a hard man who would not wish to bandy words with a mere girl. Local opinion judged him shrewd and mean, and, despite his enormous wealth, not given to generous acts, unless the outcome was to his own advantage.

Nobody really liked him; most feared him. Ever since she could remember, Donna Penroze had resented his power and arrogance, not only because of the way in which he used people—and it was said women in particular—but because of her father. And Jos.

Once more, as she stood there, with the pale spring sunlight cutting slantwise from the window across her face, accentuating the high cheekbones and strange orange glow of amber eyes, she recalled the day more than a year ago, when Jos Craze had asked her to marry him—the day on which later, her father was to die. Everything had seemed full of promise on that far-off afternoon. She loved Jos, who was the son of her father's mine manager, Tom Craze, and he'd been so full of plans, talking of taking off to the Americas somewhere—Wisconsin, Colorado, Nevada—where increasing numbers of Cornishmen skilled in the working of copper and tin were becoming rich, following the great slump in Cornwall. A new life with her as his wife, he had said. And she'd thought: What more could any eighteen-year-old girl want?

Lying in the cove with his arms around her, lips on hers, gently at first then hot and demanding, traveling from mouth to neck, temples, and firm young breasts beneath her low-cut dress, she'd murmured, "Yes, yes. Oh, yes Jos . . ." unthinking in those sweet, passionate moments of what she would leave behind: her father, the grey house, Trencobban, her home, perched high on the moors, the sea—the restless Atlantic forever breaking below the gaunt north cliffs.

Even the mine, Wheal Faith—a small one according to some standards but meaning so much to her father—had counted little to her just then. Mines were failing everywhere, with the Cornish market for ore being so undercut by trading from Malaya and Bolivia. She had grown used to the depression, to the constant strain imposed on her father while keeping things going and his men employed. It was sad that throughout the countryside so many families were out of work. But it happened; it was life, and had to be accepted.

So for those few hours only the future had mattered. Her future with Jos. Her father wouldn't be left alone anyway. There was her sly puss of a sister-in-law, Jessica, who'd got her brother Luke to marry her, pretending it was his child she carried. What a trick. But it had worked, although after the baby was born, a girl, Janey, Luke Penroze had taken off to sea and got himself drowned.

Poor Luke. Like a frail shadow his sad memory had risen briefly, clouding her happiness, then as quickly gone again.

But as she and Jos were taking the track back to Trencobban, a band of cloud had dimmed the dying sun, and looking up to the right, she'd seen the dark figure of a horseman silhouetted against the sky; the distant square-shouldered form of Nicholas Trevarvas. He was watching them, she'd known that, and there was something about his static pose, forbidding and relentless, that had filled her with queer, mounting apprehension. Her hand had tightened in Jos's.

"What's the matter, Donna?" he'd said, "Seeing ghosts, are you?"

She'd laughed. "Ghosts? Don't be stupid."

But the feeling, vague as it was, had persisted. And when she reached the house, she *knew*, could sense in her bones, that something dreadful had happened; the very silence was uncanny, as though heralding tragedy and loss. She had gone with Jos to the study, and there was William Penroze—the father she'd loved and who'd loved her so much—slumped over the table, head turned to one side, half his face twisted grotesquely, with papers and accounts strewn all around him, one arm hanging down like that of some helpless dummy. Quite dead.

A stroke, the doctor had said later. And she had known why. From strain, because of the mine. The mine her father had told her would be hers one day. His gift to her.

Her heritage.

At that moment she'd changed from a heedless girl into a woman. Known too that she would never leave Trencobban or Wheal Faith which together were a commitment laid upon her that even Jos's pleading couldn't shake.

For the first time she had fully realized how deeply her roots were embedded in that narrow neck of Cornwall reaching between the north and south coasts of Lands End, and in the gray house itself, Trencobban, which had been the home of the Penroze family for so many generations. Since the age of nine, when her mother had died, she had never even been away, except for brief outings to Truro, Falmouth, and Penzance. Her education itself had been limited, undertaken under the supervision of a governess. Although it had been adequate, providing her with the necessary manners and social accomplishments considered suitable to her position as William Penroze's daughter, serious studying on her part had been minimal. Her tastes had always been for outdoor pursuits, for riding and wandering about the coast, for making friends when she had the chance, with whom she chose, rather than with the gentry, a habit that had increased when Miss Trotter, her governess, had left.

William Penroze hadn't seemed to object. Family contacts with workers had proved an asset during that mining depression of the late seventies, when so many stark relics of once thriving mines scarred the moors, and cottages stood empty because their occupants had taken off to other parts of England, or across the sea.

Her association with Jos, therefore, had come about naturally, and inevitably developed into the deep emotional involvement which she had known, that tragic evening, must end.

"Go if you must," she'd said a week later. "Go to your strange new land across the sea. Make your pile and fill your pockets with American gold. I'll be staying here on my own land. My father's land. Somehow I'll keep the mine working. You see. I'll manage."

He'd pleaded and argued, but to no avail. The following month they'd said goodbye, and she'd watched him take off for Falmouth where the mailboat sailed at regular intervals for America.

8

"I'll come back," he said, "and then it'll be different. You'll need me then. There'll be no more scrounging for shillings and pence from barren land. You wait my girl. You just wait."

But she hadn't believed him. As far as she was concerned he had gone forever. Except for Jessica, Luke's wife; the little girl, Janey; and the three servants, Sam Treleor, his wife Sarah, and their boy Ted, she was alone.

Only the house remained: a static monument of the past, a challenge to the future. The house and the mine.

For the next twelve months she had done as she intended, managed somehow, selling the silver, a valuable portrait or two, and other heirlooms, contriving with Tom's help, to keep the "tut" workers paid, and the "tributers," although dissatisfied, still in business. But it had been a losing battle all the time, and now the point of reckoning had come. She had to have money. Three thousand pounds at least, Tom had told her, to purchase the new machinery necessary for sinking a deeper shaft where precious tin lay beneath the copper. No "adventurer" had seemed prepared to invest, and a money-lender would demand far more in interest than she could ever hope to repay.

The only hope, therefore, seemed to be Nicholas Trevarvas. In the past he had refused her father's request to take up shares, even though the sum required would have been a mere fleabite in his vast income. For *that*—and other things—she detested him.

But dislike now had to be camouflagd by pride and charm—sufficient feminine charm to ensnare his co-operation, however abhorrent it might be.

Could she do it? The question, really, was quite irrelevant. She *had* to.

Pulling her mind resolutely from the past once more to the present, she lifted her chin an inch higher, turned her head this way and that, smiled at herself falsely but enchantingly in the mirror, put a little perfume behind each ear, and arranged a light shawl around her shoulders. No woman could have looked more charming, and

9

if Nicholas Trevarvas had been a different type of man she might even have enjoyed the occasion. The challenge lay in her capacity to survive the meeting without giving herself away.

Formerly they'd had little contact, none in a social sense—just brief nods and "good-days"—when they'd met unexpectedly on the road or riding on the moors, and since his wife's death five years earlier, their encounters had been less frequent because he spent a good deal of time in London, at the gaming table some said—others, in extravagant parties with loose women, though no one could prove it, Cornwall being so far away. When he stayed at his house, Polbreath, he had aroused further resentment among the natives by his refusal to "mix," and rumors circulated about orgies where too much drink was taken, and some "furrin wumman or other" presided in the place of his lady wife . . . "God bless her pore soul" . . . who had "bin driven to her grave, the pore thing through his rovin' ways."

But rumor was always quick to take up a story in such remote districts, and the truth was that little was known of Nicholas Trevarvas's private life, except that being so rich he could afford to do what he liked and go where he willed. His already tidy fortune as considerable landowner with two thriving mines Penveel way and four tenant farms, had expanded fourfold since his marriage to Selina St. Venne, the only child of the late Lord Vencarne, who had died from a strange malaise officially diagnosed as "galloping consumption." But afterward people in the neighborhood had whispered knowledgeably, if mystifyingly, of "fox-glove tea," and that had increased Trevarvas's unsavory reputation.

Whether or not Donna believed this dark rumor, she didn't precisely know. What concerned her, and always had, was his refusal to give co-operation and financial ballast when her father had so needed it—a refusal now that had to be overcome, not only in compensation for the past, but to ensure security for the loyal workers of Wheal Faith.

So her mind was sharp, her emotions under full control that day as she walked down the wide staircase and through Trencobban's front door to the drive below. The gig, harnessed by Sam, was already waiting for her. She felt confident and assured as she got in, for she had rehearsed her role numerous times before her mirror.

The day was clear, with a slight wind ruffling the air, wafted sweet from the hills with the tangy scents of young summer. Donna pulled the flimsy veiling from her hat over her eyes, so that no rebellious curls could escape to mar her careful serenity.

It was three miles to Polbreath and, after a short distance, the road cut sharply inland, leading away from the sea to a more lush area of wooded valley, where rhododendrons grew thick among the undergrowth bordering the road. Despite the warm sunshine, there was a shadowed stillness about the district, a damp cloying verdancy that mildly oppressed her after the stark, open vista of the windswept northern coast. The moorland hills, though rising on either side, were indiscernible through the thick trees interlaced overhead. She could have been in another world. A world of shadows and lurking, haunted shapes that even the mere Bess, with her head high and ears pricked, seemed to sense.

But as she entered the tall wrought-iron gates, already open to receive her, everything was suddenly different. The well-kept drive stretched in a straight line for roughly a quarter of a mile, between an avenue of tall elms to a large, early Georgian-fronted mansion above a series of terraced steps.

Donna had glimpsed it briefly once or twice when she'd passed on journeys to the opposite coast, but had seen little, because the gates had been shut then.

She realized now that the rumors of neglect and whispers that everything was going to seed must be untrue. But the knowledge, far from comforting her, only served to tighten her nerves to a pitch of intense apprehension.

Still, if she was surprised, so would he be, she thought, when he saw, instead of the wayward impetuous girl of previous encounters, a young woman of—though not *high* fashion—certainly of enough sophistication to speak up for herself and her project in a businesslike, intelligent manner. She hoped he would also notice that she had retained her feminine capacity to allure.

She was not aware, as she pulled the horse to a walk, that Trevarvas himself had already seen her, and was watching from a reception room of the ground floor as she approached the porticoed entrance. His expression was mildly sardonic, with a hint of wry amusement about the well-carved mouth. Though not handsome, strictly speaking, his dark eyes were fine, shadowed by heavy brows, his nose blunt, and chin determined, with a cleft in it. The whole face betrayed an overpowering will and a contempt of weakness that had made many enemies in the district, but few friends.

He had no sentiment where women were concerned—especially this one, who had flaunted her dislike of him on every possible occasion; but he couldn't help admiring her spirit. Damn it, he thought, she had nerve, coming all dressed up in her country finery to get what she could out of him before her whole petty estate went bankrupt. Although she had not informed him in the note delivered days ago of the matter to be discussed between them, he knew very well Donna Penroze wouldn't come within a mile of his door unless it was for money. And just how was she going to play her part? he wondered, for play-acting it certainly would be. Coquetry? Flattery? Or the offer of a mere business transaction along lines that would have been impossible for her ineffectual father. Her body for a thousand or two?

Turning from the window as she drew the gig to a halt, he went to the cabinet, took out a decanter and poured a stiff brandy. The occasion, far from irritating him as it had done at first, suddenly held an intriguing element that stimulated his gambler's instinct, even though he knew full well that he held all the cards—

background, wealth, and the opportunity to make or break her.

As he waited, he glanced around the room he'd known all his life, but had used only rarely since his wife's death. It was a fine room, high-ceilinged, with an embossed frieze, and an immense luster chandelier hanging from the center. The delicately carved Chippendale furniture went well with the Adam fireplace, gold-colored upholstery, and crimson velvet curtains. The Persian rugs, too, were in keeping with the muted, though rich tones of priceless portraits . . . one by Reynolds, another by Winterhalter, and landscapes including Constable and Turner.

A proper setting, he told himself with heavy irony, for the entrance of so great a lady. He himself had been careful to dress well, in grey cloth trousers, maroon velvet jacket, adhering still to the cravat, which he considered more elegant than the high collar and bow tie currently appearing in fashionable and artistic London society. Not that fashion normally played much importance in his life. Being so rich he could afford to disregard the trends and dictates of others. Then why today of all days had he bothered to assume the façade of gentry, when deep down he knew his instincts to be of a far more earthy order? He didn't feel like a gentleman, he never had . . . even during his marriage to Selina. He had done his best at the time because she'd brought so much that pleased his acquisitive business sense. But the truth was that for most of their few years together he'd been deadly bored. In their marriage bed she'd been, though outwardly desirable in a fragile pink and white way, a complete loss, shrinking at his touch, cringing on the few occasions that he'd forced her into submission. Her tears, following those rare, unwelcome sexual interludes, had finally hardened and driven him elsewhere for restoration of his male esteem. After the birth of his younger child, a daughter, he'd left her alone altogether, until her early death at the age of twenty-four.

Naturally, he had been no monk for the past five

13

years, but the anticipation of having this proud young madam, Donna Penroze, at his mercy, was certainly stimulating.

He had mentally prepared himself for a little polite badinage at the beginning of their talk before the proper bargaining began, but his first close glimpse of her, face to face, as she was shown into the room, took him for a second, unaware.

She was quite lovely, he thought, in her strange way. Not beautiful, but intriguing, with uptilted features and deep amber-colored, almost orange eyes, under the absurd pushed-back veiling of her silly hat. Well proportioned too, slim and seductive, despite the incongruous velvet gown and jacket which no doubt she considered fashionable.

"Come in," he said, as she paused just inside the doorway. "And sit down . . ." indicating a chair.

"Thank you."

"Oh there's no need for thanks. Better for us both to be comfortable than ill-at-ease. Though I must confess to being at a loss to understand what we can have to talk about. Still—what will you drink? Brandy or sherry? Most women prefer sherry I believe."

"I don't drink, Mr. Trevarvas," she answered calmly, a faint flush staining cheeks which had been pale when she set out, partly from stress, and partly thanks to carefully applied rice powder.

"Never?"

"Not when there's anything important to—to discuss." Her voice faltered slightly under the cold, intimidating glance of his eyes.

"Oh? How important?"

"Very. I wouldn't have asked to see you otherwise."

"No. I can quite believe that. In the past you've made it only too obvious that we've nothing remotely in common."

"That isn't quite true," she told him more sharply than she'd meant. "If you'd shown an interest in my father's affairs when he needed it so badly, we could have been friends, perhaps."

14

"Perhaps," he agreed dryly.

"I . . ." she broke off, realizing with annoyance that the interview was not going entirely as she had planned. He waited, fingering the stem of his glass absently, savoring pleasantly her discomfiture, assessing her . . . mentally undressing her.

"I'll come to the point," she said abruptly. "It's about the mine. Wheal Faith."

"Yes, I assumed that."

"I need money. A loan, that's all—for machinery, so that a deeper shaft can be sunk. There's tin under the copper. Tom Craze knows it. My father knew it. But because he hadn't the backing—well you must know what happened—it killed him."

"No. I didn't know it," Trevarvas said. "Men don't die because a business project fails. They write it off as a bad deal and start again on something else. Your father perhaps was too old for that, but he should have realized the position long ago. Mines—and larger ones than Wheal Faith—have been closing for years. It was unfortunate for him that he hadn't the sense to face facts earlier, instead of killing himself over a white elephant—if indeed that *was* the reason."

"Of course it was. He was only fifty years old. The mine meant everything to him."

"And that's why you're so dead set on keeping it going?"

She stared at him, with a hint of contempt in her glance. "Yes. Mostly. What mattered to him matters to me."

"And what sum have you in mind, Miss Penroze?"

She swallowed before answering. "Three thousand pounds."

There was a drawn-out pause during which she waited, hardly daring to breathe, watching for any slight indication of emotion on his face—some clue of promise or refusal to her request.

There was none. His face, hard and implacable as stone, betrayed no flicker of feeling whatsoever, although she could feel him assessing the situation

15

through narrowed dark eyes. Just as though he enjoyed having her under scrutiny, she thought, rather like a cat watching its prey before pouncing. Beneath her thin gloves—the one pair she possessed, merely for respectable occasions—she could feel the palms of her hands perspiring uncomfortably. Her back, too, was moist. And as she unconsciously lifted a hand to her forehead—a characteristic gesture of hers under stress—a strand of hair broke loose in a curl across one temple, making her suddenly appear younger, more vulnerable.

Then he said coolly, with a brief, sardonic smile twisting his lips, "Three thousand pounds. That is what you said, isn't it?"

"Yes," she answered, lifting her head an inch higher, though a sense of shame mingled with irrational anger quickened her heart, making the pulses race in her throat, half choking her. She waited, steeling her nerves for his reply, longing at the same time, to be away from the lofty luxurious room, the closeted atmosphere of wealth and power that for a few dizzy seconds threatened to enclose her claustrophobically, or drive her to some wild action or speech that would have spoiled the whole thing.

The pause seemed interminable. Then at last, he remarked, "You astonish me. You really do. Do you imagine for one moment, Miss Penroze, that I am the type of man to hand out such a sum even to so charming a young woman as yourself, without adequate collateral?"

She was about to speak, when he silenced her abruptly, with an arrogant wave of the hand. Just as though she were some servant, she thought, hotly. Some skivvy before him to do this or that at his command. She jumped up suddenly, no longer able to control her anger, and would have gone to the door if he hadn't continued in clear cold tones, "I didn't say I wouldn't advance a loan, under certain conditions of course. On the other hand, don't you think an explanation's due?"

"Explanation?"

"Oh please." The contempt had returned to his voice. "Naive you may be, but don't try the complete innocent on me. I'm no country yokel or tin-miner's son to be ensnared by your obvious charms. I have a fair knowledge of people, women in particular. And you must have had some scheme, some bargaining proposition in your pretty head, or I'm sure you wouldn't have gone to such pains to impress. Your dress, for instance, is quite elegant, if slightly outdated. Still in the country, one does not have the opportunity of being completely *au fait* with current fashion."

"If you're trying to be insulting . . ."

"Oh no, no. The contrary. But had you arrived here looking like your usual wild wayward self in the yellow dress worn for rustic intrigues—if you'd come, saying 'I hate you, Nicholas Trevarvas, because of your wealth and my lack of it, but I need your help, will you give it, yes or no?' I might have agreed more quickly than I've a mind to now. Obviously, though, you had other ideas. Now what, I wonder? You see you have me intrigued."

His tones had softened, his voice had an ironic, teasing quality that brought a swift, high color to her cheeks. She had a longing to bring her hand smartly across his face, and would have done it, if the issue hadn't been so important. Instead, clenching her hands so that the nails bit through the gloves into her palms, she said, contriving a veneer of icy tartness, "You're quite right of course about our not being friends. But there's no need to try to humiliate me because of it. I had just hoped you'd help. We are neighbors, and there was no one else."

There. It was out.

"Thank you."

"For what?"

"Telling the truth. I'm your last resort. You have no relatives with any wherewithal, no friendly adventurer even, willing to invest in Wheal Faith, nothing but debts, the upkeep of a decrepit old house and mine, and the responsibility—though God knows why—of sup-

17

porting the whore your brother married, and her bastard child. On the other hand, you *do* have something. . . ."

His voice trailed off while he regarded her speculatively from under half-closed lids. She waited, stiffening her body under his scrutiny, trying desperately to control the threatened trembling of her limbs. Even her jaws ached from tension.

"You have the devil's own cheek," he said at last, "and for that I'll make a proposition."

Her temper flared suddenly, sending a stream of hot words from her lips.

"You've said enough. I don't want your propositions or your money, or your—your—or anything that's yours. And you're wrong about me. I have connections. . . ."

He laughed.

She swept past him toward the door, but he was there before her.

"Sit *down*, Miss Penroze, and stop playing the *grande dame*."

"I . . ."

"Sit down I say. Your airs are getting tedious."

He stood there, back to the door, so close that she could feel his hot breath on her face, knew he had noticed the rather poor quality of lace at her throat which she had cut from an old dress and pinned cunningly with the cameo, to give an impression of elegance. She had an impulse to push past violently, take him by surprise, and rush out down the steps into the chill spring air and waiting gig, leaving Polbreath and its detestable owner forever. It would serve him right, humilate him perhaps for the first time in his life, show him that there was one woman at least with the courage to defy him. Courage? Yes. But sense?

As the thoughts raced through her head, she realized that she was beaten for the moment. With an attempt at graceful bravado, holding a fragment of her skirt in one hand, she turned, assumed indifference by a shrug of the shoulders, and went before him to the same chair

18

she'd left, adjusting her gown and dabbing her forehead with a shred of handkerchief sprayed with cologne.

"That's better," she heard him say. "Would you like the window open? Do you feel the heat?"

"Not at all. Why?"

"I thought you looked a trifle put out, disturbed. However, although you say you never drink, I'm sure a glass of sherry wouldn't come amiss. And please madam—no protestations. If we're going to come to some agreement you'll have to cultivate a more sophisticated approach to life than you've shown so far."

Agreement? Well, if that was true, she thought, maybe a drink might soften the bargaining on both sides. So she said nothing, and when he passed her the salver with two delicately stemmed cut-glasses on it, she took one obediently, and waited as he picked up the other, replaced the tray, strode a few paces to the vast mantelpiece, and with one arm resting on the cold marble, the other fingering his glass absently, stood a moment or two before remarking, "A toast. To the future, shall we say?"

She didn't answer, merely lifted the drink to her lips, taking, in her emotional state, more than was wise in one swift gulp. With difficultly she restrained the cough in her throat; her color rose, then died again, as the intoxicating liquid set her thighs quivering, then her knees. Did he notcie? Hardly. Although, when she faced him, noting the tilted half-smile on his lips, the amused glint in his hard eyes, she was so sure. She'd put nothing past him; nothing. It was as though he had already mentally disrobed her and was savoring each throbbing curve of breasts, thighs and buttocks, but with an impersonal lust that, despite his cultivated veneer, held nothing in it of sensitivity or appreciation.

"He's beastly!" she told herself. "I hate him, *hate* him." But at the same time she was aware of a curious mounting excitement that Jos, even during their most passionate moments, had never succeeded in arousing.

She fought against it, struggled for composure, while

19

the seconds ticked by, until he said suddenly in the detached, shrewd manner of a purely business associate, "Now, Miss Penroze, let us get down to brass tacks.

"You want money. I've got it. But I don't give it away to anyone. Neither do I speculate on a risky deal. However, I am willing to meet you halfway provided that we draw up a contract that will be legally sealed and signed by both of us."

"What?"

"You shall see it in due course; if you choose to agree. The terms in brief are that you make yourself available as hostess at my home when, and as often, as I consider necessary, to preside at parties and any social occasions when you are needed. Also, to keep an eye on my rather wild children when I deem it necessary. In short, to be at my serivce, at any time in any reasonable sphere, when called upon. Notice I said reasonable. An ambiguous word perhaps, but you needn't fear I shall ask you to scrub floors, cook meals, or act in any way beneath your level of birth and breeding. Do you understand?"

"I'm not sure," she said coldly, though she did, only too well.

As if sensing her thoughts he continued more slowly, a little lazily, "Don't mistake me. I've no dark intentions of seduction or of impairing your doubtful virginity. Women, however intriguing, bore me, and can be a damned nuisance. I just want what I said—a hostess, Miss Penroze. And I shall, of course, if the deal goes through, need the assurance of Captain Craze and perhaps a more skilled engineer, that the proper equipment is adequately installed at Wheal Faith. There will be other more concise details to be discussed. But there in short, are my terms. And very fair I think. In fact on my part, damned generous."

"That depends," Donna said with a renewed spurt of spirit. "I mean . . ."

"Yes?" he interrupted quickly, "Just what do you mean?"

"Well . . ." She floundered a second before continuing tartly, "You haven't really explained what being a hostess, as you call it, implies. It could be—anything."

"So it could. That's my price. You get the value of your three thousand for a proper contract and receipt drawn up at my direction, under the supervision of your bank manager: who, I believe, is also mine, John Crebbyn himself, of Crebbyn's, Penzance."

"And when? Do we meet there?"

"I suggest next week some time, at the bank."

With her thoughts in turmoil, face pale again now, strained taut from frustration and danger, she answered recklessly, "I shall have to think about it. Do you mind?"

He shrugged. "Not at all. Wait a day or two, then let me know. Perhaps in the meantime one of your rich connections may turn up with a more acceptable proposition."

Color suddenly replaced the marble pallor of her cheeks. After insulting her he was now mocking her. She! the daughter of William Penroze, whose family, after all, had been land-owning gentry—of however minor a caliber—for centuries, before even the fifteen eighties when her family had known men like Sir Walter Raleigh, Lord Warden of the Stannaries. Their fortunes, it was true, had declined from time to time, and the first copper works on Penroze property suffered heavily during the nineteenth century. That was due largely to the depression caused by trading from the east, and the great copper output of the cheaply worked Parys mine in Anglesey, which had so disastrously lowered the price of ore throughout Europe, and hit the Cornish industry badly.

The discovery of a new lode at the cliff face on Trencobban land however, had revitalized and enriched Wheal Faith once more, and for seventy years it had kept going, despite the discovery of immense mineral deposits at Lake Superior and the Spanish Peninsular mines, including Rio Tinto.

For its continuing survival and the employment of the men who worked Wheal Faith she was fighting now, suffering the humiliating taunts and barbed comments of Trevarvas, whose roots had sprung from mere farming stock—a hardy family made rich in the past not only from agriculture and ambitious marriages, but dubious smuggling activities, and—if rumor could be relied on—far worse things, including the ruthless wrecking and plundering of ships.

Yes. Ruthless.

How dare he? she thought with a sudden violent hammering of her heart, how dare this dark-eyed savage-featured man, with not a whit of cultured blood beneath his harsh exterior, play the condescending gentleman to her.

For a few moments all fear of him, of his capacity to make or mar her future, was swept away in a tide of outrage at his audacity. Her breathing quickened. A brilliant, swift flame lit her amber eyes; a pulse fluttered wildly in her throat above the froth of lace as she said clearly and very coldly, "Certainly. I'll contact you when I've properly considered your terms Mr. Trevarvas."

Getting up, she swept past him with a swirl of skirts to the entrance, not realizing that never before had she looked so beautiful or so desirable. She paused momentarily as he stepped in front of her, saying with mock gallantry, "Allow me," and then he opened the door for her to pass through.

With her chin a fraction higher, skirt raised slightly by one hand, in the elegant manner of a lady of fashion, showing a glimpse of toe and white petticoat, she went forward and without another glance in his direction walked very erectly down the hall as the man Sarne appeared from a recess to see her out.

"What an actress," Trevarvas thought, watching the swing of dress and perfectly poised figure silhouetted above the steps against the velvet shadows of trees and garden. "And what a damned little madam into the bargain."

There was a tentaive half-smile on his face, an admiring speculation that would have surprised her, had she glimpsed it.

But she didn't. Her one thought was to be away from Polbreath, to feel the wind freshening her face, dispelling the confusion and humiliation of the interview that she'd had to endure.

Trevarvas! she thought as she got into the gig. I'll make him sorry. One day I'll shame him more than he shamed me, somehow . . . sometime.

She set off at a brisk pace, driving more recklessly than was strictly safe, from the avenue into the winding rough road leading northward towards Trencobban.

The action released some of the tension, and as the familiar line of high moors dotted by ruined mine-stacks came into view, memories of Jos's departure invaded her mind with a stab of indignation, and a sense of loss. Why did he have to leave her, she thought, just at the moment when he'd been so needed? He had said he loved her, he had promised marriage, and she had agreed. There would have been difficulties with her father of course; they'd known that. Cornwall, though a remote, hard land—perhaps because of it—observed a strict social code dividing the gentry from the workers.

Jos, a mere mine manager's son, however well respected, belonged irrefutably to the latter, and would not have been considered a suitable match for William Penroze's daughter.

This hadn't mattered to her, though. They would have got over it together, and anyway, America was a long way off. America! The idea seemed fantastic now, because her father was dead, Jos was gone, and she was alone. Alone to fight her battle like any man, only in a different way, because she happened to be a woman with heavy commitments laid upon her.

Why couldn't Jos have loved her better? she thought, with renewed longing. Why couldn't he have been there to protect her interests and save her from the power of Trevarvas? The intimidating shadow of the dark horseman of Polbreath had seemed to dominate her life recently. Now it was a very real force in her future. A threat which nevertheless held a hint of male arrogance that excited and confused her, leaving her emotions at conflict. A restless tide seemed to ebb and flow within her, giving her no chance of peace, no hope of coming to terms with the situation confronting her.

Peace! The very word was a mockery.

And so she drove on wildly, forcing the mare to gallop, while her heart cried again, thinking of Jos, "Why couldn't you have loved me more . . . ?"

And the rising wind seemed to carry his answer in chilling condemnation . . ." Or you, Donna, have loved yourself less?"

But that wasn't true, she told herself fiercely. She had loved him, she had and she did. But the past was past, and no one could put the clock back. It seemed to her then, driving back under a darkening sky already spitting with rain, that with the afternoon's interview, a phase of her life, perhaps youth itself, was already ending before it had properly begun.

Later, taking out the yellow dress that she'd worn on that fateful day with Jos in the cove, a lump rose in her throat—grief, suddenly turning to anger, rebellion, and something stronger, a ruthless determination to let nothing, ever, stand in the way of her goal. She would win despite Jos's warning, and Nicholas Trevarvas's greed. Her pride demanded it. Her father's memory.

And so with lips set in her white face, eyes burning, she took her scissors and stabbed the material mercilessly, slashing it from bodice to hem, and again and again, until it was nothing but a tattered, forlorn remnant lying in pieces on the floor.

Then she threw her coat over a chair, and undid her velvet gown, and let it fall to her feet.

Her shoulders and neck rose firm and cream-skinned above the curving breasts and the constricting corsets. I must be free, she thought. I will be. And, in the end it's Nicholas Trevarvas who'll pay. Without thinking, she had unlaced the absurd corset and pulled the petticoats and frilled bloomers from her thighs. The warm blood pulsed through her limbs in a wave of certainty and power as she saw herself in the glass, naked, filled with such a conflict of emotions she could not even begin to assess their significance; only deep down she was already loking forward in a fierce, feminine way to the challenge ahead.

CHAPTER TWO

Two days after Donna's meeting with Nicholas, Tom Craze called at Trencobban and asked to see her. Feeling irate and on edge after an unpleasant scene with Jessica, who had contrived to spend most of the small sum allowed weekly for Janey's care on gaudy but worthless baubles for herself, she went downstairs grudgingly to the sitting-room where Tom was already waiting for her.

He was a broad, thick-set man in his fifties with a friendly air about him. He was shrewd-eyed, not given to conversation unless it had a point, and he had the knack of assessing—generally correctly—any mining problems arising, of seeing the two sides of every question concerning Wheal Faith, and of dealing with each on its merit. Donna's first impulse had been to inquire about Jos. But one glimpse of his face told her it was not the time. Her heart sank. What had happened now? What fresh trouble to sort out—even if only with delaying tactics? Tom appeared unusually serious, addressing her as "mistress" instead of his habitual "Miss Donna."

"Well, Tom?" she said, when they were both seated. "What's the matter? Tell me. Get it over with; you're worried, aren't you?"

"I've lived with that for some time," he told her. "But things can't go on as they are for much longer. At the end of the week the men will be wanting their month's wage packet. We've only two left on tribute, and last month's taking by each of them amounted at most to one and six a week. The tut workers are about in the same boat. They're loyal men, most of 'em, but you can't expect them to continue without some guarantee. And what I want to know is, can you give it, mistress? Without the new shaft and engine Wheal Faith's not only dying but dead. And if we can't supply them, the sooner my men know the better. Tempers are frayed already. Families are suffering, and we've a trouble-maker on our hands—that Jed Andrewartha—who's all struck on the new union and as like as not rousing violent action if he thinks fit."

"Then get rid of the man," Donna retorted quickly, recalling him well, a burly red-faced worker who bullied his frail wife mercilessly and scattered his bastards about the countryside. A crude, domineering, loud-mouthed creature with a lascivious leer who more than once had eyed her in an offensive manner.

Tom shook his head. "No. Not that. Only harm would come of it. It'd be like setting a match to a load of smoldering timber."

Donna sighed. "Then what—what, Tom? Sometimes I think—I wish . . ."

"Yes?" The manager's voice was gentler. A strong vein of compassion in him sympathized with this head-strong young woman whom he knew to have been fonder of his son than she should have been.

". . . I wish I'd gone with Jos to America," she said dully. "He wanted me to, you know. To marry him. Or didn't you?"

"I guessed," Tom answered. "But it wouldn't have worked. And in spite of the trouble you're having now, I reckon you wouldn't really want to leave your home, Trencobban. What's in the blood, mistress, generally wins in the end. There's too much of the Penroze in you to run away."

"I know."

"All the same we've got to take some action over the mine. Either close it, or . . ."

"Hope for a miracle," she interrupted.

"That's about it. And a quick one."

"Well," Donna got up, walked to the window, and facing him again, said steadily, "the miracle's happened

27

Tom. In another week—two at the most—I can promise that the men will be paid, new equipment and machinery ordered for sinking the shaft, and on top of that—she hesitated, swallowed nervously, before concluding—"there'll be some compensation for wages lost. There, is that enough?"

Tom paused before telling her slowly, "I don't know, mistress. I really don't know. We've been going on so long in this way. And promises don't feed hungry bellies or pay for the care of men laid off sick through poor food, heart disease, and sikes."

"But if I give credentials," she said desperately, "if I can prove the loan's available?"

"And how can you do that, Miss Donna?"

"Nicholas Trevarvas has promised me the money," she answered with cold, deadly precision, knowing that with those words she had truly burned her boats.

"*Travarvas?*" That one word, and his manner of saying it eloquently expressed his surprise, and was a true assessment of Trevarvas's reputation in the district. Awe. Dislike, contempt, and hatred for his ways and reputation, yet beyond all this, a grudging kind of admiration for the power of the man.

After a long-drawn-out pause in which Donna could guess the trend of her manager's thoughts, he said with no trace of expression in his voice, but with a searching look in his eyes, "Are you sure of that?"

Her lips snapped together. "Quite sure."

"And for what . . . ?" He broke off in mid-sentence, continuing abruptly, " 'Tis none of my business of course."

"No," she told him, "not yet. Not until the meeting."

"Meeting?"

Turning her face from him to the window which faced the high moorland road leading to the small fishing port of St. Inta eight miles away, and resisting the impulsive desire to confide the whole affair then and there to him, she said calmly, "At the bank. Crebbyn's; You'll be wanted I expect when Mr. Trevarvas shows the document. You'll have to tell—about—about machinery, what it will cost and what the engineer said—you know, that man who came to see my father from Birmingham, about the tin."

"I'll not be able to do that, Miss Donna, no man could, exactly. We'd have to get a firmer expert than me to deal with the expense business."

Her heart sank. "Oh. But I thought you said . . ."

"I said roughly, what I'd been told, and what, in my judgment would be needed for shaft sinking and a new man-engine. It's a tricky proposition, and it'll take time. There'll be labor and wages to be thinking of on top of everything else, remember."

"There won't be any difficulty over that," she said with more conviction than she felt. "I know, Tom. I know."

"And how do you expect me to tell the men? Say a certain greedy landowner's come all over generous of a sudden, and is willing to give a handsome hand-out to every one of you? No, mistress, it wouldn't wash. There'd be jeers and mud-throwing in my face. You know that as well as me."

"Can't you put it in another way then?" she persisted, "If you gave your word . . ." her voice had softened, become pleading. "Please, Tom. I wouldn't deceive you. If you could keep the men satisfied for just another week, or fortnight, perhaps, everything will be settled. And the engine, it doesn't have to be paid for all at once does it? I thought just a premium at first . . ."

Her eyes, bright and brimming like clear amber forest pools lit to darkest gold from the sun, had their way with him, as they always did in such a mood. After a little more arguing and discussion he gave way, telling her he would try a bit more soft-soaping for an undertaking they would stick at their jobs a bit longer.

When he had left she relaxed into a chair for a bit, thoroughly exhausted. Then, knowing what she had to do without wasting further time, she went to the chest and took a decanter from the cupboard, with a glass, recalling ironically how she had told Trevarvas that she seldom drank—which had been true at the time—and how, later, the alcohol had revived her, bringing their interview to a more sucessful—though doubtful—conclusion, than she'd hoped for.

She was amazed to find hardly any sherry left in the decanter. It had been almost full the last time she'd seen it, merely a week ago. Jessica, she realized instantly. Her sister-in-law had become increasingly addicted to the bottle since William Penroze's death, which explained why she so frequently appeared flushed and unable to concentrate on the simplest household task and so immersed in her own vanity that little Janey was frequently left alone, or to the care of Sarah.

With her first rush of anger over, Donna sighed, and poured a small drink which she tossed off quickly, guiltily, in an effort to dispel this further problem of Luke's wife and child. Not that she had ever really believed the little girl to be Luke's, and the older she grew, the more unlikely it seemed. Though dark in coloring, Janey's was an alien darkness, with almond eyes and a pale golden skin that had none of Luke's ruddiness. Mercifully she bore little resemblance to Jessica either. Jessica, brashly good-looking, was fair. The fairness had a brilliance about it owing more to artifice than to nature, but her eyes were good. Bright blue with a hot light in them set to inflame men.

Because Donna was fond of Janey, she did her best to make excuses for Jessica, who must have found life at Trencobban frequently boring, having nothing in common with the wild expanse of bleak brown moors scattered only with remote gray farms, nor with the huddled mining hamlets—so many of them now derelict—and the rocks and monoliths of the distant hills. To Jessica there could have been no stimulus, no thrill in hearing the Bal maidens singing at six o'clock of a morning as they made their way, neatly clad in garibaldis and white aprons, from their homes to a long day's work at Wheal Faith, no challenge, or sense of achievement in watching the pump rod's rhythmic rise and fall against the sky. She was a different breed. A "furriner" to the Cornish. Donna often thought pityingly that she deserved a little consideration because of that, cheat though she might be, and despite the fact that they'd all have been better without her, especially Luke, who would probably have been alive today but for the yellow-haired stranger.

Not that Luke would have been much use in mining affairs. The sea, from his earliest youth had been his love—sea and adventure—without the responsibility of having to deal with accounts, debts and endless speculation about financial hazards and the future of Cornish ore. That he'd been a disappointment to their father she'd always known, just as their own mother had been—the only daughter of a well-to-do antique dealer in Truro who had never been able to accustom herself to the bleak environment of the north Cornish coast. But William Penroze had been devoted to her, and Donna still, at odd moments, recalled her beauty—the delicate features, the massed fair hair and strange tawny eyes that she herself had inherited.

It was understandable that a woman so gently reared should wilt in the harsh environment of Trencobban. But Jessica—Jessica was different. At least she could have tried, instead of endlessly complaining that she hadn't expected Luke to take off and die. She hadn't wanted him to make her pregnant, and leave her penniless without kith or kin and no job any more to keep her in the way she was used to.

What this job was Donna had never exactly fathomed. There had been airy references to hotel work, and having others to do her bidding. But Donna had reduced such flowery terms in her mind to barmaid or some servant in a tavern, Plymouth way, and guessed shrewdly enough that poor Luke had been trapped while in his cups.

However, none of this seemed to matter any more, and as Donna made her way upstairs, after the crucial talk with Tom Craze, irritation with Jessica had subsided into a mounting impatience to get through the rest of the afternoon which now must somehow include a "chance" meeting with Nicholas Trevarvas, lest he changed his mind about his proposition.

She set off ten minutes later, wearing her conventionally styled dark green riding habit, with a small hat perched forward on neatly coiled hair. Usually she wore Luke's breeches and shirt and felt free to ride like a man astride Saladin, Bess's two-year-old colt sired by her father's fine old stallion, Starlight. Saladin, like his namesake, was a proud-looking creature and preferred a fierce gallop to a canter. But because of Nicholas, and wishing to appear her best, she had decided on Bess for this occasion.

By the time she had crossed the road above the house, and taken a straight course up the hill, the late afternoon sun was already sinking in a ball of fiery gold toward the western horizon, sending long-fingered shadows from the summit of the moor. There the cromlech stood, a gaunt relic and memorial to a bygone age, guardian of secrets never completely plumbed by man, although the locals believed that Druids had once held their sacrificial ceremonies there.

Sniffing the air appreciatively, Bess's pace increased as they left the furze and gorse behind, and reached the stretch of short hill-turf dotted only occasionally by the immense tumbled boulders that were so characteristic of that part of Cornwall. This was the way Nicholas Trevarvas generally chose for his ride at that hour. The view, from the top, was truly magnificent, taking the eye past Rosebuzzan Hill to the south as far as Mounts Bay, where St. Michael's Mount itself stood regally medieval, an island castle at high tide, and then, turning back to the north, providing a panoramic vista of the opposite savage coast which encompassed the whole of St. Inta's Bay, including Hayle estuary, and the rugged cliffs clawing westward toward Land's End.

Before reaching the summit, Donna drew her mare to a halt, and glanced back at her own familiar scene, the granite house, Trencobban, standing square-fronted to the road. It was a distinctive building, constructed in an L shape at the back, which was the sea side. From where she was it seemed to stand on the very rim of the cliffs, as did Wheal Faith half a mile further on to the west. Much of the land thereabouts was sparsely cultivated by tenant farmers in a patchwork pattern of miniature fields bordered by stone walls. The nearest hamlet, Gwynvoor, was half hidden in a fold of the slope. But around it clob cottages squatted, blending into the scene almost as naturally as the round boulders that had been washed by the elements into curiously smooth contours.

Donna was suddenly filled with a wave of emotional pride and sense of belonging that temporarily swept all thoughts of Trevarvas aside. For a few moments she was able to relax on her mare, forgetful of the battle and problems that lay ahead. Then a streak of cloud dimmed the sun's last glow, plunging the scene into deepening gray desolation. She glanced back, suddenly apprehensive, and saw the static figure of a horseman silhouetted on the hill's crest against the dying light.

He had come then, as she'd known he would, and was waiting there, a symbol of dread and threat to her freedom, yet the only hope of saving her heritage before it was too late.

She turned, kicked Bess forward, and as she approached the rim of the moor he cantered down at a leisurely pace to meet her, drawing his horse to a halt when they came face to face. Her head was lifted proudly, her face set and tense, his was expressionless, save for the speculative glint in narrowed, dark eyes, which told her nothing.

"Good evening, Miss Penroze," he remarked. "How lucky we meet at this propitious moment."

"Propitious?" she queried lightly, professing to ignore the irony. "But I planned to see you. I thought it would be easier for me than having to call at Polbreath."

"So you're aware of my movements?" he said with a faint smile that tilted a little more to one side of his mouth than the other, fleetingly giving him the taunting look of a satyr. Yes, she thought, with the familiar stab of annoyance his presence always caused her, he was trying to rouse her again. He enjoyed playing with her. Well, she wouldn't let him know he had, this time.

"It would be hard not to be, wouldn't it?" she parried, with her eyes unflinchingly on his. "As you're so often looking down on Trencobban."

He gave a short laugh. "Well said. It's good you have a smart tongue. Wit and a clear head are frequently necessary at my rare social gatherings. Of the proper kind, of course. But then I wouldn't expect gauche behavior from the daughter of William Penroze." He paused, savoring the beauty, the vivid rush of color to her cheeks, and sudden hot blaze of her eyes in the fading light. As though sensing her mistress's resentment Bess gave a quick pull at the reins. Donna placed a soothing hand on the mare's neck, saying, "Shsh Bess. Good girl now," as he continued, "I take it that's why you so charmingly interrupted my lone canter, to discuss or dismiss any plans for our mutual future."

"Our mutual future?"

"Naturally. If you condescend to be associated with my household, the arrangement must obviously be a mutual one. Or had you decided that you couldn't oblige?"

He waited, knowing full well during the short pause between them what her answer would be, just as she knew he was aware of it.

"I've no choice," she answered abruptly, "and there's no point in trying to pretend. I accept."

"Good. Very well then; the meeting will be at Crebbyn's Bank, the day after tomorrow, Friday, at eleven thirty precisely, and I'd be obliged if you see that that manager of yours, Craze, is also present."

She was dumbfounded for a second, staring at him speechless. Angered, yet in a queer way fascinated by his audacity, conceit, and the sheer animal magnetism of this man who could surely not be more than thirty-five, but acted as though he had a lifetime of power and experience behind him.

"You mean you—you've already arranged with Mr. Crebbyn, without telling me?"

34

His jaw stiffened before he said coldly, "I plan what is expedient in good time. As you've already said, you had only one choice. You can withdraw from the arrangement if you want. It's entirely up to you."

If only she could. For a brief moment she hesitated, wondering what his reaction would be if she told him that she had reconsidered and the condition of the loan was no longer to her liking. It would have amused her immensely to see him disgruntled and put properly in his place. Unfortunately he held all the cards, so she replied coolly. "Very well. Friday, eleven thirty."

She was about to turn Bess back toward Trencobban, when he said, "I'll accompany you to the house. It's growing dark. I wouldn't want my new hostess-to-be to meet with an accident or a fall."

"I'm not in the habit of falling," she interrupted quickly, "and I'd rather be on my own if you don't mind."

She had a brief glimpse of his shrug, sensed his annoyance at the rebuff, before she'd kicked the mare into a swift canter down the hill, taking the track she knew so well, between furze and heather scarred by intermittent rocks and thorny gorse bushes.

When they reached the short drive bordered by windblown sycamore and elms that led to the porticoed entrance of the granite house, it was almost dark, with massed clouds mounting in the sky.

She dismounted, and taking Bess by the reins along the wide right-hand path that led round the back to the stables, was startled to see a dark male figure lurching, presumably from the yard, toward a side entrance in Trencobban's sturdy wall.

Leaving Bess to make her own way placidly to the stables, and thinking at first that the intruder was some poacher or vagrant out to thieve a cheap meal or whatever he could lay his hands upon, Donna rushed after him, shouting, "Stop! What are you doing? Come back."

But he took no notice and she might not have caught up with him if he hadn't stumbled over a stone and

35

fallen with a torrent of blasphemous oaths on his lips, leaving a heavy reek of whisky on the air. When he righted himself Donna was already there, furiously breathless, hat fallen from her head, leaving a stream of tumbled hair about her shoulders. Rage deepened in her when she discovered the man to be Jed Andrewartha who must have left work at Wheal Faith only half an hour ago.

He swayed on his heels, surveying her lecherously, as a rumble of laughter caught his throat.

"A pretty pullet and no mistake," he muttered thickly. "First, are you Mistress-high-an'-mighty Penroze? Or lustin' for a bit of love maybe?"

Though it was impossible to define his expression in the half light, she could imagine the avaricious thick lips above the heavy jaw, the bleared eyes bloodshot with drink and sexual desire, and she instinctively lifted her riding crop in defense.

But it was too late. As her arm swung upward, it was caught above her head in a grasp of iron. She struggled ineffectually, pummeling his sweating chest with the other fist, until that too was caught and his body was heavy against hers, pulsing and demanding, while the breath was torn from her lungs in gasps, and she tottered backward, helpless, with his hands brutally enclosing her breasts, coarse fingers bruising the tender flesh, where the jacket had been torn. She tried to scream, but the sound was smothered by his large palm across her mouth.

Then, suddenly, there was a thudding from nearby, the sounds of hooves dying to a halt, followed by a dark figure leaping from the background, and after her swift release, the confusion of two bodies at each other, until, with a sickening thud, one lay on the ground, with the other looming over him, sending the stinging lash of a whip whistling across the groaning, sniveling creature that was now Jed Andrewartha.

Donna, pulling her jacket together, leaned against the wall, struggling against the wave of faintness that rose sickeningly, as her heart, from its wild beating, slowed to a cold pace. She found her jaws chattering, and could not control the trembling reaction until a male voice—Nicholas Trevarvas's—said close to her ear, "Are you all right, Miss Penroze?"

With an effort she straightened herself, saying, "Yes, yes. I . . ."

"Well, you don't look it. Here take a drop of this."

She felt the sting of spirit against her lips, as life miraculously flowed back into her veins.

"You could have killed him," she said.

"And I would have, if I'd had less sense and more guts," Trevarvas answered grimly.

"Is he . . . ?" Her voice wavered.

"There he goes, the drunken oaf, and I'll wager he'll do no more attacking of defenseless women for many a night. Who was he by the way? I didn't get a direct look at his face. Do you know?"

Recalling Tom's warning, and with a brief glance at the shambling form now disappearing into shadow across the patch of grassland beyond the wall, she said, "A farm laborer perhaps, a miner, or tramp, or just a thieving poacher like I thought. I don't know. But I do know he was up to no good, so I went after him, and then . . ."

"And that was a damn silly thing to do, wasn't it?" Trevarvas interrupted grimly, adding sharply, "Where the hell were the servants? Or haven't you got any?"

"Of course I have. But the kitchens are right at the back on the other side. They'd hear nothing. I couldn't scream." She didn't explain that Sarah was getting on in years and completely deaf in one ear and that Sam was probably dozing by the fire. As for their boy, who was slightly simple, heaven alone knew where he was. Neither did she reveal that whereas, when the mine was prosperous, seven or eight servants had been employed at Trencobban, those three were now the only ones on the premises.

Anyway, Nicholas had probably assessed the position accurately for himself. She also suspected that he wasn't entirely satisfied by what she had said about Jed. Now

37

that the first shock was over, the whole incident was becoming acutely embarrassing, and she was about to thank him curtly and take her leave of him, when he said abruptly, "I won't delay you further, Miss Penroze. You must be wanting to wash and have a rest. But I think you'll agree I was right when I suggested accompanying you. It was a good thing I took it into my head to follow. I don't want your gratitude, but just think yourself lucky, that's all. Rescuing fair damsels in distress is not my accustomed role. Next time I might request a taste of what that oafish blackguard was after as a reward."

"I won't forget," she promised sarcastically.

He waited until she'd disappeared safely into the house, mounted his horse swiftly, and was away in a flash over the darkening shade of the landscape, cutting upward across the moors around the side of the hill toward Polbreath.

What kind of a man was he? Donna wondered as she made her way upstairs, this man whom she detested and who could infuriate her as no one else had ever done before, but who could in the same moment set her pulses racing like any simple-bred adolescent meeting an attractive man for the first time.

Yes. He was attractive. She hated to acknowledge it, even to herself. But his very arrogance combined with the strong features, the erect square-shouldered figure, the brilliant dark eyes and his way of dominating a tricky situation, had awoken a dormant need in her. A need to put her trust in someone stronger than she, a yearning for the burdens of her inheritance to be shared. And something she could not bear to admit yet—a longing to be conquered as a woman. A longing that she would fight every inch of the way if need be.

She knew she should be grateful to him for his participation in the evening's vicious event. And she was. But he needn't think that left her forever at his mercy to obey his every whim.

Oh no, indeed. She remained still the mistress of Trencobban and would follow his instructions only on the strictly practical basis of a business deal. Though her senses might respond to his masculinity, she still hated him for what he'd done—or failed to do, for her father. As she remembered her father, her feelings toward Nicholas Trevarvas resolved themselves again into intense dislike—something she determined to keep firmly in mind during the months ahead.

As she turned along the landing to her bedroom, a feeling of depression—reaction to her ordeal—descended on her. Except for a small light burning, the oil lamps had not yet been lit, and queer shadows patterned the floor, creeping up the walls like ancient phantoms risen to bewail the increasing penury of years, to mourn the empty spaces where valuable paintings and portraits by famous artists like Winterhalter and Reynolds had hung. There had been a Landseer too, one of her father's favorite possessions that she had been forced to sell, a Wilson, Constable, and others, all gone to London and now hanging in the great galleries or housed in private collections.

Exhaustion overcame her. Her knees again felt weak and shaking. She was about to turn into her room when an insidious odor crept along the wide landing from her sister-in-law's bedroom, filling her with distaste, and in her overwrought state, a sickening anger.

Donna rushed ahead, half stumbling as she went, and tried the door. It wasn't locked. She went in. Jessica was lying on the bed dressed only in bloomers and a corset which revealed ample too-full breasts; her yellow hair was unpinned, straggling over the pillow, her flushed face was turned toward Donna with a simpering, bland stare in her china-blue eyes. There was a candle burning on the chest nearby, where an empty bottle stood with two glasses. Two! And the air stank of drink combined with something else—not only perfume but the reek of man, of lovemaking.

In a flash everything was clear. Donna knew exactly what had been taking place: Jed! and this—this wanton Luke had married! Jed Andrewartha had been here at Trencobban in her absence—not more than a quarter of an hour at the most and in that time they'd lain and lusted with each other, ignoring all rules of decency, taking Donna for a fool. Where had old Sarah been to let things come to such a pass? Oh, God, she thought, it couldn't go on this way. She'd have to get other help in somehow, someone with all her wits about her to keep an eye on the household.

"Get up!" she said suddenly, shouting so shrilly that her voice nearly broke. "Dress yourself and never let that man in again, or I'll throw you out and let you fend for youself. You disgusting creature! to allow such a— a—filthy oaf to have your body in my house, under my roof. Luke's widow . . ." she broke off breathlessly.

"Luke!" Jessica sneered, half drunkenly. "Precious good he's done me, or Janey."

"Where is Janey?"

"In bed," came the answer. "I sent her there, after a good hiding. She stole my scent, and broke the bottle. Then when I took it from her she shouted, so I put her over my knee and gave her what she damn well needed. That child's getting out of hand. A lesson's what she wanted—d'you hear, madam sister-in-law? An' it's my business, see. . . ."

Donna brought her hand swiftly across Jessica's face, and in icy tones said, "Don't ever touch that child again, or you'll have no roof over your head. Not a penny of mine either, and no credentials. I'll see your name's dirt through the district and none employs you. You're nothing but a whore, and a cruel one at that, not fit for decent society."

Her words must have struck home. Jessica's face blanched. There was a different note in her voice as she pleaded, "I didn't really hurt her, Donna. Young ones've got to be disciplined. And I didn't ask Jed up here. He just—just came."

Well, she might be telling the truth there. Donna thought wryly, there was nothing she'd put past that man.

She turned wearily and went to the door, saying, "There'll be no more drink at my expense in this house

40

either. So just pull yourself together and try and show a bit of responsibility."

"I'll try. I really will, Donna," Jessica said. "It isn't easy for me either, you know, seeing how things are, and with you always off visiting the gentry."

Donna looked back sharply. "What's that? What did you say? What do you mean by visiting the gentry?"

Her sister-in-law winked knowingly. "Oh I don't blame you. That Mr. Trevarvas. Setting your cap at him."

Refusing to answer the insult, Donna went out, slamming the door smartly behind her. Incredible, she thought, that Jessica had learned of her visit to Polbreath. Not that it mattered. In a short time the news of her commitments would somehow leak out. And perhaps the sooner the better. She was sick of trying to keep up a front, a pretense, and giving ambiguous answers to problems she had no way of solving on her own. Sick of the violence that seemed to have gathered lately on every side—Andrewartha, even Jessica toward her own child—a violence that at times seemed to be lurking in the bowels of the very earth itself, reflected on wild days in the angry tides lashing the gaunt coast, and storm-ridden skies, tempting the emotions of human beings to savagery and hungry lust.

She shivered as she entered her room, pausing to light her lamp before going to the mirror where she contemplated her reflection. She felt a stab of recoil. Untidy, tumbled black hair straggling over forehead and shoulders where a trickle of blood oozed from Jed's hard hands, flaming eyes in a white face, torn bodice gaping to show the bruised flesh. Thank heaven Jessica had been too drunk to notice.

She fetched water and washed herself quickly, scrubbing hard so that the effort should erase the memory of the bestial incident and make her really clean again. Then she changed into a cotton lilac-colored dress, combed her hair and pinned it neatly to the crest of her head before making her way to Janey's room, carrying the small lamp in her hand.

41

She found the child sitting up in bed, her face against a shabby stuffed bear. Hearing Donna's entrance she turned, with an enigmatic, remote look in her dark-lashed eyes. The faint glisten of tears still hovered on her delicately formed cheekbones, but her manner was restrained, too old for her years. A rush of sympathy took Donna quickly to her side. She looked so defenseless, fragile almost, yet accepting life as it was, with the unnatural composure of one who could expect nothing better.

"Hullo, Janey," Donna said, planting a kiss on the child's temple. "I'm sorry you've been in trouble. Never mind, you'll soon feel better."

Janey shrugged. "Mama spanked me. I took her scent. Then the bottle broke.'

"Oh dear."

"I'm glad it did," the little girl continued, with a flicker of malice in her voice. "She hasn't got any more."

"Now that's not a very kind thing to say is it?"

"Oh no. But I'm not kind. Neither is Mama. She's a beast."

"Hush." Donna put a finger to her lips. "You mustn't say such things or even think them, Janey. Everyone gets cross sometimes. Even you."

"You don't."

"Oh yes. I'm a real firebrand when I'm roused."

The little girl sighed, turned her head away and said, "I wish . . ."

"Yes?"

"I wish something nice could happen sometimes."

And Donna, thinking the same thing, said, "Tell you what then, we'll go out one day just you and me, on a picnic, in the cove perhaps. Would you like that?"

Janey nodded. "Oh yes, Aunty Donna. Please. But . . ."

"Well?"

"I don't suppose Mama will let me. She's like that."

"I can promise you your mother will agree," Donna

42

replied. "And things are going to be better soon. We'll have more fun. There's school to think of too."

"School?"

"Of course. Unless we have a governess here. You've got to learn things sometime haven't you?"

"Have I? Why?"

"Because your name's Penroze. And . . ."

"What difference does that make, Aunty Donna?"

"All the difference in the world. You see . . ." her voice faltered. "Oh well, never mind now. One day you'll understand."

But would she? Donna wondered a little later when she went back to her own room, leaving the little girl comforted and on the verge of sleep. There was something disconcerting about Janey—that "unknown quantity" perhaps—the question which could never properly be resolved—of her ancestry.

Back in her room she flung herself on the bed, a Regency one that had belonged to her grandmother, with a needleworked pattern in the headboard, stitched in an intricate design of roses, leaves, and lilies. Her riding habit lay carelessly flung over the back of a chair, and as the lamp placed on the bow-fronted chest of drawers spilled its mellow light over the wrenched jacket, revulsion filled her again, and she wondered if she would ever again be able to wear it without recalling the evening's hateful incident. Glancing at the china clock on the mantelpiece she saw that but half an hour remained until the mealtime. Sarah would already be busy around the kitchen getting the crockery and dishes ready. Her heart sank at the prospect, recalling the time when meals had been pleasurable, comparatively relaxed affairs, with her father at the head of the table, his very presence somehow flooding the atmosphere with security and well-being, despite the mining and financial problems. Even Jessica, then, had been subdued, affecting a certain air of decorum. Nowadays, more often than not she would appear either overdressed and too chatty for complete sobriety, or sullen and uncommunicative. Tonight probably she would not appear at all. In

43

any case the meal would be a lonely affair without William Penroze.

With a sudden desperate longing for his reassuring presence, Donna got up, went to the chest, and took a letter from a pigeonhole inside the front drawer. One that she'd found addressed to her from her father a few weeks after his death. It had fallen to the back of the desk in his study where it had lain wedged between the wall and wood until something had dislodged it. It was not a business letter, so she'd told no one, retaining it as her secret private property for just such a moment as this.

She took it back to the bed, where she sat down and reread again the precious words.

"My dearest daughter,

"I trust and hope that you will not have occasion for some years yet to read this letter. But I have been unduly tired lately, and if called upon to leave this world for whatever other life there may be, I want you to know that my only regret is for yourself, who are and have been so dear to me, and on behalf of my friends the miners and their families, whose loyalty, at considerable sacrifice to themselves, had induced them to bear hardships these last few years with the minimum of complaint.

"You, I know, will continue as far as you can, to see justice for them, and I hope and pray that Wheal Faith may somehow survive. But if you find the responsibility weighs too heavily on your young shoulders, you must put yourself first, and let those versed in legal matters advise you what is best to be done. It is regrettable that you have no other kith and kin to turn to.

"Remember, though, that in the 14th century your ancestors were Lords of the Village, Gwynvoor, cooperating with their humbler neighbors in agriculture and cultivation of the area. Trencobban Court, then, was the medieval manor, and the Penroze family, from what records we have, much respected, with a name for justice and sympathy for the less privileged.

"Copper was not discovered on our land until the late

44

fifteenth century, when the early type of mining, including streaming, was undertaken. Wheal Faith therefore, has ancient roots, although the mine as it is today, is of comparative recent origin. Much of this you already know, from what I've told you. I wish to emphasize the importance of co-operation and a friendly atmosphere between workers and their employers, while retaining each their rightful and proper places in the social structure.

"Without such understanding, nothing worthwhile can endure.

"My dear child, whatever happens, have courage. I am with you always, if only in spirit.

Your devoted father,
William Penroze."

For a few moments after rereading the note, Donna sat silently, controlling with an effort the threatened tears that brought a lump to her throat. What would her father think of her now? she wondered. Would he understand the storm of conflicting emotions that had driven her to seek Nicholas Trevarvas's aid? Recognize the inward struggle after Jos's departure for America that had turned her from a light-hearted happy girl, into an outwardly hard woman prepared to take risks he would never have condoned?

She didn't know. What way was there of telling? He had said he was always there with her in spirit. But the spirit was a nebulous thing in the face of reality, especially to one as vital and eager as herself.

Sighing restlessly, she folded the piece of paper, returned it to the envelope, and after putting it back in the chest, she went to the window which overlooked the moors.

After warming the earth, the spring day had left a veil of mist in a rolling vapor of milky gray over the huddled line of moorland hills, molding the landscape into eerie uniformity beneath the night sky. A gentle wind had risen, fanning the curdling damp into the semblance of fleeting ghostly shapes which quickly receded, fading into the general scene. She was about to turn and pull the curtains, when it seemed to her that something else was there, watchful and waiting against the moor—the giant shape of a horseman, symbolic to her heightened fancy, of so many things—her life in the years ahead, the unknown destiny from which now, she knew, there was no escape. Then, while her eyes were glued to the hill, she saw the apparition disintegrate and fade once more into mist.

She turned and went back to the mirror, tidying herself absently for the meal. Later, when she went downstairs, Jessica, now fully recovered from the earlier scene of debauchery, was already waiting in the dining room, looking, apart from the slight puffiness under her eyes, as radiant as a full-blown rose. She held Janey by the hand.

"There now," she said to her sister-in-law, "everything's forgiven, isn't it, Janey pet, and just for a treat she's going to have dinner with Aunty Donna and Mama."

Janey nodded obediently, and inwardly Donna surrendered. Perhaps after all there was some sort of deeply embodied affection between the two. In any case it was obvious that Jessica had taken her threat to heart, and with luck there'd be no further unwarranted physical punishment on the child.

That night Donna's sleep was disturbed by confused dreams, of terror and rape and the looming figure of Jed pursuing her, of screams and abuse and of falling, falling, until she was submerged in a welling tide of blackness that also held desire in it, and a great longing to be at one with the thing that claimed her. The thing she hated but was also in her and of her. Man to her womanhood. The vision followed by the passion and the pain.

At first there was no face. No sound but of her own heart beating, and great hooves of a stallion thudding through the air. Then, the darkness lifted and two eyes burned, holding the blackness of night and the fiery glow of morning. Nothing else. No features, but she knew. And the knowledge filled her with a queer sense of loss and shame, because by rights it was of Jos she should have been dreaming. Jos whom she'd thought she would love forever.

CHAPTER THREE

The following day she reached Crebbyn's Bank punctually. She and Tom Craze had been driven there by Sam. Donna was wearing the same clothes as she had for the meeting at Polbreath, but this time she had draped a flimsy "Bertha" round her neck, hoping to lend the dress a mature dignity, even though such accessories were more usually worn with evening attire.

Nicholas, to her surprise, was already there, ensconced in John Crebbyn's office with the two documents prepared and laid ready for her inspection on the table. Tom, to her disappointment, was taken to another room and told to wait there until his presence was required. Then after a few preliminary formal remarks between them, the main agreement or deed of contract, as the manager called it, was handed to Donna for her approval.

It was terse and to the point, stipulating that Donna Penroze, for the advancement of £3,000 to be used specifically for the purpose of purchasing the machinery, engine, and equipment necessary, together with any extra labor needed for developing tin production at Wheal Faith, would in return guarantee to give any reasonable services required of her at Polbreath, including those of acting as hostess for Nicholas Trevarvas, until such time as benefits from the mine enabled her to repay the loan.

There was more. Details concerning Tom Craze's part, outlined in a further contract, which entailed his taking full responsibility for the working of the mine, and his willingness to be questioned and advised should a matter arise beyond his immediate ability to deal with it. If he rejected the terms he should be replaced by another with the necessary engineering credentials to fit the position.

Donna read the main document fleetingly. She knew she would sign anyway, and hoped fervently that Tom would do the same. She was fully aware that Nicholas, too, knew it. But she was surprised when, with her signature still damp on the thin parchment he said, "And now, Mr. Crebbyn, it will help all concerned if you would transfer further credit, of another two thousand pounds *unconditionally* from my account to that of Miss Penroze for her specific personal benefit. Such a sum should enable her to repay debts owing, and to get her affairs into order, including any back wages due to the miners. She will naturally need to equip herself with a wardrobe suitable for her situation in my household, and no doubt has a few plans for her own domestic comfort."

Donna was breathless. She felt the color ebb from her face, then rise again, in a flooding tide of crimson. John Crebbyn averted his eyes. She realized what he must be thinking, but at that moment it didn't seem to matter. Just for a heady period of time she felt exultant with relief. She was rich—rich beyond her wildest dreams. £2,000 wasn't a fortune. But it would enable her to be free of anxiety as she had never been since her father's death.

"Thank you," she said, almost in a whisper, lifting her orange eyes to Trevarvas.

There was no flicker of expression on his face. He merely inclined his head slightly to show that he'd heard, and then said in formal remote tones, "Now we had better have Craze in."

John Crebbyn touched a bell at his side, and a few seconds later Tom entered. The shorter second document was put before him, and he did not sign quickly as Donna had done, but perused it several times before lifting his hand to take up the pen.

Donna sighed with relief. There. It was over. For

49

good or ill the matter was settled, and she would be able to sleep in her bed that night without worry, for the first time in many months.

Trevarvas did not accompany her when she left with Tom, but remained for a further session with John Crebbyn, ostensibly on other business. Sam was waiting outside patiently in the carriage. He flung her a speculative glance, no more, as she stepped into the vehicle with Tom following. But one glimpse at her face told him all was well, and that was a welcome change, he thought, flicking the mare to a brisk start. Soon they'd left the main street and Penzance behind, striking upward in the direction of the hills. The road narrowed presently, becoming a mere thread of a lane climbing steadily between wind-blown hedges towards the opposite coast.

The air was fresh, heady with the scent of spring and pulsing earth; Donna wished briefly, in her elated mood, that she was riding Bess instead of behind her, so they could have paused when they wished, to have a view of the country, of the outlying area of Trencobban which now she would be able to refurbish, and give many homes that had been long poverty stricken a certain security.

When they'd taken the turn around the base of Rosebuzzan Hill and were mounting the slope again, Donna said suddenly, "Wait a moment. We've time to spare."

Sam drew the carriage to a halt, and she jumped out to view the scene, noting, against the changing pattern of spreading sunlight and scudding clouds much that was not good. "See that," she said, indicating a cluster of cottages huddled to the left of the valley near the stark shape of a lifeless mine, Wheal Joy.

"Aiss, mistress. I see it."

"We'll not be having that at Wheal Faith, now, thank God," she went on triumphantly, "it's all going to change, Sam. Better wages in the future, shorter cores and no deserted cottages on our land. I'm not an expert about these things. But you know, don't you, Tom?"

Tom nodded. "Yes, Mistress Donna. I've seen only

50

too much of the bad side." And he remembered how only a few years previously men and women had lived and worked contentedly at Wheal Joy, on the surface and down the dark shafts, despite long periods, sometimes of ten hours up to a stretch, including the tributers, who took what was due to them from coinage. Now most of those same cottages were empty shells or occupied by families hanging to life by a thread against the tragic odds of hunger and sickness.

"Johnny Chenoweth and his mother died only last month from the consumption," Tom added grimly. "And George the father's left jobless with four younger ones to look after. Charlie the eldest's only fourteen, but he walks eight miles and back every day to act as shaftsman's assistant at Penjust. And they're not the only ones hereabouts. Ruth Couch has lost three of her children, all under five, in the last three years. Yet when I was young, the folk of Wheal Joy seemed thriving. Their houses were clean and well cared for, although the ground's swampy, but when you get a cottage built of clob, it lasts well. That's what the old folks've always said. But how can anything last, without the strength and means to give it care?"

"No," Donna said thoughtfully. "Perhaps . . ."

"Yes?"

"Perhaps—I was wondering if we might do something now, just a little, for those poor people."

"No," Tom stated firmly. "All you have, Miss Donna, will be needed for your own property, our own miners, and Wheal Faith itself. No use going philanthropic all of a sudden, just because things look better. Your father would have said the same, if you don't mind me saying so."

"I expect you're right," Donna agreed doubtfully, recalling the letter her father had written about cooperation and friendliness in the district. But then he had been referring to Trencobban lands. Oh, she thought, with a sudden wish to free her mind from tragic subjects, it was all confusing and rather depressing looked at from one point of view. She had no inten-

51

tion of being depressed that day, however, and returning to the carriage quickly, said, "I'm ready, Sam. We'd better be going. Heaven knows what will have happened in our absence."

Her remark, so lightly spoken, proved to have serious justification later. For when they reached Trencobban it was to find Sarah and the boy waiting in the hall with Janey and her mother in the background, the child peering like a frightened elf from behind her mother's skirts. One glance at the little group told Donna something was amiss.

"What's the matter?" she demanded. "Sarah—Jessica—come along. Speak, can't you?"

Her eyes widened in dismay when Sarah said, wringing her hands against her ample breast, "Oh mistress, some knave have thrown a great lump of rock through drawing room winder. I didn't hear et till Mrs. Luke came downstairs, and with you and Sam being off to Penzance there was nothen' to be done."

In a voice cold as stone, Donna said, "Did you see who it was? *Any* of you?"

Sarah shook her head. "Not a thing, mistress. By the time I got theer everythin' was quiet as the grave. An' like death et was, to see all that beautiful glass scattered about the floor with the wind blowing through that poor winder as though the devil's doom had fallen on us."

Without another word Donna hurried down the main hall taking the wide corridor to the right, which remained an orginal wing of the house as it had been in Tudor times. The arched drawing-room bay projected onto the drive outside, and had always been considered of great artistic and historical beauty, made, as it was, of such delicately selected colored glass, patterned in heraldic design.

Donna, shocked at the outrage, was silent for some minutes, picking the larger pieces from the still luxurious but worn carpet. The drawing-room was not one usually used nowadays, but kept only for those special occasions that had been practically nonexistent during recent years. Many expensive items once housed there had been sold since William Penroze's death, including miniatures, china from the glass-fronted Chippendale chest, and embroidered stools and small chairs. A Louis Quatorze gilt and china French clock too, and other small things, for financial reasons.

This, though, was desecration, vandalism calculated to show hatred of Trencobban, of what it stood for, most of all, she guessed, for herself. And by whom? For what real purpose?

Jed Andrewartha?

"Do you know anything at all about the affair Jessica?" Donna asked her sister-in-law a little later, when they'd eaten a quickly prepared meal and Jessica stood idly by the window, scanning the sky which had clouded now, with Cornish unpredictability, to dull gray.

She swung round. "Me? Why should I?"

"You know very well," Donna answered quietly. "As far as I know only one person bears a grudge to us—or rather me, someone you're on rather more than just friendly terms with."

Jessica's eyes widened. "You're surely not suggesting Jed?"

"But I surely was," Donna told her acidly.

"You must be mad."

"Why?"

"Why?"

"He wouldn't be such a fool. Oh I admit when he's had a drink or two Jed can be a bit—explosive. But he knows which side his bread's buttered. He's got a head on him, or this committee of his wouldn't give him the power it does."

"What committee?"

Jessica shrugged. "Why ask me? I don't know a thing about committee business or anything of that sort. Boring I call it. But it's clear he's thought highly of. A real man, Jed, whatever you may say. Not the kind to act like a half-witted brat. And anyway . . ."—her face was sullen—"what right have you got to go flinging accusations about when you've no proof of anything at all?"

It was on the tip of Donna's tongue to blurt out the story of Andrewartha's unspeakable behavior to her two nights ago, and to ask what sort of a "real man" would act in that way, but she kept silent, realizing that her sister-in-law had been far too drunk at the time to have an inkling of what had happened.

Later, when Jessica had taken Janey sullenly upstairs to change her frock (which she said got "messed up" by scrabbling about on the drawing-room floor) Donna, on impulse, changed into Luke's breeches and shirt, drew her hair back with combs and a ribbon, and went to the stables where she saddled Saladin for a gallop over the moors.

It was some time since she had done this, and the sturdy pull of the colt at the reins, his burst of exhilaration as Donna gave the animal his head, so filled her, too, with freedom and release from strain, that she could have shouted with joy. Though the clouds were lowering, and the first spots of rain spattering the earth, she didn't care. This was her natural self—to be out in the air, abandoned to the elements, at one with the moor and the lonely sky, with the wind and rain against her face, young, carefree, heedless of what lay ahead, as she'd been that day a year ago, when she had lain with Jos in the cove.

On she galloped, on and on by rock and furze and flaming gorse, the wild tang of heather mingled with brine carried from the sea, sweet and heady in her nostrils.

When she reached the high crest where the cromlech stood stark on the horizon, its ancient stones formidable suddenly, emitting an ancient power no civilization had conquered or dispelled, she drew Saladin to a halt, and waited, looking over the vast scene.

Her pulses were still pounding, dark hair tumbled from its ribbon now, falling loose about her neck and shoulders, wet from the increasing rain which instead of subduing and depressing her, only increased her sense of belonging, of being one with the wild elements which her ancestors had known for countless centuries. Maybe they had even known it before the Roman invasion. The Romans had never completely conquered the small dark men, the original Celts of Cornwall whose blood could still run in her veins. She felt for those few minutes, with Saladin rearing and pounding the earth, that this must be so, and that the legions of those long passed away were with her—the early inhabitants of Chysauster, the prehistoric village over the hill that one day, perhaps, would be resurrected by archaeologists to provide a further link in history. And the dwellers of the Beehive huts further to the west, followed by the very early miners of "streamers" who had first discovered the red precious ore on their territory.

Cornwall. A magic land; old as the hills, filled with legend, and history, Her land.

How could Jos have left it? she wondered, not for the first time. Love? He had not loved her. Or he would be here beside her, in the thickening rain. They could have thrown their clothes off and lain abandoned to the downpour, their bodies close and soaked, yet warm with each other, laughing at the elements, letting the sweetness of life and desire drench their tongues and flesh. Through longing she could almost feel physically, the thrust of passion, the leap of nerves and womb, as he went into her.

Then, abruptly, she stiffened, and jerked Saladin to movement. No. Not Jos for her. One day she might give herself utterly to some man. But it would not be Jos Craze.

To whom then?

There was no way of knowing. But as she tore back astride Saladin towards Trencobban, it seemed that another rode with her. Featureless in her imagination, but implacable and strong, the man who, however staunchly she might deny it, had already become a symbol in her life of desire and conquest, and ultimate subjection.

When she reached the house she stabled Saladin, and went in through the back door. Sarah threw up her hands in astonishment as the dripping figure passed through the kitchen to the back stairs. "I doan' know what's come over you," she said, "goin' out like that in all that theer rain. You'll catch cold sure 'nuff, ef you're not careful."

Donna hardly heard. She went up to her room, flung off the wet male breeches and shirt, scrubbed herself well in the rather primitive bathroom, dried herself thoroughly, then changed into a low-cut gold-colored gown, one of her mothers that she'd kept. It was outdated, but still becoming enough to transform her from an impetuous girl into an alluring woman—the woman who one day, and perhaps very shortly, would play elegant hostess at the dinners and social occasions arranged by Nicholas Trevarvas.

"My!" Jessica exclaimed when she went downstairs. "All togged up, is it? And what for? Quite the grand madam you look."

Donna, who had not informed her sister-in-law of the outcome of the morning's meeting, merely answered calmly, "In future we must all try to look and behave our best, Jessica. Things are happening to Trencobban that will be to the advantage of all of us. There's a meeting, I've heard, either tonight or tomorrow at the Count House. And who knows? Someone might want to see me."

She walked away leaving Jessica staring after her, round blue eyes wide, mouth slightly open. There! Donna thought, with a burst of triumph. That will give her something to think about.

And it did. But Jessica's thoughts wandered more to what Donna had said about Jed after the discovery of the broken window, than to her sister-in-law's show of bravado. Was Jed involved in the incident? Had Donna inflamed or rebuffed him in some way? Everyone knew he had an eye for women. If so, why? She had an uncomfortable feeling that something had occurred after Jed's surreptitious visit to the house, that she didn't know about. She would have to wheedle it out of him somehow. To have Donna at Andrewartha's throat all the time could be a nuisance. Jed was the only consolation she had these days in the dreary old house, alone except for Janey, stuck-up Donna Penroze, and the miserable old servants. Clandestine meetings when she and Jed met on the moor, in secret places of the cliffs, or very rarely at late night hours in her own bed, just about made things bearable, and that was all.

She had been tempted many a time to persuade him to take off with her somewhere—Bristol way preferably, where he could get a job at the docks, surely better paid than working in the dull mine and going back most nights to his thin shadow of a wife. But though she'd steered the conversation in that direction, he had not taken it up. Instead his lips had tightened, and last time he'd loosed her suddenly—when a moment before, one large hand had been fondling her buttocks.

He had said, "Now don't you go getting ideas. There's no wumman in the world I can't do without, so just you remember. When I want you I'll have you, or else *git*, and go elsewhere. See?"

And with her thighs aching for him, lips thirsty for his kisses she'd said, "I know, I know, Jed. I was just wanting you, see?" And after a studied, reflective moment, he'd flung her down in the heather, exposed and desirable, taking her in a fierce stab of avaricious lust.

But it had been good—good; although she knew only too well that her high and mighty sister-in-law would disapprove. Well, let her. What business of hers was it anyway, how she spent her days? No conversation but . . . "Perhaps you'd help Sarah a bit this morning, Jessica? Perhaps it would be a good idea if you busied yourself about the house more." Or, "Janey's dresses need mending," and, "her hair looks as if it needed a good brush."

Janey, Janey. If only Donna had the first inkling of what a plague the child was to her. How secretly rebellious and sly. If this new talk about schooling came about it would be a good thing for all concerned, for herself especially. Of course there were times when she felt a primitive, instinctive bond with her offspring, even occasions when she wished things could have been other than they were. But it was hard to love a young creature so completely different from herself, especially with no clear proof of who the father was. Anyway, she argued to herself in rare moments of conscience, it was just possible that Janey was Luke's, although she had a shrewd idea that she wasn't, and under the circumstances she'd done the best she could for the girl, making her a legal Penroze.

She only hoped that what Donna had implied before she flounced out was true, and that better times were ahead for all of them. Otherwise—pictures of Bristol, and company, and taverns, bright lights and laughter, the company of men and compliments—though they had to be paid for later—swam temptingly through her head. She wasn't a bad sort, not at heart, not really, she told herself. If it hadn't been for her drunken swine of a father who had taken off to foreign parts with a colored woman, leaving her downtrodden, frail mother to fend for herself and her child, she could have made something better of her life. But with her mother's death when Jessica was but fourteen years of age, and ill-equipped for any job but scrubbing floors or using her youth and good looks to their best advantage, she had chosen, naturally to take the primrose path.

Even then, if it hadn't been for—but at that point, always, her trend of reminiscences broke off in a wave of horror. This especially dark period in her existence hadn't yet lost its power to fill her with terror. Only Luke, later, had saved her from complete degradation and possible madness. He'd been young, headstrong, and so filled with liquor the night they'd met in the bar of the Flag and Goat, that only her rich, fair looks had registered; he had seen none of the unsavory experience lying beneath the luscious façade.

Getting him had been easier than netting a defenseless fish in a pond. Perhaps the marriage would have worked, too, if they'd had more time. Perhaps, although she doubted it. It wasn't for nothing he'd taken off to sea again so soon after Janey's birth. And so sly about it too, without a word to her at the time, or even his precious father. Obviously he'd not thought her good enough then, for the toffee-nosed Penroze family. None of them had. The only one who'd tried to be kind and reasonable had been William, and she had a shrewd notion it was thanks to him Luke had ever married her, simply because she'd have made a scandal if he hadn't, her being so conveniently pregnant, and William, like most of the gentry, not caring for scandals of that kind.

Oh well, viewed in retrospect, her past was certainly a patchy affair, fitting her more to Jed's ways than life at Trencobban. And Jed, she thought wryly, would only fancy her so long as it suited him. A bird of passage she was, as someone had told her in the old days; the trouble now was that her wings were so uncomfortably clipped.

That evening the rain thickened, so the meeting referred to by Donna, was held in the Count House instead of outside, which was exceptional, as the mine office was normally reserved for the twelve-week review of the "cost book" when the purser dealt with finance and paying out of monies due. Dinners had been held at those times in the past, when Wheal Faith was prosperous enough to have adventurers interested, and smelter's agents present to sample ore.

Now, gradually, the custom had declined to such a minimum it was practically nonexistent. The mere fact that this evening so many had assembled to have their say in what was afoot, told Jessica that Donna's prediction of important happenings could very well be true. So before the evening meal, Jessica, determined not to be outdone by her sister-in-law's show of finery—just in case the mythical visitor should appear—attired herself in the best clothes she had (a crimson silk retained from the time of her brief marriage) painted and powdered herself more than necessary, which gave her the look of some exotic foreign blossom rather than the luscious full-blown rose variety endowed on her by nature, and sailed downstairs, smelling, overpoweringly, of the perfume kept hidden in her chest safe from Janey's inquisitive fingers.

The effect on Donna, who was looking almost regal, was electric.

"Heavens, Jessica," she exclaimed sharply. "What on earth's this in aid of?"

Jessica, preening herself before the glass, answered with a calculatedly refined accent, "You did say, dear sister—or sister-in-law—that we might have company tonight. And I should dislike to disgrace you."

This brief speech, though an effort, was so well delivered that Donna's mood changed to amusement. But she restrained herself from showing it, merely remarking calmly, "Obviously you've taken trouble, Jessica. You look very . . ." Her voice trailed off.

"Yes?" As she turned sharply, Jessica's white bosom seemed about to burst from the tight fitting red silk.

"Ravishing," Donna replied shortly.

"I should, shouldn't I, in this?" Jessica retorted mockingly. "A real scarlet woman; that's me. Anyway, who's this fine company you're expecting?"

"I'm not expecting anyone now, in such a downpour," Donna said, although she'd wondered if Nicholas Trevarvas might call, to see what was going on. Miner's talk had a way of spreading, and it was quite possible news of the special meeting had reached his ears.

"Oh," Jessica's bravado vanished like a pricked balloon. "Then you were just having me on. I should've known."

"No. I'd no reason. What I said was true; things are going to be different."

"How?"

"More money."

"Where from?"

"That's my affair."

"Oh yes. Of course. I just wondered, that's all. There's been so much dreary talk of economy, and not having this and not having that, not even able to have a bit of a fling now and then, and being made to feel an encumbrance as though you had to carry all the world on your back. Now, suddenly . . ." Jessica shrugged

60

her plump shoulders, "Well, what do you expect me to say?"

Donna, relenting slightly, paused, before taking the bull by the horns. "Mr. Trevarvas is taking an interest in Wheal Faith, if you must know, he . . ."

"God's nightgown!" Jessica exploded, before she could finish. "Him! That's an achievement and no mistake. For you I mean. How did you do it, Donna? Flutter your lashes at him and play the innocent? Or was it more than that, eh?" Her blue eyes had narrowed, become shrewd. There was a faint smirk on her lips.

Donna flushed. "Hold your tongue. You just can't behave decently, can you? Not everyone, remember, goes about things the way you do. Some people have pride. Proper pride." Her tawny eyes were smoldering. Her lips tightened in a thin line.

"And I haven't, of course. True enough, not your sort. I'm loud and common, and call a spade a spade. Sorry."

"I didn't mean that. I . . ."

"Of course you did. You always have. You've never liked me ever since Luke brought me back here. If you'd been a bit nicer it would have made things better all around—for Janey too. How do you suppose I feel, knowing that she runs to you every time I say a cross word or try to correct her? Aunty Donna, Aunty Donna . . . always high-and-mighty Aunty Donna. No wonder I lose my temper with her sometimes. You make a great show of affection for her, but has it occurred to you, Donna Penroze, that because of it there's many a time I can't stick the sight of her?" She broke off, breathing heavily, the warm blood bright in her face, almost as bright as the scarlet dress that for a few moments coarsened her, taking all semblance of youth away.

Donna was shocked. No, she'd never thought of the relationship from such an angle, but Jessica's tirade, she had to admit, could have some truth in it.

"It hadn't," she admitted quietly. "I mean I never imagined you felt like that."

61

"It's time you started then, isn't it?"

"Perhaps we could both have a try," Donna replied.

"At what?"

"Making things pleasanter at Trencobban."

Jessica laughed mirthlessly. "Oh yes! That would be fine! But how? You're not exactly going to become a millionaire suddenly, are you?"

"No. But Nicholas Trevarvas is going to help us in many ways. Not for nothing you understand?"

"Oh I understand. That's one of the things I do know about. Men."

Ignoring the implication, Donna continued. "Let's get things straight from the start. You may as well know now as later. I'm going to repay certain financial help for Wheal Faith, by assisting him when he needs it at Polbreath. Socially. And with his children at times."

There was a pause, before Jessica said knowingly, "Oh. I see."

"I don't think you do, not for an instant," Donna retorted. "My duties at Polbreath have been made specifically clear. Everything will be on a completely business basis, whether you believe it or not . . ."

"If you say so. . . ."

"I do. I do say so," Donna answered, with her temper rising. "And you'd do well to remember it, or I shall change any plans for next week and just leave you out of them."

"Plans? What plans?"

Donna took a yellow rose from a bowl, held it to her nostrils delicately and paused before saying with a veneer of coolness she did not feel, "I'd thought of taking a trip to Penzance and seeing a seamstress there. There's a skilled one I've heard who used to work for the Godolphin's. I'm badly in need of a new wardrobe, and I thought you might like something new. Who knows—she might have one of the new fashion magazines showing the latest Paris styles. And there's a boutique store in Falmouth where you can buy almost anything—stockings, shoes, hats, and dresses already made on the new sewing machine. If funds can run to it,

I don't see why we shouldn't visit both if necessary."

Jessica was speechless, as her color turned from crimson to palest cream tinged only by two bright spots of pink. Then she gasped, "Oh Donna. Do you really mean it?"

"Yes. If you pull yourself together. Try to behave reasonably, and keep off alcohol."

There was a long silence while Jessica struggled with a desire to placate and plead with her sister-in-law, whose tempting references to Paris fashions and new clothes on the one hand intrigued her and on the other made her long to defy the schoolmarmish conditions with a tirade of unbecoming language. The former emotion won, as she envisaged herself arrayed as luxuriously as any high lady of fashion, frequenting a society that boasted such elevated personages as the Prince of Wales himself.

The idea went like champagne to her head.

She said sweetly and meekly, "Of course, Donna. I won't let you down. I'm not really stupid you know."

You're certainly not, Donna thought to herself, noting the ridiculous, suddenly demure look on her sister-in-law's face. But really not very clever either, if she believed Donna could be so easily taken in.

The conversation was cut short there by Sarah entering the room to say that Tom Craze had arrived and wanted to see her.

"Oh very well," Donna said, "take him into the library. I'll be with him in a moment."

At the door she turned and said. "Sorry it's only Tom this time, Jessica. But probably I won't be long, and then we can have a little toast together."

In cold tea I suppose, Jessica thought ironically when her sister-in-law had gone. Still, she'd wait, just in case. Even that hard-faced Mr. Trevarvas might come poking around. Who knew? To her knowledge he never had visited Trencobban, but there was always a first time. What a joke if he should appear when Donna was closeted with that dull mining captain and found her in all her splendor, far more willing to please him than her

63

stuck-up sister-in-law. People said in those parts that he was a hard man. But she was used to hardness, and had never failed to soften any male hungry enough to look at her twice. Except—the cloud descended on her mind again—the one great horror of her life, which in moments of solitude was wont to roll like a great fog from the past filling her with fear so sickening and overpowering that she had the instinctive impulse at such times to crawl into a cupboard, under a table, or hide herself in any dark corner available until the pounding and terror of her heart had ceased.

No one knew about this. No one ever had, not even Luke. Most of the time she suppressed it herself, through alcohol, or any other activity calculated to give confidence and forgetfulness. When she was with Jed and physically satiated, it subsided altogether. But when left to her own resources with only Janey to talk to, and the disapproving servants eyeing her as though she were the plague descended on the house, she felt as though only some rash act could save her from madness.

It was not so bad when she was dressed up, flaunting her body's rich charms. The scar, reaching from one shoulder blade to buttock was mercifully hidden. It had faded now from a jagged bright line into a puckered, whitish disfigurement that looked as though it had been stitched by a great needle that had left dark spots where it had pierced the flesh. In the daytime it was never visible, and in the dark no one saw it—no one had access these days except Jed, and even if he had noticed he wouldn't have cared, concerned as he was only with her throbbing warm limbs and need of him.

Still, she reflected, if the chance did come to better herself, her involvement with Jed would have to end. He would make no fuss. In fact she'd thought several times recently that he'd appeared a bit on the sullen side, and when their love-making was over, too anxious to be rid of her.

So Donna's surprise might be coming just in the nick of time.

Half an hour passed before her sister-in-law reappeared, and during that interim Sarah looked in twice, grumbling and rubbing her hands on her apron. "Dinner 'bin waitin' too long for its own good. I can't keep apace with such delays. Giblet pie an'all in th'oven. What's goin' on's beyond me, what with Sam's hints, an' the mistress skippin' heer and theer like a dolled up lamb that's lost its mother. An' all this dressin' and prinkin'. An' that theer Tom Craze actin' secret an' callin' at such an hour with such importance on him you'd think he'd a ton of gold at his back."

"Perhaps he has," Jessica answered knowingly, enjoying having Sarah at the end of a string. "Heigh ho!" apeing the manners of a weary duchess, "We'll find out in good time I expect."

But when Donna appeared at length, she was dissappointingly uncommunicative and in answer to Jessica's flood of questions, merely replied, "Everything's gone off very successfully; the men have agreed to stay at work. Back monies will be paid. And Tom's going next week to the foundry to see about machinery—Harveys at Hayle."

"Oh," Jessica remarked. "And shan't we see anyone else tonight then?"

"I don't suppose so for a minute," said Donna equably. "But that's not important, is it? I know you've dressed specially. Still . . ."

"Yes?" Sensing criticism, Jessica's voice was sharp.

"That color's really too brilliant for you. Blue would suit you so much better."

"Blue? Blue's a little girl's color. My ma used to dress me in that. Peace and holiness, she called it. That's how it seemed to her. What a laugh!"

"Well I wouldn't make such a mistake as that," Donna said acidly, "but it is your color. It would bring out all your best points."

"Make me look more ladylike you mean?"

"I wasn't thinking so, though it's true. You see your eyes are lovely; they really are. Haven't you the sense to see it? They don't need paint, or parring shades to fight them. Just blue to emphasize their own natural color."

Jessica was silent for a few moments, then she said, "Do you know, Donna, I think that's the nicest thing you've ever said to me."

Donna, not wanting to be involved in a sentimental scene, turned away abruptly saying, "Touch the bell, Jessica. Sarah will be getting on her high horse if we don't get on with the meal soon."

Later, at bedtime, before snuffing out any unnecessary candles and turning off the oil lamp (a duty Donna had undertaken since the reduction in domestic staff) she remarked, "We'll be going into Penzance next Tuesday. Sam shall drive us in the carriage, and we'll take Janey too. We'll have a meal out at the Dancing Bear, and see the seamstress about clothes for us all. In the meantime, for heaven's sake don't get involved in any scenes or scandals with Jed."

"As if I would," Jessica said, apparently astonished that such a thing should even cross Donna's mind in the exciting new circumstances.

She probably meant what she said, Donna thought going upstairs—for the moment. But how long would it last? And how long would it take for Donna to accustom herself to all the intricacies involved in the revival of Wheal Faith's prosperity? To the entertaining that would be expected when engineers came down from Derby and Birmingham again to assess its potential productivity and analyze amount of ore to be worked? There would be more workmen about the place too, at a time when she was also under obligation to be at Nicholas Trevarvas's beck and call. She had a shrewd idea that he might be fair and not press her until Trencobban affairs were properly in order. But afterwards?

Her mind boggled at the prospect, as it did also when she tried to assimilate even a portion of Tom's remarks concerning new adits and shafts, and the necessary man-engine required with other accompanying machinery. What did she know of tin mining? Costing? Coinage? Smelting, and the rest? She had pretended to, under Tom's shrewd and businesslike eye. But most of it had been mere mumbo-jumbo to her; and with her senses strained and eyes tired, her thoughts had wandered, at intervals, to other things—to the sweep of moor outside, and scent of heather in her nostrils. To Jos far away in the Americas, to her dead father, and long hours spent wandering about the granite rocks and coves with her glowing dark hair free about her shoulders, and the gulls crying ceaselessly over the pale shore. She hadn't wanted to grow up. Youth had been sweet. But circumstances had forced her to maturity before she was ready. And maturity held other visions including that of a strong male face with smoldering dark eyes under heavy lids, and of an erect square-shouldered figure that seemed to be forever poised above her on the rim of cliff or sky—the figure of a man for whom she felt no tenderness, only a kind of smoldering, resentful fascination which impelled her each hour toward an insidiously frightening destiny.

CHAPTER FOUR

The weekend passed comparatively quietly, with no sign of Nicholas Trevarvas. On Tuesday, Donna, who had another appointment at the bank, took Jessica and Janey to Penzance, as she'd promised. It gave rise to a few grumbles from Sarah who remarked that her husband was seldom there to help her these days. " 'Tedn' as ef the daily girl's any good," she said. "First chance she's got when my back's turned, and off to the stables she is, gettin' round my boy Ted. An' I've only one pair of hands. Not so young any more either."

"I know. I know, Sarah," Donna soothed her. "It's been very hard for you. But everything's going to be different." And how often had she said that, she thought ironically, during the last few weeks?

Sarah moved off, grumbling. She'd never thought much of Mr. Luke's widow and had made it apparent from the start. But seeing her titivated up, with that "wisht" child of hers dragged by the hand, irritated her still further. Do a job of work, she should, she told herself irately, instead of lounging about as though she owned the place, and with always a bottle handy somewhere. That kind never did anybody any good. And one day Miss Donna would regret treating her so softly.

Donna well knew what old Sarah was thinking. She was of the same opinion. But it pleased her to have the rare opportunity to play the Lady Bountiful—if only to Jessica. And at least the trip would prevent any clandestine meeting with Jed Andrewartha.

The rain had cleared, leaving the morning fresh and cool under a paper-pale sky. Sam drove smartly across

68

the wild tongue of country, arriving at Penzance soon after eleven. Donna left Jessica and Janey seated in the carriage outside the bank and went into Crebbyn's to settle a few financial dealings with the manager. Janey was fidgeting quietly, but Jessica's blue eyes sparkled bright as forget-me-nots in her pink and white face, her yellow hair drawn tidily under a small non-too-fashionable hat, which was dashingly decorated with a liberal assortment of artificial flowers. Donna, wearing a high-necked purple alpaca dress under a plaid wine-and-blue-shaded fringed shawl that had been her mother's, was far less flamboyant, but with her dark hair shrouded only by a flowing piece of veiling, over a boat-shaped creation of black velvet, she looked lovely and proud enough to put any gaudy bird-of-paradise in the shade.

Jessica, quite unaware of this, smiled complacently when she asked, "Where do we go now, Donna?"

"Sam will deposit us at the coaching house," Donna told her. "We'll book a meal there, then go and have a look at the shops."

"And what about the seamstress?"

"We can see the seamstress later when we've an idea of what's being worn," Donna told her firmly.

The shops, however, proved disappointing. They displayed none of the up-to-date clothes Donna had expected, but obviously catered for ordinary Cornish women who wanted value for money rather than style, practical service instead of fashionable display.

The seamstress seemed bewildered by their requests, although she did produce one or two out-of-date magazines showing styles still favored by the gentry of the district—ladies whom Donna guessed were more likely to be the wives of rich farmers than members of the aristocracy.

"Oh I don't know, Miss Payne," Donna said after studying the fashions for some time, "I rather think— haven't you anything a little more—well, exciting than these?"

"Exciting, Miss Penroze! There are some here actually copied from the Bertarelli Collection in France. Herbert and Van Acker displayed them in their own shop . . ."

"I don't care two pins about Herbert and Van Acker," Donna retorted sharply, to the great satisfaction of Jessica who thought the styles dry as dust, and the colors dull. "I'm sorry, Miss Payne. I can see your *work* is excellent. But the fashions? No. Not any of those. And the materials; I wanted something richer and more elegant—for both of us."

"And me?" Janey piped up.

Donna squeezed her hand. "Yes, you too, my love."

Eventually the matter was left unsettled. Donna suggested they have a look round Falmouth, one day soon, and see what styles and materials were available there, but she also promised that if they found anything suitable, Miss Payne should be given the opportunity to make up the garments. Her needlework was undeniably excellent and she had two girls training to work the up-to-date sewing machine in her back room.

After their session with the dressmaker, the three of them strolled along the harbor—busy that day with merchant vessels unloading cargo. There was a fresh wind blowing from the sea, and after a look at St. Michael's Mount with its causeway only half submerged by the rising tide, they took the road back to the town again, and the coaching house where they were to eat.

The meal was good homely fare, and to suit the occasion Donna permitted them each a glass of wine, with just a taste for Janey.

As they were leaving, Donna inadvertently caught the heel of her shoe in her dress. She stumbled and would have fallen had not a pair of masculine arms quickly caught her. After a quick glance at the disarrayed petticoat and the slender ankle it revealed, a pair of gray, quizzical eyes traveled appraisingly to her face.

Astonishment, admiration, and something else undefinable flooded the handsome countenance of Donna's rescuer. Although embarrassed, she couldn't help noting how extremely attractive he was with his small golden beard, swept back fair hair, and a fashionably slight moustache. He was wearing a stove hat, with a white silk waistcoat, an immense golden brown bow tie, and a fitted tail coat.

A young man of fashion obviously. But it wasn't simply that which impressed her. It was more his eyes, which in the first revealing moment quickened her heart quite ridiculously. They were so penetrating and deeply set. Clear, light gray eyes, which, though superficially cold, held depth and an underlying warmth that she sensed would suddenly light to flame.

Her lips were tilted whimsically when he said, "Pardon me. I hope your foot is undamaged?"

"Oh yes. Yes thank you," Donna answered, recovering and straightening herself. "I'm—I'm most obliged."

He gave a slight bow. "I'm sure all flattery should come from me." There was a pause before he added, "May I see you to your chaise, or perhaps offer my own?"

"That's quite unnecessary," Donna answered. "Our own is waiting over there," indicating the vehicle with Sam waiting in front, "I'm most grateful, though."

After a brief touch of her arm, while she assured him again she was not in the least hurt, he passed on, lifting his hat, and at the same time added, "I hope we may meet again sometime."

"Yes," Donna agreed, "perhaps." She hoped so too, but did not consider it very likely.

A few minutes later they were cantering along the lanes leading back to Trencobban. Jessica, although disappointed by the inconclusiveness of their visit to the dressmaker's, had nevertheless been sufficiently stimulated by the morning out to say before they reached home, "Thanks for the outing, Donna," adding after a pause, "did you do that on purpose, by the way?"

"What?"

Jessica gave her a nudge. "You know—that young fop. Which way was it, eh? Did he trip you up, or you him?"

"For heaven's sake don't be ridiculous," Donna said

71

shortly. "I just caught my heel that's all. Anyway, I'd forgotten the incident."

But she hadn't and Jessica knew it.

"I think you're a sly one," she said, "but I don't blame you, not one bit."

They had not been in the house more than a few minutes before Sarah came into the hall saying in a hushed, secretive way, *"He* came, mistress. Not half an hour after you were gone. Left et theer by the door he did, so I took et to the kitchen jus' to see no prowler was around."

Donna drew her brows together. "He? Who do you mean? And whatever is it?"

Sarah lifted one hand, beckoning.

Donna followed her along the hall down the steps to the basement, where the flagged kitchen quarters were redolent with the tempting smell of baking mingled with roasting from the oven. "There 'tes," Sarah said, indicating a large cardboard box, near the door to the erstwhile butler's pantry. "Not heavy." She sniffed. "Looks like et has finery or hats or such like in et. But o' course he wasn' saying. Well he wouldn't be would he? Probably dedn' know hisself."

"For heaven's sake, Sarah, who's *he?"* Donna asked impatiently, bending down with one hand at the string, eyes peering at her name printed clearly on the lid. *Miss Donna Penroze.*

"The man," Sarah told her. "That theer Mr. Trevarvas's man. Drove up in fancy attire like as ef he was a duke hisself. 'Do you mind seein' Miss Penrose has this' he said, all haughty like. 'You leave et theer,' I told him. 'An' I'll be attendin' to et. Everythin's left in *my* charge,' I said, 'is looked after properly, and gits to its right owner. ' *That* made him take heed. He just gave a polite bow, an' touched his hat as he should an' off he was again in that fancy-looken trap, as quick an' bold lookin' as the devil's messenger."

Donna laughed. "Well, you've been very patient,

Sarah. I think if I'd been you I'd have had a peek. I couldn't have resisted it."

"Very temptin', Miss Donna, I do admit it, an' once or twice I caught that wench Libby fiddlin' with the string. But no harm done; after a good sound box on th' ear she learned her lesson an' kept off."

"Come along then, help me open it," Donna said. "Have you any scissors?"

Sarah brought a hefty steel kitchen pair from a hook on the dresser, and in a minute the box was opened, revealing at first only layers of tissue paper, with a note in an envelope on top.

Her name, written this time in a strong slanted hand, stared boldly up at her. So like himself, she thought, arrogant and self-assured, as though it were already his right to bestow gifts, just as her duty was to accept them. She was still staring at the envelope when she heard Sarah saying with an important edge to her voice, "Well, mistress? Aren't ee goin' to see what's beneath?"

Although she would rather have viewed the contents on her own, Donna felt at that point bound to allow the old servant a glimpse as well. Slipping the envelope into her pocket, she pulled the layers of paper off, and her pulses quickened with excitement. Even Sarah was awed into silence.

Materials. So varied, and so much of them; silks, satins, velvets, lace, together with an assortment of ribbons, thin chiffon in every shade one could imagine—luscious rich purples, crimsons, blue, soft greens, gold, and yellow. Where, she wondered after the first shock of surprise, could anyone, especially a man, have purchased such a fine choice of luxurious material?

She still had not spoken, but was letting her hands stray sensuously over the soft surfaces, savoring the smooth impact of rippling silk and satin, lingering lovingly on the thick velvet, when Sarah said, echoing her own thoughts, "An' *where* may I ask, did a man such as him find all that? An' for *what,* mistress?"

"London perhaps," Donna answered, almost mechanically. "Nicholas Trevarvas goes to London a great deal."

"And elsewhere no doubt," Sarah retorted darkly. "Wouldn' surprise me ef the likes of him was about many a time round the coast of a dark night when they Frenchies come. An' for what? 'Cept to make a packet. Plunder, smuggling. Aiss an' always *some*one to meet 'em. Or maybe that Trevarvas do leave others to do the dirty work for 'en, an' takes the reward hisself. You have no truck with 'en *or* his presents, Miss Donna. Whatever they say 'bout the railway and steam bringin' civilization to Cornwall, the old habits go on, an' will do, so long as gentlemen rogues like Trevarvas and his comp'ny have power in these parts. Besides, 'tesn' as ef he's courtin' ee, es et?"

"Oh Sarah! Really!" Donna laughed, but all the same she was momentarily discomforted. What Sarah said could be true. Cornwall was still very much a law to itself, even in this late period of the nineteenth century, and despite the achievements during the past thirty years of men like Brunel and Paxton, who had built the gigantic Crystal Palace in London. A building which was regarded as symbolic, Donna had read in a much respected newspaper, of all that man and spiritual inspiration could achieve in the world of art.

Those things were very much the other side of the Tamar but she was not prepared to let Sarah's gloomy observations spoil her pleasure in Nicholas Trevarvas's gesture. Anyway, she thought wryly, preparing to take the box upstairs, there would be even more moral condemnation from Sarah when she revealed the extent of her commitments to the enemy camp. She decided to do it that very evening. If she didn't, Jessica would probably let the cat out of the bag first.

When she was safely back in her bedroom with the key turned in the lock, she opened the note.

"Dear Miss Penroze," the letter ran, "I hope you may find the enclosed material suitable for equipping yourself with your required wardrobe. I suggest you do

74

not run to wild extravagance in style, but concentrate on being fashionable and at the same time dignified enough to impress my guests.

"I shall be pleased to welcome you a week hence, June 6th, to introduce you to my children, and give further instructions and help—I hope—concerning what is expected of you in the future.

"Three thirty would be a good time for me, and unless I hear to the contrary I shall expect you then. My man will call for you by chaise at Trencobban by three ten which should allow comfortable time for the journey.

"Yours sincerely and in good faith,
Nicholas Trevarvas."

For a moment or two after reading the note, Donna's pulses pounded, and the flush in her cheeks deepened to vivid spots on each high cheekbone. Her tawny eyes smoldered. The *nerve* of the man, she thought, in a rush of temper, to think he could order her in this way, demand her appearance at Polbreath without even asking if it was convenient. The impertinence of questioning her taste in clothes! She had a brief, violent urge to fling the materials he'd sent back into the box, and tell Sam to take it back immediately with the message she did not require the material, she had plenty of her own, and that perhaps some other day would suit him for their meeting, since she was engaged on the date stipulated.

Then, suddenly, she knew their was no point.

She possessed nothing of the proper quality to make attractive garments; besides which there was nothing really offensive in the manner of the note. The whole truth was that she resented its impersonality—the mere fact that he could already be treating her as just another employee or personal acquisition—to be displayed in order to inflate his own ego in the sight of others.

Nevertheless, when the initial hot reaction was over, a stimulating vision of herself adorned as grandly as any young duchess, returned and brought a secret smile to

75

her lips. For some time she idled about her room, swathing herself in turn with each of the varied materials. Gold and russet to emphasize the amber of her eyes, green satin for enhancing her cream skin, lush crimson velvet perhaps for winter evenings when the light of chandeliers and candles would play on the changing tones of her hair and cheeks. And blue . . . but no. Blue was not really her color. Jessica perhaps might have something made of that.

Then the chiffons and flimsier materials! In a sudden wave of exhilaration she unbuttoned and pulled off her dress, standing in her corsets and petticoat for a moment, before draping a length of thin mauve muslin from a shoulder over her chest and thighs, leaving one breast free except for the constricting chemise. She pulled it away recklessly, leaving the flesh warm and pulsing, pale yet glowing from an inner fire, which tinted the nipple as deep a pink as the fresh bud of a rose about to open into bloom.

I'm beautiful, she thought, regarding herself as though for the first time. Really beautiful. If Nicholas Trevarvas saw me . . . Her thoughts broke off abruptly, filling her with quick shame. How could she have permitted even one small reminder of him to invade her thoughts just then? Only a moment or two before he had been no more than a dark symbol in her mind.

It wouldn't happen again she told herself determinedly. In the future her attitude toward him would be remote and businesslike, with her senses always steeled and on guard against emotion.

She must forget, either, that in a very short time she had to present herself at his home where her appearance would be arrogantly scrutinized.

Suppose she were rebuffed? Suppose she were to turn the tables on him by looking like some ragamuffin gypsy girl, or wearing Luke's breeches with a boy's shirt? Would he want her in his household then? Or would he take the whip to her as he had to Jed? No, not that. But he would certainly see through the ruse and

76

pay her out somehow. Nothing would be gained by attempting to infuriate him. He had already purchased her services, and she had given her word.

The impish streak in her must be quelled—at least for the time being. She would act as her father would have wished under the circumstances—being a Penroze, and having made a promise—the least she could do was to keep it, provided that he too, honored his. But would he?

The question still lingered in her mind as she turned her head before the mirror, this way and that, admiring herself, although she knew it was unladylike and would have been frowned on by Sarah and other respectable women. But then she, Donna, wasn't all respectable. Was any beautiful girl completely so? And what was respectability anyway, but a mode of manners, a veneer so often of goodness, when goodness wasn't really there?

"Oh botheration!" she exclaimed as a pin scratched her shoulder. She let the chiffon fall to the floor, and at that moment there was a tap on the door. As Donna unlocked it Jessica entered.

"My!" she exclaimed. "What on earth are you doing? And what's all that?"

Donna picked her dress up, tugged it over her shoulders, and replied acidly, "What does it look like? And why did you come in without warning? You should have waited."

Jessica didn't seem to hear, just stared at the collection speechless, eyes riveted greedily on the luxurious array of silks, velvets and chiffons. Then she managed to say, running forward to the box where a shawl straggled over one side, "God in Heaven! What's . . . ?"

"Don't swear." Being dictatorial helped Donna to put aside the guilt she felt at the erotic fantasies she had been encouraging a moment or two before.

"And don't be so prim, Donna. Don't pretend anyway." Jessica's blue eyes had a shrewd, calculating look in them as she continued, "From your middle-aged admirer? Or should I say protector?"

"How dare you! Hold your tongue. Mr. Trevarvas isn't middle-aged, and he isn't my protector."

Jessica shrugged. "No? Well, obviously he has hopes. Anyway, you've done well for yourself. Some women have all the luck." She sighed. "I suppose you were thinking of taking it to that pie-faced Miss Payne on your own and getting a whole new wardrobe made up for yourself?"

Donna relented, knowing how envious her sister-in-law must be.

"Miss Payne? Probably—she's clever with the needle—and that new machine. But I was planning for you, too, Jessica."

"You were?"

"I thought some of the blue silk would be nice for special occasions, and maybe the gray cloth made up for daytime—perhaps with a toque of some kind, and a fitting jacket. Or even a cape. Capes never properly go out of fashion. And your figure would carry one."

Jessica didn't know what to think. Toques, capes! She was further bewildered when Donna added, "I saw a copy of *La Vie Parisienne* on a table at the dressmaker's, just as we were leaving. Why she didn't show it I can't think. It's a most elegant magazine, Jessica, and I'll certainly want a look at it when we go next. I know French, thanks to a stuffy governess when I was young. We'll see that both of us are quite up-to-date. I promise you."

Jessica, too awed to register the full excitement she was feeling, merely said, "When is it? When shall we go to Penzance?"

"When I can arrange it. Soon. But we can't expect poor Miss Payne to have things done instantly. And first of all I've got to think what to wear for next week."

"Next week?"

"Mr. Trevarvas wants to see me," Donna answered calmly, averting her eyes. "To present me to his children, and show me around the estate, so that I have a good knowledge of what lies before me in my . . . my social duties."

The term cost an effort, and Jessica well knew it. But in view of the rosy future so obviously intermixed with her sister-in-law's commitments at Polbreath, she was careful not to show that, and curbed any sarcastic comments in favor of a complimentary, "I'm sure you'll do well Donna. You've got such a manner with you when you feel like it."

Yes, Donna thought wryly, and it was her manner more than anything else that would have to impress Nicholas Trevarvas on the next visit. He'd seen her in the only really smart attire she had, and there'd certainly not be time for her to acquire anything different within the week. Unless—she suddenly recalled the chest in the attic upstairs, where a few relics, treasured by William, still remained, including a mauve high-necked satin with a full skirt, embroidered hemline, and a fitting jacket, heavily embroidered and braided down the front like that worn by the Princess of Wales in 1860. Eloise Penroze had had it copied from a photograph, or fashion plate, following one of her rare visits to London with William.

Satin of course was not usual for everyday wear. But the full skirt could be taken in and drawn to the back to give a flowing type of bustle. She could redecorate her small hat, and wear her mother's embroidered shawl about her shoulders. Such garments had been considered sacred in her father's lifetime, but it was surely wrong now for them to remain idle and unwanted in a dusty, forgotten room, when they could be put to such practical use.

And so, during the next few days, she set about the necessary alterations herself, to the concern and disapproval of Sarah, who by then had been told of Donna's forthcoming post at Polbreath.

" 'Tesn' right," she said stubbornly, setting her lips primly. "Not usin' the dear mistress's—your respected mother's gown—God rest her dear saul—for such a dark purpose. What d'ee think the folk roundabouts will be sayin'? Eh? An' Parson Treeve hisself? Oh I knows you edn' inclined for church matters these days. But you bein' the daughter of William Penroze should have regard for religious opinion."

"Parson Treeve?" Donna echoed contemptuously. "Let him say what he likes, the old hypocrite. He does plenty in his spare time I've heard; things that would scare the pants off the Archbishop if he knew."

"You shock me. You really do," Sarah said, flinging her hands up in the air. "To think I'd ever hear the like, from the daughter of dear respected master, and him responsible for the living of Gwynvoor, too. Or was." She lifted her apron to her eye.

"He didn't choose old Treeve," Donna said tartly. "And he'd no illusions about him either. So for pity's sake stop the waterworks and leave me in peace."

Forgetting that she was a servant in the house, Sarah's show of sentimentality turned to swift anger. "You watch yourself Miss Donna," she cried. "Ef I was an older woman an' you a year or two younger in a different station of life I'd have my hand 'cross your backside so you'd never forget et. I can't for the life of me think what's got into you. Unless et's that coarse creature your brother married. I knowed no good'd come of 'er. An' et hasn't . . ." She broke off breathless, her plump cheeks gradually fading from vivid crimson to a grayish pallor that was the color of lard.

Donna was about to speak when she saw the older woman gasp and fall back against the table, one hand at her heart.

Any scolding Donna had been about to give was swallowed up by fear.

"Sarah!" she cried, fetching a chair for her. "Sarah—are you all right? There now. Sit comfortably and I'll get the brandy." But when she'd located a bottle in the cupboard, kept there for cooking purposes and for just such an emergency as this, Sarah was already looking better and refused it.

"No think you, mistress," she said primly. "I'm quite all right, an 'tedn' my habit to be drinkin' spirits in daytime. I lost my temper an' that's that. I do apologize to 'ee, because et edn' my place to go tiradin' at my bet-

ters, such as you. So ef you'd rather be lookin' for someone else in my place, 'tis for 'ee to say so now. Sam
an' me will be all right. There's always . . ."

"Oh stop it," Donna said, half smiling. "How do you
think we'd manage without you after all these years?
You're part of the family, and always will be. But . . ."

"Aiss, mistress?"

Donna's voice was gentle as she continued, "Because
we have to have money, and because an opening for
earning it has been offered to me, I have to take it
Sarah. I've already told you of Mr. Trevarvas's proposition and that I've accepted it. Quite an honorable position, I can assure you, just for helping with his children,
and socially sometimes. I realize you can't bring yourself to approve. But I think my father would have understood. In fact I'm sure he would. So the matter's settled, and other things will be, quite shortly. I shall
arrange for you to have better help at Trencobban—
yes, yes." As Sarah made a gesture of dissension.
"There's going to be no argument about that. Understand?"

Sarah hesitated before replying, "Ef you do say so,
mistress."

"All right then. And now we'll forget this little scene
shall we, and get on with the day's work."

The episode, coming as it had on top of her elation
about her mother's dress, left Donna feeling curiously
tired. If the weather had been fine that day she would
have eased her mood by a swift gallop on Saladin. But
it wasn't. From a thin drizzle in the morning, lowering clouds had brought heavy rain which pounded with
rhythmic, dreary monotony through the trees, spattering
the ground with puddles and rivulets of water. The
formless line of sea and sky had become swallowed
into one—a mere indistinct suggestion of lighter gray
merging into a sullen, darker gray hanging like a pall
over the Atlantic. No ship was visible, there was no
sight or sound of gull or wild bird from the bushes—
only an immense gathering cloud of oppression, a
haunting sense of doom and loneliness that made her

81

wonder momentarily if her efforts had been worthwhile. Even a glimpse of Trevarvas astride his horse would have been welcome just then. But there was nothing. No indication of life at all except the faint clatter of pots from the kitchen. Sam and Ted were probably in the stables, and Janey in her bedroom playing with her crayons and the new box of paints bought for her in Penzance.

Perhaps, after all, it would be a welcome change going to Polbreath. A vision of the dark horseman flashed through her mind quickly, and was as speedily replaced by the memory of another, younger face. That of the fair young man who had so romantically and unnecessarily insisted on helping her in Penzance when she'd briefly caught her heel in her gown.

CHAPTER FIVE

The next morning Donna woke knowing that she had business matters to attend to. Tom Craze would arrive early at Trencobban with an accounts sheet of the sum needed to reimburse the workers at Wheal Faith. It would include his estimate of a fair proportion to be set aside for the tributers, whose percentage of coinage had been distressingly low in recent months, because the copper they had salvaged had been so thin.

The weather had cleared during the night, and the lifting mist was already silvered by the fitful glint of the the rising sun when she went downstairs to breakfast. Janey was sitting at the table in the small room that adjoined the larger dining room where they usually had meals. Jessica was with her, and both of them were looking considerably neater than usual. A gesture, Donna guessed, to future prosperity and her own promises of fresh clothes and jaunts to Penzance and Falmouth.

"What's this in aid of?" Donna inquired trying not to smile. "There's no outing today you know. I have to see Tom here presently. It will be a business sort of morning."

"Of course," Jessica replied with hypocritical meekness. "But as Janey and I have to look our best when we can, there's got to be a start sometime. And Janey's going to be a good girl from now on, aren't you love?"

Janey's solemn, strange eyes rested thoughtfully on Donna for a moment before she replied, "Yes, Mama."

"Well—don't be too good," Donna said sharply, "or

I'll be wondering what you're up to. Small girls are allowed a few pranks. Isn't that so, Jessica?"

The bright smile on Jessica's lips belied the sullen expression of her eyes, as she replied, "Of course. As long as it's not stealing my scent or fiddling about where she shouldn't."

"I won't take any more scent, Mama," Janey promised.

"You won't have to," Donna promised. "When we go into Penzance I'll buy you a tablet of that new sweet-smelling soap with a French name; then you can wash yourself and be perfumed all over at the same time."

Later, when the meal was over, Jessica said to her sister-in-law, "I wish you wouldn't spoil the child, Donna. It'll be nice having a few new clothes for her. But it's no help to me, as I've told you time after time, having her think every time she wants anything or I've checked her, she can go running to Aunty Donna. It's not fair. She's mine, after all, and I know what's good for her. She may appear as though toffee wouldn't melt in her mouth, but there are things about her you don't know."

"Yes, I realize. Her father for instance."

Jessica's lips tightened. "There's no reason for you hinting and prying. Why can't you let things be? And just when I thought things were going to be better between us."

"They are," Donna asserted firmly, "as long as you keep off the bottle, and your hands off Janey."

"I told you I would, didn't I?"

"Well then, that's all right. Now," in an effort to change the subject, "I thought we might drive into Penzance tomorrow morning. What do you say?"

"I suppose so," Jessica answered sullenly.

"Oh well, if you don't want to . . ."

Jessica's surliness lifted like magic. "I do want to; of course I do. To be fitted do you mean?"

"Well, look at styles, as I told you. And have measurements taken, I expect."

The mere prospect so delighted Jessica that she was

84

all radiance as she left the room, appearing despite her brown, out-dated dress, as magnificent as any fashionable courtesan. Her full yet well-proportioned figure was thrown to advantage against a streak of sunlight from the window; her pink and white skin lapped to rosy gold, and yellow hair to silvered flame, holding that elusive quality so sought after by portrait painters of the past.

No wonder Luke had fallen for her, Donna thought as she went out through the door. However shady her profession had been, her charm in early youth must have been intoxicating indeed.

She touched the bell a moment later, and when Sarah appeared, told her she was expecting Tom Craze.

"I'll see him in the library," she said. "I've always noticed men are so much more at ease there."

"Yes, mistress," Sarah said, wondering how it could be that the young lady of Trencobban could be one day so wild and unpredictable, the next as sober and well-mannered as any of the highest gentry in the land. There was no understanding William Penroze's daughter, and that was a fact.

Tom arrived half an hour later, presenting, a little doubtfully, a full account of the immediate monies required, and for what purpose.

"I've bin over it several times," he told her. "It seems a good amount but it's required if you're going to get the idea of stinting and bad times out of the men's heads. They've gone on too long for too little in their pockets and bellies, to take kindly to anything less than I have here. And this is just for the interim period, Miss Donna. A little later, as soon as we can arrange—I'd like that man down from Derby—the expert, to advise. And he won't do it for nothing. Then the machinery. That'll cost a deal of cash. But Harveys at Hayle will probably do it on a premium—the engine anyway."

"Yes. I realize all this."

"But does Trevarvas?"

"It isn't his affair," Donna retorted stubbornly. "We

have the money, and you have the go-ahead. What more do you want?"

"The expense of a proposition like Wheal Faith can't be judged accurately until you get down to the actual job," Tom said. "On top of everything else we'll have to get extra labor in."

"Naturally. Where's the problem in that?"

Tom shrugged. "Just that I hope we've enough in hand to see us through without worrying."

"If the cost is higher than we expect there's something at the back of me, now, Tom," Donna reminded him.

Tom relaxed. "Very well then. Just so long as you know what you're doing. And now, about this account?"

"I'll give it my blessing and signature," Donna told him, "With a note to John Crebbyn for him to hand the sum stipulated over to you."

"So be it, ma'am."

"I just don't . . ." She paused, before continuing with a sudden longing to be done with figures and estimates and matters that were quite beyond her grasp, "I just don't want to have to rack my brains trying to think bothersome finance out, Tom. I trust you. Trevarvas does, and the men. By taking this side of things on your shoulders you're helping me so much. Can't you understand? My father would have. He'd have said, 'Let Tom deal with it. Tom knows all there is to know about practical mining.' He said so in those very words, many times in the past."

"Well, I'm honored to hear you say so, Miss Donna," Tom told her with a hint of emotion in his gruff voice. "I'll be taking off then. Joe Paynter's taking the cart into Penzance with some vegetables, and will give me a lift."

"But you could have the gig."

"No need for that. Joe and I'll have a drink when we've got our business done, and come back together."

"Very well." Donna wrote the note for John Crebbyn, and five minutes later watched Tom's sturdy figure walking down the drive to the main road, where the Paynter home stood around a bend on the opposite side; a small granite-faced square farmstead, overlooking Gwynvoor.

She sighed with relief as he disappeared. Money affairs not only worried but bored her, especially with so much else to think of, including the meeting ahead with Nicholas Trevarvas.

The next two days passed quickly enough, and at the appointed hour the Polbreath chaise drew up at Trencobban, the driver elegantly attired in stove hat and yellow coat, much to Sam's contempt, who happened to be in the side drive at the time.

"All swagger and common show," he grumbled to Sarah later, when the vehicle had driven away again, with Donna seated within, wearing her mother's fine mauve attire.

"She's up to no good," Sarah affirmed, "our fine young madam. You mark my words, Sam, evil will come to this house unless we do take great care, put our faith in the Almighty, and keep as careful a watch on 'en as us can."

Sam grunted, and turned the conversation into other channels, as he always did when it came to one woman arguing against another. Jessica, meanwhile, was staring from the upstairs window of her room and caught just a glimpse of the chaise as it took a turn along the moorland road to the right, cantering at a smart pace toward the west.

Lucky thing, she thought, to have all that money—which she must have, to be taking off to Nicholas like that. Lucky too, to have everything in front of her, good living, drink, and rich men in the future, no doubt, to dance attendance on her. No more having to stint and scrape—not that Donna knew the first thing about that, really—no fears or insecurity, no horrible dark image from the past lurking always at the back of the mind, ready to spring out if she gave it a chance, and set her trembling.

God! if only she could rid herself of it for good.

She turned, looking automatically for the bottle. But of course it wasn't there. Donna had been really mean lately about seeing nothing alcoholic came her way.

Jed then. Jed was the only answer. She wanted him. Her thighs ached suddenly, the hidden pulse of her womb leaping, subduing the fear of her mind into a longing of the flesh. To forget—forget . . . "Jed," she whispered, sinking the nails of her hands into the palms, "Jed, help me."

She flung a black shawl over her brown dress, and scurried along the landing, almost knocking Janey over as she turned the corner by the stairs.

"Mama—are you going out, Mama . . . ?" She heard the little girl saying, "Can I . . . ?"

"No. No! You can't. Leave me alone. Go to Sarah. Sarah'll give you a cake. Quick . . . d'you hear?"

The child's eyes widened, though Jessica didn't see. "Yes, Mama," she whispered obediently, "I'll go," and fled like a frightened rabbit back the way she'd come, as Jessica went ahead to the wide front staircase, which, after one abrupt turn under an arched glass window, led straight into the hall and front door.

There was no one about. She cut in front of the house to a side path leading directly to the moor, and eventually to Wheal Faith, standing bleak against the rim of cliff and sea. It would be two hours at least before Jed's core, toiling along the dark levels, was finished, but she would feel safer knowing he was not too far away. Jed was strong. With Jed she would forget who she was, where she came from, and when he had her she'd be at peace—until the next time, which could be the following day or six months ahead. She had no knowing when the "thing" would return.

She hurried on, with the path becoming narrower, until it was only a thread stretching through heather and furze, sloping downward now so the sea was clear beyond the cliffs, still and bright as a sheet of glass under the afternoon sky. The mine, to her fancy, then, had assumed its own identity, a somber, hungry shape demanding food it couldn't have, with its slits of flame-streaked eyes, and pumping rod thrusting and falling—thrusting, grasping, grasping—her hand instinctively went to her neck. She shivered, although the air was warm, and leaned against a boulder, watching. Then she started off again, and continued walking until she reached a twisted thorn where she could remain huddled in the shadows around its trunk with the black shawl over her fair hair, so that no one could notice. Sometimes she sat, sometimes she walked a few yards and back, while the sun gradually crept a little lower in the sky and a veil of cloud crept chillingly from the sea, shrouding her figure deeper in oblivion.

When at last the bell rang, she tensed herself to meet him. One or two Bal maidens came first, cutting up to the road, and singing as they went, though their voices were tired. Then the straggling column of men began to appear, knees bent ploddingly, heads thrust forward under their miners' hats. There was not much talk, and no laughter. One or two chatted together before they broke up, crossing the moor in different directions for their homes. Most making for Gwynvoor. Jed was about the last to appear, and he was alone.

She waited, still with the shawl over her head, until he passed by above, then went after him rapidly but unobtrusively, until she was close enough to call, "Jed . . . Jed . . ." in a soft but carrying voice.

He turned abruptly His expression was not pleasant. "What you want? At it again are ye?"

Her breathing quickened as she drew the shawl from her head allowing the yellow hair to cascade over the brown dress. "I need you Jed," she whispered. "Can I talk to you?" Her hand touched his arm. He laughed, shaking her off.

"*Talk?* With *you*? I told you wumman, when I want you I'll have you. An' that's not now. See? I've a wife sick at home. An' a wife's a wife. *You*. You're only a slut."

She rushed at him, tearing and pulling his coat, lashing him with a fury of words torn in breathless whispers from her throat. "You cur. You filthy creature you.

You think that do you—well it's a lie—a lie do you hear? And you'll never lay a finger on me again, Jed Andrewartha." Her voice was rising to a scream.

He laughed again, and lunged at her, pushing her down into the bracken. "I'll have you, like I said, whenever I feel like it. An' d'you know why? Because you'll be lustin' sick for me. So take yourself off now, and leave me be."

He strode on, followed by another man she had not known was there. He must have heard. If word were carried to Donna there'd be no new dresses, no home, no roof over her head. Without these where would she be but back where she started, only worse because of the "thing" she dreaded, that in moments such as this seemed to envelop her. A menacing shadow of retribution that with each day that passed, each month and year, moved a little closer. No. Donna mustn't know. She had been a fool to come, and so near the mine too. She'd been a greater fool to plead with Jed who had no heart, no softness, only body and his appetite for a woman when the mood was on him. The wretch, she thought, as she stumbled on, almost running, toward Trencobban. But she'd learned something. She'd never expect anything of him again. The next time he needed her he could look somewhere else, or come pleading and begging so she had the power for once. Never again, she thought, rushing ahead, never again like this—knowing, though, that if he stepped before her now, with that smile crinkling his rough large face and the hot light in his eyes, she would have no strength to fight him for long.

But Donna! The rising fear that some of the men might have seen and recognized her, returning to override temporarily, everything else. She'd have to think up something, be ready for any blunt sudden questioning from her sister-in-law. Janey perhaps. Bribe Janey to say Mama had been in her room reading stories to her, or some such thing. This possibility made her feel better. Anyway, she decided, as she slipped in a side door of Trencobban, she'd probably been worrying unnecessarily. The light had been bad during her confrontation with Jed. And with her in the shadows, wearing that dark shawl and dress—no one could have seen her features. No one but Jed. And he wouldn't say. As to the man following, it could only be her word against his if anything came up, and all she would do was to dub him a liar and cheat who'd been trying to blackmail her, and that would be that.

Her characteristic resilience had already asserted itself as she crept quietly up to her room. But her body, thankfully, was tired. Tired enough for her to fling herself on the bed and fall asleep almost instantly, but not before wondering lazily what Donna was doing, and picturing herself, instead of her sister-in-law, being shown around the awesome precincts of Polbreath.

In fact, at the precise time of Jessica's return to Trencobban, Donna, after a brief survey of Polbreath's sumptuous ground floor, was waiting with Nicholas in the conservatory. She was to be presented to his two children, Ianthe, aged six, and Jonathan, three years her senior, who were both in the care of a governess for their rudimentary education.

"Jonathan is to go to Rugby next year," Nicholas said, "and high time too. As for Ianthe—well, we'll see. She's a trifle hot-headed at the moment but I'm sure you'll appreciate a young girl's moods, especially one with a will of her own and no mother to curb it."

With the uncomfortable feeling that duties were already being assigned to her that she'd not bargained for, Donna said quickly, "That's surely the business of the governess?"

"It should be," Nicholas agreed. "But Miss Pullen isn't exactly endowed by nature to charm a child of Ianthe's character. You may well have more success."

Flushing at the implication of his words, and lifting her chin an inch higher, Donna said, "I've very little knowledge of children, Mr. Trevarvas, and I didn't think my involvement was with them, but as hostess in your house."

She was staring straight ahead, but she could feel his

eyes assessing her once more, shrewdly, yet with a deeply personal interest which was somehow discomfiting. He got up abruptly, walked to an assortment of potted flowering plants on a shelf, plucked an exotic orange colored bloom, which he brought back to her, saying, "Take that ridiculous thing off your head, Miss Penroze."

She gaped, with one hand going to her hat automatically. "I . . ."

"Take it off, I say," he repeated in a remote, cold voice "It's quite ridiculous. More suited to a charade than civilized society. And though we may be somewhat behind the times in this part of the world, there's no point in advertising the fact. You don't have to put on airs you know, although you've plenty of them I've no doubt. But in my house I'll expect you to dress in accordance with your position—and your own natural beauty."

That last compliment, coming as it did after what amounted to an outrageous insult took her so aback that she found herself somehow taking the hat she'd considered so smart from her head. The muted glow of early evening combined with the glimmer of a lighted chandelier from the adjoining room, gave a softened glory to the dusky hair, bathing her figure with a gentle radiance, that, had she known it, filled him with desire. He bent down, placed the flower behind one ear, where it rested like an orange star that reflected the shade of her eyes.

"There," he said. "That's better. You look at least—possible." His tones, remote and dry, damped any feeling she'd had that he admired her. Annoyance combined with a dull sense of disappointment that flooded her nerves and body.

"Thank you," she said politely, as her hand, faintly trembling, touched the waxy petals. "I'm sorry you don't approve of hats, Mr. Trevarvas. I'll remember in future, and wear only veils, dark ones preferably, like a well-mannered widow."

Her last answer, she realized a moment later, was ab-

92

surd and childish. And it was obvious that he thought so too. His lips had a wry, amused tilt when, playing her own game, he replied, "If you feel like that, certainly. Your commitments to me do, I suppose, appear rather as a death-in-life ahead, for one so young and unversed in manners as yourself. Never mind, Miss Penroze, we'll sort things out somehow."

She was spared the effort of thinking up a quick and suitable reply by the entrance of the two children and their governess. Donna's first impressions were electric, of surprise, almost shock. The girl was so beautiful— extremely dark, with a golden skin touched by rose at the cheeks, a wealth of thick black hair caught loosely back by a green ribbon, and large violet eyes fringed by thick dark lashes. Her parted mouth was firmly set over a dimpled, stubborn little chin, and her gaze, as it rested on Donna, was direct, almost bold. The boy was different. Fair, slim, tall for his age, with slanting hazel eyes that had a hazy appraising look in them, as she said, holding out his hand, "Hullo. How do you do."

Donna touched his fingers briefly, aware at the same time that the governess, who looked a pale uninteresting creature, was prompting Ianthe to do the same. But Ianthe shrugged. "No. Why? It's silly."

"Do as you're told," Nicholas said abruptly, with a note in his voice which compelled her to obey.

"Hullo, both of you," Donna said, adding impulsively, "Don't worry. I'm not an ogre."

"Of course not," Ianthe retorted, "ogres are men, silly."

Disregarding the child's remark this time, Nicholas merely said formally to the governess, "Miss Pullen, this is Miss Penroze, who in the future will preside as my hostess on such occasions—socially—when I consider it necessary, and will also be able to relieve you a little where my children are concerned."

He broke off, watching the reaction of both women as they faced each other, shaking hands politely with the usual formal greetings on their lips, and veiled dislike in their eyes. Pity in Donna's who thought it odd that such a thin, nondescript female should have strayed into Trevarvas's household, and in Agatha Pullen's something more positive, a swift instinctive hatred that changed their narrowed greyness to brilliant cat-green.

Nicholas was amused, thinking how diverting it would be to see the thin-breasted bantam, as he had dubbed her, sparring with such a desirable opponent. It would do her good. Make her smarten herself up a bit more. He knew very well that if he so much as cocked a finger in her direction she would come running. When she had first arrived there, he'd had half a mind to visit her one night. He had seen her shadow reflected through the half open door on her bedroom wall. Whether it had been intentional or not he had never known. But she'd been younger then, with a slim neck and tiny breasts like half-grown apples; something fragile and pathetic about her had touched him, briefly.

Thank God he'd thought twice about it. Seduction of a penurious parson's daughter would inevitably have meant marriage, and that would have landed him in an intolerably dreary position. Poor Pullen. He'd wondered in idle moments if any man had ever looked on her with desire or touched her lips in passion, and decided not. Lately he'd been aware of her increasing dedication to the needs of his family—and himself—and he was beginning to find it embarrassing.

Now, with Donna a part of their life at Polbreath, she might learn to busy herself in other directions. He hoped so. He had no wish to hurt her, but if she continued to pursue him as she had done recently, he'd have to send her packing. The idea was distasteful to him. The following year he intended that not only his son, but also Ianthe be sent away to school. School would mean a natural termination of Agatha Pullen's services.

As for Donna—he had a shrewd idea that she would be a match for his wayward offspring. Jonathan would certainly be no trouble. He could see admiration already registering in the narrow eyes that were too knowledgeable for his years. A haughty, supercilious boy—a true Vencarne, who one day would inherit the title that was now held by his great-uncle, the younger brother of Nicholas's late father-in-law. Trevarvas had very little in common with the son who had the unfortunate knack of reminding him of Selina. Ianthe was a different matter.

If he was capable of fatherly love, he reserved it for her, and the emotion was passionately reciprocated.

During the quarter of an hour that followed he took note with dry shrewdness of the interaction between the two women and his children. Then he said abruptly, "Come along, Miss Pullen. We'd better leave my new— help—to get to know these two brats of mine." And to Donna, "why don't you allow Jonathan to show you the tower? You might be interested."

With a sense of relief Donna watched Trevarvas and Agatha Pullen leave the conservatory and go out through the adjoining room that was by then ablaze with light.

"Do you want to see the tower?" Jonathan asked, staring at her intimidatingly. "There's nothing there except my things—stamps, and butterfly cases, and goldfish, and guns."

"Guns?"

"Oh yes. I collect them. But they're never fired. Still if you're frightened . . ."

"Of course I'm not frightened," Donna told him. "All right. Yes. I'd like to see your domain."

"Domain. I like that word," the boy said. "I shall call it that now—always." Adding, after a short pause. "For a woman, you're not bad. I mean you seem to have ideas."

"Thank you."

"Come along then, I'll show you. We shall have to go outside—it's rather dark now, but only a few yards down the path. Would you like me to take your arm?"

Donna almost burst out laughing, but controlled herself. "Oh no, really. I'm not a tottery old woman you know."

"Like Pullen," Ianthe said sharply, hurrying along by her side.

"Miss Pullen isn't old at all," Donna said calmly, but with a rebuke in her voice.

"She looks old," the little girl said. "She pretends she isn't because she's after my father."

Donna, taken aback, replied shortly, "I never heard of such a thing. You've been listening to people talking, I suppose. Well, remember, Ianthe, it doesn't do to believe what everyone says."

"Oh I don't. But I see things."

"What things?"

"Ah." In knowing tones, "I shan't tell you. Except I know why you're here."

"What do you mean?"

Ianthe shrugged, and as they reached the door of the tower which jutted out from the high wall of the house six feet or so across the drive, she asked pertly, "Are you going to share my father's bedroom?"

Too outraged to speak at once, Donna paused, with the lamp from above shining down from the squat tower, lighting her eyes to orange flame. "How dare you speak to me like that? If you ever do again, do you hear . . ." She grasped the child's arm and shook her before concluding, "I'll box your ears and tell your father, who'll take a whip to you. Do you understand, miss?"

Hot cheeked, controlling a desire to stick out her tongue, Ianthe retorted "All right. I won't say things. But I'll think what I like."

She turned to go back to the house. Donna caught her by the shoulders and propelled her to the front behind her brother. "No you don't, Ianthe Trevarvas, you go straight up those stairs with Jonathan; I want to see his collections and goldfish. And you're coming with me."

After this brief exchange of words and wills, Ianthe subsided into sulky silence.

The tower, which, despite its name, reached little further than Polbreath's top floor, had a flight of stone steps with a handrail stretching directly upwards to one largish room with a cubby-hole of an attic leading off it. In the room, already lit by one oil lamp, were books, a table, two chairs, a large bowl with fish in it on a ledge beneath the window, which was of narrow gothic design, and a number of cases on shelves lining one wall, filled with butterflies, stamps, and relics of bones and ancient instruments probably from the grounds or coast. Donna, who disliked seeing winged creatures so pinioned, turned her eyes to the stamps, and afterwards said, "What about the guns?"

Jonathan led her proudly to the small attic. "There they are," he said, indicating an assortment of firearms including a couple of dueling pistols arranged on a narrow table, and above it on the wall.

"Very impressive," Donna commented. "How did you get them all? Some are very old, aren't they?"

"Oh yes. My grandfather gave me one or two. Heirlooms, he said. But father doesn't like them; he's not very interested in tradition you know. But I'm different. I shall be Lord Vencarne one day. Did you know?"

"No I didn't. But I'm sure you'll fit the title." And her words held no hypocrisy. It was really true, she thought, facing his unswerving stare, proud set of the head, and well-modeled, but thin, tightly set mouth.

Ianthe who had been so silent until then, piped up very clearly, "Being a lord's nothing. Lords all come from bastards. That's what Abraham said."

"Who's Abraham?"

"A gardener we had. But he's left now. He lives alone in the woods in a funny hut sort of place with two goats." Her voice sounded reflective. "I liked him. I'd rather live with old Abraham than that silly Pullen woman. Abraham knows everything about foxes and badgers, and what the wild flowers are called. He can whistle birds and they come when no one else is there. One day . . ." her voice died wistfully.

"Yes?"

"One day I think I shall run away and be a gypsy."

"Sometimes I've wanted to do that myself," Donna told her, taking her hand.

"You have?" The child's voice was incredulous.

"Oh yes."

"Then why don't you?"

"Because when you're grown up other things happen and you're not free any more," Donna answered.

"I think that's wrong, don't you?"

"Oh stop your silly questions, Ianthe," Jonathan interrupted before Donna could reply. "Come on, I've had enough now."

"I'm not that sure I have," Donna said thinly. "Don't try your lordly airs on me, young man. I'm going to take a look at the view first," she added firmly. "Then we'll go."

"But you can't see anything. It's dark."

"Not quite. Anyway there's no such thing as complete darkness."

She returned to the large room and crossed to the window which overlooked the trees and the moors, stretching far away, it seemed, to Trencobban. Everything suddenly seemed dramatic and lonely, giving her the impression of being cooped up in some remote prison with freedom near but always a little beyond her grasp. Yes. She well knew what the child Ianthe meant about longing to run away, and for a moment was amazed with herself, not merely for becoming indebted to Trevarvas, which under the circumstances was inevitable, but for the dark emotional involvement that was already spreading its net about her, making it impossible for her to predict or even properly assess her own feelings.

Presently they went downstairs again and back to the house. Miss Pullen was waiting in the conservatory room, her small mouth tightly shut, face grayish-pale under her smoothed-down, light brown hair. So stupid of her to wear gray, Donna couldn't help thinking, if it was green now . . . she smiled involuntarily, watching a faint color tinge the high cheekbones as the governess said, "You've been a long time, children. It's almost time for your supper. Come along now."

"Oh, but . . ."

"No buts. Your father is waiting for Miss Penroze in the drawing room." Her voice was cool, polite. But her eyes were the greenest Donna had ever seen. Perhaps she has more to her than one would think at first glance, Donna thought. She might even be a bit of a bitch at heart.

The idea was stimulating. A bit of a duel with another woman might provide amusing diversion—especially with Nicholas Trevarvas at the heart of it. She'd have preferred friendship, but if that wasn't to be—well, to hell with the dry-as-dust creature. She'd show her, on the first opportunity what beauty allied with brains could do to a man. At that point her resolve faltered. Whatever else Trevarvas might be, he was certainly no fool.

No. Her best course was to appear dignified, and well bred, as befitted William Penroze's daughter. Later, when she was properly initiated and in control of her duties at Polbreath, she could relax and let herself go a bit more.

With Donna in this mood, her last encounter with Trevarvas that day proved to be a polite formal affair, with little indication on either side of what the other was thinking.

But as he watched her driving away in the chaise, profile silhouetted through the window against the wan light of a rising moon, with the ridiculous hat perched once more on her head, a conflict of emotions stirred him which he had never previously experienced in quite the same way.

Turning from the window he saw the star-shaped orange flower he'd given her lying on the floor, its petals wilted and stem crushed.

He picked it up involuntarily, holding it to his nostrils. A dying perfume lingered there insidiously reminiscent of youth too soon gone sour. Himself?

Through the gilt-framed mirror he studied his face

critically, strong dark features, too stern mouth, and shrewd eyes at that moment consumed by a veiled inner passion he'd never, until then, allowed to shatter his equilibrium. He wanted her, this proud Donna Penroze. Wanted her as he'd never desired any woman in his life before, and sooner or later, he'd no doubt, she would come to heel—unless the miracle happened, and she delivered herself willingly and tenderly to the passionate love he knew was in him to give.

Still, much would have to happen before that. He shrugged, turned, and was about to throw the flower away when on impulse he took it instead to a crystal bowl filled with roses, and placed it there, before pouring himself a stiff whiskey to relieve the tension of his mind.

It took him by surprise to realize that a week had gone by and yet he was still unable to erase her image from his thoughts. On impulse he sent a note to her, by Sarne, saying that if possible he would like her to come to his home the following Saturday. He would have a friend from France staying with him for the weekend with his daughter.

"Annette Rouget is quite young, having just left finishing school I'm told," he wrote, "and for six months I understand they are traveling about Europe. If you could be present it would be a help. I am not adept at entertaining young ladies of her type, and if you could take her off my hands for a bit I would be free to discuss certain business with her father, Paul Rouget. Don't think of this in any way as part of future social duties, but merely as a favor to me . . . if you can bring yourself to do it.

"Unless I hear otherwise I will presume you agree, and will send the chaise for you about seven.

Yrs,
Nicholas Trevarvas."

When she received the letter Donna was at first resentful. Why should he expect any favor of her, when her commitment had been arranged on a purely business basis? And to entertain a boring schoolgirl into the

100

bargain? She had a quick impulse to refuse, telling him she had a former engagement, but on second thought, dismissed it, realizing he probably wouldn't believe her, and that to show obstinacy at this point might jeopardize any future help.

So at the appointed time she was already hovering about the hall waiting for the chaise to arrive, dressed with care, and modestly in a tightly-waisted gray silk dress with a high neck that, had she known it, only emphasized the budding curves beneath. Her gleaming black hair had been caught up by a shred of gold chiffon, and her only ornament was a gold locket containing a curl of her mother's hair.

To her surprise, she found Annette Rouget vivacious, amusing, and charming. She had no visual beauty, being sallow, slight, and less than five feet tall, with too wide a mouth, and rather small dark eyes beneath heavy brows. But she was intelligent and lively, and her English, except for a perceptible accent, excellent.

Her interest, Donna soon learned, was flower-painting, and an intensive studying of the flora of certain districts and countries.

"One day," she said to Donna after an animated conversation following dinner. "you must come to France. Yes? And I will show you all the books I have, and my paintings too . . . though they are not clever, you understand? Just line drawings filled in with water color."

"I'd like to very much," Donna answered, "and if I can I will."

Paul Rouget had his daughter's coloring and lack of height, but there the likeness ended. He was portly with sensual lips above an imperial black beard, and fierce birdlike eyes under heavy lids which continually appraised Donna while his attention appeared riveted on what Trevarvas was saying. A sensualist, Donna guessed shrewdly, and when later he engaged her in conversation, this impression was confirmed.

"I am *enchanté, Mademoiselle*," he said more than once, though by what, she did not know. "It is such a great pleasure to talk with you," and she knew full well

101

that her conversation did not matter to him a rap, but that his lascivious nature was obsessed with her body.

When she left at about nine thirty, Nicholas escorted her to the door. They stood for a few minutes waiting for Sarne to appear with the chaise.

"Thank you," he said, taking her arm. "You were quite a success."

"I think it was Annette who was that," she said, not looking at him. "I liked her. She was fun, and so knowledgeable and lively." She waited for him to take his hand away, made a faint gesture at withdrawal, resenting and yet subtly enjoying its possessive impact.

"Annette? Oh. Yes, I suppose so; but very plain."

"Looks aren't everything," Donna remarked quickly, at the same moment wrenching herself free. "And please don't . . ."

"What?"

She didn't reply, except to ask, "Why is Sarne so long?"

He stiffened. "Is my company so tedious?"

"I didn't say that."

"No." He paused before adding, "You certainly imply it. However as I know very little about wild-flowers or painting, you no doubt find my conversation extremely limited. By the way . . ."

"Yes?"

"I didn't know you were so well versed in botany."

"Why should you? After all . . . you don't really know a thing about me. Nor I about you."

"True; except for a certain manner of bargaining on your part which I'm beginning to think is far subtler than I'd believed."

Donna laughed artificially. "You're imagining things that aren't there. I wish you wouldn't. I've quite enjoyed tonight. But after all, what we have is just a business arrangement, isn't it? I wouldn't expect you to be concerned in what Annette and I talked about, and I certainly wouldn't choose her father as a friend."

"Didn't you like him?"

"We hardly spoke."

"He was attracted by you, I think."

"How unfortunate for him," Donna murmured.

Trevarvas touched her cheek lightly. "Miss Penroze, for all your pretense of innocence, I've an idea you know full well what you're doing when there's a man around."

She stared at him blankly. "Are you implying . . ."

"I'm implying nothing. Consciously naive you may be. But underneath you've all the knowledge of Eve at work. In short, you're no saint, and no potential nun, my dear, which with luck I'll prove to you one day."

Stifling a hot retort, but with her pulses quickening, she pushed past him, through the door into the night air, where she paused, feeling goose pimples prickle her spine, knowing his eyes were hard upon her, willing her to glance back.

Strangely, she wanted to, but she didn't. And the next moment the chaise appeared, enabling her to hurry down the steps with Nicholas following.

His touch, as he helped her in, was once more cool, his voice remote and formal when he said, "Goodnight, Miss Penroze. Thank you for your services." But his hand brushed her thigh as she settled herself and her heart pounded in response.

Those last few words enraged her. "Services!" what a phrase to use, in front of the man too. Just as though Trevarvas were determined to humiliate and put her in her place.

By the time she reached Trencobban her flare of temper had died into mere affronted annoyance which revived her old instinct to pay him out one day for what he'd done—or failed to do—for her father.

How she would accomplish it, she did not yet know. But the chance would come some time, somehow, and then he'd be sorry. Oh yes, she was sure of that. Yet even through her resolve excitement lingered, and when she had undressed for bed, she paused for a few moments before the mirror, savoring her own naked beauty licked to creamy gold in the lamplight, intuitively letting her hand stray to the softness of thigh

103

where his touch had been. Instantly a little pulse sprang to life, stimulating all other pulses to a throb of sensuous awareness. Then suddenly she picked up a wrap and pulled it savagely around her. "I hate him," she told herself. "God! how I hate him."

But her hate was both a longing and revealment of her own primitive need—something deep down she knew, and found despicable. In an irrational wave of self-hate for such weakness she flung herself on the bed where she lay for some time with burning cheeks and fevered flesh, dismayed and bewildered by the revelation, and wondering what the months ahead would bring.

CHAPTER SIX

So much happened during the next few weeks that Donna began to lose count of the days. Engineers came from the Midlands to advise and test ore, new labor was taken on at Wheal Faith to assist in the shaft sinking. There always seemed a buzz of activity about the mine, the sound of drills and machinery, and arguments concerning the new equipment required; visits by Tom and others to the Hayle Foundry for estimates, and inspection of the most up-to-date man-engine, followed by excitement when the possibility of a natural adit for drainage of water was discovered, at a low level on the cliff face. On top of all this were visits to the seamstress in Penzance, followed by seemingly endless sessions of fittings, boring to Donna, stimulating enough to Jessica to keep her away from Jed.

Donna had come face to face with Andrewartha on odd occasions when she'd been crossing the moor. His eyes, bold as brass in his large face, stared at her unflinchingly, and with a hint of insolent bravado that stiffened her spine with momentary fear as she recalled the night of his attempted rape. The "knowing" look, combined with the habitual confidence which had once more asserted itself, warned her that she still couldn't trust him an inch, and that, given a chance, he would gladly harm her and anything else that was hers in revenge for the incident.

It was late June when she had the first summons from Nicholas. The message, delivered by his man, Sarne, requested her presence promptly at six o'clock the following Thursday in order to receive one or two guests for a small dinner party he was arranging.

". . . The chaise will call for you about 5:45," the brief letter stated. "Dress will be formal but not extravagant. The occasion will not be a very onerous one; including only two business associates of mine, also Sir James and Lady Penverrys, whom I believe you're acquainted with, and their niece Rosina. However, if there's anything more you wish to know, perhaps you'll inform me. Otherwise I shall look forward to your presence at the hour mentioned. This will give ample time for any necessary details to be discussed.

Sincerely yours,

Nicholas Trevarvas."

Donna's primary reaction was of excitement, followed by annoyance at his terse bidding. At least, she decided, he might have inquired if the date and time suited her. Their contract had not stipulated that he could call on her at any hour of any day without proper warning. This "occasion," as he termed it, allowed just two days for her to prepare herself. She would have to get in touch immediately with the seamstress who'd not yet finished the rose pink gown she'd planned to wear for her first official appearance as hostess at Polbreath.

It was unfortunate too, that Lady Penverrys should be one of the guests. Donna had met her only once or twice, each time at Trencobban, when her father was alive, and had resented her haughty, condescending ways, plain looks, long nose, and manner of using her lorgnettes as though to reduce all others present to a minimum of importance. She was a strict moralist—well, she could hardly be anything else, Donna thought maliciously, with her lack of charm and overbearing bossiness. Even her bucolic looking husband seemed afraid of her, although behind her back he certainly had a roving eye. They were not an attractive couple. Donna guessed that Lady Penverrys would soon start a flood of vicious gossip to discredit the new hostess of Polbreath.

Rosina, their niece, had been a lumpy adolescent

106

when Donna had seen her five years ago, pink-cheeked with rather prominent pale blue eyes and gingerish hair. Dull too. Heavens! she wondered, what on earth had induced Nicholas to invite them to his house. Of course they were supposed to be rich; something in shipping . . . simply rolling in money . . . *Surely* not . . . ! her mind refused to accept the notion that there was any mercenary motive behind Trevarvas's invitation. All the same he *had* got a name for "closeness." And the family had influential connections. She supposed that Rosina might have lost some of her stolid plumpness during the past few years. The idea didn't please her at all. "I hope she's stout and ugly, with pimples, she told herself, and decided, if only for that reason, to appear at her very best and most seductive.

Without informing Jessica, she drove herself in the gig to Penzance that same afternoon, and found to her delight that the rose pink gown was already finished, and could be packed immediately.

"No," Donna said, "I'll put it on here, if you don't mind, Miss Payne. Then if anything's wrong perhaps it can be altered while I take a stroll along the harbor."

"Oh . . . very well. Certainly, Miss Penroze," the little dressmaker agreed, rather grudgingly, "but I don't think you'll find anything to complain about."

And she was right.

The pink dress was similar in style to one worn by Eleonora Duse, the famous Italian actress. High-necked, it was trimmed with bands of lace that left the shoulders bare, but fell gracefully over the arms to just above the elbow. The bodice, tight at the waist, reached to a low point in front, from where it cascaded in frills and flounces, fuller at the back, to a frilled hemline. With it she planned to wear the long kid gloves that had been her mother's and have her thick ebony hair full at the front, drawn simply upwards to a knot on top.

She had noticed a print of the actress clad in a cream and orange dress like this when she had visited a fancy-work shop to purchase silk thread, and she had asked if she might borrow it.

"You don't think the pink clashes with my eyes, do you?" Donna asked, surveying herself critically in the cheval glass.

"No no, Miss Penroze. Normally I'd say golds and greens and orange were your colors. But for the evening, with lights on your cream skin and dark hair . . . oh my dear! you'll look truly lovely . . . as you do now."

"Yes," agreed Donna, knowing it was true. "Perhaps. I do hope so."

When she was back in her room at Trencobban with the gown outspread on her bed she couldn't resist putting it on again.

Jessica, hearing her sister-in-law return, and sensing that something was afoot knocked on the door, saying, "Can I come in? I wondered if you could lend me your scissors. I . . ."

She didn't finish the sentence, just pushed inside and stood staring.

"My!" Her voice was envious. "So *that's* where you've been. To the dressmaker's. I do think you might've told me."

"I hadn't much time," she said tersely. "You're going in on Friday; I don't have to ask you to accompany me everywhere I go, Jessica."

"No. That would be a lark wouldn't it? Especially when you go visiting your la-di-da high falutin' Nick Nobody."

Realizing that she was jealous, Donna didn't reply. And after a few moments Jessica conceded, "Still, you look very smart. It suits you. I wouldn't have thought so. Pink's usually for people with yellow hair, like me."

"You can wear anything as long as it's not too loud," Donna retorted. "That's what you've got to guard against . . . looking cheap."

"Thank you very much."

Donna swung around, smiling disarmingly. "Why are you so edgy, Jessica?"

Her sister-in-law shrugged. "I don't know. I suppose because some people have all the luck, and others have to sit, paws up, begging."

"That's not fair. You're having three new dresses, a costume, and all for nothing."

"Nothing, Donna dear? Oh no. That sort of thing never happens to me. I've always paid, *always*—one way or the other, and it'll be like that to the end. You see."

She went slowly to the door, turned her head and remarked, before going out, "If Trevarvas goes for you, Donna, in a big way, take him. That's my advice. Only make him catch you, not the other way around. That was my trouble, and is, and always has been. I could never wait."

Donna frowned. Now what exactly had got into Jessica all of a sudden? It wasn't only envy. There was something else. Something tired out and utterly weary that had made her look, in that short interval at the door, twice the age she really was, rather as though she'd been looking back over her shoulder seeing ghosts.

She could not know that Jessica was remembering again.

Remembering, and seeing a girl of seventeen who had gone headlong into the arms of a man more than twenty years her senior. A man with a formidable physique and fine strong face below a wide intellectual forehead, crowned by a thatch of spring gray hair. A man who came preaching the word of God to a tavern of prostitutes and seamen where she worked . . . whose eyes were fire, sending a warmth and longing through her body to belong, and serve him like a woman made new again. Good. Ever obedient and loving. A true wife.

So he'd led her through the door and set her on his horse, and together they'd galloped from the narrow streets of Plymouth's dockland, making their way to his large square-faced farm on the outskirts of Bodmin moor, where his domineering sister waited.

She'd disapproved. But he had married her, and soon the sister had packed her bags and gone. Only the house remained, a farm hand or two, a cowed simple-minded girl, too frightened by something to open her mouth except in a whisper. And Jessica had soon learned why. The husband she had thought to be her savior was a holy evangelist only on weekends. During the week he was surly and silent, treating her like a dog, besides working her to the bone; and at night . . . recalling the nights, Jessica shivered. No love, no soft touch, no tender words—nothing but warped brutality. And when she'd turned, sickened, from him, he had tied her up and thrashed her. Then they'd prayed together. And she had known, during the first week, that she'd married a madman. Then . . . her thoughts always broke off at that point and she allowed memory to recede into a dark vacuum of shadows. And when that happened, only the bottle and other men could properly drag her back to life.

If Luke had lived and not rejected her in his heart, maybe she could have dispelled the past for good. But Luke was dead. And she knew that although he'd made her his wife, it had only been because she had tricked him. Luke, in his sober moments had known it too. So he had detested her, and the dark episode lingered at the back of her days and years, haunting her with the terror that one day it would revive its ugly head, and she'd be lost. The bars would be broken and he'd be free—the one she'd married before Luke—free to stalk the countryside and moors in search of his prey: in search of the one who had testified and sworn against him in court—Jessica.

If only she could tell Donna. But Donna wouldn't understand; how could she? No one could for that matter, and she would end up in a worse plight than before, because they'd say then she was no Penroze and never had been. This was her one safety . . . being a Penroze, and sometimes being able to lose herself in Jed. Not that Jed was anything to brag about, as a character. But she needed him, and her need was a dark pool in which she could mercifully be submerged and forget . . . when he was willing.

It was seldom that Jessica let her thoughts stray so

far, and when she got back to her room, Janey, mercifully, was there to bring her back to practical affairs.
She was standing in front of a mirror with her mother's
new hat on her head, draped in the brown cape, looking
like some old-fashioned little midget in a show. The
child's first reaction was of fright. She threw the cape
off, her strange eyes widening, and mouth slightly open.
"Sorry mama. Mama, mama, forgive me. I haven't hurt
it."

Jessica rushed over to her and took the hat from her
head. "It's all right, love. Mama's not cross. But you
mustn't take my things, see? Here. Give me a kiss now;
and remember—I'm your mother, and you're all I've
got, same as I'm all you have. We're together, you and
me, until you grow up and maybe get married and become a fine lady."

Janey hid her face against the cloth skirt. But a moment later she'd pulled away. "Why haven't I got a pa?"
she said with a touch of resentment.

"Now what would you want a pa for? Stupid. Anyway, he went away to sea and got lost. And that's that.
So don't go asking such silly questions."

And as she said it Jessica realized once more that she
and her offspring had really nothing in common at all.
They never had and they never would. Janey was a
mystery with an intimidating quality about her that was
off-putting as well as disconcerting. So she dismissed the
child, telling her to wash her hands and tidy up, and
then she let her mind wander once more to Donna and
the pink dress, wishing fervently she was in her sister-
in-laws's place.

Now that it had come to the point, Donna herself was
looking forward to the dinner party, knowing that her
presence was bound to cause a furor of excitement and
speculation. "Take him," Jessica had said, referring to
Nicholas. Well, maybe she would, maybe she wouldn't,
if the moment ever came. In the meantime there were
other men in the world, including the one who had as-
sisted her outside the coaching house that day in Penzance. She didn't expect to meet him again, although

something in his words or manner had implied that she might. She was duly surprised when, on that Thursday evening, Nicholas Trevarvas's chaise deposited her at Polbreath and *his* face was the first one she saw. His eyes widened in astonishment. "Gad!" he exclaimed, recognizing her after a pause of astonishment. "If it isn't my lady of—not camelias—but roses."

He went toward her, hand extended, gray eyes so intensely full of admiration that she flushed. She lifted her own gloved one, feeling his fingers enclose it longer than was strictly necessary.

"Lucien Trevarvas at your service, Miss Prenroze . . ." he paused a moment before adding, "you are Miss Penroze I suppose? Donna Penroze?"

"Yes. But . . ."

"You didn't know I'd be here. Neither did I till two days ago. I happen to be in this country from Paris where I have a studio, and had been staying with a friend near Penzance. Then, being a very conscientious character, duty impelled me to visit my elder brother, or rather half-brother, old Nick." He smiled. Tiny laughter lines crinkled his strange eyes. "And that name rather suits him don't you think?"

Before she had a chance to reply, Nicholas himself appeared, walking from the direction of the study. "Oh, so you're here," he said abruptly. "And I see you two have already met."

"Not for the first time, old chap," Lucien replied.

"Oh?"

"I had the great good fortune, recently, to rescue Miss Penroze from what could have been a very nasty accident in Penzance. But I'm delighted to meet her again so soon."

Trevarvas, throwing him a dark glance, said coldly to Donna, "I showed you where the cloakroom is. Perhaps you'd go and take off your cape. You'll find everything you need there. Then I suggest you come straight down to the drawing room and meet me there."

"Very well." Feeling that she had been too abruptly dismissed, Donna swept past with her head high, knowing both men's eyes were upon her—Trevarvas's cold and annoyed, Lucien's whimsically amused. How handsome Lucien had looked, she thought later, as she tidied her hair, turning this way and that before the glass to insure everything was just so . . . and so distinguished in his fitting tail coat, yellow silk waistcoat, cream shirt and wide gold shaded bow tie beneath the high white winged collar. And from a studio in Paris, he'd said. He must, then, be an artist. How intriguing. Perhaps he would want to paint her. And if he did?

The smile confronting her in the mirror, though enchanting, was secretive, triumphant, and had she known it, just a little sly, because she was thinking, Nicholas wouldn't like *that* at all. He'd been quite annoyed at his half-brother's appearance in the hall, and instinct told her that he was already jealous.

So when she sailed downstairs a few minutes later, her eyes were bright, poise regal, her manner confident and assured. She paused for a moment at the bottom of the stairs where the light from a gilt statue of Aphrodite holding a chandelier blazed down upon her and haloed her figure in its rosy light.

Then, further down the hall she saw the door of the drawing room open, and Nicholas standing there, face turned toward her expectantly, his strong form looming formidably in the black evening waistcoat and high winged collar.

"Come along," he said imperatively. "I want to talk to you."

She passed before him obediently, but with tightened lips, into the large room already lit by an immense circular chandelier hanging from the embossed ceiling, and by innumerable candles.

"Sit down," he said.

She did so, resentful that when he must be aware she was looking her loveliest, he could behave to her like an autocratic schoolmaster. Or hadn't he noticed her appearance at all?

"Well?" she said sharply. "Is my dress to your liking? Or do you want me to return to Trencobban and come

113

back in black? . . . or even . . ." she hesitated before adding maliciously, "gray perhaps?"

"Why gray?"

"Miss Pullen seems to favor it," she answered.

"What's that to do with it?"

"Oh—I don't know. I just haven't an idea what you do want. I never seem to be right. There's always criticism when I appear. And I don't see how I'm going to fit in at Polbreath without a little encouragement." She broke off, hot and breathless, yet thankful that she had got the words out.

He smiled. And his smile changed him from a heavy-browed stern-faced man into a young and attractive one, with even a hint of mischief in his eyes.

"You mustn't take too much notice of my moods," he said. "And I wasn't going to criticize. You look beautiful, which, of course, you know very well."

"Thank you."

"Now," he resumed, "when the guests arrive I shall want you to receive them in here—the ladies first, who will already have been taken to the cloakroom to remove their capes. Then I shall myself bring the men in, and we'll have an aperitif before going in to dinner. As I told you before Donna—Miss Penroze—you will be seated at the end of the table opposite me. And whether you like it or not I've arranged to have Lady Penverrys near, so that you can entertain her with feminine gossip. You know how to behave, thank God, so there'll be no trouble in that way. There's just one thing however, that I must insist on."

"Yes?"

"I don't want you to get on too intimate terms with my half-brother Lucien. He's rich, as you'll have gathered—thanks to his late mother; idle, with extravagant ideas not at all suited to Cornish society. And he likes women as long as they like him. He also fancies himself as an artist."

"What's wrong in all that?" Donna asked sharply.

"I don't think it's your concern. All I want you to know is that I'd view any friendship with Lucien, seriously. In fact I won't stand for it, do you understand?"

Donna stood up abruptly. "Oh yes. I understand very well, Mr. Trevarvas. It seems to me that you don't really want me here as a hostess at all. You just want . . . you just want . . ."

"Yes? Do tell me."

"Someone to bully and dictate to," she cried, with the color bright in her cheeks. "Someone like that pitiful governess creature . . ." She broke off, aware that she had gone too far, and of the penetrating, deepening anger in his dark eyes. Quite small things registered in those few moments . . . the tightening of his strong well-carved lips above the forward-thrust cleft chin, and a sudden resentful realization of how handsome he was. His very annoyance held a magnetic quality that made her feel somehow curiously vulnerable and childlike. If he'd moved . . . made a gesture, even slapped her face, she could have retaliated and broken the tension by a quick retort or flouncing out. But he gave her no chance, simply stood there dominating her by willpower alone, while the nerves at the back of her skull tightened and she swallowed nervously, the blood quickly draining from her face again.

Although this intermission must have lasted only seconds, her mind was so churned by conflicting emotions she had no reply ready when he said suddenly with cold, cutting precision, "I must ask you never to refer to Miss Pullen in such terms again. And in the meantime perhaps you'll pull yourself together and remember to cultivate the poise and good manners necessary for your position in my household."

He turned abruptly and went out, slamming the door sharply behind him.

Donna waited until the sound of his footsteps had died, and then relief intermingled with an irrational sense of disappointment as her whole body relaxed; life returned to her limbs bringing a renewed upsurge of annoyance, not only with him, but herself for handling the situation so ineffectually.

What a nerve he had, she thought, and how pompous

115

he sounded . . . "cultivate the poise and good manners for her position in his household . . ."

Poise? How ridiculous, Donna thought, when the evening looming ahead promised to be one of bored repartee and strained behavior under Trevarvas's eyes . . . of polite hypocritical conversation with the sour Lady Penverrys, and her dreary daughter; of affecting to be in command of the situation . . . a sort of deputy mistress of the house, instead of the paid employee she really was, only enduring it all because of Wheal Faith.

It couldn't last forever. One day she would be free, and then the domineering Trevarvas would learn just what she thought of him. In the meantime there was his brother, the artist from Paris. At Polbreath Nicholas might manage, by bullying methods, to keep them apart; but out of it, he had no say whatever in who she met or what she did.

Thinking of Lucien quickly dispelled her resentful mood. And later, when the guests began to arrive, she was bubbling with high spirits that beneath her elegant façade held a hint of daring mischief.

The Penverrys family, true to convention, entered the drawing room precisely ten minutes late, having been preceded by two of Nicholas's business friends. One was Lewis Owen, a sturdy fiery-eyed middle-aged Welshman who, Donna gathered, was also in shipping. The other was an elderly cadaverous looking business acquaintance from London named John Webber.

Rosina, Lady Penverrys's niece, had grown, lost her puppy-fat, and was considerably better-looking than Donna had expected, with a good complexion, no pimples, strongly carved features. She had the kind of figure that suggested she was a devoted horsewoman and rode to hounds, a sport Donna detested. In fact, following the first exchange of formalities, Donna had a growing feeling there was much about Rosina she would detest . . . especially her condescending, rather loud voice and her habit of staring down from half-closed lids with a secretive smirk on her lips. She was wearing a cream silk dress, which, although sumptuous, emphasized her large figure, and did nothing complimentary for her ginger hair which was still frizzy, and piled on top of her head.

Nicholas, however, seemed impressed. Donna noticed that he moved from Rosina's side only intermittently to chat with his business friends, and perhaps to pour further drinks.

Lady Penverrys, as Donna had expected, attached herself like an unwelcome limpet at her side remarking in the first few minutes how *extremely* surprised she was to find William Penroze's daughter there. "You have a post here at Polbreath I understand?" she said disapprovingly. "How very odd, and . . . unfortunate for you. Of course my husband and I had heard that your affairs were in a somewhat poor state. Still, I never expected . . ." Her voice trailed away suggestively.

"*What* didn't you expect, Lady Penverrys?" Donna asked, staring her straight in the eyes.

The long nose seemed to quiver for a moment before the formidable voice answered, "That you would consider such a post suitable. There are other positions available. Still . . . you have your reasons no doubt."

Donna smiled. Not with her eyes, though, and her voice was cold when she retorted, "Yes, I have. And they are my own."

The suggestion of a flush tinted the long sallow countenance.

"My dear Miss Penroze, there's no need to take offense. Who am I to criticize anyone in a less secure mode of life than myself. I'm not narrow-minded you know. Even with my own servants I try to provide an understanding ear when any . . . problem arises."

What a bitch, Donna thought, wishing the old harridan would take herself off. As if her thoughts had registered aloud, Lady Penverrys, a fan in one hand, a glass of Madeira in the other, turned her head in search of fresh company and slowly moved away. At this opportune moment, to Donna's great relief, Lucien appeared

117

at the other side of the room, cutting straight toward her. He was smiling and evidently aware of what had been going on.

"Poor girl," he said. "What a dastardly trick old Nick's played on you. Leaving one so beautiful to deal with such a wicked-tongued old witch."

His presence dispelled Donna's annoyance like magic. "Witch?" she echoed. "I was thinking just the same, but the word began with a 'b.'"

He laughed. "What a dreary business this would be, but for you. And to think I have to return to France next week."

Her heart sank. "Oh?"

"I have a patron there," he told her, "and have already committed myself to a brief stay in his country house. But . . ." He paused.

"Yes?"

"I shall be returning. You can count on that, now." His fingers brushed her own for a second. His strange eyes were alight as he stared down on her massed hair, gleaming like raven wings, the lovely face turned up to his as her cheeks changed from ivory to rose pink, then paled again.

Glancing toward Nicholas, Donna saw, uncomfortably, that he had noticed, was frowning, and on the point of leaving Rosina and making his way toward her.

"Excuse me," she said quickly, "I'm supposed to be—what was it your brother said—mingling, and making myself sociable." She freed herself and moved to the fireplace, where Lewis Owen was on his own, with a second glass of wine in his hand. Donna's first impression of him had been favorable. He was so obviously himself—a shrewd businessman without any airs or pretenses of being anything else, and present only because of some matter of mutual interest to himself and Trevarvas.

"A good party." He observed. "But not quite in my line. Nor Trevarvas's I'd have thought. He generally chooses more . . ."

"Colorful characters?" Donna suggested.

"Let's say either stag-affairs, or the less conventional brand," he agreed with a twinkle. "I'm not one of the upper ten, Miss Penroze. Money's my line and how to get it. And I don't care a fig for names with handles to them, unless they know how to swing a packet in my direction. Penverrys of course has his uses, when he doesn't have to tag alongside with his supercilious spouse."

"And what *is* your business?" Donna asked, trying not to sound too interested. "Apart from the money I mean?"

"Oh ho, now." He tapped the side of his nose significantly. "A pretty lady like you should know better than to ask leading questions of that kind. Still, if I say trade, it would be no lie. Here, there, and everywhere, Miss . . . ?"

"Penroze."

"Yes I remember now, Miss Penroze."

"Not smuggling?" she said boldly.

He laughed. "You've got a vivid imagination. I like that. Allied to business it can be very rewarding. So if you ever feel like leaving Trevarvas's house and wanting another occupation, remember me. I could fit you in somewhere without any trouble." He took a card out of his pocket. "There you are."

She took it, read his name quickly, printed over a Cardiff address, and slipped it into her silk handbag. "Thank you, Mr. Owen. There's no knowing. I might even ask you to invest in a mine one day."

With a slight inclination of her head she moved away before he'd had time to reply.

The dinner that followed was, from, Donna's point of view, dull; the food, though well served, far too heavy. She was thankful when it was over, and the men retired to the smoking-room, leaving Rosina, her aunt, and Donna to make their way to the ladies cloakroom. There she learned that the guests were staying the night at Polbreath. "It would be far too wearying to make the journey at night all the way back to Liskeard," Lady Penverrys said, "and I believe the gentlemen who have come a considerable distance have all accepted Mr. Trevarvas's hospitality. *You*, I suppose, are returning to your home? Or does your position here entail your presence at all hours?"

"My position here is only on very rare occasions, to preside as hostess," Donna answered sharply. "And I think you already knew that."

"My dear girl, I do not make it my business to question employers concerning the duties of employees," Lady Penverrys said acidly. "And in such an unusual position as yours, one naturally wonders."

Stifling a hot reply, Donna pretended not to have heard. But she was aware of Rosina's calculating glance, and wondered if she really believed she had a serious chance with Nicholas; and if not, possibly with Lucien. Except for his wealth, of course, Sir James and his wife would have considered Trevarvas quite out of their social orbit. The Penverryses could trace their family lineage back to 1272 when they had been close associates of Edmund, Earl of Cornwall, Henry III's nephew, who had been invested with the title a month before the King's death in that year. But their estate near Liskeard was large, and through the last hundred years income for its upkeep had had to be reimbursed through chancy and somewhat vague channels described in abstruse terms as "shipping"; although only Trevarvas perhaps, could have given the complete and accurate definition of what that entailed.

To have stooped to a less affluent way of life would have affronted Lady Penverrys, who happened to be the daughter of a duke and believed that all that was required of English society was for the upper stratum to hold its head high, and retain its superiority over the working and developing middle classes. Donna had let that society down disgracefully. *Using* Nicholas Trevarvas was one thing. *Working* for him quite another. And although the Penroze family did not aspire—and never had—to the social heights of her own, Donna was at least of the breed, and it was degrading to find this wild, proud daughter of William Penroze in the dubious position of an underling. Irritating, also, that she should be apparently enjoying it, flouncing about as though she owned the place.

After pins and feathers and flowers had been adjusted in icy silence, the three women proceeded downstairs, and when they reached the hall Nicholas was already there, to receive them, with a manservant near at hand to open the drawing room door. Rosina and her aunt went in; the man retreated, leaving Donna and Trevarvas alone.

"And so you're ready to leave?" he asked with no trace of expression in his voice.

"Unless you want me to stay," she answered with equal coolness. "Lady Penverrys and I seem to have exhausted topics of conversation. But of course if you wish it I could make myself agreeable to Mr. Owen and—and your brother Lucien."

"That won't be necessary at all, Miss Penroze," Nicholas said stiffly. He glanced at his watch. "In fact it's later than I thought, well past nine. I'll tell Sarne to have the chaise brought round immediately."

Donna bowed her head slightly. "Thank you."

"Is that all you have to say?"

She looked up sharply, and the expression in his eyes confused, and at the same time excited her, setting her heart beating wildly, and her knees trembling.

"I . . . I . . . I don't know what you mean."

"Oh come now. Don't play the child, Donna."

Donna? It was the first time he'd called her that deliberately. Her eyes were suddenly enormous in the creamy heart-shaped face, changing swiftly as summer sunlight from orange to gold, then back to orange again. "But I'm not . . ." she said.

"I think you are," he insisted in gentler tones. "Or why that?" His eyes were on her embroidered bodice.

"What?"

"The racing heart," he answered. "Your damned insolent, beautiful bravado? I'm not a fool, Miss Penroze. And we're two of a kind you and I. Good. The future should be quite interesting." As the color mounted

121

treacherously to her cheeks, he continued calmly. "By the way, you left your flower behind the other day. On the floor."

"Oh. I . . ."

"Don't do it again," he said. "Next time the gift might be more valuable, and I don't like waste."

"I'll certainly remember."

Their brief conversation was intercepted by the two businessmen and Sir James Penverrys coming from the smoking room into the hall. Trevarvas summoned Sarne and told him about the chaise, then turning to Donna once more, said, "I'll see you to the carriage in a moment or two. Wait."

The four of them went to the drawing room, and as soon as the door had closed a light warm voice behind her shoulder whispered, "There's no need to stay for old Nick. Your most devoted admirer at your service, Miss Penroze."

Turning, she saw the handsome, quizzical, slightly amused face of Lucien Trevarvas looking down on her.

"He has a darned nerve that half-brother of mine," he said. "Expecting such a beautiful creature to wait around for him. Come . . ." he held out his arm. "Let me escort you."

With her thoughts in turmoil, Donna allowed him to assist her down the steps to the chaise. He was politeness personified. But as he helped her in, he remarked softly, "When can I see you again?"

"I don't know . . . I really don't," Donna whispered, thinking that at any moment Nicholas might appear. "Next week perhaps, or . . . or . . . Sunday. I sometimes take a stroll near the cove . . . below Trencobban. But it's some miles away . . ."

"I know where you live. What time?"

"Eleven perhaps; just *perhaps*," she managed to answer, before adding in clear, loud tones, "Thank you, Mr. Trevarvas." Then the chaise door clicked, and the horses started up, clattering away into the summer night.

She glanced back briefly once, and saw the slim fig-

122

ure silhouetted against the brilliant light streaming from the hall. Almost at the same moment he was joined by another, squarer, stronger, and altogether more formidable—his elder half-brother, Nicholas Trevarvas, the dark horseman of her imagination, whose influence, though she might resent and discredit it with all the will she possessed, seemed to gather more force and authority with each day that passed. But she would not be acquired by him as his property or woman to do with what he willed! She would show him—and the idea stimulated her—that he had other, more elegant rivals to contend with. He would be angered of course, by her sudden departure. Well, let him be. After all, Lucien had been right. No lady should be told to stand and wait in that imperious tone.

But then, ladies were not expected to feel as she did, with leaping pulses and pricking breasts, and a tingling longing through her whole body for strong male hands about her thighs and buttocks, claiming her to the subjection of passion.

Goodness! she thought. But I'm no better than Jessica, except that I knew how to *pretend*.

The knowledge was discomforting but not entirely unpleasant.

And so she sat with burning cheeks and tingling limbs, cheeks flushed and eyes glowing, a budding rose of a woman, filled with desire and the secret instinctive knowledge that it must one day be fulfilled. When the chaise eventually reached Trencobban, excitement still burned in her, and for a long time after she'd gone to bed that night, she could not sleep.

Then gradually reality dispelled elation as she remembered the true purpose of her involvment with Polbreath. Wheal Faith. Her heritage. The promise and dedication to her dead father, which must remain her first concern—undiverted by any selfish indulgence of her own.

CHAPTER SEVEN

On Sunday the weather was fine and still, though a thin mist hugged the coast, and the early sun was shrouded in a veil of silvered light. Donna woke up early, and was already dressed when Jessica appeared lazily at her bedroom door, wearing a flimsy looking shift that revealed her luscious curves amply outlined against the glow from the window. She was yawning, with her bright hair streaming in thick waves over her shoulders.

Rubbing her blue eyes with a hand, she said resentfully, "Sakes alive! what on earth's got into you? Going out, at this hour?"

"Just for a stroll," Donna answered shortly, wishing Jessica hadn't appeared just at that moment. "And it's not early. After ten. Sarah's cleared the breakfast away, and she's not in a good mood either. So you'll have to get your own."

"That will be a change, won't it? I generally do."

"That's your fault. Anyway, I'm off."

"Couldn't you take Janey a bit of the way? She's been a real torment this last hour. In and out of the room with her 'Please mama, I'm hungry. Please mama, can I wear my new frock? *Please* mama.' Oh God! No wonder I lose patience."

"It's your business to look after your own child," Donna told her, and as she moved away, "You reminded me of that only the other day. Remember?"

What Jessica's reply was she didn't hear, but knew that it was something uncomplimentary. So she hurried downstairs, and was out of the front door before anyone else could appear to ask questions. She took the path back by the conservatory, cutting ahead from there, past the house toward the headland, where a narrow track bent slightly in the direction of Wheal Faith, then dipped down abruptly along the side of a ravine. A stream, overhung with wild flowers and waterweed tumbled over fallen stones. The way was tricky for anyone who didn't know it. But Donna's feet were nimble as any goat's, and before proceeding down the steeper part of the way, she leaned against a boulder, slipped her shoes off as she'd done as a child, and with them under one arm, skirts tucked up, soon reached the rock-bound cove.

For a short time she idled about, feeling the beach damp against her stockinged feet, wishing her toes could be bare to the cool, salt surface of shingle. She had time to spare. Lucien might not even come. And her heart was suddenly sad with memories, recalling her dead father, and the day that seemed so long ago, when she'd lain in Jos's arms, thinking of the time they'd be married.

Jos's affection, although not expressed in fancy speech or manners, had been sweet and kind and filled with warmth. No taunting or threats, no menace of power or subjugation of her will by his . . . only a desire to possess her, to take and care for her, as a husband his chosen wife. But for circumstance, she knew she would have given in at last, and gone with him to start their new life in America.

But it hadn't happened. And now it was too late. Not only because of the ocean between them, but something else as well. Something darker and stronger that forever now would be part of her; her involvement with Nicholas.

But how stupid to be reminiscing at such a moment, she decided with sudden impatience. Her mind and body were still her own, and any moment her dashing admirer might appear, although she doubted that he'd manage the tricky descent to the cove as easily as she had.

So she stopped to put her shoes on, and although the

soles of her feet were cold, she didn't care. The thin mist, almost gone now, was fresh in her face, and a frail wind was rising, blowing a strand of dusky hair against her cheek. Below, some distance away, the ebb tide silvered the pale sand in a froth of breaking foam. Dreamlike. A scene such as Shakespeare might have envisaged when he wrote *The Tempest,* she thought romantically.

It was at that point that Lucien appeared, clambering over a jutting arm of rock, considerably beyond the entrance of the cove.

She stared in astonishment, and when he reached her, said, "Which way did you come? You must have walked miles."

"Oh no," he answered laughing, "I'm not that keen on athletics. There was a sort of stony track half a mile back past some old works near the cliff. So I rode as far as I could, and tethered my horse there. There was a fellow lurking about; a hefty chap, miner or farmer I judged, so I gave him a handsome tip, and he promised to keep an eye on my horse. Then I made my own way down."

"What was he like?" Donna said sharply. "The man?"

"Oh . . ." Lucien shrugged. "As I said, tough. Heavy. A real strong fellow."

"Did you ask his name?"

"No. He told me. Andrew-something-or-other."

Donna froze. "Was it Andrewartha? Jed Andrewartha?"

"That's right. Not exactly communicative, but assured enough. 'What I'm paid for I do, mister,' he said. 'Your mount's in safe hands.' "

"And did you tell him your business? Who you were meeting?"

"My sweetest Donna, do you really imagine I'd be such a fool? Although I'd be interested to know *why* I should or should not."

"No reason whatever," she said, relaxing. "It's just that . . . he works at our . . . my mine . . . Wheal

126

Faith. And we had an argument recently. We're not on good terms, that's all."

"Oh dear. A primitive Cornish vendetta?"

She frowned and flounced a few steps away. "There's no need to talk like that. I was merely stating facts."

"Of course." His face was behind hers, his voice soft in her ear. She noticed he was perfumed and found that she did not like it.

"Dear girl," he said. "How very beautiful you are—especially in your rages."

She turned. "You've never seen me in a rage, Mr. . . ."

"Lucien," he interrupted quickly. "No. But I'm sure you'd be adorable anyway."

She laughed, and the sound rang artificially even in her own ears. "You're very good at flattery, Lucien. I suppose that comes from living in Paris, and having a bevy of French mademoiselles trailing at your heels."

He stared at her with eyebrows raised. "What do you know of French ladies—or an artist's life in that country?"

She shrugged. "I read. I'm not stupid. I don't go about with my eyes and imagination shut. Besides, being an artist . . . you *are* an artist, aren't you?"

"Oh, I try to be."

"Well then, you must mix a great deal, with all kinds of society I suppose, in fashionable circles and colorful cafes, and poor people and rich, and . . . and . . . Oh! it must be exciting."

"It's the only life I'd choose, simply because I'm free. But even freedom can be boring after a time. You see I don't have to work. Therefore there's no cause for throwing my paintbrush at the wall and cursing to high heaven because I don't know where the next penny's coming from, or the next bun to eat. I'm an artistic dilettante I suppose, Donna—that's what old Nick says, without the artist bit I mean. And maybe he's right. But . . ."

"I'm sure he's not," Donna said fiercely. "Nicholas would say anything to get you annoyed and worked up,

127

and . . . and feeling *small*." She broke off abruptly, cheeks hot and eyes aflame, then turned her head away so he should not see.

But he had, and with his hand under her chin tilting her face up to his, said, "You seem to know my brother very well."

"I hardly know him at all."

"No?"

"Of course not. How can anyone know him when he uses anyone he likes, at any time he thinks. At least—that's how it seems."

Lucien said nothing for some seconds. Just stood there, close to her, staring into her eyes. Then, suddenly, his lips were on hers, gentle, warm, while her arms reached up to his shoulders in an instinctive gesture of desire. They stood for some moments, interlocked in each other's arms, her spine arched back, as she waited with closed eyes, for desire and a show of passion, for something that did not come.

Instead, after that long pause, he released her, but with one arm round her waist, the other hand stroking her forehead tenderly, where the damp hair clung, said, "Donna, sweet Donna. We mustn't. I have to go away."

"When? What does it matter? Why?" Her voice was angry, defeated. Not only because of the subtle rejection, but because when his face registered again, she sensed he could never be what she needed—but only a retreat from the hunger of her deepest desire.

"Why?" she heard Lucien echo, "Nick wouldn't want me long at Polbreath anyway. And you know that. Neither could I stick it. I'm not a man of rocks and sea, Donna. My roots aren't here. Yours are."

"How do you know what mine are?" she persisted.

"I don't. Not entirely. But you wouldn't fit into my world."

"Oh. So you're sure of that too."

He nodded. "If I wasn't, I might say recklessly, 'come with me to Paris. See how the artists and the women of the demi-monde live. Then, if it should work out, perhaps, marry me and learn to put up with my

128

moods and wanton ways, because you're the loveliest creature I've ever known' but . . ."

"Marry you, you said?"

"I said perhaps, and if darling. But there are too many 'ifs' about it. Not only on my side. Yours. You have your home, and your mine."

With her lips set, she turned away, saying in cool tones, "Yes you're quite right of course. I couldn't abandon Wheal Faith."

Sensing that he'd hurt her, he took her arm, saying gently, "Oh Donna . . . *darling*. I shall be back. It won't be for long."

"Long enough I think," she said, betraying her emotions by her rigid stance and distracted manner. "Come along now, I must be going. No one knows I'm down here. I've got things to do at the house. I only came, really, to say goodbye."

"Au revoir."

She managed to smile, artificially, almost like a coquette, and extended her hand. "Very well, au revoir."

Although she did not hear it, she was aware of the sigh of relief that coursed through his frame.

Walking with him across the pale sand to the point where he had first appeared around the cliff, she said, "When do you go?"

"Tomorrow I think."

"Good. That will spare you any embarrassment of meeting me."

"Oh dear." He let go the hand he'd been holding. "Now you're being rather childish, darling. I shall always like seeing you, always. And one day I shall paint you. I'll paint you with such adoration in my heart, that I'll create a masterpiece that will find immortal fame in the great galleries of the world."

She didn't answer, just walked on with him silently, until they reached the jutting arm of cliff. He paused for a moment before climbing the tumbled rocks, and made a gesture as though to kiss her again, but she raised a hand, delicately, chillingly, touching his once, with the tips of her fingers, and remarked, "I hope you find your

mount all right. If you don't, call at Trencobban, and I'll lend you Bess. She's a very easy ride."

He shrugged, thanked her formally, and a moment later was gone.

Now why she wondered, as she wandered back toward the cove, did she feel so bereft and desolate? Why had she used that last touch of sarcasm so obviously calculated to make him smart? She didn't care for him; she never could, in a deep way. There was something, on close acquaintance, dandyish about him, even effeminate, in his touch, his speech and mannerisms, and slight odor of perfume. The artist in him maybe. Oh well, it didn't matter. The next day he'd be gone, and she'd probably never see him again.

Eager to get the interview out of her system, she made her way as quickly as possible back to Trencobban, changed into Luke's breeches, went to the stables and impatiently saddled Saladin, telling Sam she had a headache, and would he tell Sarah to expect her when she saw her.

The risen sun had dispersed the mist, leaving only thin veils shrouding the valleys above the bleak brown hills. Saladin, with the wild air sweet in his nostrils, sniffed appreciatively, and they were soon galloping through the furze to the rim that stretched southward in a gradual incline toward Rosebuzzan. Once there she slowed to a canter, and it was only then that she heard the unmistakable thud of other hooves behind her. She kicked the colt on, but it was too late. She was almost thrown as Saladin reared, snorting with terror, forelegs striking the air. Then, as the animal quieted, she was astonished to see Nicholas with his hands on the reins, his own horse standing meekly by.

"Let me go," she shouted. "What do you mean by this? How . . . how . . . ?"

"How dare I? Go on. Continue," he said, without a flicker of expression on his hard face as he forced her down. She stared at him, outraged and belligerent, looking, but for the loose tumbled hair that had fallen from its ribbon, and the fiery glow of her eyes under the

thick lashes, like an angry impetuous boy. Instinctively she stooped to pick her riding crop from the ground. But he was there first and handed it to her.

"I wouldn't use it, if I were you," he said. "I have a way of dealing with naughty girls which might not please you."

Breathing heavily, trying to regain a measure of dignity, she asked after a pause, "Would you mind explaining what this is all about?"

"Certainly," he said. "When you've explained your conduct with my brother in the cove."

"Oh!" Her voice was contemptuous. "I see. You were spying."

"Call it what you like, Miss Penroze. But we made a bargain I believe? And that bargain entailed a promise from you to leave my brother alone."

"That was an order. From you. There was no bargain of that kind on my part and I made no promise."

"No. Perhaps not."

"Then why did you . . . ?"

"I wasn't spying. I was out for a morning's canter and happened to be on the cliff above you when that revealing little incident occurred. My God! The airs and the graces, and then thrusting yourself at that lily-livered youth! What did you expect to get from him? I shall be most amused to learn."

"You . . ." She raised her whip, but he wrenched it from her, flinging it down on the short turf where the two animals were grazing. She rushed toward Saladin. It was no use. Suddenly his arms were around her, strong, hard, his mouth crushing hers, while his one free hand traveled her face, and neck, shoulders and slim waist, straining against her so her spine almost broke, while she fought and kicked, longing for him, yet hating him. Hating with a wild, thwarted joy that made her resist, even while she desired what he could give.

Then, suddenly, he released her.

They stood facing each other, breathless, still hot with rage, speechless because no words could describe the jealous passions so wantonly aroused.

131

Then, after a drawn-out silence, he said, "Remember in the future you will give nothing to my brother that I do not reclaim threefold. And if I ever catch you whoring after him again, you'll wish with all your heart you'd never heard the name of Nicholas Trevarvas. Understand?"

Her face was deathly white as she answered in a furious undertone, "Yes. I understand. And I know now what you are. No more than an animal when crossed."

"Good. As I said before, we're two of a kind. So get on your horse; go home and change. Boys' clothes do nothing for your charms. Next time I'll be sore tempted to tear them off. And you wouldn't want that to happen, would you? Or perhaps after all I should have taken you just now, like any lusting male after a cheap mistress. Unfortunately, where my employees are concerned, I have rather a tedious conscience, and it stopped me giving you what you deserved."

His eyes, hot as her own, compelled her through a conflict of wills, to swing her leg into the stirrup, and after one more contemptuous glance back, she was astride Saladin, galloping down the hill toward Trencobban. He waited for a time, poised against the rim of moors, watching, with a curious, enigmatic expression on his face. It was partly annoyance and regret, intermingled with admiration for her spirit, and partly something else . . . desire so strong and overpowering that his loins ached and his heart beat with a torment which told him he would never entirely be at peace until he possessed her.

The next morning shortly before lunch a letter was delivered to her by Sarah, saying, "That theer man from Polbreath brought it, for you, mistress."

"Mr. Trevarvas you mean?"

"Him?" The old servant gave a short contemptuous laugh. "Not likely mistress. That one isn' for doing things for hisself . . . 'cept maybe dark deeds he doan' want others to know about. No, that man o' his. Not Sarne . . . the other one, all toffee-nosed and high mannered. Ballard I think he's called."

132

"I see. Well, thank you, Sarah."

When the door of the sitting room had closed, Donna tore the envelope open with excited, trembling hands.

"Donna," the note began, in Trevarvas's strong slanting handwriting, "I am off to London tomorrow where I shall stay for a month. So in the meantime you will be free of any duties at my house, and need have no fear of encountering me when you go riding the moors or wandering the seashore. However if you feel disposed one day to call and see my children, further acquaintance with them would not come amiss. This is *not* a command . . . just a suggestion.

"Miss Pullen has been informed of a possible visit from you, and has readily agreed to welcome you.

"For the present, I remain,

Yours,

Nicholas Trevarvas.

"Note: See that Craze is certain to seek advice if any question arises over the mine that needs a more expert opinion. Loans do not last forever, and without a clear assessment of costing etc., money has a tricky habit of slipping down the drain."

Following the first dull sense of disappointment, a cold feeling of resentment chilled her. Money, she thought. Always money; it was clear he had no trust in her judgment, and only limited faith in her manager's. He probably thought, too, that she was dipping here, there, and everywhere, not only into her own account, but into that allocated to Wheal Faith for her personal needs.

The idea was an insult, and typical of the man. So very easy for him to assert his authority even in an area that was not strictly his, when he was off to town away from it all . . . flinging himself into all manner of diversions, no doubt, with glamorous women, probably of ill-repute. She could envisage them in their satins and silks, sighing, languishing, and fluttering their lashes in his direction, could picture the parties he would doubtless attend, given by canny society dowagers out to ensnare a wealthy husband for a niece or granddaughter, or perhaps at theatrical gatherings drinking champagne after a colorful show, from some gaudy chorus girl's slipper.

Everyone of any note, even in Cornwall, knew what London was like, and how the Prince of Wales himself savored the "high life" when he felt inclined. Not that it was easy to think of Nicholas Trevarvas in the same light. But to many women he would be attractive if he set out to be, and she could well imagine his sardonic amusement at their artful ways, and didn't doubt that he'd take, without a pang, what he wanted of any of them, so long as it was to his advantage and without commitment.

But supposing there were someone. Someone who really mattered to him? Four weeks was a long time. In a month much could happen. If he returned engaged, or married perhaps . . . ! The possibility disturbed her. She was suddenly irritated almost beyond endurance. At least one thing was certain. Any step like that would surely free her from her bargain. He could hardly expect, or want her, to act as hostess if a wife was installed at Polbreath.

A wife. One day it would happen. It was sure to. His violence on the moors the previous day, the dark demand of his body and passionate kisses were proof enough of his need of a woman.

"I should have behaved differently," she thought, illogically. "If I'd been gentler, less rebellious, perhaps he'd have wanted me in another way. Perhaps he wouldn't have gone away . . ."

The suggestion made her utterly miserable. Then suddenly, setting her jaw firmly, she thrust all thought of him aside, telling herself it was a good thing he'd gone. Her business was with Wheal Faith, not the disagreeable, arrogant man who, through a business deal, had made the survival possible.

That same afternoon, she decided, she'd take a walk across the moor and see for herself what was going on. New labor was already installed there, the engine ordered, and the shaft sinking started. Eighty men in all were employed. By the new year everything should be ready for salvaging the precious tin.

And it was now high summer. Soon the first tang of autumn would be in the air. She loved that season in Cornwall most of all—the scents of brine, bracken, dead leaves and fallen blackberries—of damp earth beneath the year's decay already pulsing with new life to come.

The landscape, too, was starkly breathtaking then, with the moorland hills turned deepest russet tinged with purple, under yellowish skies, and the sparse windblown trees bent and dark, their branches almost bereft of leaves, and in the high winds suddenly blown from the sea stretched grotesquely like witches' arms. Jessica, on the contrary, had always hated summer's decline, with the long dark evenings ahead, and mornings filled with cloud over the cold sea. Days when daylight never properly came, but lurked secretly between land and sky—a giant shadow of brooding fear which filled her with unease and a desire only for brandy-soaked forgetfulness.

Even when Donna was about to set off for Wheal Faith that afternoon, Jessica was on edge, filled with foreboding and unease.

"Why can't I come with you?" she begged. "Please Donna, don't leave me alone."

"You can't come because of Jed, and that's that," Donna told her forcefully. "Besides, you've nothing to do with the mine. You'd get in the way; and you're not alone. You've got Janey and . . ."

"I know, I know. I've got Janey and Ted and Sam, and old Sarah who's half senile anyway. What good are they?"

"Soon there'll be more help in the house," Donna promised. "I'm going into Penzance this week to see a woman and her daughter who'll help Sarah. Mrs. Paynter her name is, and she's quite qualified to act as housekeeper; only I couldn't let her go over Sarah's head. Not after she's been with us so long. Eventually of course, when Sarah realizes she's too old to shoulder any responsibility, Mrs. Paynter will fill the post naturally. In the meantime she'll act as assistant. I have to explain all this when I see her. But I'm told by the agency she's a most respectable and well qualified person, also practical and good tempered."

"She sounds an angel without wings," Jessica commented dryly.

"A little of that won't do Trencobban any harm," Donna replied tartly. "There's another thing, too, that I have to see about. The window that was broken. Oh, we're going to be a tidier, better household in future, I can promise you."

"You have no idea how pompous you sound, Donna," Jessica said.

Donna's lips tightened. "Practical you mean. Someone around here has to be. Otherwise we'd be in Queer Street . . . me, you, and Janey. There's that too. Her education. Boarding school's not right for her yet. I've decided she'll have a governess and remain at Trencobban."

"You've decided!" Jessica said shrilly. "You, *you*. What right've you got to say what's good for my own brat."

"Every right. If it wasn't for me you'd be dragging her around the mean streets of some murky city or else land up with her in the workhouse . . . or worse."

"You've no call to say that."

"Perhaps not. You'd go for something more sensational I suppose, like soliciting in dockland . . ."

"You . . . bitch!" Jessica whispered through her teeth.

Donna laughed. "Between you and me, I can be, if necessary. But for heaven's sake drop it. Come on now Jessica, life isn't too bad here when you think about it. Food, a fine roof over your head, a little money in your pocket, security, and new clothes, with other things to follow."

"You despise me though, don't you?"

"Only when you sink so low I'm ashamed Luke married you . . . like lying with Jed Andrewartha. Yes, I

136

despise you then. Not otherwise. Now, I'm off. By the way . . ."

"Yes?"

"I found a pair of earrings when I was going through some trinkets of my mother's the other day. They're sapphires, and don't match my eyes. But they'd suit you. I meant to bring them down earlier. But you'll find them on my dressing table. As Luke's widow, I think you should have them."

Jessica's sullen expression lifted as if by magic. "Oh Donna d'you mean it? Really?"

"Of course. Go upstairs and try them. But no poking about my things. Understand?"

Jessica nodded. "I won't. I promise you." And she sailed out of the room as if she were a queen about to be crowned.

Donna smiled. There was an appealing quality about her sister-in-law sometimes, which, despite her full-blown maturity (and she was a whole seven years Donna's senior) made her momentarily vulnerable and childlike. At such times Donna found herself wondering whether she and Luke might have found marriage workable had he lived. Luke, after all, had been no saint himself.

She was still ruminating over her sister-in-law as, suitably clad in boots and cape, she made her way along the rough path toward the mine, wondering why Jessica was so ridiculously afraid of being alone. If only Jessica trusted her, she thought, not for the first time. The fact that she didn't was ominous; it indicated that her fear not only had its roots in the past, but in the future as well.

Jessica, meanwhile, was preening herself before the mirror in Donna's bedroom, turning her head this way and that, admiring the brilliant blue flash of sapphires, where the earrings glittered below her bright hair, imagining what it would be like to wear diamonds on her full white breast, and a glistening tiara on her head. If only she were a duchess or some great lady! Then, perhaps, she could be really good, and not always in need of a

137

man's hands upon her flesh, and the thrust of his hardness into her body to drown memory.

Jed. Oh God, Jed! she thought. Why can't you be here? She took the earrings off absently, put them into her pocket and went to the window, staring out, but seeing there nothing of the sea or landscape—only an immense, dull cloud of gray, humped like the dark, crouching shape of an immense man. She put her hands to her eyes, shivered, and went downstairs unsteadily to the kitchen. There was no one about. Sarah was probably having her half hour's rest in the small back parlor, and the girl was away for the afternoon looking after her sick mother. So, after a quick look around to make sure neither Sam nor Ted were hanging about, she went to the dresser and opened the cupboard where she knew that cooking sherry and brandy were kept.

Her hand was trembling as she lifted the brandy bottle to her lips. No one would notice what spirit was missing, and if they did she'd say she knew nothing about it. Once she had had a stiff drink she felt better and returned almost immediately to her own bedroom.

Janey was there, solemn-faced, with the eternal question in her eyes. "Who am I? Where did I come from? Does anyone want me?"

Jessica stumbled toward her and caught the child into her arms. "You're all I have Janey," she said thickly. "Tell me you love mama. Tell her, pet."

"I love you, mama," Janey said obediently. But her voice was cool, impersonal. With a burst of impatience, Jessica thrust her away, and flung herself on the bed, where she lay with a dead, hopeless expression on her face, staring at the ceiling.

CHAPTER EIGHT

With Nicholas away, Donna, freed from emotional conflict for a time, realized how many of the practical duties she'd meant to deal with at Wheal Faith—especially the welfare of the miners and their families—had been neglected.

I've been selfish, she told herself one morning in a fit of conscience. I don't know what my father would think. I meant to achieve so much when I first got the loan, and I've done nothing but parade and argue with Nicholas, buy myself a wardrobe of new dresses, and interview possible servants. Any hard thinking has been left to Tom; I haven't even been to see the Bordes.

The Bordes had been a hard working mining family in the past, who'd dedicated their labor to the service of William Penroze. But when the dreadful smallpox epidemic of 1870 had swept the district, the father and three of their sons had died of the plague within a fortnight, leaving only Maria, the wife, two younger boys, and a daughter of fifteen, Thamsin, whose health had already been undermined through poor food, insanitary living conditions, and too little sleep. From eight years old she had worked hard pulling radishes at an adjoining farm for 7d a day, later going as Bal maiden to Wheal Faith.

The surviving boys, Jim and Peter, had gone down the mine when they were both under ten years of age. Maria meanwhile, thanks to William Penroze's influence, had managed to obtain a small quillet of ground where she'd grown pillas, a type of small yellow grain similar to rye, but finer, which she'd boiled into the

139

porridge known locally as gurts. This, with a minimum of potatoes, and an occasional gift of pig's leg, providing a treat of knuckle pie, had been the mainstay of their diet during those hard years.

Sometimes, through the night hours, Maria had labored at plaiting hats from the fine straw, selling them at Penzance and Penjust for a meager sum to supplement their inadequate income. William Penroze had done what he economically could to assist them. But with so many in similarly hard circumstances, wisdom had prevented him showing obvious favoritism.

Then, only last year, further tragedy had befallen the family, when Peter Borde had met his death through a fire in the mine caused by a dropped lighted candle at a level near the shaft. Now Thamsin was sick of consumption, and it was feared could not survive more than a few months.

Donna at heart was frightened and revolted by sickness. But it was clearly her duty to go, to find out if there was anything she could do to relieve, even at such a late date, a little of their suffering.

She set off, wearing boots and her most inconspicuous attire, with a basket of goodies and a chicken from the larder. Sarah had grumbled until she knew who they were for.

"There," she said to Sam, watching Donna make her way cross the moor toward the Borde cottage, "our young mistress's found she has a heart in 'en after all."

"'Twas always there," Sam said with sturdy loyalty. "You have to make allowances for young things. Hasn't been easy for her by any manner of means, having to oblige that rich fellow up at Polbreath."

"Hm. *Oblige*. As long as et's only by honest work, I suppose no harm'll come of et," Sarah retorted. "But I wouldn' trust him an inch. An' 'tis my belief, Sam, she's got a soft spot for 'en already. I never did like her takin' all that ill-gotten silk an' satin from 'en."

"Now you've no call to call it ill-gotten," Sam told her sharply. "Mr. Trevarvas is in business, and no one's to say what, or criticize what he do make of it. So be

140

careful of your wumman's tongue, and doan't go making mischief. Whether you like et or not, Trencobban owes a great deal to him, I'm thinking."

Sarah, wise enough not to argue, merely indicated her mood by a cough and snort of disbelief, remarking after a pause, "Borde's daughter's beyond helpin' now I've heard. Sad. She was a fair pretty cheel in her young days."

Actually Thamsin Borde's prettiness was still there, only changed now into an ethereal beauty tinged at the cheekbones by the bright flush so common with her disease. When Donna was shown into the humble clob cottage by Maria she was shocked to see the painful thinness of the girl, shocked also by the cramped, sparsely furnished interior, which although clean, felt damp and cold after the warm sunlight outside. A bed for Thamsin had been arranged in the single downstairs room which served as kitchen, bedroom and sitting room as well. The one table was narrow, the chairs straight-backed and uncomfortable. A long bench was pushed against a wall, facing a shelf containing earthenware crockery. The only heating came from a meager wood fire burning fitfully on the open stone hearth beneath the drafty chimney. The thick glass of the one tiny window had been broken and was stuffed with rag. The floor was lime-washed, filled with knots and holes which had to be avoided carefully. How the family had managed to live there when they were all alive, Donna couldn't guess. There was only one tiny room upstairs which would be occupied presumably by Jim, leaving Maria to make shift downstairs on the long bench at nights. The toilet facilities were so bad as to be almost nonexistent. Donna had noticed a dung-pit close to the door when she went in, and a lingering smell from it pervaded the whole of the tiny interior, making her almost sick.

Yet the girl smiled when she went in, and Maria's gratitude expressed itself with a sudden rush of tears to her eyes, and the heartfelt words, "Miss Penroze. Nothen' I do say can thank 'ee enough. See Thamsin,

141

see what Miss Donna have brought'ee . . . a real chicken an such goodies as would make a queen's mouth water."

"How are you feeling, Thamsin?" Donna asked, trying not to show what she felt.

"Oh I bin haven' a good day, miss." Thamsin said. "Better than yisterday edn' I , mam?"

Maria nodded. "She coughed yesterday reel bad, Miss Penroze, an' a lot of blood came. But today, with the sun so bright an' you appearin' . . . well, we do have a lot to thank God for I do s'pose, although there was a time when I did curse the Almighty for the grief that was sent upon us. Parson Treeve have bin kind though. A real good man, whatever folks do say."

"Treeve?" Donna said, recalling the portly overfed clergyman, who, it was said, had sired two bastard sons in the district, despite his watchful plain spouse, and had frequently preached from the pulpit when he was the worse for liquor.

"Oh yer, mistress. He've bin plenty times to see our Thamsin, an' always with sumpthen in a bag . . . a bottle of real wine last time, an' a joke or two with it as well. Not like that Methody man who no doubt's as holy as they come, but with a long face an' too much preachin' by half 'bout God's will an' the next world. Our Thamsin don' want that. What she needs is a bit of a laugh, an' good nourishment inside of her."

And fresh air and proper attention, Donna thought. Egg-nog too and all the expensive little extras anyone as sick as that deserves. A sudden idea struck her. An idea characteristic of her impetuous nature—which no doubt her father would have advised her to think twice about.

"Mrs. Borde," she said, "How would you like to move to Trencobban with Thamsin? You could help in the house, and Thamsin could have every attention necessary to . . ." Her voice faltered ". . . to make her well again. Jim could come too. We've plenty of room. Oh please. You'd be no trouble, and the air at home is so good. . . ." She paused, waiting for Maria's reaction, hoping she'd take the suggestion as it was intended, and

142

not as an insult to her pride. Mrs. Borde did not reply at once. Then she said quietly, "I don't think that'd be practical, Miss Penroze. It'd mean leaving the cottage, an' although et's a poor place by some standards, et's ours; we're used to et. Jim'd take unkindly to goin' away. He's . . . proud I reckon."

"Yes. But . . . for Thamsin's sake."

"I know. I know. The girl would be better in another place. This here's all right when you do be well. But in her state . . ." her voice wavered before she continued, "I do badly want to do what's best for the girl. But we havin' no call on you Miss Penroze, an' . . ."

"It's not a matter of that," Donna told her, touching her arm with her hand, gently, "It's because my father thought a lot of your family. And I know he'd always want to do what he could for any of you. Especially now, when Thamsin so badly needs a lot of things I can afford to give. If you want to stay here—and I can understand agout Jim—why don't you let Thamsin come to Trencobban for a good long stay. I'll have my own doctor to see her, and she'll have all the treatment and attention necessary."

In the silence that followed, no sound registered but Thamsin's harsh breathing and the scuttling patter of a rat somewhere under the floor. Then Maria said with an effort, "Ef there was a real chance of her gettin' well . . ."

"Of course there is. Of *course*," Donna said emphatically. "Especially if Thamsin wants it. And you do, don't you Thamsin?"

The girl nodded. "Yes, miss. Oh yes!" Her eyes were brilliant in her thin face, filled with such expectancy, such sudden hope, that Donna was inwardly stricken, knowing she'd created a vision that could never be. Already the ghostly hand of death shadowed Thamsin's brow. This her mother must know, and had accepted.

However, in the end she gave into Donna's offer. Arrangements were made for the girl to be moved as soon as possible to Trencobban, and Donna left a little later,

143

relieved to be in the fresh air once more, although the shadows lingered in her mind, along with the knowledge that she'd acted hastily and the uncertain feeling that Sarah would probably object.

But Jessica was the first to show resentment when Donna imparted the news, "Consumption? But it's catching," she said indignantly. "Supposing Janey caught it? I think it's wrong of you. Really wrong, Donna. 'Tisn't as if she's anything to us here. Why've you got to go riskin' the lives of all of us just because of a girl you don't really know's beyond me. I can tell you one thing—your father wouldn't have agreed. Not ever."

"You don't know what my father would have done," Donna said stubbornly, although by then she had a shrewd notion Jessica was probably right. "Anyway, it's done now. I shall do everything I can for poor Thamsin while she's with us, and there's no reason for anyone else to be in contact."

As things turned out, the argument about Thamsin proved superfluous. Two days after Donna's visit she collapsed and died following a violent fit of coughing and hemorrhage.

She was buried three days later in Gwynmoor churchyard, where her father and four brothers already lay. Donna, wearing a sober black dress with dark veiling over her head, attended, and was surprised to find so many of the miners' families present. The weather had changed and the skies were leaden, filled with a spattering of thin rain. No one seemed to pay much attention to her, but she fancied she could detect an air of silent reproach among the mourners—reproach to the rich, and regret for those who'd worked and died for so little reward.

She was grateful that Jed was not present, and thankful when the sad little ceremony was over, leaving her free to drive back to Trencobban.

"Won't 'ee come in for a bite, an' a cup o' tay mistress?" Jim Borde asked politely. "You'm welcome."

Donna shook her head. "No thank you, Jim. I've

things to attend to, and you don't need me. I'm not family."

He didn't contradict her, and after a few words of consolation to Maria, Donna went to her gig and started Bess up into a trot over the damp ground, knowing that a handful of mourners were watching, feeling their dark eyes on her as though probing to her very soul.

When she got back to Trencobban she felt deflated, and utterly tired, not physically, but in spirit as though all life had been drained from her. Jessica, as usual, was on the watch for her.

"My goodness," she exclaimed. "You do look washed up. I can't understand you. Going through such a dreary business . . . especially when you weren't asked."

"Funerals are never pleasant," Donna answered shortly. "I suppose I felt guilty."

"What on earth for?"

"All the things I haven't done."

Jessica drew a deep breath of impatience. "I'll never understand you, not ever. With me it's the opposite. If I could undo my life and start all over again there are a whole lot of things I'd leave out."

"Luke?"

"No. Luke was about the best that ever happened to me. And that's the truth."

"Yes. Well, I believe you."

Jessica went to the sitting room window, staring out over the moors bleared by rain. "When is *he* coming back?" she asked, "Trevarvas?"

"A month or so."

"Hm. A pity it's so long. At least he seems to get things going. So it'll be some time before you go up to that big place."

"Not necessarily. I've got an invitation to visit the children."

"Oh. Will you go?"

"Yes, I might," Donna answered, feeling suddenly brighter. "Tomorrow probably. And there's no need to be dull. The new housekeeper, or *assistant* I should say, will probably be here next week, with the girl. You won't have to feel alone any more when I'm out. You'll like that won't you?"

"It depends what she's like," Jessica said, hoping she wasn't some busybody with eyes all around her head and forever on the lookout when Jed was about. Still, no one could be drearier than old Sarah with her moralizing and forebodings. Like a prison it was sometimes, cooped up with her and Sam.

Prison.

Though she didn't realize it, her hands were clenched at her sides, her mouth set. "Why don't you have a drink, Donna?" she said, on the spur of the moment. "Couldn't we have a brandy for once, together? I feel like something the cat's brought in, myself."

After a quick look at her, Donna agreed. "All right. Just this time. Why not."

The spirit revived and relaxed her. And presently she went upstairs to change from the black dress into something more becoming, wishing irrationally that Nicholas were there to approve. For the first time she realized she actually missed him, which was odd, considering how they always seemed to be at war when they met. In the future, if he didn't goad her, she'd try to be gentler and behave more decorously in his presence.

Decorous?

The warm blood flooded her cheeks as she recalled their last meeting on the moor . . . his kisses, the hard pressure of his body against hers. Forget it, he'd said, or something to that effect. But that was the trouble; she knew she never could. And her heart quickened, just through remembering, while the echo of hooves seemed to ring through her head, temporarily obscuring the sadness of the Bordes' tragedy.

The next morning the air was still damp with thin drizzle, but by afternoon the sky had cleared, spilling pale sunlight through the drift of remaining clouds. Donna drove to Polbreath and endured a stiff hour drinking tea with the governess, Agatha Pullen, and Nicholas Trevarvas's children, Ianthe and Jonathan.

Their hostility made her uncomfortable and she heaved a sigh of relief as she reached Trencobban. To her surprise Jessica met her with a playful, knowing look on her face, saying that she had a visitor—a gentleman waiting for her in the drawing room. Someone she was sure she'd like to see.

Mystified, Donna removed her outdoor clothes, and after tidying her hair in her room, went downstairs again, thinking to meet some engineering authority, or one of the officials recently seen by Tom Craze.

To her astonishment she discovered Lucien standing by the mantleshelf, looking extremely—unconventionally—smart, in a dark crimson velvet jacket, gray trousers, white waistcoat, and spats to match.

"Lucien!" she exclaimed, going to meet him with extended hand.

He took it, bent his head, and graciously kissed it, then said, staring at her ardently, "I should have let you know, but when I heard old Nick had definitely gone, I couldn't wait a single moment. Donna . . . you look adorable." His compliments, after the recent sadness, sent her briefly and recklessly into his open arms.

"But I thought you'd gone," she said when she'd freed herself.

"So I did. Just as far as Truro for a few days, where I stayed with a colleague of my student days. I wrote to my patron, telling him I'd been delayed by family matters for a time—oh very tactful I assure you. So tactfully I was certain he wouldn't take offense. Then I waited, thinking things out. When I heard old Nick had really taken off to town I soon packed up, and—here I am. The fact is I just couldn't tear myself away after our last parting, Donna. I behaved gauchely; maybe you thought me cool, but I wasn't. Merely, shall we say—momentarily practical."

"And now?" she asked, so softly that her voice was almost a whisper.

He paused before answering. Then he said, "I'm

staying at the inn in Penzance. But I've still a few days to spare and it occurred to me that in such time I could make several sketches of you, and start a portrait perhaps."

"A portrait?"

"Yes. Don't look so surprised. I mentioned it before."

"Yes. But how? When? I mean, are you sure you want to?" she asked, both confused and flattered at the same time.

"Quite sure, darling. And the sooner the better as far as I'm concerned, with old Nick safely out of the way, and no one else coming to poke their noses in at every sitting."

"What do you mean by sitting?"

He laughed. "A sitting means you just in front of me, and me with my pad and materials ready to sketch you first, from the most attractive angle, then getting down to the real thing."

"I see," she said although the whole business of painting her sounded rather bewildering. However, feeling that she was due for a little excitement and recreation, she eventually complied, recklessly agreeing to meet him the following evening at about five thirty, not in the cove this time, but in a small secluded bay a little further to the south. It was generally sheltered from any strong winds by its picturesque background or of rocky cliff-face, and had a few convenient boulders about where she could satisfactorily pose.

"What shall I wear?" she asked before he left.

"As little as is necessary, but enough to keep you warm."

She blushed. "You're not expecting me to behave like those . . . those cheap creatures they call models and that I've read about, are you?"

"My dear Donna," he assured her, taking her two hands in his, "as if I would."

"Oh I think you're quite capable of it."

He shook his head. "You're wrong in each case. Models, to begin with, are never cheap. They're

148

damned dear. Secondly, I'd never expect you to behave as anyone but your sweet self. Satisfied?"

"No," Donna replied. "But I'll come all the same."

He drank one glass of Madeira then bid her adieu, kissing her hand flamboyantly once more before leaving Donna to her own thoughts. They were a curious mixture of excitement and anticipation mingled with a tinge of apprehension that she couldn't quite assess, but was intensified by Jessica's probing.

"I think you're up to something. What is it? What did he want?"

"Oh nothing much. Just to paint me sometime."

"When?"

Donna shrugged. "Oh, it's one of those things in the future that may never happen. Sometime I said. When I feel like it."

"You be careful," Jessica said. "There's something fishy about that one. And don't ask me what; I couldn't tell you. But there is something. I feel it."

Donna laughed, but she had to admit uneasily to herself that Lucien was certainly unlike anyone else she'd ever met.

Before going to bed that night she tried on an assortment of clothes, and decided to wear an amber-colored linen dress that she had had made recently by the seamstress. It had a tightly fitting bodice, low-cut to show the subtle shadow between her gently swelling breasts and a full skirt left to fall freely over a frilled petticoat.

And if the weather's not good, she thought, I won't go at all. I'll take it as a sort of omen that Jessica's right.

But the weather proved to be perfect, still and dreamlike, warm with not a quiver of wind in the air, and the sea so still it could have been a sheet of glass under the golden haze of the late summer sky.

Lucien was already waiting for her when she made her way carefully, slippers in her hand, between the boulders bordering the thrusting cliff beyond the cove. As the tide was out, it was simple, and when she saw him she dropped her skirt modestly, perched herself on

149

a rounded slab of granite, putting one foot into its light shoe.

Lucien stopped her. "No," he said. "Please, darling. I want you like that, only . . ." his voice trailed away uncertainly. The light in his eyes was curiously disturbing.

"Well?" she said, with a note of doubt in her voice. "What were you going to say, and why are you staring so?"

He rushed forward, knelt by her knees, and lifting both hands to her face, loosened the thick hair so it fell in its tumbled ebony mass about her shoulders.

"You're so beautiful, Donna," he said. "Oh lovely— lovely one. I hardly dared hope you'd come."

"I told you I would, didn't I? If I hadn't meant to I'd have said so. Anyhow, you haven't even said hullo, or . . . or . . ."

"Kissed you?" As the teasing smile tilted his lips, she felt his charm once more stealing over her, and she instinctively lifted her lips to his. For moments, or was it minutes, his mouth was on hers, sensually savoring the sweetness of that long heady embrace. Then he released her gently, got up, and walked away to where a collection of paints, canvases and sketching materials were piled carelessly by a boulder.

"I must capture you as you are, before the light changes," he said. "Just a sketch at first—but without shoes, and with your bodice down—Aphrodite I shall call you, Aphrodite of the waves."

"Oh but . . ." one hand went to her bosom protectively. "I'm not going to undress," she said. "Not that. I did say so, in the beginning. No, Lucien."

He ambled toward her again, lazily but purposefully, with the smile gone from his face, his expression intense and set, as though impelled by an inner dedication no words of hers would shake.

"Donna," he whispered. "Please."

"Please what?"

"Do as I say. For art. For my sake. For me, Donna."

She jumped up quickly. "Don't talk like that. Why

150

should I? I hardly know you. And I don't care about art. In fact, I should never have come. I think we should go, Lucien."

He shook his head. "Oh no. You don't mean that. Come now." As she backed away from him, he followed, quickening his pace. She turned and tried to run, but he had her suddenly by the shoulders, with his slim hands, those hands that looked so elegant, biting into her flesh. She could feel his breath against her cheek.

"Quietly now. Gently," he said, forcing her backwards onto a rock. "There. There you are; my most beautiful. My Donna."

He smiled again, while she trembled, fascinated and yet repelled. Some part of her responded to the caresses which followed, even while her mind rejected him. As he unbuttoned her bodice exposing the naked breasts, her heart instinctively quickened. Very gently then, as though relishing every movement, every curve of her body, with mounting excitement, he undid her skirt, removed the petticoat and lacy bloomers, the garters and stockings, murmuring endearments all the time, stroking her skin and letting his lips linger on the fiery sheen of her body—the pink nipples, thigh, traveling from stomach to naval and down to where his eyes rested, not with an artist's gaze, but with something else even beyond physical passion.

Struggling ineffectually to free herself, she shut her eyes, knowing it was useless. With her nerves and deepest pulses roused by the sensual touch of his adroit fingers, she shuddered as he murmured, "Come, darling, don't fight—don't fight—come, come."

He was trembling too; more than Donna. Trembling convulsively, bearing down upon her, pressing himself hard against her, while she stiffened fiercely with a sudden rush of awareness, against what, too late, seemed inevitable.

It did not come. Suddenly he moaned and rolled away from her onto the cold sand. Convulsive sobs shook his frame. Frustrated and revolted, she saw that he was crying, sensed there was no true manhood in

151

him, nor ever could be—only a thwarted sexual need incapable of giving love to any woman.

The flash of knowledge, the shock, were so sharp she had no pity for his torment, only outrage, and a sense of degradation that made her cry shrilly, "You horrible thing. You—*creature*. Go away, cover yourself. I loathe you, you understand? Get away; don't touch me!"

She struggled into her clothes, pulling them frenziedly over her limbs in a fury of contempt both for herself and for him. Then she picked up his coat which still lay at her feet and flung it in his face. He took it without a word, thrust his arms into it shamefacedly, and adjusting his breeches murmured only one word "Donna."

"*Go*" she hissed. "Get out of my sight. You and your art! I never want to see you again . . . never, never."

Forgetting even to pick up his sketching gear, he stumbled away over the rocks, and when his downcast figure had disappeared around the cliff, she kicked the paintbox violently against a stone where the contents spilled and rolled about the sand. Then, after making sure he'd really gone, she found a pool in a cleft of rock, and stooping down, bathed her face and forehead, letting the salt water trickle from her neck between her bodice and skin, until the wild thudding of her heart and in her head gradually eased, and she felt almost clean again.

She waited some time, unable to think coherently, noticing nothing, unaware even of the sounds of activity somewhere above, of men's voices receding into the distance and the dying singing of the Bal maidens making their way home from the mine. Neither did she see the broad, dark shape of a man poised to her right on the clifftop against the sky. If she had she might have realized she was wearing only one stocking, and that the other lay yards away with a blue silk garter.

It was only later, when at last she reached her own room at Trencobban, that she realized what had happened. Her impulse was to make the trek back there and then. But she was too tired. Anyway, she thought, no one normally clambered about such a remote spot, and the tide, except when the weather was extremely rough, didn't quite reach there. Tomorrow she'd return and reclaim the missing clothing. Lucien could do what he liked about the paints. They were none of her concern.

But when early next morning she made her way past the cove to the spot where the unpleasant incident had occurred, nothing was there. The stocking and garter had gone, together with most of Lucien's painting gear. She didn't know what to think, and was dicomfited. Someone must have come along later that night or in the early morning before it was quite light. Not Lucien. She was sure of that. He'd been far too upset to revisit the scene of his humiliation.

Then who?

The thought there could have been some peeping Tom about was sickening and somehow unthinkable. But there was no point in brooding, and her one consolation was that however distasteful the process, she had emerged whole. Now that she knew what manner of man he was, she could understand Nicholas's hostility to him.

Nicholas.

He must never know. If he ever found out . . . she shivered, with the blood running chill in her veins. By nature, she sensed, he was not a cruel man. But remembering the way he'd beaten Jed . . . Oh God, she thought. He must never know, *never*. How he'd treat Lucien if the truth came out, she could guess. But herself? There was no way of telling. His most secret self was still a mystery to her, although she'd glimpsed at odd moments a streak of tenderness that belied his usual hard veneer.

It was a touch of such tenderness that she wanted so badly now. Something to lift her from lingering shame to self-respect again, and perhaps—love. But how could she hope for love when all Nicholas appeared to want was her obedience because he'd bought her services for a few thousand pounds of his vast wealth?

Suddenly she felt unendurably tired, and wondered, not for the first time, if Wheal Faith were worth it.

She did not go down for a meal that night, pleading a headache, but instead had hot milk and biscuits in her room. Afterward, to restore her resolve and her faith in the mine, she took out her father's letter and reread it twice before putting it back into the drawer.

Contact with his memory and the dignity of his last poignant appeal to her made her feel better. In the future, she decided, she'd not bother about men or their stupid flattery. She would try to live as her father had expected her, with pride and understanding.

CHAPTER NINE

The work at Wheal Faith was proceeding as planned, and on time, but one day Tom Craze called at Trencobban to remind Donna that the expense of reaching the new tin levels at the mine would exceed the stipulated sum of £3,000.

"I told you before," Donna said glibly, "I'm not without funds any more. If I have to dig into my own pocket, Tom, I'll do so. Besides—would it be so very much?"

"It's according to what you call much, mistress," the captain answered. "I'm not doubtin' you'll have it, if required. But money goes quick when any obstacles come up."

"What obstacles could there be?"

"Well, drainage to begin with. You never quite know where you are with water until you get down to it. The cliff adit's good. But there could be other underground sources waiting to pour through, once rocks are struck. Then wages, as I've said already, Miss Donna. There can be no more cutting. And with the extra labor they'll cost quite a packet. Men aren't prepared any longer to take risks. There's the new Union to contend with, too. Of course, on the whole, folks in these parts like to remain free in spirit. The Cornish are a sturdy, independent lot, and loyal. When it comes to the families though, and how to feed them—well, they're going to look to the future. And there's belief growing that the Union's going to protect them in years to come."

"Do you believe that, Tom?"

155

He paused before saying, "I've a hunch it may be true."

"And Jed Andrewartha? It's him, I suppose, who's goading the men to ask for more and more and more?"

"No no. You've got it all wrong. Jed can be a trouble-maker, we know that. But he's a fine miner too. Tough, and his mates respect it, even though he gets their goat sometimes. He can't make trouble, remember, unless it's already waiting there for him to blow it up."

Donna shrugged. "If you say so. All the same, I wouldn't trust him an inch."

"Then try, mistress," Tom told her. "Folk generally act better if they're thought well of."

The same philosophy as her father's, Donna thought reminiscently. But then Tom didn't know of Jed's savage attack. If she told him he would no doubt believe her, but there was no way of *proving* it after such a time. Her word against Jed's! Unless she brought Trevarvas into it, and she had denied to him that she knew the culprit's identity. So it was stalemate. Her only course was to go along with Tom's advice as far as possible, hoping to keep matters on an even keel with Andrewartha. As for the money question, she'd pull in her purse strings a little. It would be intolerable to have to go begging to Nicholas for a further loan, and doubtful that he'd comply. There was the new housekeeper arriving too, and arrangements already set in motion for Janey's governess, although the appointment hadn't been decided yet.

Oh dear! she thought when Tom had gone. Why did she have to get such worries pushed at her? As if she hadn't got more than enough to bother over, without the threat of having to dwell on the complications of water that mightn't be there, men's wages, and all the talk of Unions, which didn't mean a thing to her, but was obviously calculated to make trouble.

And she'd done all she could lately to promote good feeling, visiting the Bordes, making visits to Wheal Faith, giving all encouragement possible with baskets of goodies for the Bal maids. She'd tried so hard to be one

156

of them, but realized now, that despite their bright smiles and polite welcome she never would, simple because she was of a different breed—one of the gentry, who'd never known what it was to work for a living cobbing and sorting ore, returning home after long hours of labor to additional duties of caring for children. Younger brothers and sisters maybe, generally a man as well, and sometimes a sick parent.

With her head Donna could understand. Her heart, too, was frequently stirred by pity. But what wasn't practically experienced could never be properly comprehended, and there were times, walking back to Trencobban, when she felt that her presence had served more as an insult than as a mark of friendship. The Bal maidens, like their fathers, husbands, and brothers, were proud, wanting only what was their right rather than charity—unless tragedy struck, as it had with the Bordes.

She was walking back one early evening, following a routine visit of this kind, when she met Jed striding toward Wheal Faith, where he was on night cores, being a skilled natural engineer who, with proper qualifications and education, could undoubtedly have risen to a position of far greater authority.

Her nerves contracted and stiffened when she saw him approaching across the moor. There was no mistaking his broad figure which, unlike most of the miners who were on the small side, slightly bent from constant stooping, still loomed erect and tall. Dismissing the impulse to cut away from him toward an upper track leading directly to Trencobban, Donna continued straight ahead, and as their eyes met, said coldly but with outward politeness, "Good evening." To her dismay he made a gesture to one side and stepped in her path.

"Evein', miss. On the chilly side, but not too chill for a few words, I'm thinkin'."

"A few words? What do you mean? If it's about Wheal Faith or your work, Captain Craze is the one to go to."

157

Jed shook his head knowingly. There was a shrewd, calculating look in his small eyes that momentarily unnerved her.

"No mistress. Ted'n work," he said. "I doan' ask advice 'bout that from any wumman."

"Then what?"

"A little consideration's due mebbe—on account o' what's gone before."

"I don't know what you're talking about," Donna said, attempting to pass him, but encountering one iron-hard arm that barred her way.

"Don't 'ee! Shall we put it then—my skill perhaps? The cleverness I've got, the others haven't?"

"You're getting full wages now," Donna retorted sharply, and with more courage than she felt at that moment. "You can't expect more."

"Oh yes I can, and I do," he said with his eyes narrowing, threatening. "You see, mistress, like I said—'tedn' only th' work I know things. I seed."

"What do you mean?" Already Donna's heart was beating unevenly against her ribs.

"The other night. 'Neath the cliffs. You an' that fancy chap—brother of that fellow of yours up at the big house—Polbreath. Oh I seed all right."

"Fellow of mine? Fancy man? How ridiculous. You're lying! And what's more, remember, Jed Andrewartha, if you start spreading things around the countryside . . ."

"Oh I won't. I surely won't, miss—s'long as you see reason. A little extra in my pocket would be a deal of help just now with my wife sick an' needing what good stuff she can get inside of her. You understand?"

"No," Donna managed to say firmly, although she did only too well. "I don't. You're trying to intimidate me. You've no proof of anything at all."

"No? What about this then?" From his pocket he produced the telltale blue garter, dangling it in front of her eyes for a few seconds before he replaced it in his pocket.

A feeling of sickness rose in her, causing a momentary sense of faintness. He watched her silently, a sadistic twist on his thick lips. Then he continued. "There's more too. A stockin', a brooch, an' some paints an' things belongin' to the fellow—the one who laid you."

"You filthy cheat," Donna said in a whisper. "If you ever breathe one word, there are things I could say about you, about a night not so long ago, either, when you came creeping after my sister-in-law and then assaulted me."

Jed threw back his head, laughing. "Much good it would do to tell on me now. You should'a' spoken earlier shouldn' you? But you didn', no. An' I know why. Because you was frit, and maybe you had a bit of a likin' for me—however wild you fought. Maybe I should've crept into your bed some night 'stead of that fat whore Jessica's. Yes. That's what I think now. But then I hadn't seen you afore, had I, without your petticoats, or a shred on."

Involuntarily Donna's hand rose to strike his face. Then abruptly she let it drop to her side.

He nodded his head approvingly, licking his lips.

"That's better. P'raps now you understand. P'raps you're ready to talk sense, because there's quite a score I have agen you, madam high-an'-mighty Penroze—includin' that dastardly attack on me by your man."

"He's not my man. He . . . he . . ." She choked on her own words.

"No? An' he never will be, will he, if he hears what's bin goin' on? An' you wouldn' like that I'm thinkin'. It strikes me it's not only money you're wantin' from him, but somethin' else. That's it, isn't it? Somethin' a wumman has to have when the mood's on her—either in a fine bed or a ditch. Finery or rotten rags . . . underneath you're all the same. *Women!*" He drew his hand across his mouth, and then spat as a gesture of contempt.

She turned her face away, shuddering, and saw to the right two figures—miners—walking from the road toward Wheal Faith. Oh heavens! she thought, she mustn't be seen arguing with Jed. Everyone knew his reputation; they might think . . .

159

"What do you want exactly?" she asked in an under-tone.

"Pound a week for twelve month," he answered without a moment's hesitation. "Then after that, we'll see."

"A pound a week! You must be mad. That's fifty a year . . ."

"Cheap I'd have thought, considerin'."

She started to move away. "I'll have to think about it."

"You think hard and quick then," he said. "Or *else*. Bring the first lot on a Friday if you're wise, in cash."

"Where?"

"Somewhere around the Kiddleywink at the turn leadin' to the village. 'Bout five, before I goes on night cores."

"I'll see," she said. "I don't promise."

He flung her a shrewd, acquisitive look before turning abruptly and without another word, strode away across the brown moors until his hulking figure was hidden by a clump of twisted thorn and windswept, stunted sycamore.

That night Donna could not sleep. Torn between outrage and fear, her mind could see no clear course or freedom for the future. First, she was under an obligation to Nicholas. Now Jed. At one point she tried to believe she could call his bluff and refuse to pay. After all, a stocking and a garter proved nothing. But there was the brooch, with her initials on, and the things left behind by Lucien. Added to Jed's story, they could provide a pretty nasty picture, and the result not only would be to her discredit, but damning, a scandal no one of any standing would be likely to forget or forgive. She could take out a case for blackmail of course, but this would only add fuel to the fire. No. There was no way out except to go along with Jed's demands, until some day, somehow, she found a way to thwart him. And thwarting Jed would be no easy matter. He was not only a villain, but a cunning one.

What a fool she'd been.

For the next few days Donna appeared so abstracted

160

that Jessica asked one evening, "What's up? Why so sour and stand-offish? Isn't the money good after all? Or has the rich benefactor taken off with some high falutin' woman who can give him what you won't?"

"Stop it," Donna answered sharply. "The money's safe in the bank, and it doesn't matter to me one jot what Nicholas does with himself."

"Oh. So it's always Nicholas now. You know . . ." Jessica paused before continuing. "I think you're the worst liar I've ever met, Donna Penroze. I don't know about the money of course—so long as you've got it, that's all that matters. But I'll tell you one thing straight. It's my belief you're so besotted by Trevarvas that you just can't bear him out of sight and sound of that ugly great house, or not having him riding about all show and swank on that big horse of his. Oh yes, he's a swank all right. A real Lord John-Tom-Noddy, if you ask me. All the same if you feel so strong about him— why for God's sake didn't you do something about it earlier, instead of letting him slip away without nabbing him when you'd got the chance?"

"Be quiet," Donna told her. "Leave me alone. I've too much on my mind already without you trying to goad me with your stupid ideas and low talk. None of it's true anyway. Nicholas doesn't care about me. Why should he? I hardly know him. I'm under an obligation, that's all. I work Jessica, in order to keep Wheal Faith, and a home for us—you, me, and Janey. Think of it that way, or maybe you'd better start planning what you want to make of your own life. I'm not bound to keep you here you know. You're quite competent enough to carry on with whatever you were doing before you met Luke. In fact it might do you a deal of good to start a real job of work again."

Jessica's color faded. Go back? Revulsion rose in her. The lights and the busy streets—yes, that had been all right until her passions had caught up with her and sent her into the hell of degradation. But she'd never feel safe any more up there alone—not knowing who might appear around any corner some dark night, whose face might loom unexpectantly, suddenly, in a crowd or in a public house. No. Not again, never again. At Trencobban she was safe. At the edge of the world almost, it seemed sometimes, when she looked out across the rim of cliff and empty stretch of cold sea. The sea was always there. Lonely, impersonal, a waiting void of forgetfulness if the horror she dreaded crept up with her. It wouldn't though. She was safe with Donna and Janey, hidden in this faraway corner of Cornwall, which though wild and desolate, had given her sanctuary under another name—Luke's. And now here was her own sister-in-law threatening to send her away.

"I'm sorry, Donna," she said, trying to control a tremor in her voice. "I won't mention Nicholas Trevarvas again until you do it. And it isn't that I'm not grateful—it's just—sometimes I get lonely I reckon, without Luke."

"Or Jed?" Donna said coldly.

Jessica's blue eyes were enormous, filled with a haunted pleading quality that Donna found curiously disturbing as her sister-in-law answered, "Jed's a man, after all. I wasn't meant to be a nun, Donna."

"He's not a good man," Donna said, appreciating the touch of honesty. "You'd do better to keep away from him. But you must know that."

"Yes, I know it," Jessica admitted. "And I'll try. I'll do my best—truly I will."

Donna sighed. "Just so long as you remember. There's Janey to think of too. Whatever else she may be, she is yours. Even through her, you could make something new of your life, if you put your will to it."

"Don't say that!" Jessica cried shrilly. "Not about making something new of my life. I've heard it before, and it brought me nothing but harm. Never, never tell me to be made new. It's a damned, bloody lie. A trick. So . . . so . . ." She broke off breathlessly, her breasts rising and falling convulsively under the stretched gray bodice of her dress.

Donna took her arm. "Whatever's the matter? I didn't mean to preach. Sakes alive Jessica, have a bit of sense. You're making something out of nothing. And anyway I'm not all that perfect myself. There are some things I want, others I can't bear to think about, and times when I wonder what the whole thing's about. Living I mean, and trying to keep my head above water. Then do you know what I do?"

Jessica, quietened by her words, asked, "No, what?"

"I think of my father," Donna said simply, "and somehow everything begins to slip into place."

"Yes. I know what you mean. He was good to me. A real saint if ever there was one."

"No," Donna contradicted her. "No one on earth is a saint. Neither me, you, nor even my father, although he came near to it sometimes. We're all a bit of a mixture. Me perhaps most of all, because I know how you got into this mess with Jed."

"You know?"

"I'm a woman," Donna said shortly. "Had you forgotten?" and she walked away without waiting for Jessica's reply.

On the Friday after her encounter with Jed, Donna set off in good time to meet him, with the silver carefully wrapped in an old piece of cotton bearing no identification or mark to show where it had come from, and her father's pistol concealed in her cape.

She knew the Kiddleywink by sight and hearsay; a small granite dram-shop of unsavory repute, huddled in a hollow overlooking Gwynvoor. There, it was said, many doubtful deals were hatched, under the influence of liquor considerably more potent than beer. Clients were of a varied order, including some decent miners, as well as thieves, those dealing in stolen goods, shady smugglers, peddlers and tramps. The authorities had long since learned that it was wisest to turn a blind eye to much that went on there, rather than get involved in violence and possible murder. Donna had gone on foot and walked so briskly that she was a little early, so she didn't wait in the immediate vicinity, but cut down for a short way toward the sea.

The surrounding boulders were large and provided

protective shadow from the lowering sun. She was pausing, looking back toward the west where the distant stark shape of Wheal Faith stood in miniature against the sky, when she heard the crackling of furze behind her, and turning around, saw Jed clambering up toward her. His hateful face had an expectant grin on it.

"So you've come, mistress," he said. "That's as well for you. Got the silver, have ye?"

With a contemptuous gesture Donna flung the money at him. He caught it adroitly. "Now now. That's no way to go on," he said. "Throwin' good silver about. S'posin I'd dropped it, eh?"

"You'd soon find it," Donna retorted. "It's all tied up. I'm sure you're not the kind of man to waste a single penny for the want of looking."

"You're gettin' to know me," he told her. "Goin' to be a bit nicer now. Eh? A cuddle or kiss? He stumbled toward her. She brought the pistol out, holding it straight at him, hoping he'd not notice her hand trembling.

"It's loaded," she said.

He laughed. "Put that thing away. Think I'd risk being dead, just when I'm on to being rich? You keep your bullets, mistress, an' I'll keep the silver. Only just you remember to be here next week, same time, same day, with the same silver, or I'll make things so hot for 'ee roundabouts you won't want to show your face ever again afore your so-respectable gentry."

She winced at the hatred in his eyes and for a moment thought he might attack her. Then suddenly, he turned and was striding up the slope toward the Kiddleywink, leaving her with such a sick feeling in her stomach that she wanted to retch. Her legs felt heavy as she made her way back to Trencobban, and a sense of despair filled her when she reached the house. She went in by a side door, cutting quickly across the hall and down a corridor to the back stairs, before anyone could appear to question her.

Once upstairs, she flung herself on her bed, lying there for some time before attempting to wash and

164

change her dress in preparation for the evening meal.

She made no particular attempt to brighten herself, but took out a gray dress—one William had liked, that was simply cut with no pretension to fashion, and when she went downstairs later to the small room where the family had mostly taken their meal since William's death, Jessica, who was hungry, and already waiting by the window, said critically, "You look a bit dreary. You haven't worn that drab thing at all lately."

"There are a lot of things I haven't done lately," Donna said shortly.

"Such as?"

"Seeing about certain—matters—in the village."

Jessica's eyes widened. "What matters for heaven's sake?"

"Church to begin with. I never liked Parson Treeve; but after the way he helped the Bordes when Thamsin was so ill I've been thinking I may have misjudged him."

Jessica laughed jeeringly. "Him? Don't you believe it. From what I've heard . . ."

"What you've heard is of no account," Donna interrupted. "Every day someone hears something to another person's discredit. Anyway, it shouldn't matter to you. *You* won't be drawn in, have no fear."

"I haven't. Not of that kind. And what's the use of pretending? If I was to put so much as one foot inside the church everyone else would go out, or else turn away with their noses so high in the air you'd think there was a bad smell there."

Donna was about to turn the conversation to another channel when Sarah appeared with the food.

Jessica ate heartily, but Donna had no appetite.

"You are feeling off, aren't you?" Jessica persisted, when her sister-in-law's plates went back, hardly touched.

"Tired. That's all."

"Hm. Well Sarah won't like it."

"Whether she likes it or not I can't help it. I've got things on my mind."

165

Jessica said nothing to that. But a shadow crossed her own mind as she thought, so've I. And worse than you'll ever know.

Before they went up to bed that night, Donna said, "Mrs. Paynter comes on Monday. For my sake try to get on with her, Jessica. She's a proud sort of woman, very respectable."

"Oh, the dull kind."

"No, I wouldn't say that. More—reserved. The daughter's about fourteen. A nice girl."

"If only there could be a man about," Jessica burst out impetuously. "It would be a bit of a change. Young Ted after all . . . he's a bit simple, thinking of nothing but horses and stables and messing about with manure. As for Sam, you can't call him stimulating now, can you?"

Donna agreed. "No. But worthy."

Jessica snorted. "A fig for worthiness. I thought you said when you got the money from Trevarvas there'd be more company about."

"We've had plenty I think," Donna told her. "The engineers were quite pleasant men. Concerned with their work of course. But it's bound to be like that for some time yet. Later, when we get on our feet, and the mine properly started up, there'll be a change I promise you. And then there's the governess for Janey. I've heard of someone in Falmouth wanting a job. We could drive over there one day next week and see what we make of her. What do you think?"

"Oh I'm all for an outing," Jessica agreed readily. "Although I think I should have the first say if she's suitable or not."

"You'll have no say at all," Donna told her imperiously. "It's my money that will be spent, and I mean to see it's not squandered. No feather-brained hussy to take on your daughter's education. She happens, as well, to be my niece, by law, anyway," she added with a touch of malice. "And it's up to me, under the circumstances, to see what can usefully be made of her at Trencobban. So if you come with me, Jessica, you'll

166

keep your mouth shut if anything controversial crops up, or else not go at all."

"Very well, madam," Jessica said, with heavy sarcasm.

If Donna noticed the irony she didn't appear to. Jessica's alternating moods of depression, excitement, cheerful good humor and sharp-tongued malice now left her cold. If only she kept off the brandy, she thought, the relationship between them could drift on more or less satisfactorily.

Beth Paynter duly arrived at Trencobban, with her daughter, the following week. She was a dark-haired, striking looking woman in the mid-forties, with an educated voice and a manner that suggested she knew her place, and would keep well within it. The girl, Phyllida, was tall, slender, rather colorless, but attractive in a shy fawn-like way. Sarah took to her immediately, although she explained to Donna, when they were alone that Beth—she insisted on calling her Beth from the start—had a bit of a snooty way about her that she'd better not use on her, as there'd be bad blood between them.

Relying on Beth's tact to keep things on an even keel, and after emphasizing that Sarah was still in full control, Donna felt a weight fall from her shoulders, until she remembered Jed.

On the Friday she set off as before with the silver and pistol safely hidden in a pocket, but this time astride Saladin and wearing Luke's breeches and jacket. Let them see, she thought. She was entitled to take a ride across the moors at any time she chose, and there was nothing peculiar in having a chat with one of her own miners.

Jed was waiting for her in the same place, and was clearly taken aback when he saw the boyish figure and proud black colt facing him.

"Here you are," Donna said, handing him the silver carefully tied by string in its cloth bag. "And in the future don't expect me every Friday. I may have other things to do."

"Tryin' to fool me, are ye?" Andrewartha said, with a suspicious glint in his eyes.

"If I could, I would," Donna told him. "But I won't try it—yet. You shall have your pound of flesh, Jed. Blackmailers often get away with it for a time. It won't be forever though. You can rely on that."

"We'll see, missie, we'll see," Jed said, attempting to take Saladin's reins with one great hand. The horse reared, snorting belligerently, a magnificent sight, but one that sent Jed backing away with a flush of fear and surprise flooding his fleshy countenance.

Donna laughed. "Don't try any tricks on Saladin, Jed. He's like his name . . . vicious when he feels like it."

"I can see that. And much good will it do you. One day someone could put a bullet through that creature on a dark night when no one's about."

"I'd have a good idea who it was, Jed, and see he swung for it."

"They don't hang for the shooting of a mad animal, wumman. Now, let's get down to it. When'll you be back again, eh?"

"Friday if I can. Saturday if not," Donna answered. "Take or leave it."

Without waiting to hear his muttered comment, she turned, jerked the colt to a fine speed and was soon galloping away, in the direction of Trencobban, her figure silhouetted against a cloudy sky.

The quick interview with Jed, and the knowledge that her male attire and Saladin's ferocity had given her the upper hand for those brief few minutes, made her feel better. That, and the reminder that soon Nicholas Trevarvas would be back. She hadn't realized until then quite how much she'd missed him. And missing was hardly the word. His presence at Polbreath meant far more to her than she yet admitted, even to herself.

It seemed so long since he'd gone. And so stupid of her to care, when only a few short months ago Nicholas Trevarvas had been no more than a symbol of dislike and vengeance in her life.

But it had happened. The thing she wanted most in the world—to desire a man so completely nothing else counted in comparison. The only thing missing was the knowledge that he felt the same about her. And he must, he *must,* her heart cried, remembering the impact of his kisses, the dark hot flame of his eyes. She'd loved Jos. Or thought she had. But this was different. Something so compelling that she felt without it she could die.

Yet he'd left her and gone off alone to London, leaving the lingering torment of their last meeting churning her emotions into unbearable conflict and despair. Only through action and by setting her mind to domestic affairs and the problems of Wheal Faith could she force herself into a more normal state of mind. It was in solitary moments, as now, that his form and face were all she saw, and she felt they would forever haunt this land of hers—this wild Cornwall where the winds moaned through heather and around cromlech, disturbing the wanton gale-blown clouds.

CHAPTER TEN

Autumn came, passing from September to early October, with the moors turning to a patchworked glory of russet, dying gold, and deepest purple. The early mornings were dark, and the evenings fell quickly, enclosing the landscape in shrouds of mist, or throwing it into stark relief with a fitful moon. Sometimes gales, heralding the winter ahead, lashed the harsh coast, and moaning threateningly against Trencobban's sturdy walls.

Donna and Jessica drove to Falmouth to hire a governess for Janey. And still Nicholas did not return.

Donna, uneasy and resentful at his absence, though she knew she had no right to feel so, spent most of her time riding Saladin to the wild summit of the hill where the cromlech stood, or busying herself in mining affairs of which she had no practical knowledge. Her temper was edgy and Jessica became sullen, depressed by the lack of congenial company, and by the hard-faced newcomer, the governess, Zenobia Bray, whose intimidating presence appeared to be striking a wedge between Janey and herself.

One day Tom Craze called at the house and, as tactfully as possible, suggested that Donna keep away from the precincts of the mine for a while.

"The men aren't used to women inspecting and asking questions whenever there's a chance, mistress," he said. "Not that it isn't your right if you're determined. But the hours they keep . . . the way they go on . . . their welfare, an' wanting to know what this and that's for—even questioning 'bout their families when they leave of a night—oh I know the mine's yours, and they

170

know it. But it's a man's world, Miss Donna. And the Count House . . ." he broke off, shaking his head ruefully.

"Yes?" Donna queried sharply.

"You'd do best not to be present at meetings unless it's a very special occasion. Money affairs are the purser's business, an' my pardon please for sayin' so. All of us know it's from your pocket the cash comes. But the master always left such matters to those dealin' with it. Remember too, we've taken on one or two new tributers, an' they don't much appreciate a woman wantin' to know the ins and outs of coinage and ore, and suchlike."

Donna's lips tightened. "I see," she said shortly. "You mean I've been a nuisance. Poked my nose in where I wasn't wanted."

"Yes, Miss Donna," Tom said firmly.

"Oh I . . ." Donna suddenly felt dejected, depressed—put in her place like a child who'd unknowingly done wrong. "I'm sorry," she said. "I didn't mean it. I suppose I was trying to be important and show interest."

"Of course, mistress," Tom assured her. "And we all know that. I had to put in a word though. You see . . ." he broke off before continuing. "Most of our workers are a decent straightforward crowd. But men are men, and a few might get wrong ideas. That's another thing."

"Wrong ideas?"

"About why you should so often be nearby when they leave cores, mistress. Men like Jed an' a crony or two of his. 'A bit of skirt around' as they put it means only one thing to some. I can't think of how else to say it, an' I hope I haven't offended you, Miss Donna. But being a Penroze and your own father's daughter, it'd worry me to hear you joked about in that way."

Of course, Donna thought, Andrewartha; she might have known . . . she could imagine his lewd remarks when her name cropped up. Naturally he would be careful to keep any financial deal between them secret.

171

But he wouldn't be beyond talking insultingly about her if the opportunity arose.

The suggestion caused her to say resolutely, "Thank you for pointing out what I should have known, Tom. You're quite right. And I'm grateful. I'll keep away from meetings and not bother myself about Wheal Faith problems. I should have had the sense to realize how things were before. So let's leave the matter there, shall we? I know you'll always contact me if there's anything to discuss."

"Of course, miss." Tom sighed with relief.

Donna smiled. "Have you heard from Jos?" she asked, changing the conversation into more friendly channels.

"Yes. I had a letter the other day. Doing well, he is, over there. Wisconsin's the place. Already quite a crowd of Cornishmen settled—'Cousin Jacks' they call 'em, who've struck it rich."

"Jos always said he'd do well," Donna said absently. "I remember . . ."

In a friendly, fatherly way, Tom patted her shoulder. "It was all for the best, Miss Donna. The right thing for him to go, and go alone. It's different there. You'd have found it hard, I'm thinking, to get accustomed to such new ways, and money in the pocket doesn't compensate for giving up what you was born to. Not one like you, anyway, with so much of the past remaining your own, the house, the land, the mine. Oh no, midear. Your place is here. An' I think you know it in your heart."

She did, but after Tom had left, a sense of loneliness fell on her, which she could only dispel by thinking of the future—of the day when Nicholas would return, and of the darker problem of her unsavory commitment to Jed.

It was getting increasingly difficult to conceal her regular absence from the house on Friday evenings. The days were closing in more rapidly, and her plea of wanting a breath of air when the weather grew damp and dark didn't always ring true. She made an effort to take herself out at the same hour on other days of the week

172

in order to allay any suspicion among the servants. But Jessica noticed.

"Always prowling about in the twilight. What's the idea?" she asked pointedly, one night when Donna returned wet and tired to Trencobban. "Are you meeting someone, or what? Come on, let me in on it, Donna."

Donna shook her arm away. "Don't be so stupid. Who would I meet on a night like this. For God's sake stop watching me."

"Oh dear. Hoity doity!" Jessica sniffed. "You've got it badly and no mistake. Sorry I asked."

She flounced away, leaving Donna uneasy and at a loss to know how to manage things in the future. The only way, she decided after a session of hard thinking, was to pay Jed monthly. If he didn't agree, then she could challenge him to do his worst and threaten to take him to court for blackmail. He might refuse at first, but in the end he would comply, because he wanted to be sure of the money, and although a case against him might ruin his reputation, it would also put him behind bars. In fact, if she had more courage, she thought, she would refuse there and then to pay him another penny. The trouble was that he'd pay her out in some other way—somehow he would hurt her where she was most vulnerable—through her association with Nicholas Trevarvas.

Nicholas. She couldn't get him out of her mind. And the more she fought against her feelings, condemned herself for being weak and childish, for behaving as sentimentally as any brainless girl just out of finishing school, the stronger her longing grew.

"I *love* him," she thought one day, pausing astride Saladin by the cromlech, her eyes turned to the west. And aloud, to her colt, "D'you hear that, Saladin? He's wild and strong, like you are sometimes, with the devil's darkness in him. But I *want* him. Want him so much I could die." She patted the horse absently. "All right. All right boy—come on now."

She kicked her mount to a sudden wild gallop along the high ridge, with her hair flying free as the horse's mane, chin lifted to the afternoon sky where a rim of sullen clouds were spreading from the sea. The air was sweet and wild about her; her senses, with the elements, seemed to be singing and responding to the unfettered primitive force that drove her inexorably toward the fulfilment of her most secret need.

On she rode—faster, faster, until suddenly Saladin stumbled on a boulder. She was pitched headlong and thrown. She had landed on a tump of dead heather, but with one ankle bent under her, and her horse streaking away in the distance along the far horizon.

The pain was excruciating. But after a time she managed to raise herself, and sit up, finding presently that the ankle, though badly strained, was obviously not broken. She waited for a time, hoping Saladin would return. But he didn't, and eventually she forced herself on her feet, her eyes searching for a possible prop, a fallen branch of tree or furze to help her down the hill. She could see nothing. She took a step forward gingerly, and then a sudden wave of sickness from the pain brought a rush of faintness, and she fell back again, with the sky revolving into a vortex of darkness above her, taking her into oblivion.

While she lay there she dreamed.

The spirits of the great stones took identity and became a force of gray ones marching toward her from that faroff unknown past. They wore wind-blown shrouds of garments with wild locks and beards straggling around burning eyes. And in their hands they carried knives. There was a curious chanting in the air as they closed about her, and the far-off wild thudding of giant hooves. She struggled, with her hands outstretched before her, trying to ward them off.

And then she screamed.

The shrill sound was caught up by the thin high crying of a gull. The figures receded into the fleet of lowering clouds above the earth. Beneath her she could feel softness and the gentle easing of her form into comforting arms. At first she thought she had died. Then, slowly, miraculously, as she opened her eyes, she saw the eyes of another staring down at her. Not harsh or condemning this time, but filled with sympathy, and undeniable anxiety.

Nicholas.

He was holding her in his arms, and when she had properly come to herself, she heard him saying, with a hint of the old irony in his voice, "To think I came back but yesterday evening, and the next morning the first thing I find is my new hostess lying thrown and bruised in the bracken." She noticed then that he'd removed the boot, and the ankle was already swollen.

"I'm not bruised," Donna said, "at least, not much. Just my ankle. It's sprained badly I'm afraid. I . . . I . . ."

"You're an infernal nuisance aren't you?" he said, and smiled. "Oh Donna, for God's sake! why on earth can't you take care and act like a reasonable woman?"

"I'm not very reasonable I suppose," she said, with an answering gleam of mischief in her amber eyes.

"No," he agreed. "And maybe that applies to me, too." Almost before she realized it he had bent his head, and was kissing her, not fiercely as at their last encounter, but lingeringly, tenderly, as though he could not bear to release her. She closed her eyes momentarily, savoring rapturously each heady wonderful second, forgetful of pain, shock, and any former conflict between them; content for that short interim to be at peace in her longing, drawing the sweetness of passion into her lungs and heart, with the moorland tang of earth and air, wishing never to be free again, but, for the first time in her life, entirely submissive.

Never before had she sensed such flowering of both sense and spirit . . . of surrender to a deeper, more potent force than her own.

Then, reluctantly but purposefully, the pressure of his lips was withdrawn from hers. She glanced up wonderingly, longingly. There was a hungry look in his eyes and about the whole set of his face. Now that its defensive arrogance had gone, his expression was aflame with desire, but it was desire mingled with a curious shyness

175

that had something of fear in it . . . fear of acknowledging the secret bond between them, and perhaps of having it broken forever.

"Donna . . ." he murmured, "oh Donna . . ." as the wind lifted her hair and caught the one word into a sigh, drifting through the blown undergrowth and furze with a gentle dying sound. It seemed to her that something followed . . . or was it her imagination only . . . a mere illusion that he whispered "love"?

She never knew, because suddenly he had pulled himself away, lifted his head, and was saying with maddening practicality, "Now, Miss Penroze, the sooner I get you back to Trencobban the better. It seems I'm fated to appear just at the very moment you're either swooning in the bracken or fleeing from some madman. How the hell you do it is beyond me. If that ankle wasn't such a swollen sight I might think . . ."

"Yes?"

"Never mind. Come along."

He lifted her onto his horse, while she gritted her teeth in pain. Then he took the reins. "Hold on, and try to relax. Pluto's quiet enough. It's a tidy walk, but safer this way."

Together they made their way down the hill to Trencobban. Little was said; Nicholas relapsed into silence, and when they reached the house his remarks to Sarah were detached and cursory.

"Your mistress has had a fall. If the pain doesn't subside soon it would be advisable to let a doctor see it. A lucky chance I happened to come across her. And in the future . . ."—with a glance at Donna—"do ride the mare if you have to ride at all. Seems to me that colt of yours isn't yet broken in enough to take any woman safely over such wild country."

Donna, for the first time since her fall, thought of Saladin. "Where is he?" she asked Sarah quickly. "Saladin. Did he get back?"

"Oh yes, mistress. He's safe in the stables. Arrived 'bout five minutes ago. Sam an' Ted were just startin' off to look for you. You look a real mess, an' no mistake."

"I quite agree," Trevarvas said with no trace of expression in his voice. "But when women act and dress like boys it's to be expected."

A few minutes later he'd gone, and once Donna had been attended to, with the ankle bathed, liniment applied, and expertly bound up by Beth Paynter, Sarah said grudgingly, "Well I s'pose we have to be grateful to that man, more's the pity. You're beholden to him enough, an' too much already. That's what I do think. An' I didn' fancy the way he looked at you."

Donna blushed. "Oh don't be stupid. He hardly looked at me at all."

"Hm! you say so. But I saw what I saw. An' 'twasn' dignified. Especially you in those breeches. You shouldn't ought to go about in such a way, really you shouldn', Miss Donna."

"Thank you, Sarah. I'll do what I choose," Donna said reprovingly.

"Oh you will, I'm sure. I doan' need tellin'. But what about the doctor? Mr. Trevarvas said . . ."

"Doctor? Fiddlesticks!" Donna retorted. "I shall be all right in the morning."

But she wasn't. Although the swelling had subsided considerably, the strained ligament still pained her, and Donna had to resign herself to the fact that her activity might be curtailed for several days.

On Thursday, which was Sarah's half day, when she went to Gwynvoor to shop, Mrs. Paynter knocked at the sitting room door and presented Donna with an immense bunch of bronze and yellow chrysanthemums.

"A man servant brought these from—Polbreath—I think he said ma'am," she said. "There's a note there too."

"Oh thank you, Beth," Donna replied, with her heart quickening. "Would you mind getting a vase and water. There's a crystal one in the drawing room—tall, on the small table near the window."

177

Beth withdrew, and with her hand trembling, Donna tore the envelope from the string and opened it.

"Donna," the note ran, "Please accept these with my good wishes and hopes that the ankle is better. I intend having a small gathering at Polbreath on Friday, a week tomorrow, at which I hope your presence will be possible.

"However, don't take any risks. To do so would annoy me almost as much as your absence would do.

"Yours,

Nicholas Trevarvas.

"Note. I thought the Chrysanthemums, though hardier and less sentimental flowers than roses, would more suit your flashing amber eyes and willful temperament."

Donna lifted the flowers to her nose appreciatively, drawing their earthy, tangy scent deep into her lungs. How like him, she thought.

She was still standing with them crushed against her cheek when Mrs. Paynter came back with the vase. "Lovely aren't they, miss?" she said. "Aren't you lucky to have such a kind gentleman thinking of you?"

"I suppose so," Donna agreed, not adding that Nicholas was also thinking of himself. She had only a week before he expected her to preside once more at one of his aggravating and probably boring parties. Who would be there this time? she wondered. Not the Penverryses, surely, or the haughty Rosina. Heavens! She hoped not. *Rosina.* The mere thought flooded Donna with jealously. Had Nicholas ever given her flowers, she wondered, and thought it quite likely, if he thought she would be useful to him. They wouldn't be chrysanthemums, though. For Rosina there would be roses or camellias, or something more exotic.

Oh botheration, she thought, moving suddenly so that her ankle stabbed viciously with renewed pain. Why on earth did she have to think of Rosina just then? Why, when something pleasant had occurred, must other disagreeable visions follow on? Such as Rosina, and—and Jed.

Like a cloud descending, and depressing her, she remembered that tomorrow was the day on which Andrewartha expected his weekly payment. She would certainly not be strong enough to reach the appointed place unaided. She toyed with the idea of contacting him—sending Ted with a note. But it was too risky. No. He'd just have to wait. And if he didn't and appeared at the house, he would undoubtedly have concocted a plausible excuse for asking to see her.

She was right, although he didn't call until Saturday morning.

Donna was looking through some of her father's books in the library when Sarah knocked at the door, entered, and said, "There's someone to see you, mistress. That theer big man from Wheal Faith. Mumbled sumpthen' 'bout the mine, an' business. Said it was important. Thinkin' it funny, 'cos the Cap'n generally attends to all that, I said I'd have to see. You wait, I told 'en, I'll have to find ef it's convenient."

Trying not to show her agitation, Donna replied, "Oh, yes. It's quite all right. I expected him. Show him in here."

"In *here?*" Sarah's voice expressed more than surprise, extreme disapproval.

"I said so."

Muttering to herself, the old servant withdrew, and a minute later Jed strode through the doorway.

"Well?" Donna said, when the latch had clicked behind him. "I suppose you hadn't heard I'd had an accident that prevented our usual . . . assignation." Her voice was cold with contempt.

"No," he answered. "How was I to learn of such a thing, not movin' in your class of society? An' did you expect me to wait then, for my due, until such a fine wumman as yourself thought fit to let me know?"

"You're a skunk, Jed Andrewartha," Donna said in a low voice, through clenched teeth. "And don't raise your voice or you'll be heard. Then, whether you like it or not, I'll have you behind bars in no time."

She pointed to a wooden smoking box on a round

179

oak table near the fireplace. "Bring that here. It's lucky I keep spare silver at hand or you wouldn't get a penny this week or the next. In fact not until the following month. I've decided you'll receive your filthy lucre in a single sum every four weeks. And if such an arrangement doesn't suit you, you can lump it or have the whole thing out in the open."

He handed her the box.

She counted a pound's change and gave it to him. "That's up to date. I'll see you three weeks from next Friday. In the meantime don't dare to show your face here again."

Her bright eyes shone vividly in her white face, giving her a fleeting wildcat look. He started to say something, thought better of it, thrust the change into his pocket and strode to the door. But before opening it, he turned and muttered in a low voice, "Ef you was my wumman I'd see you was properly tamed. You see you keep your word, or you'll be sorry."

There was a sharp snap as the door closed. Donna shut her eyes, as though in doing so she could dispel the mixture of hatred and thwarted sexual desire in Andrewartha's eyes and voice. Then she got up, and, limping slightly, left the library for the sitting room—but not in time to see Jed almost bump into Jessica coming from the kitchen, as he made his way along the hall to the side door.

Jed paused for a moment while Jessica stopped, staring at him with such intense emotion on her face that Jed, inflamed as he already was by Donna's contempt, felt the lust rising in him.

"I want you," he whispered. "Understand?"

She nodded, swallowing hard. "And me. And me."

As she passed, he turned, giving her a meaningful touch on her buttocks. "Tonight in the cove."

She nodded mutely. The next moment he was gone.

That night, in the dark shadows of the rocks, unpenetrated by the milky light of a clouded moon, Jed used and took Jessica, alternately ravishing and abusing her, thrusting and crushing her time after time, pretending she was Donna, while she moaned and writhed beneath him in the culmination of insatiable passion.

And that same evening, a criminal escaped from Bodmin Gaol—one who'd killed many years ago, but still lived, thirsting for revenge. No ordinary man, but clever, with the gift of words and the capacity to plan. To slink and hide and lurk in unknown corners until the moment came to pounce and strike with infinite cunning.

No one knew which way he went, or who housed him. The moor was large and villages sparse. As for Bodmin, Launceston, Turo, the folk there were careful of their own, shutting their eyes to things they feared, and their ears to disturbing whispers. There was no point in bravery when a cutthroat was around. No sense in seeking trouble until it came. Besides—most who remembered the tale said that the bitch herself had been responsible. If a woman lay with a man not her own she was asking for it. Lust and fornication had been condemned by the Good Book itself. Let events speak for themselves. The affair was nobody's business but those concerned.

And so it was that when a shadow passed a lighted window of a night, no one saw.

When a large humped form stretched a greedy hand for a piece of bread not properly hid, no one cared. Rumors were adrift, and the eyes of the law alert. But without co-operation the law was powerless, and in the secret hidy-holes of his numerous retreats, the outlaw listened and learned, and smiled his madman's smile, knowing that in the end he'd find her, and then—God, or the devil—help them both.

CHAPTER ELEVEN

Donna's ankle recovered more quickly than she would have thought possible. When the time came for her to appear at Polbreath again she was quite strong, and stimulated at the prospect of seeing Nicholas once more.

On this occasion, for a change, she wore black chiffon, cut daringly low at the bosom, with dropped lace sleeves, and a finely woven, thin shawl dotted with gold spots to drape her shoulders. The bodice was tightly cut, the skirt voluminously full over a series of fancy petticoats. In her piled hair she wore a white flower to match her elbow-length white gloves.

She looked beautiful, and knew it.

Therefore she was acutely disappointed when Nicholas greeted her with a veiled, cold glance and a critical note in his voice as he said, "You're late. Still, I believe you've met my brother before, and as . . ."

"Your brother?" she interrupted with astonishment.

"Yes. He's here until after Christmas. He was taken ill in Paris. However as I was saying, or about to—my other friends are staying here, so ten minutes here or there doesn't matter. But I would be grateful if you could be punctual in the future. I was wondering if your ankle was still bad."

She lifted her head, staring him straight in the face, and answered with what she hoped was equal coldness, "It's better thank you. I was not quite ready when the chaise arrived. I had things to do, and driving along rough roads in the winter is more precarious than in the summer when evenings are so light, you know. Your man didn't feel inclined to take risks."

"Of course not. Well—perhaps you'd like to go and remove the cloak you're wearing. We shall be waiting in the drawing room."

Biting her lip she answered, "I won't be a moment longer than necessary. And—thank you for the flowers. It was very kind of you Mr. . . ."

"Nicholas," he said curtly. "For heaven's sake don't be so damned formal. Keep your airs to yourself and stop behaving like a spoiled child."

Feeling angry and humiliated, she turned in silence, hurried to the dressing room, removed her cloak, and viewed herself critically in the glass. Two brilliant spots of color burned her cheeks. Her eyes held the fiery gleam of hot coals under the lamplight, adding allure to the soft cream sheen of skin and dusky hair. She had meant to keep the lacy shawl over her shoulders for modesty's sake. But in a fit of temper she now removed it, and was pleased by the effect of her softly swelling breasts, her full, firm neck arched proudly below the stubborn, delicately formed chin, and her pouting lips. The flower in her hair added just the right touch of virginal purity.

She felt suddenly mischievously assured and daring, knowing intuitively that Nicholas would certainly not approve, but would be quite helpless to do anything about it.

When she sailed into the drawing room a few minutes later, she was surprised to find so few present. Only Lucien, who gave her a tentative smile, and two others—a portly red-faced middle-aged man with white hair and bushy eyebrows, and a woman who was very blonde, very painted, very overdressed in pale blue satin.

"My dear," she gushed, as Nicholas introduced them, "I've been so longing to meet you. This dear boy Lucien told me all about you . . . absolutely *all*. How beautiful you were . . . how excessively individual and charming. Which you *are*. Of course you are. And

183

so far away from the world, too. One wouldn't have expected it. Still . . ."—She patted a place beside her on the Louis quatorze chaise-longue,—". . . do come and tell me about yourself. You've heard of me of course. Or don't you go to the theater . . . ?"

"Miss Lamont, Regan Lamont, is to appear in a new play at Drury Lane next month," Donna heard Nicholas saying, still in the steel-edged voice he'd used to greet her. "No doubt she could give you many tips about London life and manners. And this by the way . . ." indicating the large man, "is Mr. Emmanuel Frobisher, agent and theatrical producer."

In a daze Donna felt her palm gripped by an immense hand, so heavily ringed that the fingers cut into her flesh before he dropped it and bent his head to kiss her own hand.

Nothing seemed quite real any more to Donna. The conversation sounded artificial and contrived, and the presence of Lucien, whose eyes seemed forever turned in her direction, intimidating. She could not understand how he dare look her in the eyes after what had happened during their last meeting. But at one point, when Nicholas was out of the room, he approached her and murmured in her ear, "Please forgive me, Donna. I was a brute. If I hadn't been ill I should still have come to plead your understanding."

Knowing that Regan Lamont's eyes were on them, Donna replied with a shrug, "Of course. I understand perfectly." Adding in an undertone, "Don't look at me like that Lucien. Someone will notice."

Lucien withdrew, but not before Nicholas's return, and from the tightening of his lips she sensed that he had seen. He walked toward her. "Put your shawl on," he whipsered furiously, his lips hardly moving. "And don't dare expose yourself in such a manner again. I'll see you later."

Subdued, but with a delicious thrill of anticipation running up her spine, Donna complied. Jealous was he? At first she thought so. But later in the evening she began to doubt. He was very attentive to the gushing actress, for whom, she gathered, he was sponsoring the forthcoming play. He hardly appeared to notice Donna at all.

Oh well, that was his affair, she thought, trying to pretend she didn't care. And if he wanted to ignore her, she could do the same to him. So she slipped off the shawl again, and flirted outrageously with Lucien and Emmanuel Frobisher.

Lucien was enchanted. "Donna," he whispered, some moments before she left. "You are adorable. And so beautiful. So kind too. I shall recover now. I know I shall. Everything's all right between us, isn't it?"

"As all right as it will ever be," Donna answered. "We must be brother and sister Lucien, and . . ." She broke off as she saw Nicholas approaching, then, making a swift apology, slipped into the cloakroom where she waited until she felt secure enough to steal out quietly, already clad in her cloak for the homeward journey to Trencobban.

No one was in the hall but the manservant. "Please give my apologies to Mr. Trevarvas," she murmured. "Tell him I'm feeling unwell, and am leaving quietly so as not to disturb the party. Is the chaise waiting?"

"It will be in a minute, miss." The servant said doubtfully. "Only a few moments if you care to wait."

But Donna did not take the risk. Instead, as the man disappeared down the hall she slipped out of the door and down the steps, to find the carriage already drawn up for her departure.

Once they were out of the drive gates, the rapid beating of her heart eased a little, and when they reached the ridge overlooking Trencobban she was already regretting her impulsive conduct. She could have told Nicholas himself that she was leaving and have bid goodnight in a civilized manner to his guests.

But then . . . she wasn't entirely civilized, and for that matter, however much Trevarvas might talk of social gatherings and correct attitudes, neither was he. It was strange, she thought, that in his own home, with his own acquaintances around him there was always a gulf between them, and that their only moments of real contact seemed to be on the moors. But life itself was like that. A mixture of opposing elements, fire and water, and great gales beating suddenly over a calm landscape, whipping the earth to fruition and new life, blowing the dead leaves away so that spring could blossom from winter's sleep.

In all such things, Donna found something of Nicholas, knowing in her deepest self that however much either might deny the truth, they were already bound by something stronger than reason, wilder than any social code. In spirit they were united, although their opposing wills might make havoc of any mutual future.

For the next few days Donna lived in a tense state of apprehension and anxiety, fearing, yet hoping, to see Nicholas. Longing to have a word from him, but worrying what any note might say. There was no sign of him though. Not even on the moors above, where she ventured out on Bess one afternoon, correctly clad in her best riding habit—the one Andrewartha had damaged.

The bodice had been mended and Jed's image was so submerged by memories of Nicholas as to be almost blotted from her mind. He no longer scared her. Sometime, she told herself, she would either face him and dare him to do his worst, or tell her solicitor to threaten him with exposure unless he ceased his financial demands.

She had put the business of Jed and finance firmly out of her mind, when one morning in early November she received a note from John Crebbyn asking to see her at the bank.

Now what on earth for? she thought, starting at the brief note, with her brows drawn close over her eyes. Was there anything wrong with her account? Had a check gone wrong? Or surely . . . no! It couldn't be Nicholas. However annoyed he might have been at her abrupt flight from Polbreath on the night of the party he couldn't be so mean as to withdraw his support for Wheal Faith. There was no way, even if he wanted to. Everything was sealed and signed. The mine was due to reopen properly—with the deeper shaft sunk earlier than had been thought possible—in just another two months.

She questioned her manager later on the same day. "No, mistress," Tom told her. "Except for bills being a bit heavier than we'd counted on I can't see anything to worry about. Not where the mine's concerned anyhow."

"That's all right then," Donna said, almost gaily. "John Crebbyn's a bit of an old woman isn't he? My father always said he never took a chance."

"No bank manager can afford to, Miss Donna."

"Well I'm not worried," Donna retorted. "It's a nuisance having to go into Penzance. But I shall get Sam to drive me over early and have a look at the shops before the meeting. I only hope we have a nice day."

But in the morning thin rain was falling from lowering clouds which hugged the landscape into dreary gray. Donna's spirits were at a lower ebb than usual when Sam deposited her outside the bank. On the journey, with no sun or pleasant view to stimulate her, and no prospect of an hour's window shopping or a stroll along the harbor, her thoughts had strayed constantly to Nicholas and to the distasteful memory of his attentiveness to the colorful, effusive Regan Lamont, when she stepped into John Crebbyn's office, a first glance at his face did nothing to cheer her.

"Do sit down, Miss Penroze," he said, indicating a chair that was placed with its back to the window allow him to study every expression of her face.

"Now," he said. "I must apologize first of all, for the . . . weather." He laughed, but to Donna it sounded more like a wheezing rattle. "I should have ordered a nicer day for you."

"I expect you have a great deal to do without that," Donna answered unblinkingly, "so please don't apologize."

He looked up at her, momentarily startled, then cleared his throat as though determined to come to the point. "I don't like having to worry you at all. But it's your current acccunt, Miss Penroze."

"My account?" Her eyes were wide; her voice afraid.

"Oh yes. I'm afraid so. You seem to have been— digging into it—rather deeply lately. You must have read your statements?"

"Well I . . . I'm not certain," Donna confessed. "I should have done, I suppose; I don't remember exactly when the last one came."

"Ah. You should have everything of that nature properly filed and in order," he told her. "You are not, of course, yet overdrawn. But if you continue to draw upon your reserves at the speed you've done recently, that day, I'm afraid, is not far off. If you start economizing now, you'll probably get through until the spring. The problem is though, to retain enough capital to see yourself comfortably through any difficult patches."

"Difficult patches?"

He shrugged. "My dear Miss Penroze—even when the mine is properly on its feet it will take a little time to pay dividends. Obviously I didn't put the position clearly enough to you earlier. The facts are there."

He proceeded to read statements and calculations of figures dealing with payments and expenditure, to which she listened with a growing sense of dismay, hardly taking in details, but having to accept the facts which told her in no uncertain terms that she'd been paying out far more than she could afford, and that she would be in a financial mess again unless she retrenched severely.

"All right Mr. Crebbyn," she said when he'd finished talking. "I'll do what I can to economize, although I've been forced to take in extra help, and also have a governess to pay—for my niece. However . . ." with a touch of shrewd insight, "if you're not prepared to give a little financial—licence—" She paused before getting up, sighed, and drew on her glove, "I can always put the position to Mr. Trevarvas. I think he would understand."

The bank manager rose to her bait immediately.

"Oh there's no need for that at all, Miss Penroze, at

the present. And I'm sure there won't be. In any case I don't wish to harry you in any way, and I don't doubt that now you know how things are, you will use a little judgment."

He smiled thinly, offering her his hand. The next moment she was in the street where Sam waited for her with the chaise.

She felt profoundly depressed by the interview as they drove back. She might have bluffed her way through it by haughty references to Nicholas Trevarvas, but she knew that he was the one person from whom she dared not seek help. She was already too deeply beholden to him.

When she arrived back at Trencobban it was still raining. Except for muted sounds from the kitchen everything seemed very quiet. Donna went upstairs, and looked in on Jessica, who, as she'd expected at such an hour, on such a day, was lying on her bed, not yet dressed, with a magazine and newspaper at her side.

Without stopping to be tactful, Donna said tartly, "You ought to be up and dressed. Why can't you behave like a reasonable human being? It's downright lazy just lying there . . ." She broke off, puzzled and a little frightened by the expression on Jessica's face, which was set, glazed, as though she'd glimpsed not one ghost but several.

"Jessica . . . what's the matter? Are you all right?"

Her sister-in-law merely stared. She had something clenched in her hand. A piece of newspaper.

Donna took it from the cold, clasped fingers, and after straightening it from a crumpled ball into half a page of readable print, let her eyes travel through the main paragraph. It was headed "Murderer's escape from Bodmin Gaol," and went on: "Silas Flint, who was condemned to death eight years ago for the brutal murder, by stabbing, of his wife's lover Patrick Trywerne, and later reprieved, yesterday escaped from prison, where he was serving a life sentence, and is thought to be making his way south or toward Plymouth, where all shipping is being carefully watched. The reprieve, on the grounds of unreasonable provocation, was considered by many at the time to be unjustified. Flint was by no means uncultured, and had proved himself, through the extreme brutality of the crime, to be an excessively violent and dangerous character. He had professedly religious inclinations, and it was because he had returned to his home a day earlier than usual, after preaching at a service in an adjoining town, that he discovered Trywerne and his wife cohabiting in one of his own barns.

"At the trial he quoted lengthily from the Bible, and was thought by some to be insane, although this was discredited by the authorities. The whereabouts of his wife, if she is still alive, are not known. But should he locate her before recapture, there are fears for her safety, and it is therefore important she should contact the police immediately, and that anyone having any clue whatsoever about the whereabouts of Flint also co-operate with the law as soon as possible."

Donna's pulses quickened as she said, "Where did you get this?"

For a while there was silence. Then Jessica replied, "Ted had it from somewhere and Sarah showed it to me."

"Well? What about it? It's horrible, but nothing to do with us. Oh Jessica, for heaven's sake. I suppose you've . . ." her eyes searched her sister-in-law's face, but they showed no sign of bleariness or dissipation, only clear, cold fear. And there was no hint of drink in the air.

"Did you know this man, Jessica?" she asked, in deliberate, steady tones. "The truth now. Did you?"

Jessica blinked, sat up suddenly, with color returning to her cheeks. "Of course not. What a thing to ask. Know him . . . him?" She was almost screeching. "Why would I know a creature of his sort? How can you even wonder such a thing?"

Her vituperation was so intense that Donna had to accept the reply "I didn't say you did. I didn't even think it. I only asked."

"Well, don't ever ask again," Jessica snapped.

"You needn't bite my head off," Donna told her sharply. "You looked so odd there when I came in, just lying and saying nothing, and with that bit of paper screwed in your hand . . ."

"I was tired." Jessica's voice became sullen. "And anyway, it's not nice knowing a madman's prowling about, and a murderer too."

"He's not prowling about here."

"How do you know?" Without either of them realizing it, both Jessica's hands clutched Donna's wrists. The fear had returned to her eyes again making them more brilliantly blue than ever.

"Oh stop it. You're being plain stupid. There are lots of dangerous men about, but they don't generally make it a habit of visiting places like Trencobban."

"No?"

"Of course not; anyway I'm tired of this ridiculous conversation. Do get dressed, Jessica, and come downstairs. I know the weather's dreary. But I feel like a bit of company myself. Come along now, up. And we'll have a glass of something together in the sitting room."

A little of the tension left Jessica's face.

"Very well. Yes . . . I suppose you're right."

Donna turned and left the room, hoping that she was, and that Jessica had told her the truth. But she couldn't be sure. In Jessica there was an unknown quality, a legacy of mystery, that, despite her extrovert temperament, Donna could never fathom.

Still, the truth probably was that the childish streak in her had got the better of her, after reading the sensational newspaper paragraph. It had sent her wallowing into morbidity simply because she had nothing better to do. Once again, feeling herself weighted by insoluble problems, Donna's thoughts turned to Nicholas. She wished fervently she could see him, and even that she could apologize for her last hasty exit from Polbreath.

It was not till November, however, that she was taken by surprise to see him walking, from Wheal Faith with Tom, of all people, across the moor toward the

191

road above. Donna had made one of her rare visits to Gwynvoor, where she had called on the vicar to make her peace, and give plausible excuses for having neglected church for so long. Tom was evidently explaining something to Trevarvas—waving his arm first toward the coast, then to the west in the direction of Polbreath. These gestures were followed by nods and apparent agreement by Nicholas, who turned suddenly, after the brief conversation, and set off along the high road toward his home. Tom immediately cut back down to the mine. Now what on earth, Donna wondered, had they been talking about? Although she knew full well their business was none of her concern, curiosity got the better of her, and she was presently hurrying at a sharp pace away from the ridge hiding the hamlet, toward Wheal Faith, taking a straight track past and below Trencobban.

When she arrived, some twenty minutes later, Tom was standing with a few workmen near the face of the new shaft. "Well Miss Donna?" he said, rather curtly, moving away from the little group.

"I saw you talking to Nicholas. To Mr. Trevarvas," she said bluntly. "Up on the moor, by the road. There's nothing wrong is there?"

Tom eyed her disapprovingly. "Now I told you, mistress, that I'd tell you if there was anything going on you should know. Mr. Trevarvas had a few questions about the new adit on the rock face. It's not far from the coast boundary of his own land. Natural for him to put a few questions to me, about that, and other things."

"Oh. Other things?"

"Expense, mistress."

"But that shouldn't worry him."

"No? Well, that's a matter of opinion, seeing it's mostly his money financing Wheal Faith's problems."

"His money? But it isn't, Tom. You know very well about the agreement. The capital's in my name at the bank. He can't . . ."

"But with all respect, Miss Donna, you had it from

him. "You can't expect him to sit back all the time not knowing what's going on, or what he might be asked for in the future."

"He won't be asked for anything," Donna said stubbornly, "and what he's loaned to me, I'm earning, in one way or another." A moment later she wished she hadn't made the last remark. Tom gave her a probing, strange look, before he remarked with compressed lips, "The conditions of the loan are your own business, mistress, and I don't want to know any more details than I've already got. But as I pointed out the other day, men have to talk over things together sometimes, and that's just what Mr. Trevarvas and I have been doing. The estates join, and nothing's going to alter that. Cooperation, mistress. It's very important."

With that, Donna had to be satisfied, although she was irritated by her manager's refusal to discuss the problem properly. Not that she'd have understood. Most of the technicalities of mining were still a complicated mystery to her. Talk of man-engines, plunger pumps, high steam, the Cornish boiler, interested her little.

When it came to the land, however, and boundaries, it was a different matter. She knew exactly the lines bordering Trencobban and Polbreath territory. The Polbreath estate—though cutting back toward the east in an abrupt line from the valley very near the coast to Wheal Faith—extended mostly in the opposite direction, toward Penpeel. Most of the visible moorland above the road was Trencobban's. In the past, there had been many quarrels between the two families about that: arguments when the Trevarvases had tried to lay claim to what was not rightfully theirs. But Donna's father and grandfather had chosen peace rather than war, and the dividing stretch of moor had become generally accepted as common to both, except for one small tenant farm which was indisputably on Penroze land.

Donna recalled her father's words to her once, "Land is land, whoever's name it may have. But remember Donna, no one can really possess it. It belongs to itself.

Human beings can only care for it and take what it has to offer. But it was there before people ever trod it. Unless you realize and respect that, you'll never know the best of it."

And it was true, she thought that day, as she left Tom at the mine and walked home. She was an interfering busybody; her father would not have approved at all. If Tom had been talking to anyone else but Nicholas, she'd have had more sense.

Why did Nicholas not get in touch, she wondered, as she made her way upstairs. Even his scolding would have been better than the silence. Perhaps he wouldn't want to see her at Polbreath again. Perhaps he would rebuff her when they next met, telling her after all that she obviously wasn't fitted to be a social hostess and that therefore her services would be dispensed with. She thought it only too likely, and the possibility sent her into a mood of dark depression.

Jessica, when she saw her later, did nothing to alleviate it, flouncing about the house with untidy hair, the bodice of her dress not properly buttoned, and with sagging dark rims under her eyes.

Donna guessed that her frowsiness was due to lack of sleep, and perhaps exhausting secret sessions with Jed. That they'd been together more frequently of late was only too obvious. On several evenings, after Jessica had gone upstairs to bed pleading a headache, Donna had gone up to her room and found no one there. Once, glancing through the window, she had seen her sister-in-law creeping furtively through the moonlight in the direction of the cove path, and guessed why. On another occasion she'd overheard her in Janey's room saying in a furious undertone, "If you so much as tell a soul I was out, I'll take a slipper to your behind as I used to, and you'll wish you was never born."

Donna had no way of knowing that Jessica's words were caused not by selfishness or cruelty, but by fear . . . of the past, and of the future, which seemed so much more menacing with the arrival of dark evenings. There were times when despite the servants' and Donna's autocratic presence, she felt herself to be completely alone, without protection from the dark threat that nowadays—except when she was with Jed—clouded each moment of her waking life.

When she went out of the house by herself, she had to fight the impulse to look around, in case something or someone was lurking behind the bushes or rocks. Reason told her it was highly unlikely that Flint would track her down. Even before her marriage to Luke, she had changed her name from Lucy Flint to the more glamorous Jessica James. And it had worked. In a new seaport, with an ever changing population, no one had connected her with the adulterous wife of a murdering Evangelist farmer. No one was looking for trouble, anyway. And no one had cared, so long as she gave what was wanted of her of reasonable payment.

But now—now Silas was free—instinct that was stronger than reason told her she'd never be safe until he was behind bars again.

She longed, as always, to confide in Jed. But last time they'd lain together in their favorite spot—the tiny cavernlike place under the cliffs where winds or rain never penetrated—he'd seemed surly and withdrawn, as though he were beginning to tire of her again.

"What's the matter with you?" he'd asked suddenly, withdrawing his hand sharply from her legs just as she was getting excited and eager for him. "Frit are you? Why are your teeth chattering so?"

"I'm not frightened. Course not. With you here . . . oh Jed, Jed . . ." She'd pressed toward him, exposing her breasts, stomach, and thighs, smothering his face with her thick hair. "Love me Jed," she'd whispered. By then, lusting for her, he'd taken her without a word.

But afterwards, glancing at her calculatingly, he'd said, "Don't use that word, love, to me. I've got no love for you, nor ever will have. An' what was that you said about not being frit with me. Why me? No one knows do they? You ain't gone and spilled it about have you?" The anger was so quick in his voice and red face that she'd shaken her head, realizing it was useless. She

195

could never tell him. If she did he would push her off and not come near her again.

So for the most part she spent her time alone in her own room or wandering about the house, with her eyes constantly turning to the windows—seaward—and to the moors above. But she kept vigil. Most of all when the weather turned wild, and the cold east winds lashed through furze and undergrowth, roaring and sighing so fitfully that if unknown feet approached from somewhere in the shadowed dark, they would not be heard. If a latch clicked, its sound would be but one of all the other sounds tapping and beating about the walls of Trencobban.

Sometimes when it was fine and bright she persuaded Donna to walk with her to Gwynvoor, where she bought a weekly newspaper.

"I don't know why you want that thing," Donna said once, "It's only local, and mostly trash, except for deaths and weddings. What's the idea, Jessica?"

"I like to keep up with things," Jessica answered vaguely.

"Hm. You never did in the past if I remember. And if it's reading you want, there are good books in the library."

Jessica didn't reply, and shrugging the matter off, Donna forgot the conversation, her mind once more wandering to her own affairs. To Nicholas.

She was angry with herself for allowing him to have become so important to her, and furious with him for making it quite obvious she was merely incidental in his life. She had no idea how frequently he was tempted to ride from Polbreath to the cromlech, and how determinedly he kept out of her way, simply to teach her a lesson.

If haughty Miss Donna Penroze wished to flaunt her ill temper and bad manners before his guests, let her work off her ill humor on her own. She was a spoiled little spitfire, for all her pride and precious family name. And damn it, he wasn't going to have her throwing her tantrums about in his house.

One day, she would come sweetly of her own accord, with her tawny eyes alight with the fire he wanted—lips all soft with longing, and then he'd show her what he was made of. But until such a time he meant to keep full control, with the situation as he'd planned, on his own terms. There were several lessons she had to learn first, including the fact—whether she liked it or not—that there were many other attractive women in the world. The trouble was that in most of them he found no fire or unknown depths to plumb. No beauty or true warmth. He remembered his wife, Selina, and her shrinking from his every touch, driving him at least to infidelity. The more he thought of Donna, the more torn he was by intense longing for her. If she'd been a gypsy wench walking the moors in rags, he'd have felt the same. Other considerations such as wealth, family, or reputation, had no bearing on the situation. The recognition on his part had been electric. And despite her taunting pride, he guessed that with her it was the same. Then why the devil had they to be so at cross purposes?

The answer was simple. He'd take no wife to Polbreath wanting to rule. If she came, she would come to him knowing full well what she was going into. Kindness and tenderness were in him to give and give fully, so long as she accepted her role as a woman, with no hope of donning men's trousers. He didn't want her that way, and dammit he'd no intention of showing the weakness gnawing his heart and loins, until she was prepared to unbend and accept.

She didn't even have the manners to apologize for her unwarranted behavior to Regan Lamont . . . leaving without so much as a goodbye or handshake. The minx.

CHAPTER TWELVE

It was quite by chance that he met her one morning, riding Saladin, not along her favorite route above Trencobban, but on the other side of the hill, facing the valley leading to Polbreath. He was out for a short canter before a day's business trip to Bodmin, and quite suddenly there she was rounding the bend, a slim figure in her trim riding habit, raven-dark hair whipping her face under the saucy hat, cheeks bright from the sting of cold air.

"Well!" he exclaimed, as the two horses were brought to a halt. "How delightful to meet you again, Miss Penroze. I'm sorry I've no hat on, or I'd certainly doff it."

"There's no need for sarcasm," she said quickly.

"No. But there's need for something I think," he retorted. "And don't dare try your Cinderella act here. The moors are wide and open, and I'm a very fast rider indeed. So unless you intend providing an amusing piece of drama for the countryside, get off that colt so that we can talk."

With her heart hammering uneasily, Donna complied, as he, too, dismounted.

"Well?" she said, facing him with her chin out.

He stood, hands on hips for a moment regarding her speculatively. "You've a damned nerve haven't you?" he said at last. "Running off as you did, hiding yourself away . . . not a word of apology, doing nothing but burn my gold and fritter your attentions elsewhere."

A wave of fear chilled her. Had he seen her that evening with Lucien in the cove after all? Been merely playing with her until an opportune moment arose to fling it in her face? And if so . . . "I don't know what you're talking about," she said. "I left a message with your butler, or your man, or whoever he was . . . telling you I was tired. Did you expect me to bob into the drawing room oh so very politely—and plead excuses to that gushing Lamont woman? I'm not your servant, although you seem to think so."

Nicholas suddenly laughed, and his laughter enraged her far more than any scolding would have done.

"Oh Donna. Really. I believe you're jealous," he said. "That's it isn't it? Jealous of Regan?" He took her chin in one hand and tilted her face up to his own, which was amused and full of mockery. She brought her hand up sharply and struck him smartly on one cheek. Then before he'd properly realized it, she had broken free, swung herself onto Saladin, and was away, with the wind behind her, galloping back to Trencobban.

He made no attempt to follow, but unperturbed, mounted his horse and returned to Polbreath, invigorated by the chance meeting and also amused. It was the tonic he had wanted to put him in the right mood for the afternoon's business, which involved the capture of a French crabber caught by the Revenue with an illicit cargo of brandy near Sennen. A tricky business. But with valuable co-operation from one or two people in high places, no doubt he'd succeed in getting the French skipper vindicated and freed.

Trevarvas knew that every time he took a chance of this kind, he was tempting fate. But he couldn't live without a challenge. Perhaps because it was bred in him from ancestors who, in the past, had not only farmed their land diligently, but had made full use of their sea-coast—either lawfully or unlawfully. In Nicholas the old instincts still lingered beneath the civilized veneer. Most of the country folk sensed it. Some knew. But none, however much they resented his power, would give him away. He was rich, "close," and powerful. But he was a true Cornishman, and, as such, respected.

As Trevarvas rode on, his thoughts turned back to

Donna Penroze. Love was not a word common to his vocabulary. Until now he had never believed in it. Now he knew it to be a reality, discomforting, aggravating, and damned difficult to accept. But this wayward daughter of William Penroze had inflamed his emotions to such a degree that life without her suddenly seemed a gray and sterile business indeed. All that remained was to persuade her to see it too.

The subject of her thoughts was, in the meantime, analyzing and reanalyzing the scene on the moors. First she thought she would pay a visit to Polbreath, and apologize. Then she decided that he deserved no apology. On the contrary, he should apologize to her for his revolting arrogance. Finally she told herself that when he sent for her to Polbreath she'd go. But not before. Let the lot of them—including the children, the pie-faced governess, Nicholas himself, and the handsome, wretched Lucien—get along without her, as they had before she arrived on the scene. Her life revolved around Wheal Faith and Trencobban; her first duty lay there, and she must really sit down to work out ways to economize. The questions were how and where?

So far, Miss Bray had proved efficient at her job; Janey was beginning to take an interest in her studies, and there seemed no justifiable excuse for dismissing her. Beth was a gem, and her daughter Phyllida a great help to Sarah. She couldn't suddenly say to any of them, "Look, I'm so sorry. I'm not so well off as I thought, so I'm afraid I can't afford to keep you on." There was no wild extravagance in household expenses. In fact Donna, who had expected to be able to brighten Trencobban a little, had done very little to the house. Several of the rooms needed redecorating. Repairing the broken stained-glass window had cost more than she had anticipated. And even now it looked inferior to its original beauty. She had thought, at the beginning, when Nicholas had given her two thousand pounds for personal expenditure, that she would be rich. But she wasn't.

She was already on a tight financial string. And on

200

top of everything else there was Jed. She had nothing and no one to turn to. Unless she was forced to ask a further loan from Nicholas, and that would be intolerable. She was still pondering over the question when Beth knocked at the sitting room door to say that there was a Mr. Trevarvas wanting to see her.

Donna's heart quickened; her face brightened to a wild rose glow as she exclaimed, "Oh! . . . well, send him in please . . ."

"It's not . . ."

"Well? What are you waiting for? I said send him in," Donna echoed, not realizing how sharp she sounded.

With a slight tightening of her lips Beth withdrew, and a moment later Donna was astonished to see Lucien enter. Her first reaction was of shock, then acute disappointment and dismay. And when the door had closed, she said, "What is it? Why have you come here? You should know after . . . after what happened, you'd be the last person in the world I would ask to my house."

He lifted both hands out helplessly, shaking his head—his very handsome head—in a gesture of almost childlike supplication.

"Donna—may I sit down?"

"As you're here, I suppose so," she agreed. "But I can't understand why you've come."

He moved to a chair, seated himself, after she'd taken the one opposite, and answered simply. "I had to of course. I thought everything was all right between us—at least I did hope—after the dinner party at Polbreath. You seemed so . . . so kind."

"I could hardly have been otherwise, could I? In your brother's house, and under the circumstances. To have been deliberately rude would have roused suspicion. But I would have thought you'd have at least the sensitivity to avoid meeting me anywhere else. Did you really imagine for one moment that I could ever forget your unspeakable behavior in the cove?"

"No," he agreed quietly. "That would be expecting

rather much. But if you remember, you said, or implied, that you'd forgive me. And something about being as brother and sister. That's true isn't it?"

She sighed. "What I said then isn't important. It's just . . . I don't want you calling at Trencobban, Lucien.

"Because of Nicholas I suppose?"

"Well, partly. I'm sure he'd be very annoyed."

"I know. And it matters to you doesn't it? What he thinks?"

Without giving a direct answer she said, "I should think it must matter to you, knowing his character."

Lucien gave a short laugh. "My dear Donna, what Nicholas thinks, or however much he pretends, and would like to have an influence over me, the fact is that he has none at all, materially speaking. I'm well off, you know, thanks to my mother. Considerably better off, in fact, than my dictatorial half-brother. That I come to see, and visit him sometimes is due only to a lingering sense of family, and as now, when it suits me to recuperate from an attack of the miserable malady I suffer from at intervals."

Donna's interest was aroused. "And what is that, Lucien?"

"Lung trouble," he answered briefly, "among other things. That's why, I suppose, anything so beautiful and brimming with life as you fills me with such admiration and envy. Oh yes, I envy you Donna . . . envy your years of life ahead—your future, whatever it may be, even if you waste it in those earthy arms of my lusty half-brother."

"Lucien!"

"Wait," he begged. "Just listen to me this once please. I know I acted unspeakably. I don't expect even to be able to erase the thing from your mind. But I want to make amends in some way if I can."

"There's no need."

"I think there is. You're beholden to Nicholas, aren't you? Or you wouldn't be acting for him as you were at Polbreath?"

202

"I don't mind that. I . . ."

"You needn't tell me. There's a thrill in seeing him. His rugged ways stir and attract you as they do most women. My darling Donna, do you think I haven't seen it all before? Do you really imagine I haven't watched more beauties than one fall under his cocksure spell? Still, that's your affair. But what I don't like is your dependence. You see, I've made inquiries."

"How *could* you?"

"I've made inquiries," he echoed, ignoring her interruption, "and I know you're under financial pressure all the time. So what I want to do is to make my own contribution—call it recompense if you like, or a mark of the esteem that I have for you. I would like to deposit something in the bank to your credit. No one will know. John Crebbyn is vowed to secrecy, and I shan't miss it. Anyway, in view of the fact that my life is not reasonably expected to be a very long one, what does it matter? I would offer you much more, if I thought there was a chance of your accepting it. Marriage . . ."

"Marriage?"

"Certainly. I might not make a very satisfactory husband in some ways, but I'd try my best. By now you'll have gathered I've not been entirely successful with the opposite sex. *You* though, you're different. The only woman I have ever felt I could truly love. And love, remember, is of the heart as well as of the body. Oh yes, I'd willingly marry you, if I had the chance and you'd take the risk. Remember that. In the meantime, with no strings attached, none at all, darling, will you, as a generous gesture to me, allow me to assist you in this one way I can?"

Donna got up and walked to the window, her mind torn between pity, gratitude, and the tempting vision of being free from Jed's payments, and from her commitment to Nicholas. Before her eyes the stretch of brown moors lay bleak under the cold sky, a windswept vista, empty of all but withered undergrowth, gray boulders, the far distant outline of a mine stack, and a few bent skeleton trees overlooking Gwynvoor. Something in her always responded to its harshness, but for that brief moment she envisaged what real wealth could mean: the luxury of rich hotels when she felt like it, traveling abroad in the winter to warmer climates, indulging herself without a pang, buying whatever priceless jewelry and clothes she wanted. And above all, being able to see and sustain Wheal Faith's prosperity out of her own pocket—or at least the pocket of a wealthy husband's. Yet, even while toying with the possibilities, she knew the whole thing was a fantasy. The mere suggestion of marriage to Lucien was absurd. Even if she could dismiss from her mind his distasteful and hysterical outburst in the cove, any attempt on his part at lovemaking would be offensive now. She admired his looks, could be sorry for him, and grateful for his offer. No more.

"I don't know what to say Lucien," she told him after a pause. "You must know that I couldn't marry you. As for helping me—I'm sure that wouldn't be right."

"Right? What has that got to do with it? You mean you won't allow me to, because of the past? You want to make me suffer."

"No. That's not true. You've explained this afternoon a lot of things I didn't know, and I accept them. I mean—there's no need ever to think of what happened that evening. I was to blame, too. So, please, shall we call it quits?"

"Very well," he said doubtfully. "As long as you can look me straight in the face and say nothing's worrying you. Can you do that? Look at me, Donna?"

With an effort, she raised her eyes to his, and knew she couldn't deceive him. Just for a moment or two the brilliance of her wonderful eyes faded, leaving them clouded with brimming misery. Then she looked away, saying, "It's all right. There's nothing I can't handle. Don't worry please. It . . . it gets on my nerves. Being questioned I mean, and made to feel so completely helpless."

He waited before answering. The silence was so strained and complete that every other small sound seemed to register: a faint tinkle from the kitchen, the screaming of a gull outside, and the rhythmic ticking of the grandfather clock, even the faint drift of wind stirring the carpet from under the door. As they stood there, she could sense, too. Lucien's thoughts could guess how his mind was darting this way and that, trying to plumb her thoughts.

"You haven't answered me, Donna."

She swung around, suddenly defiant. "All right then. All right, if you must know. Someone saw us in the cove that evening. And ever since I've had to pay."

Lucien looked horrified. "Good God! you mean . . . blackmail?"

"That's what it's called isn't it? And it's no good saying go to the police. I can't afford to. My name, and yours would be mud."

"Names aren't given in such cases."

"Things leak out. They would in this case. He's . . ."

"Oh. So it's a man. Who?"

She shook her head. "I'm not going to tell you. No, Lucien. You can't make me, and I won't. Whatever you say."

"I'll find out then," he told her, "And when I do . . ."

The way he spoke, the sudden tightening of his lips reminded her fleetingly of Nicholas. She touched his arm. "Lucien, I don't want you involved in this. I shouldn't have said anything if you hadn't been so . . . dogged about it."

"But I am involved. It's damned well all my responsibility. And to think I got you—you of all people into such a confounded position." He put a hand to his forehead, then took her by the shoulders impulsively, dropping his hands abruptly when she flinched.

"How much?" he inquired.

"One pound a week. For a year."

"Very well, if you won't let me help you in any other way. I shall hand over fifty pounds to you in cash to cover the twelve months. Before that we should somehow manage to bring the blackguard to heel. I shall also put a sum to your credit at Crebbyn's."

"No." She was surprised how intensely she felt about this. "If you do, I'll never speak to you again, Lucien. The money for—for the creature—that peeping Tom, yes, I'd be grateful for that. As you say, it was partly your fault. But nothing else. It's kind of you to offer. I appreciate the thought. It just happens, though, that I couldn't bear your charity."

"I see. You'll take from Nicholas. But . . ."

"I work for Nicholas," she reminded him. "It's different."

"It would be different anyway, wouldn't it?"

She shrugged. "Perhaps."

"I thought so. He has got around you. You're infatuated."

"Think what you like, Lucien. It's none of your business."

He sighed. "I suppose not. I suppose you'll always despise me?"

"No, I don't despise you. I just want to forget, as far as possible, what happened. And taking gifts from you, especially money, would be a reminder all the time. If you can't understand, I'm sorry. I don't want to hurt you. But I don't really want to think of you at all."

"You're honest anyway," he said bitterly.

"You forced me to be."

He left soon afterward. Donna watched him riding away up the moors leading westward toward Polbreath, and felt a strange relief, due not only to the fact that Jed, anyway, would no longer be a strain on her pocket, but to see the last of Lucien for the time being. It was strange how detached she felt now. He no longer had any power to touch her. She wondered what Nicholas would say if she told him that Lucien wanted to marry her. Well, that was one card she had up her sleeve. She hoped she would never have to use it.

Remembering his kisses, his ardor, even under the guise of fiercest criticism, her spirit and body longed with a terrible aching passion for his nearness, and arms around her. Without him she knew herself, in a torment of revelation, to be only half alive . . . a creature human, but torn apart. As apart as the looming rock coast was from the tempestuous seas, and sullen winter skies overhanging Trencobban. If this was love she felt, then it was also an anguish and hell of unconquerable doubt and uncertainty.

The only course therefore was to cast it aside by will, concentrating her whole energies into the more mundane but necessary business of Wheal Faith. She must and she would do it, not only for her heart's sake, but for sufficient sanity to continue, apparently, her normal everyday life.

This she succeded in doing, up to a point.

But sometimes at night, when the cold and brilliant moon spattered the sea to fitful dark glass and the moors above and below Trencobban to a wild panorama of changing light and shade, her whole being was resolved into but one thought.

Nicholas.

She wanted him so frenziedly her body froze with desire as she stood at the window, watching and waiting . . . always waiting for the clouds to gather into one shape, one image . . . that of a horseman riding the night sky to claim and gallop away with her, taking her to oblivion and consummation. In these moments she knew her secret self to be completely primitive. If he ravished or even beat her, she would not care. All she wanted was to be *his* . . . his woman most desired above all others.

Just so long as he loved her. Loved her so much that eventually sweetness and understanding would flower from the dark seeds of passion, giving fruition through those that came after them.

CHAPTER THIRTEEN

Christmas came and went with the usual festivities at Trencobban. For Janey's and Phyllida's sakes Donna did her best to make it a cheerful one, although Sarah seemed forever grumbling and looking back to "the master's day" when things were so different. Donna could easily have said the same, but she didn't see any use in being depressed. Besides the mine was planned to be fully working by the end of January. The shaft was sunk, new labor arranged, and the engines and equipment already installed. An added expense had been that the level of tin was lower than the cliff adit which opened naturally to the sea, so that water had to be pumped up to be released. But Donna didn't worry about this. Although she'd refused Lucien's proferred financial help, the fact remained it was there, and in an extremity she could accept it.

During the first months of 1881 Tom Craze seemed withdrawn and over-thoughtful whenever they met, although he assured Donna that all was progressing satisfactorily at the mine, and according to plan. He had appointed a new underground captain: a German called Franz Leibert, who was particularly skilled in the engineering side of tin-mining, and because of it, had been accepted by the men. Only Andrewartha was jealous and resentful. There had been a celebration dinner at the Count House for the opening of the deeper shaft. Donna, despite Tom's earlier assertions that all was well, was only too aware of Jed's surly glances at Leibert. She trusted Tom Craze implicitly, remembering how successfully he had handled difficult situations in her father's day. But on this occasion she could not help noticing how preoccupied he looked, nor quell her deep feeling of unease. Although she had resolved most firmly to do as he asked and keep her woman's nose out of things, she decided that she would seize an opportunity to draw him aside and ask what was on his mind.

Tom sighed as she did so. "Only the old problem, mistress, of cash. And this isn't the time to air it, if you don't mind me saying so. But since you're determined, here's facts. This new project is going to cost more in the end than we've bargained for, partly because water has to be pumped up to the level of the cliff adit. It's all down in the book and it's more than likely I'll have to go to the bank or contact Mr. Trevarvas himself, if things turn out as I suspect."

"But the tin is all right, isn't it?" Donna asked.

"Oh yes. Should be, according to the experts. But I don't count on anything like ore, mistress, until I properly have my fist on it."

Donna thought hard for a moment, then said firmly and recklessly, "I'll be responsible for that Tom, if necessary, as I've told you so often. You can rest assured. I've . . . someone else at the back of me now if things get too pressing. You have my word for it. Do you understand?"

"When you give a promise I have to accept it, Miss Donna." Craze said reluctantly. "And I do. Perhaps I'm getting too old and wearied for my job. I'll admit I fret more than I used to over the whys and wherefores."

"Well then," Donna flashed him a brilliant smile, "for my sake, for Wheal Faith, and because of—of my father—what he'd have wished, cheer up and don't worry."

"I will," Tom promised. "I'll try, mistress."

But a feeling of foreboding haunted Donna ever after that dinner, a sense that things weren't right, in spite of Tom's fresh efforts at reassurance. This unwarranted sense of depression could certainly not have been explained away by the weather, which though cold, was bright and clear, with snowdrops starring the earth of

Trencobban, and the bushes glittering with frost in the pale light of morning sunrise. The new mine engines were working, the pump rod's rhythmic motion against the sky was a magnificent symbol of future prosperity.

Yet the queer feeling of apprehension still clouded Donna's mind. Perhaps she was tired, she told herself. Perhaps her strange mood was partially due to uncertainty about Nicholas; or perhaps it stemmed from a combination of her debts to Jed, Tom's admission that he was feeling his age, and the revelation of Lucien's illness. There was Jessica too, and her sullen, queer fears that cast an air of melancholy over the house. Everything and everyone somehow seemed united to sap Donna's characteristic vitality, making her acutely conscious of the primitive darker aspect of Cornwall which was as much a part of her heritage as her driving will toward a better future.

She made it her business, during that period, to visit the homes of several miners' families, trying hard to be one of them, and knowing, despite their appreciation of her interest, that she'd never succeed, but remain always, William Penroze's daughter, the young mistress of Trencobban.

Occasionally, longing to be free of it all, she rode Saladin over the moors, where the cold wind stinging her face, the colt's pull at the reins and flaring nostrils greedy for life and speed, flooded her with fresh energy and renewed joy of living.

But as soon as she had stabled him and returned to the house, dejection descended again in a pall of unease.

She recalled then, how in her early years when she was not more than eight or nine, an old gypsy woman selling brooms at the door had told her she "had the sight," and would know through her life when danger was threatening herself and her own. "It's writ on thee darling," the crone had said. "Thee'll never escape thy destiny."

Donna had wanted to give her a penny, or a piece of cake from the larder; but the black-eyed, dark-skinned creature had shaken her head, muttering, "No no. Not from thee," followed by a few words of Romany, and she scurried away into the shadows as quickly as a fox or hare.

From time to time Donna would recall that strange incident—especially when a premonition proved correct—and then she would dismiss the notion as a mere fantasy. But this time the feeling persisted so strongly that she couldn't help dwelling on the dark prophecy. Her intuition told her that whatever now lay in store had nothing to do with herself or Nicholas. Nor even Jessica. Then who, or what?

The answer came in a terrible manner a fortnight later. The weather turned suddenly to high winds, and lashing rain from the west, which poured in rivulets down the moors to the coast, soaking the earth, dislodging stones, driving and beating the undergrowth as though the giant rider himself, the legendary dark hooded demon of Cairn Kenidzek, the Hooting Cairn was abroad on his fiendish horse, bent on destruction.

Jessica alone seemed unmoved by nature's onslaught. "He won't come in this," she muttered more than once. "This will stop him. He won't come now."

"Who won't come? What do you mean?" Donna said at last, exasperated and depressed by the sight of her sister-in-law's standing interminably at the window, eyes riveted to the teeming rain. "What's got into you, Jessica, talking to yourself, staring—are you mad or something? If you go on like this everyone will say so. For heaven's sake come away from that window. And stop such stupid talk. Do you hear?"

Roused by the sharp voice, Jessica turned reluctantly saying, "Let's have a drink then, Donna, just to celebrate."

"Celebrate what? Your idiocy?"

"No. Safety."

"Well! of all the . . ." exasperation made Donna speechless, until she suddenly gave in. "All right then. But the toast will be to the mine, and I hope—to your sanity."

"If that's what you want it's all right by me," Jessica replied.

So for a little while, with the blinds closed, and each with a glass of good vintage wine to cheer their spirits, tension relaxed.

"It's sure to be nice tomorrow," Donna said. "And if it is we'll get Sam to drive us into Penzance."

But the next day the ferocious weather still persisted and continued with increasing rain and gales for another week. After that the winds slowly died, and with them the rain, which became a drizzle before fading into heavy mist.

The earth now was soggy, and patches of bog blackened the moors. The Bal maidens no longer sang on their way to work and back, but stepped gingerly over stones and beaten mounds of furze in order to keep their feet dry—an almost impossible task, though their boots were covered with woollen bandages.

And beyond, beyond the road above, the cromlech stood, wreathed in its own somber shroud, guardian no longer of the grim Cornish landscape, but cold and remote, unconscious of the tragedy drawing every moment nearer to Wheal Faith.

It was Tuesday. Tom Craze had descended the shaft to investigate a query of Leibert's about an underground stream that threatened to break the wall of rock between the adit and the lower tin level which was roughly a hundred fathoms from the surface. It was a tricky problem, but one that Tom Craze had faced before. In this case he hoped, fervently, Leibert was wrong, knowing that it would completely disrupt the work in hand.

But Leibert was right. And at the worst possible moment the unforeseen happened. The heavy rainfall caused a fall of rock that started a minor landslide at the cliff face that in turn completely blocked the adit and sent water flooding to the lowest level. Tom was trapped, helpless, and unable to reach the shaft.

No one was to know what his thoughts were as the swirling waters closed over him. Probably he had none at all in his blind struggle for air, or possibly deep in his unconscious lingered the dark awareness that the mine, which had been his life for so long, had at last claimed its own.

His body, when recovered days later was so mangled and swollen, as to be hardly recognizable. Donna, in her anguish, wept. But Tom's widow remained set-faced and stony-eyed.

"It's not the end I'd have wanted for him," she said, "But he'd not have complained. He went on longer than he should, because of your father, Miss Donna, and loyalty to you."

Donna had done her best to comfort the woman, offering what material help she could. But the look in Jane Craze's eyes when she'd answered had chilled her.

"No. It's not gold I'll take from you, nor pity either. Such things don't pay for a man's life. And there's no comfort in the world when you've lost your only kin. No God either. God's nothing when you're alone."

And with this Donna had to be content, though the truth was bitter to bear.

Nicholas Trevarvas attended the funeral, with several of the miners, their families, and several farmers. Afterwards he accompanied Donna on foot from Gwynvoor Church back to Trencobban, where he had left his horse. It was an impersonal, almost silent walk.

"I don't need to tell you again how sorry I am," he said, before he left. "I've done so more than once already, and words can be an impertinence."

"Yes."

"Still, if you need advice now that Craze is gone, I'll do what I can—or find someone expert enough to give it instead."

"Thank you."

"Leibert, I believe, is a good man. Quite skilled. . ."

"But he's not Tom!" Donna cried shrilly, suddenly. "There's no one, ever, will take his place. Not to me. It isn't only the mine—it's everything, Trencobban, my father—Tom was part of my life, always . . ." she broke off, with the tears streaming from her eyes.

213

With infinite gentleness Nicholas put an arm round her and pulled her around to face him holding her close, his mouth against her hair. The contact shocked her from grief in to an electric awareness of life and a sweeping flood-tide of recognition that obliterated all else. She had wanted him many times before. But never in her wildest dreams had she known the feeling that now possessed her . . . a feeling that was also pain, wilder than hunger, darker than death. Her body swayed against him. No conflict of wills or speech any more, just a longing for the fulfilment of desire. Her thighs and buttocks yearned for his hands around them—for the pressure of flesh against flesh giving comfort and release.

Then suddenly, it was over. His hands fell away, and from a void of emptiness she heard him saying, "I'm not very good with words I'm afraid. Speech is futile. I realize Tom's death is a hard blow to you. But—you're very young. Men die every day. Craze was a fine fellow, someone to remember with respect and gratitude. Still, fretting's a waste of time. As I've said—I'm deeply sorry. But you'll recover."

She stared at him, shocked. "Y~~ ~~~~u he was unaf-
~~~~~~ by w~~~~~- might even resent them. She ~~t, he was unmarried. ~~~~~~ her bedroom mirror. And ~~ ~~oud, "Damn them both."

The quick spurt of words relieved her feelings. Her eyes were pools of orange flame as she rid herself of the heavy skirt and boots, and changed instead into a dress of her favorite olive green velvet. She unpinned her lustrous hair and let it fall over her shoulders and down her back. Then she went to the window and stared out at the early evening sky. The light was already beginning to fade into a greenish glow beyond the moorland ridge, where the cromlech was silhouetted dark and clear, a huddled circle of atavistic images rekindled to life from the past. In an age long gone, women like her could have been taken there as a sacrifice to the primeval gods. She almost saw herself laid flat upon the stone altar before the sword fell and the fire kindled her to stopped. You'll admit I'm right when you think it over. Goodbye then. Probably you'll be hearing from me soon."

There was a snap of the latch, followed by the opening and shutting of the front door. Then he was gone.

Donna stood motionless for a moment, before moving to the mirror where she viewed herself with scorn and self-contempt. How could she have done it, she wondered—allowed herself at such a tragic time to be used as plaything and as the symbol of one man's wretched power?

Trevarvas. He was just as she'd imagined him at the start of their strange relationship—uncompromising, hard, never satisfied until he had all and everyone he wanted squirming beneath his touch. That she had ever thought otherwise proved how blind she had been. But then hadn't she known the truth all along? Known it and not cared?

Well, in future things would be different. She'd see she was on guard against any intrusion into her personal life, fight him on his own ground, with any weapon she had.

The difficulty was that her moods, as variable as the wanton Cornish winds, could so quickly change and betray her.

This must no longer happen. It *would* not, she told herself fiercely.

CHAPTER FOURTEEN

One week after Tom's death, Donna walked across the moor to see Franz Leibert, and arranged for him to meet her at Trencobban the following day. He arrived at about half past nine in the morning and was shown by Phyllida into the library, the room generally used for interviews since William Penroze's death.

The windows were large, but the light was comfortably subdued on that February morning by a thin line of cloud behind the early budding trees. The grayness in no way detracted from Leibert's looks. He was striking, if not exactly handsome, with his thatch of fair hair above very brilliant ice-blue eyes. There was a certain detachment about him, that told Donna he was unaffected by women—might even resent them. She knew he was unmarried, lodging on the moors somewhere with an elderly woman who had lost both her two brothers and her husband at sea. But that was all she knew except that Tom had praised his mining skill highly.

She came to the point quickly, realizing that there was no need for small talk or flattery. The man already knew his own worth.

"I'm wondering if you're interested in—in being Captain of Wheal Faith, now Tom—my manager's gone. It's a responsibility as you know, especially at the present moment. But the pay would be better for you."

"I'm not so interested in the pay," Leibert answered bluntly. "Mining's my job. Tin—and how to work it with the maximum efficiency. Yes. I'll take it on, Mistress Penroze, providing I have my choice of Underground Captain."

Taken aback momentarily by Leibert's abruptness, she paused before saying, "And who do you suggest?"

"Andrewartha. Jed Andrewartha."

"Oh but. . ." Donna's heart sank. She might have known. Andrewartha, of all people. The one man she'd have had out of the way at a moment's notice if she dared.

"Yes?"

"I don't see—isn't there anyone else? Someone more popular with the other miners? He's not exactly a likeable character I've heard. Inclined to be a troublemaker, that's what I . . ."

"You can't believe all you hear," Leibert interrupted coldly. "Andrewartha's the only one capable. Anyone with any knowledge of Wheal Faith would admit that. As for your talk of trouble. There'll be trouble enough if he doesn't get it."

"Why?"

"Because, for a start, I'm not prepared to work with anyone less skilled, and the others wouldn't have it either. Down a mine, mistress, it's capacity that counts, and the guts."

"My father always said co-operation was important," Donna said quickly. "Tom too."

"That's the ideal. But you can't always get things, or people, just the way you want. Jed may not be the romantic idea of a leader. But the men will take his advice. The work will be done. You can't ask for more under the circumstances."

Knowing that she was beaten, Donna said grudgingly, "All right, if you say so."

Leibert got up. "Thank you. I'm glad you agree. There'll be a meeting, I suppose, to confirm all this? Or are you going to do the informing?"

"I'll do it," she said. "Meetings aren't much in my line."

So the matter was settled. But Donna herself felt no sense of achievement in the new arrangement, only a gathering sense of oppression because things would never be the same again. Wheal Faith might flourish, but the traditions that had meant so much to her father were slowly being destroyed. She had no intention of abandoning it. That would have counted as failure. All she could do was to persevere and concentrate on making it succeed—however often the thought of her heart might stray to Polbreath and Nicholas.

She met Trevarvas one afternoon by chance on the moors, but although he stopped and spoke to her, his manner was remote, holding no hint of warmth, no challenge, no scolding, nor any gathering desire in his eyes. He could have been a mere acquaintance, she thought; his only interest was in the mine and the promotion of Leibert and Andrewartha.

Her mind switched to jealous memories of Rosina Penverrys and Regan Lamont, his apparent interest in them both, and the assets that she didn't possess. Regan with her sophisticated theatrical background and bevy of male admirers, her fame, press notices, and the glamour always attached to her name. Then Rosina, whose pedigree and wealth were enough to tempt any man who was lusting for power.

Damn them, she thought, as she flung off her jacket, and stood staring at herself in her bedroom mirror. And then aloud, "Damn them both."

The quick spurt of words relieved her feelings. Her eyes were pools of orange flame as she rid herself of the heavy skirt and boots, and changed instead into a dress of her favorite olive green velvet. She unpinned her lustrous hair and let it fall over her shoulders and down her back. Then she went to the window and stared out at the early evening sky. The light was already beginning to fade into a greenish glow beyond the moorland ridge, where the cromlech was silhouetted dark and clear, a huddled circle of atavistic images rekindled to life from the past. In an age long gone, women like her could have been taken there as a sacrifice to the primeval gods. She almost saw herself laid flat upon the stone altar before the sword fell and the fire kindled her to

218

flame, could hear in imagination the moaning and chanting that followed, resolved by one deathly scream. Her own.

The vision for that brief space of time was so vivid that she could feel her eyes dim, and the pounding of blood in her ears. But when her senses registered normally again she knew it all to be a delusion: a trick of the imagination, no more. Those old men of the past were still there, but stones merely. She had given them life because she herself wanted it so. Wanted Nicholas.

She was about to turn when she saw his shape returning around the western bend of the hill, riding leisurely, as though hopefully, on the watch.

She didn't move, just stood there. He halted, and for a second or two remained static against the sky, as he had been on that evening long ago when she'd returned with Jos from the cove. Then he turned and went back in the direction of Polbreath.

She knew once more that he was as much a part of her—even more than Trencobban, the mine, or the land itself. Nothing would quench her desire for him but death. And even then, in her last conscious moments, she felt something of him would be there to carry her away into the darkness.

Presently she moved and went downstairs, still in a kind of dream.

Later she forced the mood away, in a wave of self-contempt. As if any man could matter that much. It had been reaction, no more, reaction from recent sadness and shock.

But oh God! How lonely she was. And how heavily the responsibilities of Wheal Faith weighed on her spirits!

It was in the middle of March that the final blow fell to destroy her courage, and she remembered, too late, the words of Tom Craze. "I don't count on ore mistress . . ." he'd said, or something like it . . . "until I've properly got my fist on it."

A fresh survey of levels by experts showed that the tin lode, which had promised such riches, was in fact only a thin streak that was in imminent danger of petering out. Wheal Faith's days were numbered.

Donna could hardly believe it. After all she'd fought for, gone through, and puzzled over, to be defeated at last!

And if it was true—if the mine was really on its last legs, how was she going to cover her debts and current expenses? Lucien was the only answer, but her pride shrank from asking him.

Trevarvas? After their quarrel on the moor and his coldness, she could not bear the thought of begging his help. And honesty forced her to admit that there was no conceivable reason why he should come to her aid. He had made it clear that she was less than adequate as his social hostess, and there was nothing else that she could offer him.

She could only hope that the engineers had been mistaken, and that the old mine would yet prove itself worthy of the toil, energy, tragedy, and ballast that had been poured into it. But she was wrong.

And at the end of the month, when gales swept the coast and moors, and high spring tides flung their fury against the bleak cliffs, Donna set off in her carriage, driven by Sam, to put the position to Nicholas Trevarvas.

CHAPTER FIFTEEN

Donna was surprised when Nicholas himself opened the door to her. He looked stern and tired, and his eyes were condemning when he said, "This is a surprise indeed. If you expect to see my brother I'm afraid you'll be disappointed. My man has just driven him to Penzance. He's off to London for more medical tests."

"I didn't come to see Lucien," Donna said clearly, although her whole body was already churning with nerves. "It was you."

As he stared at her, his eyes darkened, and his mouth tightened before he remarked with heavy sarcasm, "Indeed? I shall be gratified to learn why my company has suddenly become so important to you. Won't you come in? I'm sorry you can't be greeted with more ceremony. But I'm alone this afternoon. The servants have all gone off to see some charade or other put on by a group of players in Penzance. Do step inside, Miss Penroze."

Miss Penroze, she thought, how ridiculous! And also, how intimidating. He was obviously still angry with her. She wondered how she was going to broach the difficult subject of Wheal Faith.

She stepped through the door into the hall with as much grace and aplomb as she could muster, holding her chin elegantly tilted upwards, one hand lifting her gray skirt lest it trail on the dusty floor. She had purposefully dressed in subdued shades in case he thought her extravagant or that she was flaunting herself to gain his help.

The study into which he ushered her was a comfortable, unostentatious room, with upholstered leather furnishing, a desk, an Adam fireplace where logs and coals were burning cheerfully, for the weather was still cold, and a series of hunting prints on the walls. There was a decanter on the table, with a glass beside it, paper, and a book or two.

"Not very tidy, I'm afraid," Nicholas said, "and hardly where I'd choose to receive a lady. A man's room. Mine. But anyway, you don't really care whether or not you are regarded as a lady, do you?"

"I . . ." Donna opened her mouth to explain, an apology for past blunders on her lips, but he silenced her.

"Sit down."

Trembling, she obeyed him. He went to a corner cupboard, took out another glass, brought it to the table, filled it from the decanter and thrust it at her silently. It smelt like brandy.

"I don't think I . . . I don't think . . ."

"It doesn't matter a damn what you think," he told her curtly. "Drink it up."

He poured one for himself, turned, tossed it off, and leaning against the table said, "Now—what's this visit about? What little game have you in mind now Miss Penroze?"

"Game?" She could feel the brandy stinging her throat, reviving her courage so that a hint of the old temper flared as she continued, "It's not a game. Do you think I'd have called on you, of all people, if I were playing?"

"I really don't know what to think about you," he said, watching her from under his dark brows with no quiver of expression in his eyes, no softening on the lips, or hint of how his mind was working. "At one time I'd an idea that I was dealing with a beautiful but headstrong girl who would honor her obligations with courage and integrity. Now I find that's not so. In fact you have done all you can lately to fling your airs and graces about on every possible occasion—whether it's slapping my face, or acting the coy charmer to my brother when I had specifically asked you not to. Are

222

you really surprised that I have no idea why you are here?"

She wondered whether to try and soften him by pleading, or to come directly and boldly to the point, and decided on the latter.

"Wheal Faith is failing," she said simply. "The tin there isn't enough to make it profitable. Soon there won't be enough money to pay the men. And there are other debts."

There was a long pause, while he walked away from her to the window, where he stood staring out, his broad back rigid and unmoving. The set of his head and face when he turned was as relentless as it had appeared that first time, almost a year ago, when she had asked for a loan.

"And what do you expect me to do about it?" he asked. "Put my hand obligingly in my pocket again, and say understandingly, 'Poor Miss Penroze. How very awkward for you. But you can count on me. How much do you need?'"

She sprang to her feet, a surge of hot color flooding her face, her eyes brilliant with mortification and irrational anger.

"No I don't! I should have known, of course. Known you'd grasp the chance of humiliating me—of trying to make me crawl to you and obey your every word, as you have from the very beginning—ever since you got me to come here as your . . . your so-called hostess. Well, I won't, and you can't! It's over now. Say what you like, be as insulting as only *you* can be. I'm finished. Done with you . . . do you understand?"

She broke off, breathless, watching him move toward her slowly, purposefully, with something in his eyes she couldn't understand. She waited, too proud to run to the door, even though she wanted to, until he was looking down on her with a twist of irony on his mouth, eyes as hot as her own.

Then he said, "And just how do you think you're going to manage that? A dead mine? Debts that can't be honored? A family—of a sort—to support? It seems to

223

me I'm very important to you at the moment. So important that you can't possibly afford to do without me."

Too angry for discretion, Donna turned away and took a few steps toward the door. "I shall manage," she said, glancing back. "Don't trouble about me. I have other means. Someone else to turn to."

In an instant he had overtaken her and stood with his back to the door, facing her, noting the stubborn set of her chin, the challenge, the triumph in her eyes.

"And who?" he said, "If I may ask?"

She smiled sweetly. "Lucien. Your brother."

There was a pause so absolute that she could hear the clock ticking, and the bumping of her own heart against her ribs and in her throat.

Then, grasping her shoulders suddenly, he asked in a low furious voice, "Repeat that, will you? Who did you say?"

"Lucien."

"I see. You mean that all this time you've been plotting and scheming together behind my back. You had your plan carefully laid from the start. If Nicholas won't oblige, you thought, Lucien surely would. You jade. You contemptible double-dyed little hypocrite."

"No . . . no," she gasped, trying to free herself. "It wasn't like that. I haven't been playing, and Lucien was only trying to help. He wants to marry me . . . it's all . . . all . . ."

"Marry you?" His hand was over her mouth, one arm tight around her body. "My God, Donna, when I've finished with you, no man of any honor will want you as wife. For months you've had me at my wits end wondering how to treat you, thinking one moment you needed a good beating, the next kindness and understanding, and all the time you were weaving a very cunning little net of your own."

He carried her, gasping, to the sofa and flung her down, where she lay helpless and shivering from nerves, astonishment, anger, and desire all merged into a conflict of emotion to which she had no strength or will. He wasted no time either, in stripping her of the

224

bodice, skirt, and clumsy underwear, until he had her white body beneath his, licked rosy in parts from the warm glow of the fire. She made an attempt to resist, then the tenseness in her gave way to submission, as his lips pressed hungrily into her flesh, lingering hotly on breasts, thighs, and navel, burning not only her body but spirit itself, as he murmured, "You're mine, *mine* Donna, and heaven help anyone who comes between."

His tongue sought hers. Her senses responded as she arched herself to receive him, while the room spun and darkened to a vortex of pulsing life and abandonment, a thrill of mounting passionate climax with the dark horseman of her imagination taking her from exquisite pain to ultimate fulfillment.

Then it was over. She lay there spent and exhausted, until her eyes opened slowly and saw the room coming into focus again. He had eased himself from her, and was standing half dressed, his broad, naked back revealing the strong ripple of muscles as he pulled his shirt over his head. She didn't move, but lay there passively watching, her amber eyes bemused, her face pale between the masses of tumbled, rich black hair. Small pulses were beating in her body. Her lips were moist and glistening in the fitful light, still needing him. But she said nothing, half fearing his answer.

Then he turned, came back to the sofa, lifted her up, and with one hand on her breast, the other tilting her chin so she was forced to look him in the eyes, said, "That wasn't too bad was it?"

She shook her head. "No. But . . ."

"No buts any more," he said firmly. "It's decided."

"What?"

"Unless I've ravished a wanton you should know. And I think you do. There'll be no Lucien in your life, darling, and no swinging your delectable hips in any other man's direction for what you can get out of him. You'll marry me, like it or not . . ."

"There's no need for you to . . ."

"No need for me to act like a man of honor? No. Except that it pleases me to on this occasion."

225

He kissed her on the mouth again, then picked her clothes up from the floor.

"Get dressed, Donna," he said. "If anyone should call unexpectedly the outcome might be embarrassing— especially as the Penverryses, I believe, are still lingering about the neighborhood lusting for wedlock, and might not appreciate the position. Truth to tell, I find Rosina somewhat of an encumbrance."

"Is that why you've asked me to marry you? To be free of her?" Donna demanded.

"But I haven't," he reminded her.

She jumped up quickly, reaching for her underwear.

"Don't play with me then. Don't think, now that you've got what you want, you can have me at the end of a string, teasing and trying to catch me out. I won't . . ."

"You won't marry me?" Nicholas interrupted. "But I think you will. And, as I've just said, I didn't ask you. I told you."

Pulling a garment round her, Donna lifted her head challengingly.

"Just like that. I see." Her voice was bitter, lips compressed and stubborn now, unlike his, which were warm and teasing, with a faint smile lingering at the corners.

He nodded. "Just like that; because it's what you want and what you need. If I didn't think—know it—I wouldn't have laid a finger on you, however exciting you might be with your beautiful body, and tantalizing ways. Now hurry up, don't stand there like that, or I'll be tempted to start all over again."

She dressed automatically in a kind of dream, angry, confused and exhilarated at the same time, wondering if any girl before could have experienced quite such an odd proposal. No "will you marry me?" no sentimental words of endearment or affection. Just downright seduction followed by an assumption on his part that she would comply with whatever he had in mind.

Marriage. The idea was not only ridiculous, but, on his part, conceited and audacious. Although in other circumstances she might have complied with unuttera-

226

ble joy, his attitude after that passionate scene had revived all the old resentment and defiance. Why should he think, how *dare* he, that he could win her so easily? Acquire her like some desirable collection piece for Polbreath? Was that, after all, what he'd intended from the beginning? The situation for which she'd prepared herself from the very start of their acquaintance . . . the one she had determined to avert at all costs?

Yes. Without knowing it, she'd fallen into a trap. The trap of indecision, of longing for him, yet hating him at the same time: hating his assurance and insensitivity—his habit of obtaining anything he wanted in the world, for a price. In this case, herself.

She felt suddenly tired and bruised, not only in body but spirit. Her pose was limp, a little abject. When attired again and ready to leave, she stood at the door saying, "Please don't bother to let me out. This has all been a ridiculous mistake. I'm sure you realize that I couldn't possibly take you seriously."

He caught up with her quickly, taking her by both shoulders, forcing her to look at him. His face now was serious, his eyes soft with a dark warm fire in them that caused her pulses involuntarily to quicken. "Donna, I meant every word of it—about marrying me, I mean. I'm not adept at speeches. Sometimes I have to act and put on a kind of front to save embarrassment. It's my way. I haven't Lucien's gift for pretty words and flattery. But if you'll be my wife I'll do my damnedest to make you happy, because I want to. Because I need you. Think about it will you? Or don't—maybe that would be best. There's a good deal in the past that both of us should try to forget, and looking back doesn't help. But the future could be good Donna, for both of us."

She waited indecisively until his hands fell away; then she said almost in a whisper, "All right. I'll think. If that's what you want."

He stepped back, hesitated, then made an abrupt movement to open the door for her. As she passed through she could sense his body relax, knew that he was regaining control of the situation.

But she? At the moment she had no way of assessing her position. She simply didn't know, was aware only of a torment of indecision and emotion draining her of power and energy.

A few minutes later she was on her way back to Trencobban.

That night she hardly slept at all, and when she did, it was fitfully. She woke at intervals throughout the night with the problem still unresolved, her mind a vortex of doubt and conjecture. One moment she was eager to accept his offer, the next despised herself, not only for considering it, but for the circumstances leading up to it. She should have resisted instead of giving in to his passion so willingly. What would her father have thought? With a stab of pain she remembered his gentleness and his unfailing trust in her. But now she had failed him—she had betrayed all that he stood for by her few hasty moments of indulgence. The realization tortured and shamed her. If only her father were there to advise her now, to let her rest her head on his shoulder, his hand stroking her hair comfortingly as she poured out her troubles, knowing that he'd understand. But she was no longer a child, and her father was dead.

She was alone, with only her own wild heart to guide her, and the heart was a wanton thing sometimes—untamed as the elements, stronger than morals, memories, and any man-made standards of behavior. Yet marriage! So final and absolute. Convention dictated that she should not hesitate after what had occurred, but she didn't really care a fig for convention—not deep down. All she wanted was to be herself and to pacify her deep longing for Nicholas Trevarvas. This didn't necessarily mean tying herself in bondage, to be used and ordered at will by someone she actually hardly knew as a person. Oh! If she could only get her thoughts clear. But her body still burned and ached from his ravishing, and her brain though on fire, was heavy for sleep.

Once or twice she went to the window, staring unseeingly into the darkness of moors and sea and sky. But there was no relief there, no comfort, and at last, after going downstairs for milk and biscuits, and seeing Jessica's light on in her room, she knocked and went in. Her sister-in-law was sitting up in bed, her night-shift fallen from one white breast, a glass of water in her hand. In the candlelight, with her bright hair tumbled over her forehead and shoulders, she had the luscious, sleepy look of some ripening adolescent waking to flushed maturity.

"What the . . . whatever's the matter?" she asked impatiently, but with blatant curiosity in her voice and cornflower-blue eyes. "All night you've been prowling about—up and down, up and down. Sakes alive, what's come over you? Are you sick or something? Out with it . . ." patting the bed. "What's up? Tell me."

Donna slumped, sat down, sighed, and said, after hesitating briefly, "Nicholas has asked me to marry him."

Jessica's eyes widened. "Goodness! Really?"

"Yes."

"I see. And you accepted of course." If her voice was slightly grudging, Donna didn't notice it.

"No."

"No? You mean you refused? You must be mad!"

"I didn't refuse. I didn't say I would, though. I just put it off."

"But why? Don't tell me you're not wild about him; I've eyes in my head. Besides, any woman with an ounce of sense would be. He's got all any man could have, and more—looks, wealth, and a gleam in his eyes fit to drive you crazy. My God! If I had the chance . . ." Jessica's voice ended in a sigh. "But then I haven't. I'm just not the sort a man like him takes seriously. You make me sick with jealousy Donna. D'you realize it? All the same I don't really hate you for it. Envy. That's what it is, and to think you didn't fall for him at one go! Why? Why?" Her outburst died in a sigh of exasperation.

Donna shook her head. "Because I'm not sure."

229

"What about? Marriage, or . . ." Jessica's eyes narrowed shrewdly. "You do look washed up I must say. There's something behind all this isn't there? Something you've not told."

"Quite a lot," Donna admitted, "but that's not the point. It's him."

"What do you mean 'him'?"

"I don't really know him, well hardly. And when I think of my father . . ."

"Forget your father for heaven's sake. It's life that matters," Jessica said bluntly. "I told you before, snap the man up if you've got the chance, and quick as you can. Mark my words, you're not the only one with an eye for him, and don't tell me that's not true, either. When he's around you're as restless as a cat about to have kittens, and when he's not you're broody as a sick hen, a real bore. And that's God's truth."

In spite of herself, Donna smiled faintly. "Thanks for your advice, anyway. I only wish things were so simple."

"They will be," Jessica said prophetically, watching her sister-in-law get up and go to the door. "And do you know why? Because you want him, and there's nothing in the world that is going to stop a woman, when she feels as strongly as you do. You're a dark one, Donna. All prim and pie sometimes, but underneath as lusty as they come. Oh maybe that's not polite talking, but you know what I mean all right. And you'll marry him, mark my words. The trouble is—what'll happen to me and Janey? That's what I'd like to know."

Donna didn't answer. Her mind was too full of her own concerns to be bothered just then with Jessica's problems. She merely went out, closing the door behind her firmly and returned to her bedroom.

Very slowly, as the hours ticked away, the first light of dawn streaked the sky, rising in a rim of pale silver over the horizon. By then Donna was too exhausted to conjecture any more. But her mind had been forced at last to its inevitable conclusion. She knew that, despite the past and all forebodings, she would marry Nicholas. Not because of security, the mine, or even the future of

Trencobban, but because as Jessica had said, she wanted to.

The next day, when Nicholas rode over, he received the answer he wanted, the answer for which he would have given if necessary, all else he possessed—though she had no notion of it, and would have found it hard to believe if he'd told her.

Nicholas and Donna were married quietly a month later in Gwynvoor Church. Jessica, roused from her brooding mood, and stimulated by a smart new outfit of periwinkle blue, was maid of honor, a somewhat incongruous term in the circumstances, and Lucien, ironically, best man. Agatha Pullen, wearing unbecoming green, and Janey were all present, as were a handful of miners, including Franz Leibert, and, of course, the staffs of both households. After the ceremony there was a reception at Trencobban, attended by the vicar, and another one later, at Polbreath. Although the Penverryses had been invited as a matter of courtesy, only Sir James thought fit to be present. His lady wife had sent a frosty note of apology regretting that due to her own migraine, and the fact that her daughter unfortunately had another engagement, they could not be there, but wished the couple happiness and good luck in their life together.

"The good luck had a touch of acid about it," Nicholas observed shrewdly, before the party split up.

"I expect she thinks you need it—with me," Donna said.

"And I expect she's right," he agreed.

Lucien stated in confidence to Donna that he considered the luck was all on old Nick's side.

"He's a lucky devil if ever there was one," he told her, with a hint of regret in his voice, "and remember darling," his voice softened so that no one else could hear, "he is a devil, whether you like it or not. So watch your step, and if things get too hot for you, remember I'm always in the background."

Donna was annoyed. "Don't joke, Lucien."

231

"I thought one generally did on such occasions—weddings, I mean."

"Not this one," she said shortly.

"No. Well—I was just making the best of things. I can't quite wipe out . . . remembering."

She turned away, saying abruptly, "There's nothing to remember. Or to forget any more. And please . . . here's Nicholas coming over . . ."

"Right. Point taken."

Lucien ambled away, as his brother approached with a wary look on his face. "Very confiding wasn't he?"

Donna shrugged, knowing as she did so that the gesture only enhanced her radiant figure and the elegantly cut wedding gown of cream satin and lace. Nicholas had placed a white flower from her bouquet in her raven hair, and she had never looked lovelier.

"He was being very serious," she told him. "Wishing us well."

"Hm."

"And don't glower."

"Glower?"

"Yes. As though you didn't believe me."

"My darling, anyone who believed you—completely—would be a fool, which I'm not."

She pouted. "Nicholas!"

He laughed, placing his arm around her waist firmly, his hand sliding upwards to a soft breast. "My God, Donna," he whispered, "when is this farce going to end?"

"Be patient," she said. "Let them enjoy themselves for a bit. Everyone seems so happy."

"Except me. I want you, Donna. And if they haven't taken off in another fifteen minutes I'll throw them out. So use all your charm, darling, and persuade them that they've outstayed their welcome. Please—for my sake."

She could not resist such a plea. The house, except for the servants and Lucien was remarkably quickly emptied.

Lucien, saying tactfully he was tired, went upstairs almost immediately to his room. Nicholas and Donna,

232

really alone for the first time since the ceremony, were unduly quiet until the door of their bedroom was safely locked, enclosing them in an intimacy that was itself its own world.

To Donna the knowledge was something of a shock.

The room was so vast, so richly perfect and exotic, with its elegant gold and cream decor, Louis Quinze furnishing, and rich hangings. The air so laden with the heady scent of lilies, roses, and other carefully arranged blooms. She felt, momentarily, a trespasser caught unawares and imprisoned there. What did she really know of this man, of the domineering, sensual character she had so unpredictably married? And would she have done so if he hadn't first seduced her, placing her in the compromising situation of moral obligation? She didn't know.

Fear stirred in her momentarily as she unfastened the neck of her elegant gown and released the rich, dark flood of her hair automatically. She went to the gilt dressing chair and sat there, fiddling unnecessarily with her jewelry and pins, just to waste time. Then she said tritely, "I think it was a very nice reception, don't you?"

"Very," he replied, "as receptions go."

She tried to think of something else to say. But thought somehow wouldn't come. The next moment in the glass, she saw him moving toward her. His head bent to meet hers as his hands cupped her breasts from behind, caressing their creamy softness until the nipples pricked and swelled to his touch.

"Donna," he whispered, "look at me."

Clutching her bodice, she turned to face him. He caught her up, and very gently but purposefully undid and removed first her gown and then the layers of frilled, lacy underwear, pausing at odd intervals to let his lips travel each luscious curve and hollow of her body, until at last she was naked and shivering not only with apprehension, but with a slow welling-up of desire. Instinctively she made one frail attempt to cover herself, crossing both arms over her breasts, then letting one

233

hand drop to her navel and down to cover the soft, dark triangle of hair.

He drew her arms away firmly, his eyes hot and ardent. "No, Donna. None of that any more," he said. "I've taken you once in a moment of passion. This is going to be different."

He picked her up, and carried her to the great bed, saying, "Cold, darling?"

She shook her head. "No." And indeed it was true. Her whole body by then seemed ablaze. She lay there rigidly, yet trembling wildly, as, ignoring the dressing-room, he divested himself of his own clothes, flinging them over a chair before approaching her.

Then, for the first time, she really saw him—sturdy, square and taut in his manhood, already swelling to take her—no Apollo or Adonis, but stronger and more beautiful than either, and with all the dark pulsing wonder of life's first awakening to give her.

He swung himself on to the bed, thighs enclosing hers, while his mouth sought her own before one hand reached her, rousing her to such excitement she moaned and arched her body to receive him. Then his own flesh plunged into the rich deep recess of her, where it lingered for a moment before the rhythmic rise and fall of union claimed them both in a swelling tide of consummation.

Even when it was over he did not withdraw, but remained in and on her, until at last in peace she stirred herself and lay bathed in the ebb-flow of their first true coming together.

Oh, if it could always be like this, she thought later that night, lying naked against him, at ease but still throbbing from intermittent love-making. If only life could go on in the first rapture of passion aroused and appeased, with no problems ahead, or tricky situations to resolve. She told herself that it could, but at the back of her mind loomed the shadow of reality, reminding her that there were other people in the world besides Nicholas and herself, and other forces involved in her future that one day would have to be reckoned with.

Still, all that was for another day. Tonight was theirs alone—hers and Nicholas's.

And so at last for a few hours, she fell into a deep sleep, and when she awoke it was morning. Nicholas was leaning over her, one hand tickling her breasts, a warm smile on his mouth. "You're a lazy one and no mistake," he said teasingly. "Today we set off for London, remember?"

"Oh Nicholas!" she gasped. "Need we?"

"Yes, my sweet. We certainly need. Being a mean man I don't intend wasting money on needless hotel bookings. So don't tempt me any more just now. Get up and dressed, or . . ." he broke off, kissing her hard before easing himself away from her, and springing out of bed. Almost immediately there was a light tap on the door and a voice saying, "Tea's here master . . . mistress, shall I . . . ?"

"Put it down," Nicholas called, "I'll take it presently."

Donna sighed, yawned, stretched her arms and reached for her wrap. "I'll get it. I want to. Just fancy . . . our very first morning cup of tea together."

Her naiveté and childlike pleasure in such a mundane thing as a cup of tea after the night's excessive passion, both astonished and intrigued him, and once again set him wondering about the complexities of her enchanting but wholly unpredictable nature.

Two hours later they set off for London, traveling by chaise to Penzance, where they caught the steam train for the capital. They stayed in town for a week where Donna, for the first time, had a taste of the most expensive hotel life, theaters, riding in the Row, interspersed with visits to the famous sights, including the Royal Botanical Gardens at Kew, with the Palm House built and completed by Decimus Burton in 1848, the Orangery, the Pagoda, and the Arch and Temples for which William Chambers had been responsible in the eighteenth century.

Donna was amazed by Nicholas's historical knowledge. She discovered each day a new aspect to his character that made her feel she'd married a man she didn't really know at all . . . until he once more took her in love, which was most days when they returned from sight-seeing, or touring the gaslit streets by cab, driving leisurely sometimes by Chelsea Embankment where the tugs lay dark on the water, and plane trees stretched their network branches against the yellowing dusk.

Life was a continual, dizzy whirl of excitement, filled with endless fresh experiences and enchanting sights like the glittering Crystal Palace at Sydenham, the colorful arty atmosphere of the Café Royal (where Regan Lamont took them after a party), St. Paul's Cathedral, the Tower—not to mention the various theaters, opera, ballets, and art galleries they attended.

Donna, wearing her most fashionable clothes, thrived upon the admiration she received from Nicholas's friends . . . not only on her own account, but also for his pride in her. Never for one moment did he forget her presence; his hands would constantly find an excuse to touch her. Even at the theater when his eyes should have been on the stage, they were slipping to her face every few seconds, marveling at her grace and the new sophistication, which had a magical childlike quality as rare as it was devastating. He was not musical, she discovered, though he took her to the opera once. When he asked her later in their hotel suite, if she'd enjoyed it, she replied, "I like being with you, Nicholas. But fat women rather spoil the effect . . . or don't you think so? Were you just a little bit entranced by that overpowering fair soprano?"

And laughing, he picked her up, kissing first her lips, then the shadowed hollow between her breasts where a pendant glowed, bought at Cartiers the day before. After that he laid her on the silk-covered bed and took her as though it were the first time, with all the gentleness and passion that was in him.

The National Gallery had her spellbound, although she knew the impact of da Vinci, Rembrandt, and other famous artists affected Nicholas hardly at all. He had of course been there before, and the truth was that, of the arts, only drama particularly mattered to him.

A highlight of their London visit was an evening at the Lyceum, where Henry Irving was playing in *The Bells,* with Ellen Terry as his leading lady. A year or so previously the famous actor had taken over as theater manager, but this had not diminished his dramatic ability. Though slight in build he had a magnetic quality in his role as the wicked Mathias.

Donna thought Ellen Terry quite lovely, although Nicholas said the word handsome suited her better. "One day," he said, "she'll be remembered as the most outstanding actress of her time."

And Donna thought fleetingly, with an irrational pang of nostalgia, how wide the world was—so many different facets and modes of life, so many unknown countries, and people to meet—and so little time, really, to enjoy everything. Perhaps she was tired, but a longing seized her—for the first time since their honeymoon had started—to be back in Cornwall riding the brown moors, with Nicholas beside her.

Such moods though, never lasted long, and the second part of their honeymoon, spent in France, completely erased them. Paris, bathed in spring sunshine, seemed to her a magical place. London had been colorful and exciting; but Paris was pure romance, with the tree-lined boulevards designed by Baron Haussmann in 1859, and elegant bridges crossing the river Seine.

They stayed at a conveniently situated pension, from where they visited among other famous buildings, the ancient church of St. Germain de Prés, the Louvre, Cathedral of Notre Dame, and the Place Vendôme, with its towering column—similar, so Nicholas told Donna, to Trajan's Column in Rome.

"But you're so knowledgeable, Nicholas," Donna reiterated yet again. "I didn't realize you'd traveled so widely."

"My dear love, I haven't," he replied. "It's just that I have a retentive memory. And anyway . . ." he shrugged, "I have many French business associates, such as the Rougets."

It was on the tip of Donna's tongue to mention Lucien, but she wisely held the words back, in case their present happiness should be marred by even the palest shadow.

They did visit Montmartre, the artists' quarter, however, which Lucien had described to her graphically as a place of quaint corners, and colorful cafés, wine gardens and low-roofed buildings in narrow streets, with flower baskets hanging outside. It was all just as he'd said, and she loved it, feeling far more relaxed in the genial artistic atmosphere than in the sophisticated elegance of the cultural capital.

Yet, when the time came to leave for Cornwall once again, a deep sense of relief and gladness filled her. She had enjoyed every moment of the honeymoon, and had discovered qualities in her husband's character she'd never thought to find. But home was home, and she was longing to be back, to feel the sea winds fresh on her face, and the salty tang of brine against her lips, to have Nicholas close to her in their own environment of bleak hills and lush valleys above the granite rocks of the wild north coast. The vision was so exhilarating she forgot, in her longing, the one drawback to her return, until the morning of their departure.

And then she remembered. Jed. His money had been due the previous week, and she'd completely forgotten. She tried to dispel the looming sense of menace resurrected by his evil image in her mind. But there were odd moments on the return journey when the radiance left her face and she relapsed into introspective silence, a silence tinged with uneasy fear.

Nicholas noticed. "What's the matter?" he asked once. "Tired?"

"I expect I am, a bit," she answered, forcing a smile. "Sleepy I mean."

"That's understandable." He grinned, and she was once more astonished to see how, when he smiled in

238

just that way, the years fell from him, leaving a youth and sparkle she hadn't known he possessed.

For the time being she forgot Jed again, although her thoughts did stray to Trencobban and Wheal Faith.

Nicholas had assured her that all outstanding expenses would be covered, and that the possibility of exploring a new tin level might be considered. No miner would be at a loss for wages. As for Trencobban—although, as his wife, she would be living at Polbreath, he had said that she could spend as much time there in the daytime as she wished, keeping an eye on her sister-in-law and Janey. The governess and servants could continue as usual.

"Apart from sentiment," he'd said once, "Trencobban is a valuable property, historically and architecturally. And it means a lot to you. You've got this—this family of your brother's to shoulder—though there's no real reason why you should. It's an expense I don't particularly relish—being what they call close. But because of what it'll be worth in the long run, and because of you—I'm willing to pay a reasonable amount for its upkeep. And don't thank me, Donna. You were never one for pretty speeches. So don't start now."

She hadn't. But the whole problem—the major one, had been a great load off her mind. In fact if it had not been for Jed, there would have scarcely been a cloud on the horizon at all.

CHAPTER SIXTEEN

It was typical Cornish weather on the evening of Nicholas and Donna's return to Polbreath, with a thin mist hugging the moors and cliffs, and a faint wind moaning through the spring undergrowth. By the time they reached the house it was dark, but after she'd washed and changed, Donna's eyes strayed eastward from the window of their bedroom in the direction of Trencobban. She couldn't help feeling strange at first, almost as though, in a dream she'd wandered into another—the wrong world.

She was so used to the barren wilderness of the north coast, the giant cliffs and turbulent seas, the grim outline of Wheal Faith and the gray house where she'd been born. How were they getting on there, she wondered, Sam and Sarah, and of course Jessica and her little girl? Not knowing cast a faint depression on her—one of those unpredictable feelings she had experienced from time to time since childhood, feelings which more often than not foretold disaster of some kind.

Yet if anything had happened in her absence, surely someone would have carried word to them?

In fact nothing of importance had occurred at Trencobban whilst she was away. Jessica, whenever possible, had continued her association with Jed, although on the last occasion as they'd crept by moonlight from the cove to the cliff, he'd stopped suddenly and said, "When does that fine young madam return?"

Jessica's face, white and heavy-eyed from the satiation of desire, was blank as she replied, "Donna d'you mean?"

240

"Yes. That's her. Your high'n-mighty sister-in-law."

"I don't know exactly," Jessica answered. "Soon, anyway."

"It'd better be," Jed told her grimly, "or there'll be fireworks sure 'nuff."

"What do you mean?" Jessica said, with jealousy gnawing at her. "What's she to you, anyway?"

"Never you mind," Jed told her roughly. "Nuthen' as a woman goes—'cept for what she can give."

"Give?" Jessica's voice was shrill. "Did you say give?"

"I did. An' what's more I'll give you sumpthen' unless you shut up," Jed said roughly.

Jessica went on sullenly, clawing at the furze and weeds, angered at herself for putting up with him, and outraged at his behavior. "You've no right to talk that way," she shouted when they'd almost reached the top. "Not after . . . after . . ."

He dealt her a sharp blow, sending her almost sprawling. "Get on with you. There's no one . . . least of all a lustin' female like you's goin' to tell me what my rights are."

"Is that so, Jed Andrewartha? And s'pose I ask Donna myself, then? Suppose I say, 'Please tell me, dear sister-in-law, what it is your workman Jed so anxiously requires of you?" Her voice, suddenly bitter sweet, took him momentarily aback. He stood dead still for a moment, then, grasping her by the shoulders, shook her violently.

"Don't you ever . . . ever try that on me agen," he said, with his hot red face close against her own. "Or I'll get you so no man'll ever look on your body or face agen. See?"

Terror engulfed her, not because of Jed or his threats, his bark was generally worse than his bite, but because his words reminded her of something else—someone at large who could still lurk behind any clump of bush or tree. *Silas.*

She started to tremble as the lump of fear rose thick

241

in her throat. Tears sprang to her eyes in a storm of anguish and frenzied words poured from her lips.

"Don't, Jed . . . don't. Stop it please. Oh God, Jed, don't talk like that . . ."

The desperation in her voice temporarily dismayed and touched him.

"Aw! C'mon now, girl, I didn't mean it, see? Not to frit 'ee. You're mine, aren't 'ee? We've good things between us you an' me . . ." he said, with uncharacteristic compassion.

"Yes, Jed, yes. You're all I've got."

"Well then . . ." He pinched her thigh reassuringly. "Get on with you now. It's time we wuz back. Only remember—no talk. Nuthen' 'bout me an' you. No word to your high up sister-in-law?"

"Not one, Jed. I promise you, as God's my judge."

He laughed. "I b'lieve you, though I reckon God don't come into it."

At the clifftop, they'd parted, Jessica, huddled into her dark cape, would cut across the moor to the right, Jed straight on, head jutting forward from massive shoulders, hands thrust into his pockets. Sexually satisfied, he didn't give another thought that evening to Jessica, but concentrated on the possibility of making further demands on Donna when she arrived back with her rich husband. The marriage—although he envied the stuck-up Trevarvas for his possession of that beguiling young madam—had its lucky side for him. More than ever now, she'd be beholden to him for his silence, knowing full well that if he let on about that seduction scene in the cove there'd be the devil to pay.

A golden sovereign or two wouldn't come amiss now, when there were extra things he had to get for his sick wife, just for decency's sake. Not that she was much use to him as such any more, but when they'd first wed there had been a feeling between them. Something better than anything since, because he'd expected a child from her, and the normal relationship due to a lusty husband. Effie had been a sore disappointment though, breeding no son, producing only an endless string of

242

complaints, wailings, and headaches that had sent him off in their early days looking for a bit of pleasure elsewhere. And the pleasure had paid off. He knew for a fact that he had four thriving sons in the district. But no one could prove it, whatever they guessed, and he'd made no pretension to holiness nor made out that he was a particularly moral man. Morality, to his mind, was a weakness and a sham. It was up to anyone in his position to do what he could for himself.

When he heard from Jessica that Donna had arrived back from London at Polbreath, and was due to call at Trencobban the following afternoon, he made it his business to be lurking nearby as she arrived in the Trevarvas chaise, driven by the Polbreath man in his yellow coat and top hat. At first he thought that it would be a tricky business, but then he saw her get out alone, dismiss the chaise, and stand watching it for a moment before it started off again and disappeared along the drive to the main road.

She moved toward the stables, where he guessed correctly that she'd be getting out that wild colt of hers for riding back. Presently he saw her approaching the side door. He moved from a clump of bushes, stepping quickly in front of her, with a set look on his square, broad face.

She involuntarily drew back, her eyes wide and apprehensive. "What do you want?"

"Just what's owing me," he answered. "That you so conveniently forgot. An' a bit of interest, I reckon, to make things right."

"I haven't got enough with me," she told him. "So be off, or there'll not be a penny."

"You hand over what there is, Mistress Trevarvas," he said, "That'll do for now."

Glancing round quickly to see that no one was about, she found a sovereign in her pocket with change, and thrust it out to him. "There."

"And the rest?"

"Friday. Same place, no interest."

243

He shrugged and moved away. Before his large hulk had quite disappeared Sam turned the corner from the stables. "Afternoon, mistress," he said, lifting a hand to his forelock in the customary way. "Wasn't that Andrewartha?"

Tensing herself to reply nonchalantly Donna answered, "That's right; he gave me a message about the mine."

"Did he know you'd be here, Miss Donna—I mean ma'am?"

She laughed uneasily. "Heavens no. How could he? Just a convenient chance. Otherwise he'd have had to go all the way to Polbreath."

Sam stared at her hard for a moment, then passed on. But she knew he didn't believe her. Realized too, that already a weak link in the chain of secrecy had been forged, and wondered briefly if it wouldn't be better to give Jed the money in bulk next time, pay him off for the year and be rid of the strain.

If only she could confide in Nicholas, as she had in Lucien. Dare she? He had changed so much since their marriage; perhaps he would understand if she came out with the whole thing, explained exactly what had happened, and how she'd come to be in such a mess.

But just as she was debating the point, a sullen rim of cloud rose from the west, obscuring the sunlight. The air chilled as a thin, rising wind began to blow from the sea. She shivered involuntarily, before walking back to the house. No. She knew she couldn't. Dare not. Nicholas was set in a different mold than Lucien. Even if he believed her, the truth would probably end their marriage, and this risk she couldn't take.

With the problem so heavily on her mind she found that she couldn't greet Jessica and the rest of the household naturally. Despite her smiles and vivacity, her enthusiastic accounts of Paris and London, she felt the lines of her face taut, stretched from temples to neck and drawn into a knot of pain at the back of her skull.

Jessica noticed. "You look a bit washed out," she said. "Still, I suppose it's natural."

"I could say the same of you," Donna retorted. "How have things been going?"

"Same as usual. No company, no handsome male callers. Nothing but interference."

"What do you mean?"

"The governess. You'd think Janey was her child 'stead of mine. As for education! Seems to me all she teaches her is to stick her nose a bit higher and to look down on her own mother."

"Well . . . I did say she wasn't the proper person," Donna pointed out.

"I know," Jessica sighed. "I never seem to do right do I?"

Donna, suddenly forgetting her own problem, laughed.

"Oh Jessica. Cheer up. Anyhow, the day after tomorrow, Thursday, I want you to come over to Polbreath for a sort of—a sort of celebration party—Nicholas knows all about it. Lucien should be there, he's returning from London that day. Janey can come too, if you like. But as it's for the evening. . ."

"No. Not Janey," Jessica said, her spirits rising mercurially. "Janey can come another time, can't she? And if it's just four of us. . ." She broke off questioningly. "Is it? I mean will there be anyone else?"

Donna shook her head. "Just four."

"Oh Donna. It'll be grand. What'll I wear?" She got up, moving to the glass near the fireplace, smoothing her bright hair, lifting her ample breasts between her hands, smiling so radiantly that the years of fear, disillusion and self-indulgence fell away, leaving her eyes clear and brilliant as the blue of a summer sky, the sensuous full mouth expectant and warm as that of a girl on the brink of life.

"Blue," Donna told her. "I've told you before that it's your color. You should always wear it when you want to look your best."

"All right I will, and the earrings you gave me. They'll go well won't they? I'll wear my hair tidy, all on top. And perhaps—can Sam bring me in the carriage?"

245

"No," Donna answered. "You shall come in style in Nicholas's—in our chaise."

Jessica was so exuberant about the affair that Donna was touched. For the first time since Luke had brought Jessica to Trencobban she felt guilty that she hadn't bothered with her a little more, that she had failed to regard her as more than the scheming woman who'd corrupted and cheated her brother into marriage. Still all that was over now, and possibly in the future she'd be able to bring a little more glamour into Jessica's life. In this way Jessica's association with Jed might be ended.

Before she left that afternoon, Donna went to the kitchens where the servants were waiting and agog to hear news of the honeymoon—where they'd been, and what plays they'd seen? Was the Crystal Palace as wonderful as it was said to be? Was London really such an overpowering place? And had they had a glimpse of the Queen herself? What were Kew Gardens like? And Paris? Was it true that the streets were full of artists and fallen women, and that there were shop windows with paintings in them of naked people?

Donna, highly amused, tried to describe as colorfully as possible the places that she had visited with Nicholas, the galleries, the restaurants, including the Café Royal, and the trip by boat down the Thames; but eventually she had to break off, knowing that Nicholas would be expecting her back and might even be on the way to meet her then.

"I've brought something for each one of you," she said. "But I'll have to bring them next time I come. I'm sorry—I quite forgot today. They were all ready in the hall, then thinking of you all stupidly put them right out of my head."

"We need no presents, Miss Donna," Sarah told her. "Although of course anythin' to show you've a thought for us will be treasured, I'm sure. But just a sight of you lookin' so well an' glowin' is somethin' for sore eyes, an' to be remembered."

246

"Sure 'nuff," Sam agreed.

Donna, in spite of the excitement, contrived to have a quick word with Beth Paynter before she left.

"Have things really been harmonious here without me?" she asked.

"Well—I can't say there's been anything wrong miss—ma'am." Beth contradicted herself quickly. "But Mrs. Penroze and the governess come to words sometimes, and Janey gets the worst of it, I'm afraid."

"You mean her mother?"

"Oh no. Her mother tries her best to please the child, I'm sure. But—although it's not my business—I don't think Miss Bray's influence on her is good. She's growing conceited and too sure of herself. Not that I blame the child. It's her misfortune, as I said, more than her fault. I don't wish to complain. But since you asked me . . ."

"Yes, yes. Thank you. I'm glad you've told me," Donna answered hastily, as Sarah's figure emerged from the kitchen. "I'll see about it when I've had time to settle and get things in order."

She left soon after that, and found Saladin already saddled for her and waiting, with Ted holding the reins. After a few words with the boy, she was quickly mounted and away. She eased the colt along until she'd crossed the road and was taking the path up the hill over the moors toward the cromlech. Then, giving the colt his head, she encouraged him to a gallop, while her senses responded to the sweet early spring air, laden with the fresh, heady scents of thrusting young bracken, gorse, heather, and the intangible frail perfume of spattered yellow primroses and speared heads of young bluebells pushing through the short green turf. Occasionally a gull squawked overhead, and now and again she heard the nostalgic haunting call of an early cuckoo.

At the top of the slope she drew Saladin to a halt, and paused, looking down on the distant vista of moors sloping to the coast and sea beyond, on the cottages and huddled hamlet to the east of Trencobban, and to the other side, where the land rose toward the west showing the dark shape of Wheal Faith standing secure and still working. Thanks to Nicholas it was likely to be prosperous for many years to come, although Leibert had not expressed firm hope that new levels would prove any more economic than those he had tackled already.

"There's a chance," he'd said, "no more."

To which Donna had replied, knowing Nicholas would support her, "Then take the chance. We've got to."

And Trevarvas had agreed. His generosity over the failing mine still surprised, even touched her proud spirit. She knew that he was taking this gamble simply to please her. The knowledge rekindled her warm and glowing need of him, a need that was more than desire or passion, and extended far beyond the sphere of mere physical demands. How far he reciprocated this overwhelming emotion she couldn't guess . . . until her return that afternoon.

He was waiting and watching for her at the door as she rode Saladin down the drive to the stables, and when she went into the house up the stairs to their bedroom, he was already there before her.

"Oh Donna," he said, moving toward her, arms open to receive her. "I've missed you."

She could hardly believe her ears. "Missed me? In just two hours?"

With his lips first on her temples, then gently on her cheeks, moving from neck to shoulders, he said, "Look at me Donna."

She lifted her head, studying him questioningly, closely, with her heart so full of joy she could hardly breathe.

"Oh Nicholas," she murmured.

"I love you Donna," he whispered against her ear. "More than myself . . . more than anything in the world that's counted until now. More even than life, I think . . . and that's a damn ridiculous thing to say isn't it?"

She didn't reply. What else was there to say? How

could she express the thoughts and emotions that, though so uniquely their own, must have been experienced before yet never adequately put into words by all the great lovers of history. Just to know was enough.

CHAPTER SEVENTEEN

The next day was warm and windless, with the thin mist lifting to silvered brightness under a climbing sun. Young birds chortled, and fluttered from their nests and about the bushes and trees. Seals lay sleek and supine on the rocks by the cove, and everything seemed astir with new life around the headland where fox and badger lurked, nosing through undergrowth and curling bracken. These were the mornings when the Bal maidens went happily to their work at the mine, singing with the rest of nature, their garibaldis and white aprons bright against the freshening young green and gold of the moor.

Jessica, filled with excitement and anticipation over her visit to Polbreath the next day, spent the morning trying on the new frock, arraying her plentiful yellow hair to the best advantage, and choosing from the new collection of clothes provided by Donna, a gray velvet cloak, which she had been thinking, of late, she might never have occasion to wear.

I look a lady, she thought, surveying herself in the glass. As grand as any countess or duchess. The knowledge was so stimulating that she had a sudden longing for Jed to see her in her new attire—not the dress, because she wouldn't risk spoiling it—but certainly the cloak and earrings. It would be a chance to give him just a glimpse of her, instead of having her submissive and all willing in his arms: make him respect her more, and treat her with the dignity that befitted the sister-in-law of Mrs. Nicholas Trevarvas.

Once the idea had entered her head, she couldn't get

rid of it. The problem was that Jed was temporarily off night cores, and working by day. Never mind, when the men left the mine at about six, she could be wandering around, pretending to pick primroses and bluebells. A few would look nice in a vase anyway, and when Jed saw her dressed up he'd be sure to find an excuse to stay behind and talk to her. And it *would* only be talk this time, she decided. They could just amble a bit, casually, so as not to cause undue comment during the changing of shifts. Then, when that was over, she'd explain she couldn't meet him as planned the following night, because of going to Polbreath. He'd doubtless want to have her there and then, but for once she would be calm and polite, reminding him that it wasn't safe in daylight, when one or other of the miners was always about.

So, after tea, as the sun dipped lower toward the horizon and a veiled heat-haze quivered over the rim of sea and sky, Jessica set off from Trencobban, sauntering lazily but purposefully over the moor. The gray velvet gave her an especial dignity and presence, and she walked proudly, her fair hair a bright halo in the dampening air and the evening light.

By the time most of the day men had gone, and those on night shift had disappeared into the mine-house, she had gathered a whole bouquet of primroses, bluebells and wild pink thrift. She lingered about for a time, not cowering in the bushes, as she had done months before when Jed had rejected her, but flaunting herself, pausing, then drifting on again, greeting one or two of the miners who nodded as they passed. Jed, in his position as under-Captain, was the last to leave, wearing his new stove hat as befitted his rank. He took it off to pass a hand over his hot forehead, and didn't replace it, but walked on until he saw her coming toward him up an incline of the moor.

"My!" he gasped, approaching her. "What's all this then? What's 'ee dressed up as queen for?"

She smiled, two dimples crumpling her pink cheeks.

251

"Like it Jed?" she asked, unable to resist giving a twirl around.

He looked behind him and in the direction of his receding companions before grabbing her hand and giving her a spanking kiss. "Tryn' to tempt me?" He grinned. "That it? Couldn't wait?"

"Oh no," she replied coyly, drawing away. "That's not it at all. I came to tell you I wouldn't be able to see you tomorrow. I am sorry Jed. It's just that Donna's asked me to—to Polbreath. And I want to go. So we'll have to arrange another time."

"Will we then?" His eyes narrowed. "An' suppose I say it's now or never? You let me lay you as you are, all toffed up in them fancy cloes, or not at all. Well? What'd you say to that, eh?"

She paused, then realizing that he was making a joke in his own heavy way, answered, "I don't think I'd believe you."

He laughed. "Cocksure all of a sudden aren't ye? Never mind, it suits you. I like a wumman with a bit of spirit. All right then girl, we'll say Saturday, in th' cove. A bit of waiting'll only sharpen the appetite."

She nodded. "I suppose so."

"You s'pose?"

"I'll always want you Jed," she said simply. "It's you who's the cold one sometimes."

"I've things on my mind sometimes," he said bluntly. "Heavy things."

"I know. Your wife."

"And the rest," he told her.

"The mine?"

He shrugged. "I've a hunch things aren't goin' to work out the way they think, an' then where'll we be agen? Out of work. At a dead loss. That's why I'm scrimpin' an' scrapin' to get a bit of gold in my pocket, 'fore balloon goes up."

They walked on silently together for a few yards. Jessica did not question him further because she sensed in him the familiar dull resentment of worker against employer and knew that words would only exacerbate it.

252

The mist, which earlier had been only quivering silver, had now thickened to a rising milky-white, billowing to gray, shrouding bushes and rocks in obscurity, then lifting again before resolving once more to ghostly uniformity. The air had suddenly chilled, making Jessica glad to have her cape round her. She waited, beside a clump of thorn humped against a boulder, to adjust the clasp at her neck. Then, suddenly she stiffened, standing motionless with all her senses keyed to the silence, to the intense quiet which should have been bereft of movement but wasn't.

"Come on now," Jed said, puzzled. "What's up? Seen sumpthen? Poacher, eh?"

He stared at her face—dead pale, strained, with such terror on it he thought she was about to faint. He took her arm. "What the hell's gotten into you wumman?"

She tried to speak. Did her best to lift her hand in the direction of a huddled gorse bush to her right, where the heather was massed thick with stones. But her arm was trembling so violently she couldn't, just let it drop, and thrust her head forward, half stumbling, as the twigs and undergrowth creaked, and snapped, revealing the lurching form of the thing she'd dreaded for so many days, months, and years—the menacing half-defined shape of a man, snarling and muttering with a stream of oaths as he sprang suddenly. Before Jed properly realized it, he was upon them, knife outthrust for a second, catching a frail beam of light before he plunged it first at Andrewartha, slashing his face, thigh, and upraised arm, kicking at shins and stomach until Jed, blinded temporarily by shock and streaming blood, stumbled and fell writhing into a mass of tangled briar. He did not see the rest, nor hear Jessica's high wild scream, as she rushed ahead and down to where the open ground led toward the cliffs. He had been too blinded to see the crazed, mad face looking down on him for a few seconds, or the sudden gesture that sent the grotesque form after her—running, half-bent, like an animal hunting its prey, pausing a moment, then on again, getting each second a little nearer.

253

CHAPTER EIGHTEEN

The news that after so many months the escaped murderer, Silas Flint, had been found dead with the body of his wife Lucy at the bottom of a Cornish cliff, naturally caused wide and dramatic comment in the press. And despite all efforts by Donna and her husband to keep Jessica's name out of the sordid story, the fact that she had been the bigamous widow of William Penroze's son, Luke, was fully exposed. The newspapers also retold with relish the bizarre story of the trial and the sensational events leading up to it.

Donna, with shock and disgust, read how the young wife of seventeen had been frequently grossly abused and beaten by Flint, despite his fanatical religious aspirations—how she had been discovered in a barn with one of his farm workers on the fatal night when he'd returned a day earlier than expected from a weekend preaching, and how he had stabbed the youth in a mad rage with a kitchen knife before attacking his wife. She had first been wounded then raped and thrashed mercilessly, and had borne, it was stated, the scars ever since. The young man had been kicked into a ditch by Flint, who thought he was dead. But he had managed to crawl to a cottage a quarter of a mile away, and give a brief account of the tragedy before he collapsed and died. If it hadn't been for this and the wife's testimony against him in court, the truth might never have been known.

Silas Flint was obviously a warped and split personality. The defense at the trial had pleaded insanity, but had been discredited by the jury. He had been sentenced to be hanged, but later reprieved, due to the fact that he had undoubtedly acted under extreme provocation. His wife, despite her youth, had been of dissolute character, and when Flint had first met her was earning her living as a prostitute in Plymouth and elsewhere, frequenting taverns of ill-repute and cohabiting with men. There had been little sympathy for the girl, who, in the eyes of society, had asked for all she'd got. Eventually, on the Home Secretary's order, the death sentence had been commuted to life imprisonment.

There were further lurid details which so sickened Donna when she read them, that she wanted to vomit. And when she found Janey being escorted one day from the kitchen by Zenobia Bray, who said she had found the child listening to the servants discussing the tragedy, indignation and revulsion were so strong in her she caught Janey's hand in a hard grip, saying harshly, "I won't have you listening to stories, and you're not to go to the kitchen, do you hear? Your place is upstairs in the nursery, or with me and Miss Bray."

Janey's eyes narrowed as she shook her head. "Where's mama? Is she dead?"

"Mama's having a long sleep," Donna told her ambiguously, with a feeling of guilt.

A queer, knowing look crossed the child's face. "But she won't wake, will she?"

Donna, struggling to find an adequate answer, heard Janey continue unemotionally, "It doesn't matter. I don't mind. Mama used to spank me. If she's dead she won't ever again, and I can go and live with Miss Bray can't I, Aunty Donna?"

Donna regarded her incredulously before she said, "You mustn't speak like that. And you must forget anything your mother did to hurt you. She didn't mean it. So . . ."

"Oh yes she did," Janey said obstinately. "I know."

"Janey . . . " Miss Bray interposed in a strangely gentle voice. "Why don't we go upstairs and have a game? Or perhaps I'll read to you."

257

The little girl stared mutely for a moment then replied, "All right. If you want to."

Donna was at a loss. What, she wondered, was the right thing to do for the child now? Take her off to Polbreath where she could have lessons with Ianthe and Jonathan before they went to school? Or leave her here with Mrs. Paynter, Sarah, and Zenobia Bray? There was obviously some strange understanding between Janey and her governess that, in view of Zenobia's lack of personal charm, was hard to fathom.

The answer came the following day, when Donna, on her return to Trencobban in the morning, found that a newspaper man had somehow inveigled himself into the house and had tried to interview the child.

Zenobia Bray had caught them before much damage had been done. "But I don't think it's right for Janey to be in such a position," she said primly, but with considerable force. "This sort of thing could harm her for life. I know it's not my business. You're her legal guardian now, but from what I've heard about Mrs. Luke, she was never the proper person to have a young daughter at all . . ."

"The fact remains she did," Donna pointed out dryly, adding almost immediately, "How would you deal with Janey's future, Miss Bray?"

A faint flush tinged the other woman's thin face before she answered, "Since you ask me, Mrs. Trevarvas, I think a change of scene and air would do her a great deal of good and keep her safe from unhealthy gossip. If you were willing to continue with my salary I would be only too glad to take her back with me to Falmouth. I still have my house; we get on well together. I would see that her education was continued correctly. But of course . . ." her lips closed primly. "That is entirely a matter for you to decide."

"And Janey," Donna pointed out.

"I think you'll find Janey would jump at the idea."

And she did. When Donna, after thinking the matter over, and with Nicholas's approval, put the suggestion

258

to the little girl, Janey's solemn slant-eyed face lit up with enthusiasm.

"Oh *yes*, Aunty Donna," she said quickly. "*Please* let me go with Miss Bray. There are all sorts of things in Falmouth, shops and ships, and—and lots of people. And we could go up the river on a boat . . ."

"I see. So you know all about it?"

Janey nodded. "She's told me. And—and she loves me, Aunty Donna. She doesn't scold—not much, and she never spanks me with a slipper. Never. Not even when I'm bad."

Donna gathered the young form to her, hugging her warmly for a moment, and as she did so, realized how frail and slight she was—so small and thin-boned. She reminded her pathetically of a piece of delicately formed porcelain. "All right," she said. "You shall go, for a time, and I'll come over sometimes just to see how you're getting on."

So it was arranged, and a week later, in the Polbreath chaise, Janey and a rejuvenated Zenobia Bray set off for Falmouth. Generous financial arrangements had been made for her upkeep while she was there, and if it worked—well, Donna thought, as she went back into the house after waving them goodbye, there was no reason why things shouldn't continue indefinitely in that way. Janey, she was now convinced, was no Penroze by blood but whatever her heredity, contact with a respectable, obviously child-starved woman like Zenobia Bray could only do good, and take a load of responsibility from her shoulders.

Meanwhile the problem of Jed remained. When he returned to his cottage after a month's spell in the nearest infirmary, Nicholas went over with the offer of fifty pounds a year as compensation, on behalf of his wife, to be paid from Crebbyn's Bank once a month.

"It's not that you're owed it," he told Jed bluntly. "The accident—or attack on you had nothing to do with the mine. But in view of the fact that you were with Mrs. Penroze when it happened, we both feel that

259

something should be done to help you in your unfortunate situation. There should be parish relief, too, if you're unable to take further work. And that Union of yours has funds I suppose for its members?"

"Depends on what you call funds," Jed replied grudgingly. "Still, I'm thankful for what you can spare. And the wife'll be glad too. In bed she is—up theer."

Nicholas glanced up the narrow flight of rickety steps, leading to what was presumably no more than a space above the downstairs room. It was shelved off by wooden boarding, and a floor holed in parts, that emitted light between the beams of the room below.

The smell was not pleasant, and Nicholas was thankful to get away.

When he told Donna of the interview and described the squalor of the dwelling, she screwed her brows together, then said after a pause, "Do you think a pound a week is enough?" Thinking, as she spoke, that if it were doubled, Jed might not bother her any more.

"Quite," Nicholas answered.

"How is it going to be paid?" she asked. "Of course I shall be visiting the poor woman, and could take it with me . . ." such an arrangement, however distasteful, would give her a reasonable excuse for meeting Jed.

"Certainly not," Nicholas replied shortly. "I'm arranging for Andrewartha to pick the sum up, fortnightly from Crebbyn's. I've heard that Paynter, the tenant of that small farm of yours above the road, goes into Penzance most weeks with vegetables. He will have no problem in getting there. I don't want you visiting that cottage more than is necessary. It's a filthy, unhealthy place and should have been done away with long ago. No wonder so many died from cholera and typhus in the past."

"My father knew that," Donna said pointedly. "He did his best to improve the miners' conditions. But he hadn't the money to set things right."

"Now, Donna," Nicholas's arm went to her shoulders, "don't start throwing things in my face. It wasn't my business to support your father."

260

"And it isn't yours to criticize him," Donna exclaimed hotly.

Nicholas's lips touched her temple. "Don't quarrel, sweetheart," he said, letting his lips travel from the soft cheek to the pit of her throat.

She pulled herself away irritably. It was the first time that she had reacted with such impatience since their marriage. "Oh leave me alone. Don't think you can always get your way with just a kiss and a . . . a . . . I'm not a child, Nicholas. So don't treat me like one. And don't patronize."

She rushed out of the room as she was, in her green cloth dress, without cape or hat, made her way to the new stables where she now kept her colt, pulled on a pair of boots, and saddled Saladin. Before Nicholas was aware of what she was up to, she had ridden up the lane to the moors, going at a gallop to the left and along the ridge with her heart pounding, her hair a streaming pinion of tumbled ebony. Once beside the cromlech she paused, feeling better. That would show him, she thought. Just because they loved each other, and because he had been in the position to bring security and prosperity to the Trencobban estate, didn't mean that he'd bought her, or her opinions. Nor could he ever wipe her father from her mind. Here, with the ancient stones around her, she felt released from all ties—even from Nicholas.

And then, as she drew the sweet wild air into her lungs, she saw a dark form riding up the hill from Polbreath. Nicholas.

She kicked Saladin into a gallop again, cutting along the southern ridge toward Rosebuzzan, crying, with the wind on her face, "Faster boy . . . faster . . . come on now . . ." the words torn from her lungs, as Saladin, responding gaily to the challenge, put all the power of his blood into the mad ride.

But it was not enough. Nicholas overtook them by a heap of tumbled stone where once a shepherd's hut had been. The reins were pulled from her grip, and her body tumbled into his arms, as he said, "You little wildcat. What the hell do you think you're doing?"

She didn't answer, not knowing if he was angry, but just watched him breathlessly as he freed her and tethered the two horses to the stump of a withered tree. Then he turned swiftly and drew her roughly to him, staring into her flashing eyes for a moment, before laying her down.

"Never taken you before in the heather, have I, darling?" he said. "Never taught you how to love with the leaves and grass in your hair? We've been so civilized before haven't we? But my God! Donna, you're a pagan witch if ever there was one, and witches need a certain brand of loving."

She stared up at him, half afraid, yet sick with longing, as he loosened their clothing and took her to him. Beneath him her body arched in a wanton wild desire that reached beyond love or human consciousness, pulsing with the dark flood of life until culmination came, taking her gradually into a sweet and dying assuagement of passion.

For some minutes they lay there together, breathing heavily, staring at the clear sky above. Then he said, easing himself up on one shoulder, "Feeling better?"

"Much."

"You're a damn little savage. Know that?"

She smiled. "And you?"

"I know how to handle them when I have to," he answered. Then pulling the skirts back over her thighs, "Do yourself up, or the rabbits will be shocked to death."

She giggled as they adjusted their clothes.

A little later as they rode back to Polbreath he said, "Don't goad me too far, sweetheart."

"What do you mean?"

"So long as you keep your beauty just for me, everything will be all right between us. I'll put up with your temper and tantrums for the sake of your maddening sweetness. But if ever I find you giving just so much of

262

a certain glance elsewhere, I will beat the living day-lights out of you."

Donna smiled. "As if I would. I love you."

"Yes. I believe you do," he said. "Now."

"What do you mean, now?"

As he dismounted, he said, "I'm considerably older than you, and no oil painting. Youth won't last forever. But the truth is—without you, life would be less than a husk, and the more fool I, for admitting it."

Donna's hand slid into his. "You needn't worry about that. I would never leave you, Nicholas."

And she knew that was true. The trouble was—could she be so sure about him, if he ever found out about Lucien?

In the heady rapture and excitement of her days with Nicholas, she was able to keep thoughts of Jed to a min-imum, especially now that she had arranged to place the money under a certain stone, halfway between the cot-tage and Trencobban. Occasionally she rode over from the house to take eggs and other delicacies to his wife, but that was only on fine days when she could leave them outside in a bag. Illness and poverty still de-pressed her acutely, reminding her that the world she shared with Nicholas was one of a privileged minority.

She also forced the memory of Jessica and her tragic end to the back of her mind. It was a dark episode best forgotten. There was no point in remembering. Her sister-in-law had been a constant embarrassment in life, and although hushed regrets were expressed whenever her name, or the circumstances of her death cropped up, Donna shut her ears to them, refusing any longer to shoulder the burden that Luke had thrust upon her.

Once or twice she passed Jed as he hovered by the mine, his empty sleeve pinned to his shoulder. She had heard that he'd obtained a part time job helping the purser, but his glance when he saw her was dark and malignant. He clearly blamed her for being, if only through her relationship to Jessica, partially responsible for the loss of his limb, and she guessed that his attitude would never change.

The mine meanwhile continued working. Leibert now expressed fresh hope that a new level running toward the Polbreath estate would be productive, but as autumn approached, the men became restive once more. With that sixth sense miners frequently have, they sensed that Wheal Faith was turning its back on them. Two said that they had heard the "knockers" or "buc-cas"—which were the malignant spirits of those who'd crucified Christ, toiling nearby—and not on productive loads, either. Another reported seeing a white rabbit in the engine house. It had been cornered, but disappeared as quick as a flash of lightning. The snails were about too, and everyone accepted that to see a snail on a fine day was bad.

Where such stories first originated no one knew. But they had become so much a part of tradition among those who worked underground that whether true or not, they had an insidious effect. Even Jed made sly suggestions that the mine had seen its worst day when William Penroze's proud daughter had first poked her nose in.

Even without superstition, Trevarvas himself was beginning to feel that he'd backed an ailing concern, and by late September he knew it. The new level of tin had proved as thin and disappointing as its predecessor, and one by one the tributers left. Donna was forced to meet Leibert and his colleagues in the Count House to discuss the closing of Wheal Faith.

Nicholas, who had accompanied Donna, promised the men two months' full wages, starting from the second week in November when they would have to start looking for new employment. There was room for a few of them at Wheal Joy, he said, and pointed out that skilled miners were seldom at a loss for work in the Penjust area.

The news was accepted at first in stony silence, with gratitude from some for Trevarvas's concern. But in the days following, the dark cloud of insecurity intensified and settled over the countryside, raising such questions as: Where do we go when mine's stopped? Where'll we

264

live? Cottages beant so easy as all that to find, an' what-ever that rich landowner do say, his offer's small 'ccording to what most of us have to lose."

" 'Twouldn' have happened in the auld maister's time," others remarked darkly, at which Jed murmured threateningly, "How do we show 'em then? What way is there, but to make that fine mistress o' Trencobban to sit up an' take notice?"

Leibert did his best, and partially succeeded in restoring reason.

"If you make trouble for Mistress Trevarvas," he said, "you make double trouble for yourselves. No one can give life to a mine if its juice has run dry, and if the mine's barren it's no fault of anyone's. The only thing is to go on as long as we can through the next two months."

Donna was more depressed than she admitted by the news, not so much on her own account any more, but because she now had to accept that her father's ambition was nothing more than a dead dream. Her only consolation was that both she and Nicholas had done all they could.

Life was a strange pattern, she often reflected, in that season of falling leaf, when the damp earth smelled of tumbled blackberries and brine, and decaying undergrowth hovered above the mist-hugged ground.

At Polbreath the change of seasons was intensified by the stark shapes of clustered skeleton trees. But she was glad to be there and away from the brooding forms and faces of the Wheal Faith miners who now worked only mechanically, and without ambition. Occasionally Donna, on her visits to Trencobban, made her way to the mine, doing her best to give a few words of cheer to any worker she met. But her own words filled her with self-contempt, and as the day for closing down approached, she did her best to avoid any of those her father had known.

One morning she went to see Beth and Phyllida, whom both she and Nicholas had decided were super-fluous now that Janey was gone and Donna herself was spending less than half her time at Trencobban. Afterwards she had an impulse to see the cove again, where so many happy hours of childhood had been passed, and where she and Jos had lain on the pale sand without a care in the world, thinking only of their first youthful love and romantic plans for a life together.

She was wearing Luke's breeches, and after leaving Saladin with Ted, walked over the short dried turf and heather which was crisp that day from an early frost, toward the old track cutting down by the stream through the cliff face to the cove.

But before she got there, she had a shock. There, outlined against the pale sky still silvered from the cold night air, was the figure of a man. He was coming toward her, his shape only half defined at first, gradually assuming positive identity, until she was quite sure.

Jos! She ran toward him expectantly, arms outspread, filled not with love, but with a deep, warm sense of affection and friendship, of renewal of all she'd cared for in the past. He was a symbol of her youth and the deepest ties of her childhood—her father, Tom, Wheal Faith, and the future they'd promised to share.

She was breathless when she reached him, her eyes brilliant in her flushed face.

"Jos!" she cried. "When did you get here?" She did not notice how he had matured, nor the set look of his face. "Jos—you should have written."

She waited, expecting him to take her hands. But he did not. Instead, scowling, he pushed her away roughly, saying, "I told you I'd come back, didn' I? But you couldn't wait that long. You had to find the richest man there was and snap him up as soon as my back was turned." He strode on, leaving her speechless, dismayed, and too affronted for words at first.

Then she raced after him, crying, "Jos—Jos, it wasn't like that. You went away. I never thought I'd see you again . . ."

She caught hold of his arm, and just for a minute or two he paused, staring at her with such contempt that she winced.

"You sold yourself," he told her in dull, deadly tones. "You sold yourself like any—any whore—to the highest bidder. I told you I'd do well, and I have. But I want none of you now—nor ever would—not even if you were free."

"Jos!" Her voice was sharp. "You're wrong! And if you feel like that it's perhaps for the best that you left. I didn't sell myself. You know very well, or should, that I'm not the type. I married Nicholas Trevarvas because I loved him, and for no other reason. Do you understand?"

With a short laugh he turned his back on her, saying, "Oh aye. I understand all right. But your love isn't my kind, Donna. Mine's the faithful, lasting sort, that only ways like yours can kill. So let me be now. I've a week here at the most 'fore I take off back to America, and the less I see of you the better."

He walked on toward Gwynvoor, leaving her white-faced, furious at his condemnation, and utterly miserable at his lack of understanding.

Then, presently, having no heart any more for her jaunt to the cove she started on her way back toward Trencobban. She had not gone far when she saw, to her surprise, Nicholas sauntering toward her. He was in riding clothes, and had a glowering look on his face. Donna's heart sank. Surely he hadn't seen any of the unhappy discussion with Jos.

"Quite a revealing little encounter," he said, with a jealous gleam in his dark eyes. "Who was he?"

"Oh. You mean . . ." She shrugged, trying to laugh.

"You know very well what I mean Donna," he said. "And who?"

"Nicholas, you really are being rather idiotic. That was Jos Craze, Tom's son. He's just returned from America for a week, and naturally I had to talk to him."

"Naturally. Talking is one thing, though. Running after him quite another. I happened to see . . ."

"You always happen to see, don't you?"

"What do you mean?"

267

"If I talk to anyone—a friend—any man—you seem to be just within earshot. Or eyeshot, whichever it is. It's as though you don't trust me."

"I'm not sure that I do."

"And that's quite ridiculous. Especially where Jos is concerned."

"Why Jos in particular?"

"Oh . . . because . . ."

She broke off as he interposed. "Wasn't he the young miner who pleaded with you to go off with him to foreign climes?"

She stared. "Whoever told you that? How did you know?"

"The moors have ears, darling. I was aware, too, that you'd been considering it."

"Of all the . . ."

"Was it true?"

"Not really. Whoever told you that had got it wrong. Jos did want me to marry him, if you must know, and all the time I thought I was in love with him. But that's all. Obviously I wasn't, or I'd have gone."

There was silence between them as they walked on, with the coldness growing between them. Then Donna said impulsively, stopping once more, with her face raised challengingly to his, "Look, Nicholas. I wouldn't lie to you, and if you don't believe me I can't help it. But if you go on mistrusting me everything will be spoiled. Can't you understand that?"

Her eyes were suddenly so wide and bright under the clear sky, her lips so soft and vulnerable, that he relaxed.

"No, I don't, I'm afraid," he admitted. "Not completely. But I'm willing to take your word—this time. Although I can't for the life of me see why you had to thrust yourself at him the way you did."

"I was upset. He was rather nasty."

"Nasty?"

"In what he said."

"And what was that?"

268

"If you must know . . . he accused me of selling myself. To you."

"Oh. I see."

"I don't think you do. Certainly he didn't. Or wouldn't accept it."

"What?"

"What I said, the truth. That I'd married you because I loved you."

She looked away, and walked on a little ahead. A moment later he had caught her arm, twirled her round, and was kissing her.

"You're forgiven," he said. Then, "Come along. I expected you to be at Trencobban when I got there."

"Why didn't you say so? We could have ridden over together."

"Oh, it just occurred to me that it was a good chance to get things properly settled about Beth, and that girl—Phyllida, is she called? You get on with them don't you?"

"Yes," Donna admitted, "I don't like them having to leave. As a matter of fact I'd wondered if we could get them in somewhere at Polbreath? Your housekeeper is a bit of a—a dragon, Nicholas. And Pullen's jealous as you well know."

"I do. Poor thing," he conceded. "I'm afraid she's had a raw deal, owing to my hard and careful nature. I should perhaps have bedded her just once, before I knew you."

Suppressing a hot remark Donna said coolly, "Why didn't you?"

"Because my darling, she had a greedy eye, no hips, and puny breasts. In fact from every angle she failed to tempt my lascivious nature."

"You hard-hearted wretch."

"Yes. Still—we've strayed from the point. On second thought I don't see why those two women can't come to Polbreath. We need new staff now, and Mrs. Prowse is getting rather tart and testy to carry on much longer. Nearing seventy. I've an idea for retiring her next year;

269

there's a cottage that should be available then, and it seems to me Mrs. Paynter will take on her job."

"Oh yes," Donna agreed. "I know she'd be excellent, and would probably jump at it."

"That leaves just Sam and Sarah and the boy. They could stay on at the house as caretakers I suppose? If they wanted to?"

"Well, we could put it to them, although I know Sarah's niece wants them to join her in Truro when they retire. They take boarders—not holidaymakers—permanents mostly. "Commercial gentlemen," Sarah calls them, and they have ample room."

There was silence between them until they reached the drive by the stables where Donna paused again, reliving with a pang of nostalgia all that the granite house symbolized for her: the many generations of Penrozes who'd lived there, their fears and aspirations. The emotional conflicts of love, passion, and despair which by now, surely, must be engrained into the very walls.

Trencobban. She knew, as she stood there, that she would never entirely be free of it. It was in her bones and very bloodstream. Part of the heritage laid on her by her father which would and must endure, even though the mine had to go.

As if sensing her thoughts, Nicholas said. "It means a hell of a lot to you doesn't it?"

"Yes."

"Well—you needn't worry. Even if the old couple go, we can make new arrangements."

"You mean sell, or something?" Her voice and face were suddenly full of alarm.

"Of couse not. You've just admitted it's important to you. So it is to me. Not only because of your feelings, but because of my hard-headed business sense. As I have said before, Trencobban is of historical interest, Donna. Besides, there'll be times when I'm away on business that you may want to have a change and live there. I wouldn't like to see it go."

"And I wouldn't want you to be away from me for months on end if that's what you're thinking."

270

"My dear love! Who said months on end? Whenever possible you'll go with me. But there will be times when my particular man's world would have no room for you. Can you understand that, darling?"

Donna shook her head. "I'm trying to. But there's such a lot I don't know about you, Nicholas."

"And what you don't know you shouldn't fret over," he said. "So don't give it another thought, darling. Let's go in now, and see what the domestic situation is likely to be."

It was very much as Donna had predicted. Beth, when told of Donna's new suggestion, appeared extremely grateful and accepted the Polbreath offer. Sarah and Sam both stated that for the time being they'd like to remain at Trencobban with Ted, although both asked if they could have a bit of a holiday later, to "get their second wind" as they said, following the last few months' upheaval.

Donna breathed a sigh of relief as she and Nicholas set off for Polbreath, little dreaming of the dark trend of events shaping ahead, although the shadow of her unpleasant meeting with Jos still haunted her intermittently, and she knew, despite Nicholas, she must somehow contrive to put things right before he left.

As it happened, a second meeting occurred quite naturally two days later when she was talking a leisurely canter on Bess to Gwynvoor.

The Craze cottage stood on the opposite side of the road, and as she cut down toward the village, leaving the hump of Rozebuzzan behind, Jos appeared on the rim of the slope, carrying a bag of groceries.

She stopped, alighted quickly, and holding Bess by the reins, said, as they came face to face, "Jos, I must speak to you."

"Why?" he asked truculently. "It seems to me there's nothing to talk about."

"But there is. There is. After what we've been to each other how can you bear me such a grudge? You

271

knew I only stayed behind because of my father, and because I. . ."

"Because you wanted to. Aye. I know that all right," he agreed. "And I didn't really blame you. You were fond of your father and it was a shock, enough to break any girl's nerve for a time. But I told you I'd be back. And I came. Not only on account of my mother, but for you. So what d'you think I felt like when I heard 'bout the wedding? And not only that—the other."

"What other?"

He laughed derisively. "You know full well what I mean. Your little games and trap to catch a rich man— sneakin' off like any fancy woman, dressed up in your ill-gotten finery. News gets around, Donna, and I had the lot, I can tell you."

Anger flamed in her. "I'm sure you did, and a whole lot of lies into the bargain. I took on a perfectly straightforward domestic post at Polbreath if you must know. Because I had to. For money, to save the mine, or didn't that occur to you? No. Obviously it didn't. Maybe if you'd thought about me a little more, and your own father too—you could have stayed in Cornwall and been some help to all of us."

There was a silence after her outburst while his face slowly relaxed from condemnation to discomfort. Then he remarked with an effort, "I was too quick in what I said, perhaps. If I was mistook, I'm sorry."

"All right." She smiled, offering her hand. "We're friends again then Jos?"

He pushed it away abruptly. "We were never friends, Donna, except as young ones. Let's not rake up old intimacies. Whether I should've stayed here or not doesn't matter any more. What's done's done, and when you once realize it, it's queer how the past can't hurt any more. Folk change. And lookin' at you now I feel as though I'd never known you."

"Perhaps you didn't," she said, "or I you. But at the time . . ." she broke off lamely, knowing that what he'd said was true. The thought saddened her, and for a moment regret touched her—regret for the sentimental

272

illusions of girlhood and their mutual dream which had floundered in the face of reality.

Then just as quickly, remembering Nicholas, she knew it was all for the best. Marriage to Jos would have been doomed to failure. She had never loved him. Nor ever could.

And he? Perhaps at last he realized how frail the fabric of their romance had been. He straightened himself suddenly, thrust his hand out and said, "All right. Let's shake then. I reckon I've made a fool of myself. But most men do at some time in their lives. So no hard feelings, eh?"

"None," she said, feeling her fingers enclosed briefly in his own sturdy palm. "And good luck, Jos, I hope you'll be as happy as I am. One day I'm sure you will."

"Maybe," he answered. "There's no telling; you can only hope."

The next minute he had gone and she had ridden away along the path to Gwynvoor.

Later that day, after she had returned to Polbreath, she told Nicholas of the meeting, and could see from his frown that he didn't like it.

"You went that way on purpose I suppose?"

"Not exactly. But I was pleased to see him," she admitted.

"Why?"

"Because I don't like bad blood between the Craze family and me, and because I have every right to make peace with an old friend, I think."

He gripped her wrist harshly. "You have no right to make contact at all with any man knowing full well I'd object," he told her, "and if it occurs again you'll be sorry. Do you understand?"

Her cheeks flamed. "No. You can't threaten me like a child with a spanking. I'm your wife."

"Wives, too, can be beaten when they deserve it," he said grimly.

She laughed uncomfortably. "Oh Nicholas. Really. Don't be quite such a martinet." She went up to him cajolingly, placing both hands on his shoulders, her eyes so bright and brimming that he weakened, though his lips were still stern.

"I love you," she told him softly, but with emphasis. "And you know it, or should . . . love . . . love . . ."

Suddenly his mouth was on hers, his heart pumping heavily against her breast. Then he lifted her in his arms and carried her upstairs, knowing that only by passion could he erase the ugly wave of jealousy that had so irrationally seized him.

CHAPTER NINETEEN

In order to distract Donna's thoughts from the closing of Wheal Faith, Nicholas arranged as much social activity as possible that autumn, both at home and in London, where he took her again in early October, knowing how she would enjoy flaunting her charms from a box at Covent Garden. Nicholas, well aware of her sneaking vanity, and amused by it, would flatter her simply for the pleasure of seeing the light in her strange eyes deepen from orange-brown to the fiery glow of copper touched by sun, and the gratified tilt of her exquisite mouth before she said, "Oh Nicholas, you're *teasing*. It isn't true. I'm not beautiful at all. Not really."

Underneath her shy modesty he knew that there lurked the rebellious wayward young witch he'd fallen in love with, and who, although he had not completely tamed her, was submissive now. How long it would last, he thought frequently, heaven alone knew. But at the moment all was on an even keel between them. Even Lucien had apparently gone back to Paris for good.

Lucien worried Nicholas more than he admitted. Not only because there had always been a lack of understanding between them since his half-brother's earliest years, but because of Lucien's inclination to seek the company more of fops and dandies than of what Nicholas regarded as sensible men and women. Donna was the exception, and it was a damned nuisance, Nicholas thought frequently. If it had been with anyone else he would have been delighted to see Lucien behaving like an ordinary, well-balanced young man. But where his wife was concerned he felt only irritation and mild dis-

275

gust. But Donna evinced very little interest in Lucien's activities, expressing only a flicker of surprise when she was told of an impending exhibition at a certain Paris salon which included two paintings by a young English artist, Lucien Trevarvas.

"Really," she said, over-casually. "How nice for him."

After a quick, shrewd glance, Nicholas continued perusing the letter from his brother, then said, "I'm rather surprised he never wanted to paint you. Or did he?"

"Oh. . ." Donna paused before answering lightly. "Yes, once, just casually he mentioned it. But it didn't happen. Anyway, I'd be a wretched subject to paint. Can you imagine me sitting still, posing, with a rose in my hand or something, trying to look soulful, with my eyes toward heaven?"

"No," Nicholas answered bluntly. "But I can imagine you setting out to madden any male admirer just for sheer devilment. And don't tell me you haven't had admirers. You must have started charming them from the moment you were born."

Donna smiled. "I believe I was rather good at it. I remember I generally managed to get what I wanted."

"Well, see that you reserve your charming for me in the future." Nicholas said dryly. "And for the children when they come home."

Jonathan and Ianthe had both gone to boarding school for the autumn term, and were not expected back until November.

Nicholas was grateful for the chance to start life with Donna on an even keel. But why he still employed Miss Pullen, Donna could not understand. His lame excuse that the children could be devilish little pests when they wanted to be, and that he wouldn't want her to be worried by his two brats in her first six months at Polbreath, didn't really impress her.

"*Worried*?" she questioned sharply, "don't you think I'm capable of managing two children? What a ridiculous idea. Keeping the . . . the Pullen in charge to poke her nose in, is only going to delay my chances of getting to know them properly. Surely that's the business of stepmother?"

"It's all settled," Nicholas said abruptly. "If things are peaceful between you we'll discuss Agatha's position later."

"*Agatha*? Oh, I see. It is Agatha. I always wondered if there were quite the cold-blooded relationship between you as you made out."

He laughed. "I'm surprised at you, Mrs. Trevarvas, being jealous of a thin-breasted pale, poor creature like Miss Pullen."

"Thin-breasted. Is she? You can never tell with the clothes these days. And pale women are sometimes the most passionate underneath I've heard," she was about to add more, when there was a faint tap on the half-open door, and Agatha Pullen herself entered. Her narrowed eyes shot green fire at Donna. "Can I speak to you Mr. Trevarvas?" she asked pointedly.

"Certainly. Do come in."

"Alone, if you please."

"I think not, Miss Pullen," Nicholas said suavely. "Anything that has to be said can be told in the presence of my wife."

"Very well." With tightened lips and breathing heavily, the governess waited a moment before continuing, "Ianthe is back."

"What?"

"Your daughter has just arrived by private chaise, from Penzance station in the company of a mistress. There has been some kind of trouble I believe."

"Good God. So soon. Where is she? Or rather, they?"

"In the study. Naturally I wished to inform you privately."

Nicholas sighed heavily. Women! he thought irritably. What the hell had the young termagant been up to?

"All right," he said. "I'll go and see them now. Donna . . ."

Donna hesitated. "I think Miss Pullen is quite right," she told him. "It's your affair, not mine."

"Forgive me, then, if I contradict you. As my wife,

you should be present at discussions involving my daughter, who is now also your stepchild."

So, regardless of Agatha Pullen's hostility, Donna followed Nicholas to the study. Ianthe looked very young, woebegone, and rebellious. With the faint smear of tears still on her face, she was standing by a stern-faced figure in black who had the child firmly gripped by the hand. Ianthe broke free as her father appeared.

"Oh father. It's been horrible," she cried. "They make you get up early and wash in freezing water, and do scales on the piano until your hands won't move. And if you can't learn your lessons they have a little stick. And everyone has to march with books on their heads. And . . . and the girls are horrible. They tease and pinch you, and if you scream they say it's your fault. I hate school. I loathe it. I won't ever go back . . . ever, ever. Please don't make . . . if you're bad, only a *bit* bad you have to stand in a corner for hours and hours . . ." she broke off, sobbing again, her head crushed against her father's legs.

There was a pause, until Nicholas said in an emotionless voice, "Stop crying Ianthe. Go and sit down. Now, please, Miss . . . Miss . . . ?"

"Miss Frayne," the cold voice said precisely. "I'm the housekeeper at the school, and have been requested by Miss Perkins, the headmistress, to bring Ianthe home. It's been a very distressing decision to take. But in the circumstances . . ."

"What circumstances?"

"Ianthe is a very difficult, extremely obstinate and unruly child. Her behavior, especially lately, has been such that Miss Perkins felt, and quite justly I must stress, that she is not a desirable pupil for Greystones."

"Not suitable? What the devil do you mean, ma'am?"

"To begin with, she won't learn, she won't adapt, or react to even the most severe discipline. Only yesterday her tantrums ended in a frightful scene when the French mistress had her face scratched and one leg so badly kicked that it has to be bathed, and soothing liniment applied to bring out the bruises."

Though Nicholas's voice was stern, there was a flicker of amusement in his eyes when he said to his daughter. "Well Ianthe? What have you got to say for yourself?"

"I hate them all," Ianthe said very distinctly. "If I have to go back I'll kill myself."

"There's no question of her coming back," Miss Frayne snapped. "The school will not accept her under any circumstances. She is expelled."

"Expelled?" Nicholas's voice now was ominously cold, his expression dark and set with anger. "Repeat that will you?"

"I don't think I have to," the woman answered, taking an envelope from her bag. "It's all here, in a note from Miss Perkins herself."

She handed the letter to Nicholas, who read it with the color darkening in his face. Then he said, "Donna, take Ianthe to Miss Pullen will you? I'll deal with this myself."

When the door had closed behind his wife and child, Nicholas tore the paper to shreds and dropped the pieces into a wastepaper basket. "Now," he said, "I shall reply to this—lady—myself, to the effect that the word expulsion is a misnomer and an affront. My daughter is not expelled, nor ever could be by a crowd of stupid, ineffectual women who cannot even control one small girl. I happen to be on intimate terms with Sir James Penverrys, who has, I believe, considerable influence at Greystones. If a note of apology withdrawing this contemptible expulsion order is not received by me during the next week, I shall see to it, ma'am, that no person of any social standing will remotely consider sending any child, in the future, to your school. In fact the name of Greystones will become a laughing stock and scandal throughout Cornwall. Do you understand?"

The woman's face, which had blanched, showed no sign of returning color, when she answered, with a faint tremor in her voice, "You have made it perfectly clear Mr. Trevarvas. But none of this is in my hands. I am merely a—a mouthpiece. I have to do what Miss Perkins asks me."

"I don't give a damn, madam, what Miss Perkins expects you to do," Nicholas said bluntly. "Just sit down if you don't mind, your presence offends me."

Smothering an angry retort, the black-clad figure seated herself stiff-backed on the edge of a chair, while Nicholas wrote a tersely worded letter to the effect that he had been shocked by the school's disgraceful attitude to his child, and an apology was expected immediately. Meanwhile Ianthe would be withdrawn from Greystones and her education undertaken elsewhere under more responsible tutelage.

Then he handed it to the woman, whom he privately considered a dragon of the worst order, with the words, "Now, if you'll excuse me, I have much to attend to."

He bowed slightly, as she passed through the door, an erect formidable black shadow of a creature, with not an ounce of femininity about her. What a farce the whole thing was, he thought, as the latch clicked. And what a fierce little virago he had for a daughter.

He found her presently in the conservatory with Donna and Agatha Pullen. She ran to him, with upturned eager face, huge eyes brimming with half joy, half fear.

"I'm not going back am I? Am I?"

Nicholas shook his head. "In the future you will stay here—at hand—until you're old enough to have learned what living in a grown-up world means. But no more tantrums, understand? No kicking or screaming, or I'll wallop you myself, as I walloped Jonathan when he was your age."

"Yes father," Ianthe said meekly, smiling. "I'll be very good. As good as . . . as . . ." she broke off, struggling for the right simile.

"As good as you can be," Nicholas finished for her. "That's all right then. "Now . . ." turning to Agatha, "take her upstairs, Miss Pullen, and see that she is neat and clean and prettily dressed before she comes down to meet her new mama."

Ianthe's eyes widened. "New *mama*?"

"Yes. This is your new mama." Her father held out his hand toward Donna. "We were married soon after you went to school. And I shall expect you to be good friends. Or else I'll want to know the reason. Do you hear?"

Ianthe nodded. But her eyes were stony, and her mouth sullen as Miss Pullen led her away.

"Oh dear," said Donna. "I'm afraid it was rather a shock. She didn't like it."

"She will," Nicholas answered firmly. "When she learns the alternative."

"Which is?"

"That she'll be sent off somewhere else without more ado. A real school this time, where unruly children get what they deserve and are not given the chance to kick frustrated females' shins. Heavens! What a sight it must have been."

Donna laughed. "I really rather believe you enjoyed that little interview.

"In a way I did," Nicholas admitted, "despite the blackmail."

"Blackmail?" Donna's voice was sharp.

"Not a very pleasant word I agree," Nicholas replied. "But necessary sometimes when a tricky situation has to be resolved—in this case just a noble name flung out at a propitious moment. The stupid creature was scared as a rabbit when I mentioned James."

"Penverrys?" Donna said mechanically, though her thoughts were not really on the subject of Ianthe any more, but on another . . . memory revived by the mention of blackmail. *Jed.*

"Yes, our good friend Sir James."

"Oh."

Donna's first sympathy for Ianthe had turned to subconscious resentment. The child's appearance had caused not only turmoil in the house, but reminded her once more of the shadow that hung over her life. For the first time she wished Nicholas had not been married before, and that there were no children to interrupt

281

their relationship. She wasn't jealous; after all, who could be jealous of a dead woman, a woman who in life had apparently been such a chill and ineffectual character? But if Ianthe's stormy nature were going to provoke discord, then she had a right to resent her.

The next instant Donna knew that she was being unfair. It was not the child's fault that she had been drawn into such a distressing and compromising situation with Lucien, or that Nicholas happened to be over possessive. Not Ianthe's fault either, that Jed had so easily intimidated her into paying out for something that was not really her fault. Perhaps if she'd had more courage she could somehow have been honest with Nicholas, have laughed away the whole unsavory episode as a ridiculous farce.

But then what man in his senses—especially a shrewd, worldly-wise character like Nicholas—would see anything farcical in the spectacle of his wife lying naked on a lonely beach, with his own brother atop of her? The mere thought of it now was as absurd to her as it was revolting. The idea of Nicholas getting to know terrified her, and during the period following Ianthe's return the feeling intensified.

Whenever she rode to Trencobban, which was most days, she had the lurking fear that Jed might appear. She imagined him coming toward her from the moor, or around a corner of the house, a threatening lustful figure with an additional card in his hand to play—revenge on the last of the Penrozes for his disfigurement.

The mine, which had once been the symbol of so much to both Jed Andrewartha and Donna Penroze, was now no more than an empty shell. The mine-house itself was still a fine looking building, with its rounded arched doorway, windows, and modestly ornamental façade. But the inside, though still shining and untouched by encroaching time, was dead.

Donna frequently wandered round there, staring with morbid fascination on this relic of Penroze history, thinking back to childhood, to the day of her father's death, and to Jos's departure for the Americas. She recalled, also, his last barbed comments when he had brushed her aside so contemptuously on the moor . . . "sold yourself like any whore to the richest bidder." The words filled her with shame, however untrue they were.

But she never brooded long. And after a chat with Sam and Sarah, a share of Sarah's home-brewed elder wine and slice of fruit cake, she generally took off for a sharp ride on Saladin which for a time swept unpleasant memories and imaginings from her mind.

Sarah and Sam told her that they were quite content to be with Ted at Trencobban for the time being, and would take their holiday a little later, when the weather was better. This cheered Donna. Everything except for Ianthe's intermittently sullen moods seemed domestically satisfactory, both at Trencobban and Polbreath. Beth and Phyllida had settled with the minimum of difficulty into their new duties, and there was no cloud on the horizon, except Jed.

And Jed it was, who finally and irretrievably brought past events with terrible impact into the open, causing the darkest period in Donna's life.

It happened toward the middle of December, when high gales lashed the Cornish coast, driving a fleet of sullen clouds above a darkened sea. Trevarvas had been edgy all through the day, pacing to and fro at intervals, cursing the damned wind and all it could mean to those at sea, refusing even through those restless hours to be cajoled by Donna into lovemaking.

Donna was puzzled for she felt quite at ease herself. She knew that Jed had collected his due the previous day and would not be likely to trouble her in the near future. She tried to reason with Nicholas, shutting the curtains willfully even before it was dark, saying, "Why have we got to stare out at that gloomy scene? What's the matter with you Nicholas? It isn't as though you've got a boat floundering anywhere." She paused before adding, "Or is it?"

He swung round. "What do you mean?"

"Oh darling." She laughed softly. "You've always told me not to pretend. But that's just what you're doing, isn't it? Do you think I haven't realized for some time now, that you and Sir James and . . . and others . . . including that Welshman Owen were involved in something a little dubious? What is it? Brandy? Silks? Tobacco maybe? Come on now, tell me. I don't blame you. I rather enjoy adventure. Surely to goodness you know that."

Her voice was so soft, so pleading, so amused, that he took her by the shoulders and stared deep and long into her eyes. As usual, the mischievous deep amber glow of them caught him unawares and so completely, that before he knew it his lips were on her mouth, his hands round her body, holding her close against him, until desire once more flamed into passion. After that long, heady embrace, they went upstairs and were one again in the wild abandon and security of mutual need.

Never, she thought afterward, could there have been such fulfillment of the senses and the spirit as was theirs then. Never could any woman have belonged to a man so fiercely and completely.

"I do love you, Nicholas," she murmured later with her cheek against his. To which he said, knowing at that moment it was true, "Keep it up darling, and I may yet even become a gentleman."

She shook her head, smiling radiantly. "Please don't try. Because you see . . . no lady could possibly feel as I do."

They lay there for a while, content and at peace. Then presently he was on his feet again, looking down on her with a hint of irony on his face.

"Insatiable aren't you?" he said, bending and chucking her under the chin. "Well, so am I, thanks be to . . ."

"Not God," she interrupted mischievously, "to us."

"The flesh and the devil!" he added mockingly. "So be it. If I've got you, then damnation to the rest of it."

"I'm not sure that's not blasphemy," Donna said primly. "And I don't like that."

"Maybe not. But you like the rest of it well enough.

Now get up, sweetheart and behave like a respectable female, even if you're not one. I have to go out tonight for a while and must have my senses about me."

"Out?" Donna queried, adjusting her skirts and leaping off the bed. "In this downpour?"

Nicholas, parting the curtains, looked out. "Whatever it's like, my love. And it so happens the rain has stopped and the wind is dying, which will make things considerably pleasanter."

"But why tonight?" Donna persisted. "Tell me; you must."

"There's no must about it. My business is my own affair. The house is yours. Now don't get tedious, Donna. Of all the aggravating things in the world an interfering woman is the worst."

"Oh very well. If that's your attitude," Donna said sharply. "Personally I don't consider it at all chivalrous for a husband to take off just after—after what we've had. Isn't that how men treat London tarts? Into bed and out again, then 'Thank you very much that was quite pleasant' . . . and hey presto! the slam of a door and away he goes!"

"Maybe. But an experienced London tart knows her business and how to behave when the fun is over."

Donna flushed. "Indeed! and now you're likening me to—to . . ."

Nicholas grinned, and suddenly swept her into his arms. "Stop it love. Don't tease me. When you look like that, with your eyes burning and that scowl on your delicious mouth I want to . . ." He broke off, with his jaw tightening. "No more arguments, Donna. Be reasonable, will you?"

"And if I . . . ?"

"Ah but you will," he said, before kissing her. "Because I say so. And because it's important." He took her by the shoulders and studied her face intently. "I have to go, darling. Good God! The way you're carrying on, anyone would think I was about to meet my doom or something." He paused, adding after a moment, "Come on—what's the matter with you?"

"I don't know. I just . . . I just wish you'd stay in tonight," she said. "And I'm not trying to be awkward—I . . ."

"Whether you are or not, you're damn well succeeding."

"I've got a feeling," she said, touching her breast. "Here."

"Feeling? Of all the ridiculous notions." His voice had suddenly hardened, in the old way she remembered. His gaze narrowed as he contemplated the enormous eyes and willful small chin beneath the tremulous, tempting lips. She didn't answer.

He turned away abruptly, and as he carefully pinned his tie, said, "Why don't you read a book or something? as I said—I shan't be long. By the way—how did Ianthe behave today? To you I mean?"

"She was . . . normal, for her," Donna answered ambiguously. "It's obvious she doesn't like me. But then I wouldn't in her place."

"Hm. Don't worry. Everything will work out," he said, knowing himself how trite his own words sounded.

"I suppose so."

Pretending not to notice the dejected tone, he let his lips touch hers again briefly, and then he was gone. Presently she heard a rattle and distant sound of movement above the other sounds of the night. She went to a side window, from where she could see his dark figure astride Pluto cutting down the drive to the lane. An eerie circular moon had risen above the rolling galleons of black clouds. Fitful shadows seemed to be chasing over the sodden earth, clawing in fingered shapes toward the whipped skeleton trees and looming hills above. Nicholas's figure had soon receded and disappeared, but the sense of foreboding in her heart still lingered, filling her with deepening unease.

She tried to dispel it by forcing herself to dress in an amber colored gown that she knew Trevarvas liked, and after a time, hearing the wild drive of rain once more thrashing the windows, went downstairs to the library where a comfortable fire burned. But it was no use.

Even though she found a novel by Charles Dickens that she had been intending to read, she couldn't get immersed in it, and after a quarter of an hour or so wandered up to the nursery where Ianthe was having her supper with Agatha Pullen. She tried to be friendly, but sensed an air of hostility immediately, and knew that she was resented as a trespasser in a domain that was not hers.

So she soon left, going downstairs again, to the kitchen this time, where Beth and Phyllida were helping Cook prepare the meal.

"What a night," she said listlessly. And then with forced cheerfulness, "That smells so tempting." It would have done in the ordinary way but tonight there was no relish in contemplating food, only a dragged-out, empty feeling that unless Nicholas returned quickly she wouldn't be able to enjoy a mouthful of it.

Beth looked up, smiling, saying in her tactful way, "I'm learning so much about cooking from Mrs. Thornton; so is Phyllida. As I tell her, it's a great chance for her to get a knowledge of how things should be done—from an expert."

Jane Thornton, usually a dour, large presence with no smile on her face, signified appreciation by a faint deepening of the color in her face, and relaxing her habitual concentration on the job in hand by remarking, "Phyllida's a good girl. She'll learn. And everything's all right . . . mistress." The last word obviously cost her an effort, but once out, a sigh of relief heaved her ample bosom. "You'll be getting your dinner on time. Organization, that's what I always say. Organization's the principal thing in a kitchen."

"I agree," Donna said. "But—but don't hurry too much. Mr. Trevarvas—the master—isn't back yet. And—maybe I should wait for him."

"Oh no, madam," Cook said. "He wouldn't like that. 'See the mistress has her meal,' he said before going. 'I'm not quite sure when I'll be home.' And I always see his instructions are properly followed. So in another fifteen minutes it'll be on the table in the dining room. I shall have everything waiting in the oven for him. And if he's really late we shall be off to bed prompt at ten thirty, our usual hour. He'll get it himself then. It's routine, Mrs. Trevarvas, madam. An understanding between us, as you might say."

"All right," Donna agreed. "I wouldn't want to alter your normal pattern. I won't hinder you any more."

She left then, and wandered desultorily about the house for a time, going aimlessly from room to room, looking constantly at clocks. She glanced through different windows in turn, toward the fields and paddock on one side stretching away from the back of the house, then back again to the rain-washed drive, pale and desolate under dripping trees and bushes. Her eyes strained for a dark horseman to appear from the moon-streaked shadows—the one she longed so desperately to take her in his arms and tell her that all was well.

But he did not come.

She toyed with her food, secreting some of it in a paper, for one of the dogs, and afterward went upstairs again to watch and to wait, while the minutes ticked into hours and each second deepened the queer, instinctive dread in her heart. This time she couldn't relate it to any rational fear. It was just there . . . as it had been sometimes in the past, when disaster threatened those most dear to her.

Nicholas.

"Oh God," she prayed, unconsciously. "Please keep him safe."

By ten thirty-five the house was quiet, the servants already retired. She went once to peep in the oven. It was just as Mrs. Thornton had said, the meal was warm in a covered dish, ready for him to take out when he returned.

But he still didn't come back. And by then the storm had started up again, driving its fury against the walls of Polbreath, and its anger into her very nerves, straining them to the breaking point. She went upstairs to the bedroom, staring miserably at her own amber-clad figure in the lamplight. Beautiful. Yes, despite her anxiety and

288

the haunting sense of oppressive desolation in her, she knew she was still lovely. A desirable woman needing her husband's, her lover's arms, about her. But where was he? On what dark mission, that kept him so long from her side?

She was just thinking of going to bed and trying to sleep, when she heard at last, movement below, followed by the unmistakable tread of footsteps emerging from the stairs along the landing toward their room.

With her heart leaping she looked to the door.

It opened. And what she saw shocked her. He stood for a few moments motionless, swaying on his heels slightly, staring at her with dark, glowering eyes under his soaked hair. His coat and breeches were dripping. And as he moved inside, closing the door behind him, she caught the hot stinging waft of whisky in the air.

Involuntarily she got up from her chair by the dressing table, and took a step backward, toward the windows.

"*Nicholas*," she said. "Are you . . . ?"

He grinned. But the grin was somehow unpleasant, intimidating.

"Yes. It's me. Nicholas Trevarvas. Ever your devoted servant, madam." His voice held a sneer in it. His eyes, she noticed then, were heavily ringed and bloodshot.

"What's the matter?" she said sharply. "What? Why . . . you're drunk!"

Then he laughed, before quickly moving over to her and swinging her around by one arm to face him. "Not so drunk that I can't realize who and what I've married," he said. "He was there this evening, d'you understand . . . ?"

"No . . . no I don't. Who . . . ?"

"Who? Andrewartha, of course, spilling his guineas about, in his cups, describing, oh so graphically, how he got them, and why so delectable and virtuous a young madam as Mistress Trevarvas was only too eager to supply him with the wherewithal when necessary."

Donna flinched.

"You don't understand; you can't . . ."

289

"Don't I?" He pulled her by the neck of her bodice close against his flushed face, so that she could hardly breathe. "It's not really difficult, my dear. What I find so hard to stomach is that you could have deceived me so aptly, and for so long with your innocent airs and graces . . ." He broke off, breathing heavily.

"Nicholas . . . oh Nicholas . . ."

"Shut up, damn you, or by God I'll kill you. To think I took you on trust . . . married you, *loved* you . . . yes, even that. Love. Funny, isn't it? To have loved a lusting slut who could lie like a naked whore with my own brother, for any peeping Tom to get an eyeful. And don't tell me I lie. You know I don't. I've the garter to prove it—the brooch, and other things, as well as that terrified, cowed look in your lovely eyes. You don't deny it, do you, *do* you?"

When she didn't, he shook her so her jaws chattered, then he struck her viciously on one side of the face. *"That,"* he said "for deceiving me. And *that* . . ." striking the other, "for being a liar. *This* . . . my so beautiful Donna, for daring to expose youself like any tramp . . ." he tore the clothes savagely from her body, and then flung her face down on the bed, slapping her as though she was a child. Then he turned her over and took her, not in love, but in lust—hurting and tormenting her, until she moaned fitfully like a stricken animal while he muttered thickly, "Shut up! you . . . you unspeakable little cheat . . . unless you want the servants to hear. My God, keep your mouth shut, or I won't be responsible . . ." and as the dreadful scene continued, the room darkened, swung into focus again, then faded, alternately changing from light to shade through which her numbed senses registered nothing but shame, humiliation, and pain.

Then, at last, he released her and stood over her briefly, before pulling her to her feet again. "There," he said, pointing to her dressing-table chair. "Sit down, if it doesn't smart too much."

She reached automatically for her wrap, which he

tore from her. "Oh *no*, my darling. No clothes. Naked if you please, as Lucien had you . . ."

"He didn't. He . . ."

"Sit *down*."

She did so, trembling, seeing in the mirror, but hardly recognizing, her pale, tortured, tear-stained face and swollen eyelids.

"Now," Nicholas said, picking up her vanity case and handing it to her, "put it on. Thick and heavy my love, as befits your status."

As first she didn't understand, and when she did, couldn't accept what he meant.

"Oh please, Nicholas . . . please will you listen?" she begged, "If you only . . ."

"We've had far too much conversation in the past," he said. "Put it on. Or shall I do it for you . . . ?"

Mutely, she took powder from the bowl, and applied the rouge he was already holding to her cheeks, while he watched, saying at intervals, "Heavier my dear, heavier. And now your eyes. Go on Donna . . ." for the first time his own voice sounded distressed and tortured. "Cheeks, lips, eyes . . . the whole lot of it." Then, when she'd finished, "stand up now, and let me look at you in all your naked, painted glory."

With her legs shaking so much she could hardly stand, but she managed to get to her feet. She thought at first that she was going to faint. But she didn't, just clung to the chair back for a second until the giddiness passed. Then she said, "You're a beast, Nicholas Trevarvas. I hate you."

"Good. Compliment returned," he said. "Now I feel I really know you. Which is my due, I think, don't you? As reward for the high price I paid?"

He threw an undergarment into her face, turned away abruptly, and went to the door. Then he glanced back and said harshly, "Dress yourself. The charade is over. I shall sleep elsewhere tonight. And I advise you to get on your knees and thank God I didn't take your adorable neck between my two hands and strangle you."

291

Then the door clicked. He was gone.

Donna crept back to bed and for a period lay there, rigid and shamed, and feeling she wanted to die. But after a time, volition returned to her tired limbs. She got up, washed her face, and slowly dressed in her winter clothes, with a gray traveling cloak and hood. Then, without packing a bag, but pushing a handful of coins mechanically into her pocket, she crept softly downstairs. Without a thought for the future, except an instinctive desire to reach the sanctuary of Trencobban, she set off through the side door to the drive, keeping carefully in the shadows of the lurching trees until she reached the gates.

Once outside in the lane, she started running, and ran and ran, until all breath was drained from her lungs, leaving her sick and faint and on the verge of collapse. She leaned, hunched against a tree while the rain started again, but more thinly, moistening her parched lower lip. She'd bitten it in her distress and now it tasted faintly of blood.

She forced herself ahead again, tripping and falling once. She managed after a moment to get up and go on, but stumblingly, with her heart bumping unevenly against her ribs, her throat tightened, chocking ball of nerves and exhaustion.

Then, to the left of the lane she saw the dimmed flicker of a light. As she staggered ahead for a few yards more she realized that there was a fire burning fitfully from a recess in the undergrowth that lead to a wide farm gate darkened by high hedges. Above the spitting glow a tent was rigged, enclosing dark figures crouched around an iron pot. Travelers. Romanies perhaps, or ordinary working tinkers. It didn't matter. The smell of food curdled in the damp air, and a horse was tethered to a nearby tree, with a cart behind.

Donna lurched forward. "Please . . ." she gasped, before she fell. "Can you help me? Lend me your mare . . . I'll pay . . ." And then, with the world swimming around her, she heard a woman's voice saying strange words in a foreign tongue, followed by,

"Hush now. 'Tis a Gorgio one . . . bebee . . . thee's needin' rest sister? . . . Come thee . . ." And then a softness and silence, as peace fell, with strong arms lifting and carrying her to oblivion.

When she came to herself the rain had cleared with the characteristic unpredictability of Cornish weather, and the pale moon was clearly defined in the evening sky, which was showered by a myriad of stars. As her eyes focused, Donna's brain registered the parted tent and the curtain beyond, the endless night—the lights and pinpoints shivering through the darkness. Then a lean brown face came down to hers, hawk-nosed, with a straggle of gray locks half hiding her dark button eyes.

"Feelin' better is thee?" she asked. "From where comest thou chile? And where goest thee?"

"I want a horse," Donna said in an urgent whisper, remembering. "To get home before morning. I must go . . ." She forced herself to her feet, swayed at first, then found her balance, "Look," she said, taking coins from her pocket, "I can pay."

The old crone pushed her hand away roughly. "We take no gold from thee, daughter. To all who come for gago help, we say God speed, and heaven protect thee."

"Romanies are you?" Donna said.

"Aye gago. 'Tis real Romans we be." The woman answered. "And you a fine gorgio lady by the look of thee."

"Not fine," Donna said mechanically, "And no lady. Just . . . just . . ." her voice trembled. The old creature took a hand in one of her dark gnarled ones. "Sit thee down daughter. A horse thee shall have, my son Chicknee's horse who will go with thee to thy home. But soup first to warm thy vitals."

She went to a pot and ladled a quantity of steaming liquid into a bowl. Handing it to Donna, she continued, "All will be well. Fire and flame I see . . . sadness and a great darkness of spirit. It is thy dukkerin, I tell thee. And the dukkerin dook has much to tell . . . no lies from bebee. Great truth only. Ease thy heart chile.

293

The shadow lifts. I see thee proud and happy and strong. Aiee . . . Aiee . . ." she broke off, rambling away in a wild tongue, then breaking again into English, calling, "Chicknee, Chicknee, come thee here."

A young, swarthy-looking man came around from the back of the tent. He had a bundle of sticks in his hand, which he threw by the smoldering fire. "What's this then, bebee?"

"The gorgio lady wants a horse, son. She shall have thine, for the dukkerin say so, and thou shalt lead her to her home on the moor."

Donna felt a stiffening of her spine, caused by amazement rather than fear.

"On the moor?" she echoed, "Who told you? How did you know?"

"Much is writ on thy face, daughter." The old creature said. "And we be Romans. True gagos. Don't question thy dukkerin; in an hour thou will be gone."

And it was so.

Shortly after twelve Donna, seated on a lean mare, was being led by Chicknee around the corner of the lane where it branched into the high road curving toward Trencobban. The moon had disappeared again, and she was thankful for the dark, although she wished that the gypsy had trusted her enough to let her ride by herself. She was desperate to arrive safely before Nicholas could follow.

But there was no sign of Trevarvas. No sound in the winter night but the wind moaning, and the rhythmic clip-clop of horse's hooves as they went silently ahead. The gypsy was as withheld and remote as though he was dumb.

Once Donna asked, "Where do you come from? And where are you going?"

"From places thee's no ken of, and we follow where the wind takes us," the youth answered. "Don't question me, sister. It's bad to question when only the dukkerin knows. Such things can lead to bitchady pawdel. So hold thy tongue sister, and let be."

Realizing that there was no point in trying to make

conversation with anyone who spoke such strange words, Donna huddled herself deeper into her cloak, and the journey continued with only darker shapes of rocks and the occasional tree looming against the darkness of the sky.

At last she knew from what her eyes dimly saw and her senses told her, that they were nearing the track leading to Trencobban. "It's down here," she said. "Drop me now. I'll walk the rest. Here," she handed him two coins, "thank you for your trouble and the loan of the horse."

He fingered the change hesitantly at first, then enclosed it furtively in his fist.

Muttering thanks in his own strange tongue, he was off a moment later. Donna did not wait to see his shadowed figure riding into the night, but hurried ahead, with the salty air from the sea already damp on her face. It seemed to wash some of the shame away, leaving behind a dull, unhappy anger, and renewed longing to be safe in the security of her own home.

When eventually she got there, strength had practically returned to her body. The house, bleak and sturdy in the wan night showed no signs of light or life, and she had no idea of the time, although it seemed, as her eyes turned seaward, that the first pale streak of dawn was lighting the horizon. But it was only a last fitful gleam of fading moon behind cloud, and she knew she either had to find somewhere to sleep in the stables or barn, or to rouse Sam and Sarah.

Too tired to think clearly she decided on the latter. The old couple would have to know in the morning, and Sarah would be more distressed to think of her young mistress enduring added discomfort, than by losing a few hours sleep herself.

So Donna went to the back, where Sam and Sarah had their own quarters, and hammered on the door, calling, "Sarah, Sarah, it's me, let me in, Sarah, Sam . . ."

Presently the sound must have penetrated. There was the grating of bolts being drawn, and a dazzle of quivering candlelight, as the hinges moved, revealing Sam's frowning broad face crowned by a night cap, and Sarah's, poked behind his shoulder.

Donna half fell inside against the sturdy male figure. A moment later Sarah had her arms around her and led her to the kitchen.

"Miss Donna, my dear saul. What's happened? What be wrong with 'ee . . ." she said, shaking her head, and drawing the young face to her heart. "There there. Something's frit 'ee. What is it, midear? You tell us. Tell Sam, an' he'll go for 'en with that theer iron bar in woodshed."

"No no," Donna answered, as the tears sprang to her eyes and broke free, coursing down her cheeks. "Don't ask me. It's no use. Nothing's any use. It's over."

"What my love? What?" Sarah persisted, easing her into a chair.

"My marriage. To . . . to him. That brute. Nicholas Trevarvas," she cried, in the first quick throes of reaction.

Sarah's tongue clicked against her teeth. "I knewed et. I always knowed et. But don't 'ee fret now. You just rest for time being. An' we'll let no one harm or touch 'ee, or get a sight of 'en, till you do want et. You'm safe now luvvie. Our own Miss Donna come back agen to the place where she should be. Her own home."

Ten minutes later Donna was upstairs in her old room overlooking the moors, where the bed was comfortably heated by the old brass warming pan, a hot brick, and a stone water bottle for her feet. Sarah had found a nightdress and woollen dressing gown left behind after her marriage, and on the dressing-table her father's photograph stood in its silver frame. Presently, when she was between the blankets and sheets, Sam came up with logs and coal to make a fire. Soon the room was responding to its glow, although Donna was still shivering from shock and the anguish of the night's events.

Eventually, however, she slept. And when she woke it was already past ten o'clock, with the winter sun lifting in a cold clear sky. She got out of bed and went first to one window, then to the other, where, in the clarity of the cold air, Wheal Faith stood dark and stark on the high ground immediately above the cliff. Bereft and empty now.

Like her heart. And her life.

And she was angered, not only by Nicholas, but by herself for feeling so utterly desolate. I'll never forgive him, she swore to herself, never, *never*. Her eyes now were hard and cold. Her mouth set, and mind resolved. Let him come and go on his knees to her if he cared to. She would scourge him with her contempt, so lash him with her tongue that he would never dare to look her in the face again.

But all the time, deep down, she knew such thoughts were useless. He would not come, nor plead with her. By his own words he had shown how much he despised and loathed her. In any case, Nicholas Trevarvas pleaded with no one. And neither would she.

"Don't let him in," she said, later, to Sarah. "And if he asks for me, say I never want to see him again."

"I'll do that mistress," Sarah retorted grimly, "an' so will Sam an' Ted. Have no fear, midear. We'll stay here together, as we used to be, an' 'tis my belief the spirit of the dear maister will be with 'ee too, helping you to youth again and a new future."

If only he could be, Donna thought, when Sarah had gone. But spirit was spirit, and flesh was flesh, and she could not, just then, envisage any future at all, without a man's love to sustain her.

CHAPTER TWENTY

During the days following Donna's flight from Pol-breath she stayed mostly indoors, venturing out only very occasionally in Sarah's company, to the moors and wild garden at the back, before returning quickly to the house for fear of any possible confrontation with Nicholas. She had half expected him to call within the first week, and was relieved when he didn't. Probably he no longer cared what she had done with herself or where she was. And that feeling, she told herself, she recip-rocated. She was wrong, of course. Sarah told her one day that his man had been inquiring from Sam, whom he'd met in Penzance, if the mistress meant to stay long at Trencobban? To which Sam had replied, "I've no knowledge of what be in Miss Donna's mind. But 'tis her house, and we be there to care for 'en."

So Nicholas knew. It didn't matter, just so long as she had no need to set eyes on him or submit to his bullying or pleas . . . no need any more to have her heart flut-tering every time she heard his foot on the stairs or the leap of anticipation when he lifted her into his arms.

Her hurt and humiliation were so great that after the first shock, her body felt curiously empty and drained of emotion. She didn't want him any more, and as the days passed, the memory of physical passion only caused her cold revulsion. If she'd seen him at that time, she would have felt no flicker of emotion—only hard dislike and a wish to see the last of him. Even the desire for revenge had not yet crystallized. Nicholas Trevarvas mattered not at all any more. She didn't even hate him. Something had died in her that night, taking her youth with it.

And so she spent her time wandering about the house, staring frigidly through the windows to the winter sea, and from the other side toward the bleak moors, or helping Sarah, when she was inclined, with the household chores.

Sarah noticed, and was worried. "There's somethin' more at the back o' this than a mere quarrel Sam," she said. "I never liked that theer Trevarvas, but I'd rather her a spittin' an' sparrin' with 'en than going on as she be now—so hard an' unforthcomin'. Ef only she'd say somethin'! Ef she'd confide now, as she did when she was a little thing, I could maybe give a bit o' comfort. But what can anyone do when she holds herself back so, all proud and set, an' with never a word?"

"She's a child no more," Sam said. "Let events take their course. 'Tes all we can do, wife. Things'll work out one way or other in the end, and et's no business of ours to force et."

"Ef you ask me," Sarah said darkly, "that man's done somethin' unspeakable. Remember what they did used to say 'bout the other one? . . . His first? Foxglove tea, they said. Foxglove tea."

"Quiet woman," Sam said, glowering. "Keep your woman's mouth shut on such matters. 'Twas only women started that sly talk. An' not a word of truth in et either. Don't go spreadin' unholy gossip, Sarah, or you'll make a deal of mischief that'll do nothin' but harm. An' doan' 'ee *think* of et either. Thought is mother to words. An' such thoughts as those are evil an' wrong. Lies, no more."

Sarah huffed, shrugged her shoulders, giving her short sharp cough of displeasure. "Well," she said, "it seems funny to me no sign or sight of that husband of hers have come during this last ten days. Not nat'ral. Say what you do like."

That same afternoon, oddly enough, Nicholas called, asking to see Donna. Sarah opened the door, and then, when she saw who it was, closed it again, leaving only a few inches between them. He looked strong and erect with his back to the light, a domineering figure in his buff coat and cream riding breeches. His appearance affronted her, and she set her chin stubbornly forward, not seeing the strained, haggard look of his countenance from the shadowed gloom of the hall.

"My wife," he said. "Mistress Trevarvas. She's here, I believe. Do you think ... . would you please ask if I could have a few words with her? I will not keep her long."

"The young mistress wishes nothin' to do with 'ee," Sarah told him bluntly. "Not a word or a sight, an' there be my instructions sir. Good day to 'ee."

She was about to close and lock the door on him when he put his foot in between. "I'd be obliged, nevertheless, if you'd give her my message," he said, "and take this note." He handed her an envelope, which Sarah took grudgingly.

"All right. But you wait here. I'll not have 'ee in disturbin' her."

"Don't worry woman. I've no fancy to trespass on your domain."

Grumbling under her breath Sarah withdrew, and returned moments later, saying, "I told mistress an' she says . . . she says . . . don't 'ee ever come here 'gain, Mr. Trevarvas. She doan' want 'ee an' won't see 'ee. An' ef you do so much as tek a foot inside she'll have 'ee thrown out."

Nicholas laughed shortly. "I think that would be extremely difficult. Nevertheless, have no fear. I've no liking to force my company on any sulking woman."

He turned abruptly, and walked to the left, where his horse was tethered. Almost immediately Sarah heard the sound of hooves receding up the drive, and presently, from a side window, watched him riding Pluto at a fierce gallop toward the high moors above the road.

Donna saw him too. There was no quickening of her heart, no stir of longing or affection. All that registered as she watched, coldly, from her bedroom, was raging, bitter dislike, and a sense of freezing triumph.

300

Then, when his figure had finally disappeared, she slit the envelope and read the note.

"Donna," it said, "However distasteful, I think there are matters we must discuss, which is why I am writing, in case you refuse to see me when I call.

"I am not going to express apology for my anger over your behavior with my brother, but I regret my manner of showing it, and hope very much that you will accept this as a possible basis for some sort of understanding between us. Incarcerating yourself at Trencobban cannot last forever, as you must know. Surely we can both attempt to behave as civilized human beings, and get things into perspective. I am hoping that you will agree, and, perhaps too optimistically, will send the chaise for you tomorrow, at about three o'clock in the afternoon. Think well before refusing, Donna. It may be our last chance.

Yours . . . as I always have been,
Nicholas."

The nerve of it, Donna thought, reading it through a second time. To think, after all that had happened that dreadful night, that he could inveigle her into a meeting obviously aimed at conciliation. She would never forgive him, *never*. Let him come on bended knee, beg, threaten, or plead till he was lost for words and breath, she would still dismiss him with contempt, have him wincing from her stinging tongue, as *she* had winced when he'd abused her.

For the first time since their parting, she felt the warm blood of life stinging her nerves. The devil. The brute! . . . Oh how she hated him. Hated him so much that she felt a wild desire in her again to ride Saladin until neither of them had the energy to go further—to fall, and have the earth beneath her taking her into darkness, and the death of all physical shame.

Then, as quickly, the impulse died. Resignation returned, with its sense of emptiness and recognition of hopeless future. When, next day, the chaise arrived, she sent Sarah to tell the man that she had no intention of visiting Polbreath, and to inform his master that there was nothing to talk about.

Christmas came. A shrouded lonely one, with strong winds and scattered snowfalls from the north that wrapped Trencobban in isolation and bleak unhappiness.

When the white drifts cleared from the icy ground, black patches lay between furze and stones, leaving the undergrowth and sparse trees hunched leanly toward the relentless Atlantic. Sarah, Sam, and Ted did their best to make the house hospitable and friendly, carrying in logs, holly, and mistletoe, which Donna helped to hang and arrange, thinking all the time what a travesty it was.

Parson Treeve called with a group of carol singers on Christmas Eve. Donna, trying to appear sociable, asked them in for a glass of cordial, and for a brief time the oppression seemed to lift. As Donna saw them off again into the windswept night, the vicar, as always, impressed by her beauty, and perhaps saddened by her icy distress, said confidingly in her ear, "I've heard things my dear. But don't fret too much. Many a seemingly tragic event, at the time, has had a queer knack of righting itself in the end. And God meant, surely, for you to flower, come springtime."

"Thank you," Donna said, knowing he had done his best, however futile it was.

She had cards from Zenobia Bray and Janey, the first a religious traditional one, the second, the picture of a kitten holding a card tied with blue ribbon saying, "Christmas love from me to you, lots of fun and pudding too." Signed "Janey," with the postscript, "we've got a kitty called Figaro."

So Janey was all right. Probably, Donna thought, Zenobia would wish to adopt her eventually, and that would solve the problem for good. Then another question struck her. How had they known she was at Trencobban? Reading the address again she saw that it had been forwarded from Polbreath, not in Nicholas's handwriting, but by the housekeeper. No doubt Trevarvas had gone away, to London, she decided, with a touch of irony, to confide his troubles to the ever-affectionate Regan Lamont. Or even to the Penverryses. How gratifying it would be to that insufferable Rosina and her odious mother when they learned that Nicholas's marriage was already on the rocks. Her only other correspondence was a brief note from Beth, sent from Plymouth, in which she said Trevarvas had told her she could stay on holiday until Donna's return, or come back, hoping it would not be too long, etc., and then an expensive card from Lucien, enclosing a letter.

"Dearest Donna," he said, "I have heard from old Nick that you are at loggerheads, and gather it was my fault. Don't take too much notice of his wild, melodramatic bravado. He was always a bully, and a bit of an ass. Sorry to have to say this, but I did warn you. And it was inevitable that one day our dire, dark secret must up and out. Believe me, the sooner it did, the better. Although you tried not to show it, I've known all along you've been living with a ghost, ever since my unspeakable behavior in the cove, and after all, what did happen of any consequence? Only a revelation to my cost, of my own shame. I don't like going back in this way. But I have to, for your own sweet sake, simply because I've come to the conclusion you two were meant for each other. You're both fighters. Both overbearing in your own individual ways, though I must confess that what in you is acceptable, seems ridiculous and unworthy in a man who also happens to be my brother. I intend shortly to come to Polbreath, and will do all in my power to put things right.

"Take care of yourself. It should not be long before we meet,

"Ever your devoted Lucien."

The card arrived late, two days after Christmas, followed at the end of the week by Lucien himself, who called unexpectedly at Trencobban on New Year's Day. He was carrying, as usual, a bunch of flowers. Hothouse roses, this time, which he handed to her as soon

303

as Sarah had grudgingly shown him into the library and closed the door behind her.

"Donna darling," he exclaimed, taking both hands, and kissing her lightly but lingeringly on her cheek. "How—how beautiful you look."

She gave a short, unbelieving laugh. "There's no need for compliments, Lucien. I have a mirror. I know how haggard and pale I am, and how thin."

"It suits you, though. You remind me of Bernhardt's 'Dame aux less Camellias.' So tragic . . . so sad and bereft."

"Oh Lucien." Her voice had an edge to it. "Do stop. Sit down. And have a drink will you? Madeira?"

"*Certainement, merci,*" he answered, continuing, as she poured the wine, and passed a glass to him, "You're wrong, you know darling. Much as I hate to admit it. Quite, quite wrong."

"I don't know what you mean," she said, armoring herself against any intercession on Nicholas's behalf.

"You should meet him, Donna," he told her in more practical tones. "His bark's always worse than his bite—I'm referring to my brother, of course. We had a hell of a row, naturally, when I returned yesterday, but when I wouldn't resort to fists, swords, pistols, or a general punch up, he soon calmed down—and when I explained, he dried up completely. In fact if you ask me he was not only staggered, but ashamed. He went quite—dumb."

"I'm not interested in Nicholas's reaction," Donna said coldly, "neither do I want you here pleading for him. What happened—happened. And nothing can alter it."

"Would you like to tell me what exactly did happen?" Lucien said, with one eyebrow raised quizzically. "He didn't beat you up exactly, did he? Or . . ."

His voice wavered with a question, to which she answered tersely, "No. Not exactly. But if you persist in asking me about Nicholas, Lucien, I'm afraid I'll have to tell you to go." There was a silence, in which he couldn't help noticing her quickened breathing, the tumultuous rise and fall of her breasts under the green cloth bodice, and that the lines of her neck were tensed and strained, her fists clenched at each side of her thighs, with the nails biting into her palms.

"Well—if that's how you feel, I suppose I must drop the subject," he said.

"Yes."

"A pity. Nevertheless . . ." He got up, moved toward her, and putting his glass down, lifted one of her cold hands to his lips. "I shall always be at your service, whenever and if you need me. Will you promise to remember that?"

She nodded mutely. And a few minutes later he had left.

Donna walked to the window slowly. She looked out upon the gray vista of darkened, skeleton trees against the lowering winter sky, glanced instinctively to her left where she knew, in the distance, Wheal Faith also stood, alone and as bereft as life, as she now felt. Alone, yet still remembering. Remembering the days and months of the last few years when her father, and then she herself, had so fought to keep it a living part of Cornish history. How brief the last optimistic struggle had been. How brief indeed was all life itself in the face of time. A few decades ahead, and she herself would be old, having accomplished nothing of worth, not even a fruitful marriage to carry something of the Penrozes into what should have been a rich and worthy destiny.

Suddenly, and without any warning, a wave of sickness washed over her, with it an unadmitted secret flood of knowledge. She made her way unsteadily to a chair, where she sat, waiting for the feeling to pass. She had practically recovered when Sarah, after a short, sharp knock entered.

"What's the matter with 'ee?" she queried, noticing the frightened eyes in the pale strained face. "Ill ar ye? Or be et . . . ?" The question died on her lips, as a hand went to her mouth. "Oh. Surely et bean't . ."

"No, no," Donna exclaimed. "Don't go getting ideas, Sarah. I shall be annoyed if you start probing and ques-

305

tioning. It's reaction that's all. I've been under a strain."

"If you'd tell me about et, et'd help," Sarah said huffily. "Why you have to go shutting things inside of 'ee like as ef you hadn't a soul to turn to's beyond me."

Donna reached out and touched her hand. "One day perhaps. Or some of it. And I'm not alone. While I have you I know at least there's one good friend—two, with Sam, to rely on. So please . . ."

Unable to resist the plea, Sarah relaxed. "All right my love, if that's how you do feel. But you take care of yourself, understand?"

Donna smiled. "I understand."

At the end of the month the weather softened a little, and in sheltered spots of Trencobban's wild garden, snowdrops starred the earth. At the front of the house, before the slope of land stretching to the road and lush moors above, even a few optimistic primroses and celandines came into bud, heralding spring in the months ahead. But Donna's heart did not relax. Her body was still rigid and joyless, except for these occasional moments when it seemed to her that an alien force was stirring her innermost being.

Once, accompanied by Sarah, she ventured out to visit a few of the outlying cottages of Gwynvoor where miners and their families still lived, hoping for the miracle that never happened—for some stroke of good fortune that would set Wheal Faith working again. Though polite, the men had a hint of aggression in their eyes— the women, though set-lipped and on the defensive, were doing their best to accept graciously any help Donna provided, whether in cash or gifts of food. Many of the mine's former workers had left and gone Penjust way—some farther afield. The ones who remained existed on Parish relief, Union assistance, and whatever charitable help was forthcoming.

Once, to her great distaste, Donna met Jed, as he was returning from a visit with Paynter to Penzance. He glowered at her, but his glance was furtive, sliding away quickly. She didn't know whether or not Nicholas was still paying the compensation, but guessed that he still might be, on account of the frail, sick wife, whom she had heard had not very long to live.

Nicholas. She could not entirely dismiss him from her mind. As time passed it was not the physical side of marriage she missed, so much as the emotional and mental impact of his presence. She had no one to dress for any more—no one to tease or spar with—no one to quicken her blood with the deepening dark glance of desire, or to ride with over the wild Cornish terrain. But the hatred in her, instead of lessening with the recovery of her vitality, only grew in intensity and with it an increased determination never willingly to set eyes on him again.

He called twice more at Trencobban asking to see her, but finally accepted without another word Sarah's assertion that the mistress wished no contact or word with him. He walked away abruptly, head up, shoulders squared rigidly in a manner that told the old servant they'd see no more of him.

After that there was silence from Polbreath, until a letter addressed to Donna in Nicholas's handwriting was delivered by Trevarvas's man. He told Sarah politely enough, with no shadow of expression on his face, that the master would be obliged if Mistress Trevarvas would read it at her earliest opportunity as it contained news of some importance. He then left.

Grumbling under her breath, Sarah went upstairs and handed the letter to Donna, who first went cold then had an unexpected fit of trembling that she did her best to disguise by a terse, sharp reply.

"All right," she said, "Thank you."

Sarah hesitated, hoping for a glimmer of information, but realizing that it would not be forthcoming, withdrew slowly, closing the door behind her.

Donna opened the letter.

"Donna," it said, "I am leaving tomorrow for London where I shall stay for at least a month. Therefore if you feel inclined to return to Polbreath for a time, you have the opportunity now, without the fear of encountering my hateful presence. There must be clothes and

307

other things you wish to collect, and also may I remind you—note that I say *may*—that Mrs. Paynter is somewhat confused and worried by your absence. I have had to admit that there has been something of a disagreement between us, keeping it in as light a tone as possible, but that you will doubtless be returning in the near future to discuss with her any plans for the future. She is, after all, a personal servant of yours.

"Doubtless by now you will have found enough strength to handle the affair with tact.

"I'm sorry you had not the courage to meet me face to face. It is extremely unlike you. However, your refusal to do this has left me in no doubt at all concerning your attitude to me. I can assure you I accept that all is over between us.

"Incidentally, your allowance, and for those of your dependents and the upkeep, etc., of Trencobban will continue as it has done up to date. John Crebbyn is aware—though not of details—of constraint between us, and has been informed by me to let you draw anything you need, above the amount up to a reasonable sum.

Take care of yourself,
    Yours,
    Nicholas"

Donna let the letter fall from her fingers to the floor. Such desolation engulfed her that she felt nothing in the world mattered any more.

Over. That one word was so final, so complete, and so utterly without hope that it was as though a limb had been torn from her body leaving it one vast ache. Without realizing it, the constriction of her throat brought a rush of tears to her eyes, but they did not fall. She would not weep, she told herself relentlessly. Why should she ? Over *him*? And what use was self-pity? In time she would recover and be her own self again. She wasn't poor. She was young, with years ahead in which to recarve her existence. She could do what she wanted: travel if she wished, and perhaps one day she would meet someone else . . . *No*. Not men, never again, ex-

308

cept to admire her from a polite distance, pleading for favors which she would throw back in their faces. Never more would she surrender herself to desire. The dark horseman of her imagination had effectively killed all wish in her to be possessed. She would be herself, and free, and because of it would shower contempt on any man who sought love from her.

Occasionally when she was honest with herself, she admitted that she was not proud of her own image. Even her looks had altered. From being a changing, vital creature of light and shade, and winsome, if willful moods, she had become haughty and self-contained— bitter and proud looking, with set lips and cold, steady eyes which looked more like iced peat-pools of darkness than the deep orange of sunlight on beech leaves. She could no longer bear to look on her naked body when she undressed herself for bed, neither could she contemplate the notion that Sarah's half-worded suggestion could be true. The mere thought of bearing a child— especially Nicholas's, somehow outraged her. So she refused to believe it, disregarding intermittent attacks of faintness, and telling herself that they were merely the result of her unhappy experiences.

The thought of returning to Polbreath for even a short period was abhorrent to her, but she recognized that she did have a certain obligation to Beth, and that, as Nicholas had said, there were clothes and belongings to collect. At least there she could also be free from Sarah's speculations and probings for a bit.

Two days after Trevarvas's departure therefore, she told the two old servants that she was returning to Polbreath for a possible three weeks' stay. To which, after a thoughtful pause, Sarah said, "Well then, if that's what you've decided, Miss Donna, how would et suit 'ee ef Sam an' I an Ted also had a bit of a holiday? We could go to our relations, Truro way. An' ef 'ee be comin' back in three weeks, a fortnight would give us time to be back a few days before en' just to get things fit an aired right."

Donna agreed. "A good idea Sarah. I'm sure it's time

you had a change from my—my moods and depressions. Yes. Go. I shall be returning to Polbreath on Friday. So if Sam drives me over first you could all three go on to the station afterward. You could arrange with Paynter to take you in, couldn't you? I shall know then that everything's locked up safely here."

"S'posin' you want to come back, mistress? To fetch anythin', I mean."

"I have my old keys. In a crisis I can always use them. But I hardly think that's likely. Anyway you must leave me your address so that I can contact you if necessary. And you know where I am. Cheer up, Sarah. We're not leaving Trencobban for good."

But as she spoke, the inexplicable shadow fell on her mind again, filling her with unease and a queer reluctance to leave. These gray walls which had held so much of her for so many years—the very ivy corroding the granite in parts—the wind-blown trees whose creaking and tapping at the windows had been a part of the gale-swept nights for as long as she could remember— why was it that they should suddenly seem to whisper their own foreboding and apprehension of disaster?

She was not superstitious. But the inward prophetic voice of childhood was strong in her just then, and in a moment of irrational desire for comfort she rushed upstairs to her room and took the photograph of her father from the dressing table and placed it in her valise, ready for packing with her things.

She had no doubts at all that Nicholas would be safely away when she arrived at Polbreath. Domineering and heartless he could be—and was. But a man of his word. So when she set off with Sam on Friday there was no worry in her mind that he'd be there, only a lingering reluctance at leaving Trencobban.

Sam, also, seemed a trifle sad at the parting when he left her with her bags, at the wide doors of the great house.

"Take care of 'ee-self Miss Donna," he told her, almost echoing, ironically, Nicholas's own words in his last letter to her. "An' no worryin' 'bout us. Sarah and

310

me'll be back two days or so before 'ee. You mark my words, an' we'll be glad to see 'ee back where you do belong—providin' o' course you choose to come."

"I shall," Donna asserted. "I've made all my plans, and know exactly what I'm doing."

He nodded, shook his head wryly, before getting into the carriage to drive back to Trencobban, and a moment later, after one last, quick glance at her, had flicked Bess to a canter down the drive, and was gone.

So everything was settled, Donna thought, as Trevarvas's man ushered her in before him, almost as though she was a visitor; every detail considered and in order. Ted would stable the mare at Trencobban for the night, then someone from Polbreath would fetch her the following day to join Saladin once more.

Saladin. The mere thought of him made her feel better. Her first instinct was to rush around to the stables immediately, but it was instantly quelled when the housekeeper appeared in the hall. Her manner was polite, restrained, and respectful. But her rather small eyes in their wrinkled folds of flesh emitted cold disapproval. Donna guessed that, although she could not possibly know the details of her hurried parting from Nicholas, she had drawn her own conclusions.

"Everything's ready in your room madam," she said coldly. "A fire has been burning since the morning and all is warm and prepared. Will you have tea upstairs or in the drawing room?"

It was on the tip of Donna's tongue to say that she would come down, remembering her last hateful experience in the large bedroom shared with Nicholas. Then the older woman continued quickly, "The master told me to have the rose room prepared. He thought that in his absence you might prefer it, it being cosier and a little more suitable for one person." Her lips folded primly again as she paused, waiting for Donna's reaction.

"Oh yes. Thank you," Donna answered with a feeling of great relief. "It's such a pretty room. And I'll have tea up there, if you please."

"Yes mistress." And to the man who was waiting nearby, "You know the bedroom. See there are sufficient logs in the bucket, and everything is in order. Meantime I'll go and see about tea. Early perhaps, but the light closes quickly these days, and no doubt you'll be glad of it after the journey."

"Yes," Donna answered, thinking how odd the words sounded. After the journey as though she'd traveled many miles to get there. Well, in her heart she had. Distance, after all did not seem at that point so much a matter of practical measurement as of feeling, and of entering another world from the old familiar one she had known and loved till then.

As the housekeeper reached the door, Donna said suddenly, "Wait . . . I mean . . ."

The woman turned. "Yes?"

"Will you please send Beth up," Donna said in firmer tones. "I would like to speak to her."

"Oh very well. Immediately?"

"Please," Donna said, refusing to be intimidated by the hard stare.

The door closed with a sharp snap, and a few minutes later Beth appeared, entering after a light knock.

"Beth!" Donna exclaimed. "How nice to see you. Oh thank goodness you're still here. I've wondered about you during these last few weeks." She paused, faintly taken aback by Beth's expression, by the dejection and sadness that overshadowed her. "Has everything been all right?"

"As right as things could be, without you, mistress," Beth answered. "Phyllida's happy. There's no problem. But your going so quickly left us all rather bewildered."

"I'm sorry."

"Especially the master," Beth ventured to say. "Oh, I know it's not my business, and you must forgive me for bringing the matter up. But naturally everyone's puzzled, and a bit upset. Mr. Trevarvas did assure me my position here was secure, and my daughter's, just so long as we wished to stay. All the same, when I came to Polbreath it was on your account chiefly, and with

312

Phyllida to consider I do want to feel she has a settled position.

"Dear Beth," Donna said, with momentary affection. "Of course. I do understand, but—you must try to, as well. I can't possibly explain the difficulties between my—my—between Mr. Trevarvas and myself. And I can't say exactly what's going to happen in the future, because I don't know. After a week or two, of course, I shall return to Trencobban. And if you want to join me there I'll be glad to have you. But probably you'd both have better prospects here. You see in a year or so—or rather less I'm sure, it's highly likely you'll be asked to take on the post of housekeeper here when Mrs. Thornton retires. So . . ." she broke off, sighed, and sat on the bed taking off her hat and jacket wearily.

Beth instantly took the coat and placed it on a hanger in the wardrobe.

"Don't worry," she said briefly. "I'd no business to worry you over my paltry affairs immediately after your return. Phyllida and I are both lucky to be here, and grateful, so please, mistress, forget about plans, and any bothering thoughts for the future. It's today that matters. And . . ."

"Tomorrow, and tomorrow," Donna said absently. "Yes. Very well. I don't think I can look ahead at the moment. Everything seems on top of me."

"No wonder. After your present trouble, and the mining business, and Mrs. Luke's death into the bargain. Far too much for—for one of your age. You should be carefree and enjoying this sharp fine weather. Why, do you know—this morning I found bunches of primroses growing where the frost had been only a few days ago. It's odd isn't it, how one day it can be wintry and the next filled with sun?" She paused, to continue, "A bit like life I suppose. A queer mixture of tragedy and happiness. You never know what's lurking around the corner."

Donna managed a smile. "That's how my father used to talk. I wish I could feel the same. The trouble is that it's all or nothing with me. I'm not wise or able to compromise. Not in anything."

"Maybe that's because you love too much," Beth said, showing no flicker of expression on her face.

"What do you mean?"

"My dear—and forgive me talking like this to one who's my employer—the heart's a very strange thing. Sometimes whatever the head says, it goes its own way, in spite of common sense. And no reasoning in the world's going to alter that. Well, perhaps it's right to be so. Living would be a dreary business without ups and downs, quarrels and makings up, only dull folk settle for an even keel—especially in youth."

Donna didn't answer, but from the expression on her face Beth knew that her words had gone home and a minute later she left, saying that she'd send Phyllida presently to attend her.

For the first time Donna took a real look at the room—at the brocade rose pink curtains, the pink upholstered walnut chaise-longue, elegant French chairs and fine lace bedspread over pink silk. She'd seen it before of course, but never entirely absorbed its luxurious femininity, simply because she'd been so preoccupied with Nicholas, and anyway it was a room generally reserved for guests. Now she wondered about it. Wondered who'd lain there before she left Trencobban. Regan perhaps at some time in the past? Or other women to whom he had taken a fleeting fancy, then left to go on their separate ways? No, somehow the picture didn't fit. His wife then? The cold Selina? Had she found refuge there when Trevarvas's demands had proved too much for her? Locked herself in this pink sanctuary like some frail, frightened creature retreating into its delicate shell? Without realizing it, a wave of jealousy flooded Donna's nerves and mind. Had he kept the room as it had always been, simply as a reminder, a kind of memorial to his first wife? Had he chosen to allot it to Donna now, merely to remind her that as far as he was concerned, she too might as well not exist?

She had an impulse to ring and tell the housekeeper

314

she would prefer after all not to sleep there, but return to the other, larger one—Trevarvas's. The softness and pinkness, the sheer luxury and comfort of this small domain somehow affronted her, evoking as it did an air of haunting or being haunted. It was as if another alien presence were lingering even now in the flickering shadows from the leaping firelight. Shadows that danced around the curtains and across the ceiling above, where flowers and cherubs were delicately entwined in an ornate frieze, and where delicate crystal glass quivered from the hanging chandelier.

Then common sense asserted itself. How ridiculous to imagine for one moment that she could bear to spend another night in that hated bedroom where Nicholas had so abused her. Anything was preferable to that. Anything.

But when she glanced at herself in the mirror, in an effort to tidy her hair, it seemed that someone was peering behind her shoulder—the ghost of her predecessor—pale, pathetic, only half defined, but triumphant, with a slight sneer on her lips.

Donna turned quickly, and for the first time noticed it—an oval portrait—fairly small, in a gilt frame hung on the wall to the left behind her, licked from shadows to sudden life by the firelight, and given a curious semblance of movement through the mildly contorted reflection.

She got up quickly, stared at it for a second or two with acute dislike mounting in her. Then she took a casual stool from a corner, stepped on it and lifted the portrait down. She had no intention of breaking it, but it was heavier than she thought, and perhaps because of her exhaustion, she overbalanced slightly; the stool slipped an inch or two, and although she contrived not to fall herself, the picture was jerked from her hand, catching the edge of a small table, and landed on the floor with the glass broken in several places.

Donna stared at it. Stared and stared. The jagged lines gave the delicate face a queerly satirical, lop-sided look that suddenly shocked her. She was about to pick

315

the fragments up, to put the portrait away in a drawer, when the door opened quietly without warning. Looking guiltily around, Donna saw Agatha Pullen standing there, her green eyes cold and narrowed. They were quick eyes and shrewd. Obviously there was no point in trying to disguise what had happened.

"It fell," Donna said. "I was trying to—it just fell."

"Did it?" the Pullen said calmly. "I was on my way to the nursery and heard the crash. What a pity. I'm afraid Mr. Trevarvas will be very upset. It's been there always you see. Ever since she—his wife died."

"Oh well," Donna tried to sound casual, "it can go back again when new glass is fixed and when I've left. It doesn't look a masterpiece anyway. Extremely anemic looking."

"Madam—the last mistress—was a very elegant and refined-looking lady I believe," Agatha Pullen said pointedly. "I've heard it said no artist could do her justice."

Realizing that Pullen was merely trying to irritate her, Donna controlled a flood of quickly rising temper, and went back to the mirror, saying coldly, "Please tell Phyllida or someone to come up and clear the glass away. There can't be much, but I daresay there are splinters scattered about, and they can be dangerous."

Later, after tea, when she'd changed into a scarlet dress that was not altogether in harmony with the rose shaded room, she went downstairs to get over the first slightly embarrassing and unpleasant preliminaries of meeting the rest of the staff. All except Beth and Phyllida had a closed, withdrawn look about them which was in itself condemning.

At last, thankfully, it was over, and she was free to slip on a wrap and make her way to the back where Saladin was stabled. His great whinny of joy released a sudden pent-up well of emotion in her, and she buried her face against his soft black muzzle, murmuring, "Soon we'll be safe back at Trencobban—just you and me, and Sarah and Sam, like we used to be."

The tears in her eyes mingled with the dampness and

316

sweet animal smell of him, dispelled all tension for a
time, and she relaxed, forgetting briefly that no promise
in the world, however deeply felt, could hinder for one
moment the steady approach of destiny that even then
was drawing a little nearer each hour, to thwart all
plans for the future.

CHAPTER TWENTY-ONE

After Donna's first few days at Polbreath the weather turned colder, but was fine, enabling her to ride Saladin each day, as respite from the boring and oppressive hours in the house where she had no one to talk to but Beth and Phyllida in their occasional leisure moments, and brief conversations with Agatha Pullen who had once more taken over Ianthe's education. With Jonathan at school, Ianthe had become slightly more precocious, and although, on her governess's instructions she was outwardly polite, there was a veiled, unchildish insolence in most of her remarks, and a turn of phrase accompanied by a bold expression in her dark eyes that told Donna Pullen was doing her secret best to turn the child against her.

Miss Pullen, in fact, was gathering power about her, like a cloak disguising many subtle weapons. Donna thought bitterly how easy it would be for her to inveigle Nicholas into trusting her completely. And perhaps more than that. She had won her first battle to get Donna discredited, although it was fate, that had played into her hands.

Donna thought sometimes that the whole household knew—especially when a whispered conversation between servants suddenly ceased at her appearance, and eyes that had been awed or amused became cold and veiled. Thinking back it seemed more than likely that someone with a sharp ear had overheard the undignified episode behind the marital door, and the realization increased Donna's bitterness.

Only when she was alone with her favorite horse on

the moorland hills did she feel really free. One afternoon she retraced her way down the lane to the site
where the gypsies had given her help on that terrible
night. They had gone. There was no sign of them except
the indented track of cartwheels under the thickness of
trees where the rain had not entirely penetrated, and a
few blackened twigs on a brown patch of earth that
were the remains of a fire.

She turned and kicked Saladin on until a narrow path
cut through undergrowth on her right, skirting Rosebuzzan, to the northern slope of the moors leading to the
cromlech. Once on top of the ridge she drew the horse
to a halt, holding the reins tight and pausing to look
down on distant Gwynvoor with the gray roof of Trencobban below, and Wheal Faith to the left, static and
dark.

Memories, against her will, flooded her mind, filling
her with dark unhappiness. Not only of her father and
her dear friend Tom, but of Jos as he had been when
she'd said goodbye to him on that far off day when he
left for America, and his condemning words when he'd
returned.

Of Nicholas too. How could she help it, when he'd
played so ruthless a part in shaping her life during the
past two years? And Jessica. It was odd, she thought,
that she hadn't missed her more. Strange that a character so colorful hadn't made a stronger impact. But the
fact was that Jessica had asked for it. Unconsciously
Donna had sensed that sometime life would catch up
with her. Which it had.

Nemesis. Was it also Nemesis that had forced her
own, dreadful confrontation with Nicholas? What was it
the gypsy woman had said? "It is thy dukkerin I tell
thee . . . fire and flame . . . sadness . . . and then
the shadow lifts I see thee proud and happy and
strong . . ." and something else about the dukkerin
dook. Strange words, from strange mysterious people in a
strange tongue. But meaning nothing. For she was
alone, without purpose, and Nicholas was gone.

Neither did she want him back. *Never* . . . never

more, her whole conscious being cried. Only to be herself and free, without fear or commitment to anyone. To the heart she wouldn't listen. The heart could be both liar and cheat. Henceforward it would belong to no one. No man should possess or abuse her again.

With the resolve intensified and hard once more, she spurred Saladin suddenly to action, and a moment later they were galloping back to Polbreath.

That night she couldn't sleep. A wind had risen, moaning fitfully down the drive from the high moors and sea beyond, driving through the lush new undergrowth and budding trees, sighing under the cracks of doors and lifting the pink curtains with soughing breath from window frames. The fire in her grate spat, sputtered, and finally died. But outside all was turbulent unrest—the kind of night when ships could flounder and be lost at sea. Boats maybe on some dark purpose of their own, or fishing vessels from Brittany caught by the unsuspecting gale.

At last, unable to lie there any longer, Donna got up and went first to the large window overlooking the garden, then to the side, where the hump of Rosebuzzan could be seen over the trees, stretching on the left toward the moors and the north coast. The sky from there was strangely red, the rich warm crimson was flecked with the yellow gold of a glorious fading sunset that threw the rest of the panormama into intensely dark relief. For a few moments she stared, marveling at the magnificence of nature. Then, suddenly, alarm registered with a shock. The sunlight had died hours ago. It was already past eleven o'clock. Her own watch said so, and the ornate pink and gold china clock ticking on the mantelpiece—yet the light was strong enough for her to see the time without lamp or candles.

With a mounting sense of fear and unease, Donna pulled the curtains wider, and what she saw then filled her with acute terror. Somewhere a fire was raging—a blaze greater and fiercer than any moorland furze could give. And from the direction of Trencobban. During those brief few moments that she waited, unable to tear her eyes away, a gigantic burst of flame, quivered luridly against the night sky, then leaped once more, flooding the whole horizon and landscape in its red light.

Donna turned quickly, frenzidly, pulled a wrap on, and called the servants. Then she returned to the bedroom, dressed quickly in anything she could find, including boots and a cape, and rushed downstairs, knocking into Sarne who was already in the hall with a lighted candle.

"Quick . . ." Donna gasped, "There's a fire . . . near the mine. Trencobban. It must be Trencobban. Saddle Saladin, immediately, do you hear? Then follow—do what you can."

"But mistress—if something's burnin' out there what use are we?"

"Do as you're told," Donna shouted. "Do you hear? It's a command. Hurry, man. Hurry . . ."

Her voice died as the man turned, and muttering under his breath, made his way to the stables. By the time Saladin was ready, the whole sky northward was vivid, leaping crimson.

Donna mounted the colt, although by then the household was astir, and calling upon her not to go. But if she heard, their frightened cries meant nothing. She was away even before the man could follow—galloping furiously at a dangerous speed down the drive and across the road, going pell mell, uncaring of tracks or paths, crashing through gorse and furze, driving Saladin mercilessly up the slope in a relentless urge to the ridge overlooking Trencobban.

And then she paused, knowing in the first agonized seconds that what Sarne had implied in his question was true. There was nothing anyone in the world could do to save Trencobban. Already the house was unrecognizable—a turbulent mass of blackened smoke and wanton flames, blown greedily on the tempestuous wind that filled the air with the strong tang of burning wood and masonry. At intervals, distant dots of figures could be seen hovering on the fringe of the fire, appearing to

321

Donna no more than small flies or gnats doing their best, no doubt, with buckets and hose to stem the blaze.

It was useless. Even when the fire engine arrived, Donna recognized that the elements had won, and at that same moment she recalled again the old gypsy's prophecy . . . fire and flame I see. It's thy dukkerin, daughter."

Then the agony rushed back, filling her with such savage distress that she cried aloud, "My home—it's *mine*. All I have!" before giving the colt its head and racing down to the road.

On she went—on and on, while the air thickened and curdled into menacing rosy-gray. There were screams and shouts as she neared the holocaust that enclosed her into a billowing hell of heat and destruction. The world revolved, tumbling in a snarling mass of smoke and flame, but she had no thought for herself. Danger, even her own life, during those few terrible moments were unimportant beside her torment . . . beside the agony of knowing that all she had cared for was collapsing around her . . . her home, her heritage, and every precious memento that had symbolized so much for so long.

Nothing but that was real any more. Nothing counted but the desperate urgency to salvage what she could of the past; to fight, plunge, and strike down the demonic force that was threatening her very soul.

And the more she attacked the greater her rage thrived, until sanity for that brief interim, died in a vortex of blinding pain, with the heat searing her body and spirit, blinding her eyes with the sting of smoke.

"Save it . . . save it," she screamed, urging Saladin mercilessly ahead. "For God's sake . . ." but there was a wall of darkness suddenly as the colt reared, forelegs pounding the choked air—whinnying wildly at the flames' savage onslaught. Someone yelled, while beast and girl hovered precariously in mid-air for a challenging pause of time. Then a greedy tongue of fire shot out, lighting the scene to a lurid brightness where dots of

322

figures gyrated and jerked like puppets on a string against the background of falling masonry.

In a moment of realization Donna felt herself lifted and thrown wildly, knew with a flash of insight, the meaning and finality of death.

This is it, she thought, as she fell. Darkness. The end.

And it seemed that the sky rocked with a shudder of fear, with a frisson of intense black terror, before the moaning began, the struggling and gasping for breath, the writhing and coughing. Then a face slowly registered, staring into her own as others crowded up from behind . . . pushing, staring, gaping, like a crowd of trolls emerging from the smoldering earth. She lifted a hand feebly, feeling at the same time a strong arm raising her. Life stirred again, dragging her to consciousness as though from an immense distance away, and as a cloth wiped the smoke from her eyes, she found, incredibly, that she could see.

Jed's eyes were upon her, his large face dripping with rivulets of blackened sweat, an ironic twist on his fleshy lips as he said, "Lucky you wuz thrown this way, wumman. The other would've had you a corpse in no time." She turned her head to the blaze, staring blankly, before muttering half coherently, "It's gone, hasn't it? Everything's gone?"

"Bricks and mortar ma'am. Bricks and mortar." She heard someone . . . a stranger, probably one of the firefighters, remark, "But no life, thanks be to God."

"And to him—Andrewartha," a woman added with a hint of grudging admiration. " 'Ef et wasn' for Jed you'd be naught but a cinder. Caught you he did, on the fringe of et whent that great beast flung you, and we must all thank the good Lord he had the wit and strength in that one arm o' his to act quick. You owes your life to 'en mistress, an' to the soft ground that did claim you both."

"My life? Jed?" Donna echoed, before a further fit of coughing started. She could have laughed if she'd had the capacity. But she hadn't. Reality was already becoming indifference. Despair.

She could breathe and move; her body, though shaken, was apparently still sound, her throat, rasping and dry, capable of speech and normal function. She could still hear and see, though the harsh tears were not on her cheeks. She was alive.

And even through the shock and pain Donna wondered bitterly what did life matter, when as well as saving it, Jed had taken the best part of it away?

How long it was before they got her back to Polbreath, she never knew, and by that time emotion had died completely into a cold and mute acceptance that left her rigid and tongue-tied.

Even to Beth she only answered in monosyllables, obeying the doctor's instructions also, with a resigned apathy that was far more disturbing to observe than defiance or violent display of grief.

"We should let your husband know," Beth said when Donna was at last in bed. "It's our duty, mistress."

"If you do," Donna said coldly, her eyes hard and glittering in her set face, "I'll never forgive you. *Never*. I have no husband. I have nothing any more. Neither do I want it. Leave me. And if you interfere I'll walk out of this house and no one will ever see me again."

Disconcerted by the calm, deadly tone of her voice, and by the strange, icy stare of her eyes, Beth gave in, realizing that her young mistress meant what she had said. In the morning, she told herself, it would be different. Common sense would prevail.

But in the morning all was just the same. Donna spoke and moved about the house like an automaton, answering when spoken to, but giving the impression that she had not really heard. Her mood cast a cold shadow over the house that even practical Mrs. Prowse resented. "Tesn' natural," she said. "She outer be in hospital. Depressing. That' what it is."

It seemed for the first few days that nothing would break the ice. Then, when almost a week had passed, Donna surprised everyone by announcing that she was going to Trencobban to see for herself the exact extent of the destruction.

"But ma'am . . . my dear, do you think. . . ?"
Beth began.

"Yes. I do think. I know. I'm quite recovered,"
Donna snapped. "Tell Sarne to get the chaise ready immediately, if you please."

Beth withdrew grudgingly, while Donna went upstairs
to tidy and dress automatically in her outdoor attire,
surveying herself severely yet without pleasure or interest in the mirror. When she was ready she went downstairs to find the chaise already waiting below the front
entrance.

She seated herself silently into the vehicle, and sat
there rigidly, a static figure erect and stiff-backed in
gray silk, with a small hat trimmed with black ribbon
on her swept-back hair. As they moved down the drive
she was unaware of curious eyes watching with the doleful stares of mourners at a funeral from the front windows
of the house; was unconscious also of all familiar landmarks when the chaise turned the bend toward Trencobban. Her mind was closed to everything but the
scene awaiting her ahead . . . the sight for which she
had inwardly been preparing during the past few days.

It was just as she had thought. When she walked
down the darkened track, little remained of the home
she had known, and what was left was a nightmare
scene of wanton destruction. One jagged wall of the
house facing the road still stood, with gaping holes of
windows beneath the stark outline of broken granite.
The rest was a charred black mass, holding nothing of
use to salvage.

Like a marionette she walked stiffly up the slope to
where Sarne was waiting with the chaise.

"Take me back to Polbreath," she said, her voice and
face cold and expressionless. "There's nothing for me
here any more."

Something about her frightened him. "Yes, mistress,"
he answered. Then, before starting off, "Cold are you?
Hadn't you better pull the rug round you? The air's
chilly."

She laughed shortly, ironically. "I don't think I could

ever feel the cold again." But she was shivering never-theless, as though a bitter wind had seared her very soul.

When she reached Polbreath, Beth and Agatha Pullen were both in the hall with Ianthe between them. One look at her face told Beth all she wanted to know.

"Come in now," she said, taking her arm. "You look shocked to death. I'll go to the kitchen and see about hot tea immediately."

"Thank you," Donna said, flinging her cape over a hall bench. "I'll go into the library I think."

"That's right. There's a good fire burning . . ." Beth stopped, with a hand to her cheek, "Oh ma'am—Mistress Trevarvas—I didn't mean . . . how stupid of me."

Donna shook her head. "Don't worry. I'm not a child. I have to accept what's happened and not flinch every time the word fire is mentioned."

Agatha Pullen spoke then, calmly, but with a hint of sympathy piercing her usual chill armor. "I'm sure we're all very sorry about your loss," she said. "It must have been very distressing. If there's anything any of us can do. . . ?"

"I'm afraid not," Donna replied shortly. "At least—although I'm grateful—I don't want sympathy. It would be helpful if you could try to understand."

"Of course."

Donna, instead of going up to her room first, went straight to the library and stood with her hands out-spread to the glowing logs, a slim erect figure in her tight-waisted dress. For a moment or two her limbs felt rigid, frozen. She tried to move, but couldn't. Then the door opened and Ianthe ran in.

"Tell me about it," she said in her childish, excited voice, "Was there an awful lot of smoke and . . . . burning? Did people nearly die?"

Shocked, Donna turned, but what she saw in Ianthe's wide-eyed face effectively quelled the sharp retort on her lips. No insolence any more, only an awed kind of fear.

"Not quite, Ianthe," Donna said. "Not people. Just a house. The house died."

"Oh." There was a pause, then, "Do houses have hearts and things? I mean—if they die they must, mustn't they?"

Suddenly Donna's tensed up nerves broke. She half fell on the sofa, with her head in her hands, while the tears broke free coursing through her fingers. Gently, a small hand stole into hers.

"I'm sorry," Ianthe whispered. "I didn't mean to make you cry. Do you know what I think?"

"No. What?" Donna asked, trying to smile.

"I think it'd be a good idea to go and see Abraham." Ianthe said seriously.

"Abraham? Who?" Then she remembered. Abraham was the old man who lived in the wood. He had once been a gardener at Polbreath and knew all about foxes and badgers and how to whistle birds so that they came at his call.

"Of course we will," Donna said. "I think I'd like that, better than anything."

Ianthe nodded confidingly. "We won't tell Pullen though. She says he's dirty and smells. But he's not—he washes in the stream, and his smell's nice—like . . . like grass an things."

Donna fully meant to keep her promise, but for the rest of the week she was so busy attending to business arising out of the Trencobban disaster, that there seemed no opportunity for accompanying Ianthe to the wood. There were visits from her solicitor, and the insurance company dealing with the policy, inquiries from the police, who did not yet rule out arson, and on top of all this the miserable business of trying to plan her future. An air of insecurity hovered over the household. Beth, who knew of her impending departure, asked Donna one morning if her services would be required when she left.

"If you like it here," Donna answered, "I'm sure your position will be rewarding, as I've told you before. And for Phyllida too. As for me . . ."

"Yes, mistress."

"I shall be leaving the day after tomorrow," Donna told her on the spur of the moment. "It's better for us all to have me away and things settled for good. For myself too."

"Oh. I see. And where—if I may ask—are you going, madam?"

"I've not had time to think about it properly," Donna answered. "Somewhere not too far away in case I'm needed—by the police I mean, or those insurance people. There's such a lot of questioning and probing and dipping into the stupidest details. I suppose they've got to do it. But it's all very wearing. I did wonder, though, whether Falmouth wouldn't be a good idea. I could look in on Janey sometimes, and see how she's getting on with Zenobia. There's a very good Coaching House I've heard, in the main street. I can engage a maid in the town and I could take trips up the Fal, and perhaps cross to St. Mawes. The creeks are beautiful." Her voice faded as smothered emotion gathered in the old familiar ball at the back of her throat.

"Yes," Beth answered. "The change would probably do you good. You're looking pale, Mrs. Trevarvas. Don't you think you should see a doctor?"

Donna's eyes suddenly flashed brilliant orange. "*No*. I'm not sick. I'm quite all right. Why did you say that?"

With the color rising in her face, Beth answered calmly. "No particular reason, mistress, just that you appear rather wisht—and no wonder after the strain you've been under. By the way, have they come to any decision about the fire yet? I don't want to sound impertinent, but there's gossip going on in the kitchen that someone started it."

"I've no idea about that," Donna answered shortly. "Probably we'll never know. And try to stop such stupid talk. It's no use to anyone.

In the beginning, when she'd paused with Saladin on the top of the ridge to watch the blazing building, and later back at Polbreath, Donna's thoughts had turned briefly in a wave of condemnation to Jed. But later she

328

had realized that there was no proof. In any case if he had somehow contrived to put a spark to the house he would hardly have waited about on the scene of the crime only to rescue her when she fell from Saladin. Vengeful he might be, but no fool, especially when there was nothing to be got out of it.

"If you say so," she heard Beth saying a trifle grudgingly. Of course. I shouldn't have asked."

"It doesn't matter," Donna told her wearily. "Take no notice of me if I snap. I'm no use to anyone at the moment."

When Beth had gone, Donna wandered upstairs and began to plan for her forthcoming departure. The days were slipping by. In little more than a week Nicholas would be thinking of returning. She had to be away well before then, and in the meantime she had to contact her bank, and other authorities about Trencobban, and also Sam and Sarah.

All the activity, however, rather than tiring her as she had expected, helped to take her mind off things, and at the appointed time for setting off the next day she was feeling considerably stronger and thankful under the circumstances to be leaving Polbreath for good.

Sarne was already waiting, with her valise and bags packed in the chaise as she went downstairs to the hall, wearing a gray velvet suit with a fur trimmed jacket, fur hat to match, and a cape slung over one arm. She had never looked more self-possessed and elegant, which she well knew, and never—if she'd admitted it, which she didn't—had her heart felt so heavy, so numbed and incapable of emotion. If she had allowed herself the indulgence she could have dropped the veneer for a moment, letting a few memories soften her. But she had no use for memories any more. What concerned her was the future, how to live it, and where to eventually make her life.

The small group of servants were waiting in the hall to bid her farewell. She hardly noticed them, but extended a hand to each with polite wishes for their prosperity and happiness in the days ahead. The words were automatic, her eyes cold and clear of tears, her slight smile brightly artificial. She paused briefly at the door, and then, with her head held high, went through, without another glance back.

It was at that moment that she saw Nicholas coming toward her up the steps, and despite all her resolve, all her bitterness and resentment, her hatred and indignation, the wild rich color flooded her cheeks as her heart quickened heavily against her ribs. She tried not to notice him, but in those first few seconds two things registered—the worn, haggard lines of his strong face, and the dark impelling glance of his eyes. She would have passed him by without a word if he hadn't said in an undertone, "Donna, no scene please, in front of the servants. May I have a few words with you before you leave?"

She did not reply. Indecision halted her for a second before she turned and went ahead of him into the house. "The library I think," he said.

"I really don't see . . ."

"*Please*, Donna."

When the servants had moved away she followed him down the passage to the one room where she'd felt comparatively at peace during his absence. He held the door open for her.

She went in, gathering her armor about her once more, and when they stood there, by the fire, face to face for the first time since their violent quarrel, her tawny eyes were clear, relentless, her mouth thin and set.

"Sit down please."

"I don't really see why. I haven't much time."

"You've all the time in the world if you want it," he said abruptly. "But as you obviously don't, what I have to say won't take long. I'm sorry."

"Oh!" She laughed sneeringly. "It doesn't matter, Nicholas. It's far too late for that."

"About the fire, I mean," he said bluntly. "The rest is past and done with as you've so aptly said. But about Trencobban—yes, I was really shocked for you when I

330

heard. I should have come earlier, but it was only yesterday I received the news. What are you going to do now?"

"I'm going to Falmouth, for a time, anyway," she answered.

"Alone? Without a maid or chaperone?"

"Yes," she replied defiantly. "But that's not your concern any more."

"Isn't it? Well, that rather depends. I suppose that if you choose to travel like a farmer's wife I can't stop you, but I should like your address in case anything turns up that needs sorting out between us. Also—though you may not want to accept or believe it—there are many business details which will necessitate our cooperation."

She swallowed. "In that case—well, I shall probably be for a time at the Coaching House—The Boar. But my solicitor will have my address if I move on. And I don't want to see you, or even talk with you. Is that clear?"

"Donna . . ." his hand reached out to her.

She froze.

"Don't touch me. Don't dare. I loathe you—do you understand?"

He regarded her speculatively before answering, "I should like to say in the words of the Bard, 'The lady doth protest too much, methinks.' But . . . by heaven, I believe you mean it." His voice was suddenly flat, unbearably tired.

"Yes."

"Very well. Among the other points I wanted to raise—the question of living. Polbreath is yours—and exclusively since you wish it—for as long as you choose. I can stay in London indefinitely if necessary, and will probably go abroad for a time later. So please have no worries on that score. I really mean it, Donna."

She shrugged. "I suppose I should thank you, although I wouldn't consider living here. The whole house is . . . obnoxious to me now.

He shrugged. "Just as you like. There are doubtless

many desirable houses on the market. And as I've said, you need have no fears about money."

"I suppose I must thank you for that too," Donna said bitterly.

"Not at all. The last thing in the world I want is your thanks, which you well know. I didn't marry you for that. Or for any of the reasons you're trying to believe, which is why, my dear, I'm so willing to put my hand in my pocket now. Many men wouldn't, believe me."

"Not many men would do what you did," Donna said impulsively without meaning to.

"Which is?"

She got up suddenly and went to the door. "Do you mind if I go now? The chaise is waiting."

He gave a slight, ironic mow. "By all means. Goodbye then. And good luck. I shall be here for a time if you should want me."

Though she didn't turn, or give a single glance back, she could feel his eyes watching her unswervingly until the door closed. Then, in a flurry of conflicting emotion and nerves, she went half running down the hall and out to the drive where Sarne still waited.

Once in the chaise she sat motionless and erect until the carriage had turned the corner of the drive. Then she relaxed, and found to her dismay that the tight ball of nervous tension in her throat had broken, sending a flood of tears to her eyes. So searched her bag for a wisp of handkerchief which was soon soaked and salty from a grief she couldn't understand. Then she pulled herself together, and sat for the rest of the journey to Falmouth, dry-eyed and hard looking, so that when she eventually arrived at her new destination there was no sign on her face that she'd been through any ordeal at all.

When Donna had gone, Trevarvas stood at the library window for a long time staring out. Then, driven by a wild impulse that he didn't care to fathom or question, he turned on his heel abruptly, marched to the stables, and saddled Pluto. In the adjoing box Saladin stared at him pleadingly, it seemed, from dark velvet eyes.

"It's all right, boy," Nicholas said, giving him an affectionate slap on the neck. "She's forgotten us already, you and me. Never mind, we'll have one hell of a time together."

And perhaps it was true, he told himself as he rode Pluto savagely up the moor to the cromlech. Women— even the most enchanting of them—could wreck a man's peace and sanity if he allowed it. But not him. Let the wayward jade go her own way, do what she wished with her life. It was no longer any conern of his.

The trouble was that he knew deep in his being he would never entirely get her out of his bones and memory. And the fact was that into the bargain she had spoiled all other women for him.

He waited by the great stones, until the sun sank in a dying glory of green, rose, and gold to the west. As he watched he could have been of stone itself, a relentless figure against the ancient relentless landscape and fading sky.

Then he turned and cut down to the valley which was already deepening into muted light and shade—the dark horseman of Polbreath, alone again, and wondering what he was to make of the future.

CHAPTER TWENTY-TWO

Donna's arrival at the Coaching House with neither companion, maid, nor chaperone, caused a stir that first evening when she went down to dinner wearing a subdued yet elegant crimson silk dress, which, although high-necked, with a mere suggestion of cream lace beneath the chin, only enhanced her perfect figure as she made her way to a small table allotted her, skirt held daintily in one hand.

The room, like the building itself, was low-ceilinged and obviously very old, yet large enough to accommodate twenty or thirty guests comfortably. The walls were paneled in dark oak, and at the far end, opposite the windows, was a long buffet table with a wine waiter standing nearby. The table linen and cutlery, as befitting a place of high reputation were sparkling and spotless, with silver salt and pepper mills winking in the light of gas-lit wall lamps.

Yet Donna felt alien and strange as she sat down alone, to study the menu—a monstrous, intricately designed affair bordered by a gilt pattern of flowers and fruit. The fare, though mostly simple and traditional, had a few French names interspersed among the numerous dishes, and the odors from the kitchens were certainly tempting.

But she wasn't hungry. Loneliness, in the true meaning of the word, engulfed her for the first time, as she heard herself mechanically ordering soup followed by chicken à-la-something or other, with a glass of mellow white burgundy. Her eyes instinctively, but not very acutely assessed her fellow guests, some of whom were obviously travelers passing by, wearing still their outdoor attire, with capes or jackets pushed back over their shoulders. There was no one of apparent individuality among the dozen or so people present, except one man who caught her attention briefly. Afterward, when she knew him better, she frequently wondered why, and came to the conclusion it must have been his plainnness; his complete lack of ostentation, and a certain puckish, whimsical set of features, combined with a pair of very intense, brilliant eyes that gave his face an unusually sensitive and gentle quality.

He was studying her as well, which caused her to look away quickly, and after that, though their eyes strayed to each other occasionally, she made a pretense mostly of ignoring him.

The shock came toward the end of the meal, when a highly-bred, very clear voice from the doorway shattered her composure. The waiter moved toward the table adjoining her own, and indicated two chairs politely, saying with the deference due to revered company, "This way m'lady . . . madam."

Donna hurriedly swallowed a mouthful of coffee, and with her head averted, got up, making a vain attempt to leave the dining room before she was noticed.

But of course it was too late. The eagle eye of Lady Penverrys, not to mention that of her niece, Rosina, had already spotted her.

"My dear!" The older woman gushed, as Donna was about to leave. "Mrs. Trevarvas, of all people. How strange to find you here."

"Yes," Donna said abruptly, adding, "I'm having a holiday, following the fire—which you must have heard about."

"So very sad," Lady Penverrys murmured. "And isn't it strange, Rosina," turning to her niece, "we were going to call at Polbreath tomorrow to offer our respects and sympathy. Were we not?"

Rosina smiled, if such a travesty of goodwill could be called a smile. "That's true. Mr. Trevarvas informed us when he was returning from London, and as we weren't

335

able to attend—the wedding—we thought it was the least we could do."

Donna paused a moment before saying tartly, "You'll find my husband there, or should do. He was there when I left."

"Indeed?" Lady Penverrys lifted her lorgnettes intimidatingly, and regarded Donna with hypocritical concern tinged with curiosity. "You are both well I hope?"

"My husband is flourishing. I'm naturally still shocked about the fire," Donna said coolly, inwardly raging. "Which is why I'm here, on holiday."

"Without your husband, my dear? But how . . . rather odd. Surely in such a time of great distress, it would be reasonable to expect a man to accompany his newly-wedded wife."

"What my husband and I do is our own affair, Lady Penverrys," Donna said in an undertone, knowing by then that someone must have overheard at least part of their conversation. "And now, if you don't mind, I'm tired, and am having an early night."

"Oh course, Mrs. Trevarvas. Of course. There's no need to jump at me. I really must say . . ."

What Lady Penverrys had to say was lost on Donna, who swept her lacy shawl from the back of the chair and with her long skirt held a few inches in both hands, walked quickly from the dining room, having tipped the coffee cup over in her agitation.

"Marriage certainly hasn't improved Donna Penroze's manners," Lady Penverrys said to Rosina, after the hasty departure. "And it's quite clear to me that what we've heard is true. They're separated, my dear."

"You can't really blame him," Rosina said coldly. "She was always rather gauche after all."

"Oh no my dear. Not that. Poor William's daughter was merely too charming and too undisciplined for her own good. Still she'll learn now, no doubt."

Rosina smiled, with unfeigned relish this time.

"I thnk she's learned already. I heard the most ridiculous thing. Miss Pullen was passing on the landing at the time it happened—the quarrel I mean—and from

336

what I can make out the scene was too ludicrous for words. He actually . . ." Her confidences were temporarily cut short by the arrival of the waiter, so that the listeners were spared details of further titillating gossip.

Meanwhile, up in her room, Donna was surveying herself, stormy-eyed, in the gilt-framed mirror, hating the Penverryses, and despising herself for her weak handling of the situation. How beastly fate was, she thought, to send those two officious, interfering women blundering into her affairs, poking and prying in their malicious high-bred way, and inwardly glorying no doubt in her discomfiture and misfortune. If she had been anywhere else, without others looking on, she would have taken great pleasure in slapping Rosina Penverrys's face. The toffee-nosed creature was obviously gloating and no doubt would soon be preening herself at Polbreath, forcing her sympathy and well-bred hypocritical consolation upon Trevarvas. He had pretended he didn't care for her. But apparently he'd cared enough to let the Penverryses know of his impending return to Cornwall.

Well, what of it? she thought a moment later. Let him have her, and get on with it, for all she cared. There was such a thing as divorce these days. Nicholas could be free at any time he chose, free to marry the haughty creature. It might do him good. Pay him out for the way he'd treated *her*. She couldn't see Rosina Penverrys succumbing to such ignominious tryanny as he'd shown to her. Although . . . when she considered it, the idea was slightly amusing.

For a brief moment, the picture of the stately Rosina being forced to stand naked and painted, with not a shred of clothing on after a sound spanking, touched the irrepressible sense of humor still lurking somewhere beneath Donna's cold veneer. After it, she felt better. And when an hour had passed she made her way down to the smoking-room-cum-lounge, preferring it to the smaller more elegantly confined space allotted to the ladies.

A cheerful fire burned in the grate, giving a comfort-

337

able glow to the room which was large enough to contain comfortable chairs, two writing tables with headed note paper, and a number of magazines and newspapers lying about, including *The Times* and *Sporting News.* There were hunting prints on the walls, and the comforting smell of cigar smoke hovered about the air.

Donna thought at first that she was alone, and was relieved to have avoided the Penverryses for a while. Then she saw a pair of bright eyes studying her from an alcove not far from the fire, and recognized the man she'd noticed in the dining room when she first entered.

He smiled. "Good evening. Can I get you a chair? It's not warm these days . . ."

He half rose, but she checked him. "Oh no, please. I'm not staying. I was just looking around."

"Getting your bearings?"

She nodded. "Something like that."

"And trying to extricate yourself from those abominable inquistors?"

Donna's eyes widened, becoming more brilliantly amber than ever in the colorful glow of the fire. "How did you know?"

"My dear child—pardon me—young lady—there was no secret about it, to one of my years and experience. And I admired your handling of them tremendously."

She couldn't help feeling grateful. "Thank you. I thought I behaved very badly. I should have been polite and dignified. But it's not easy, when . . ." she broke off, ending haltingly, ". . . under certain circumstances."

"I'd think it an imposition having to face them anyway," her companion told her. "And certainly not worth fretting over."

"No. But . . ."

"Won't you sit down and chat a little?" the friendly voice said. "You're quite safe from our two dragons. They left over fifteen minutes ago. So you needn't worry that they'll appear suddenly to put you through it

338

again. Besides, I hardly think females of such caliber would choose this rather dull setting."

Donna smiled as she followed his suggestion relaxing into a comfortable but rather worn-looking leather-backed chair. "No," she admitted. "Lady Penverrys likes luxury."

"*Ah*. I thought so. And obviously gossip too."

"You heard?"

He shook his head. "No, no. Nothing of importance." He smiled puckishly. "Mind you . . . I wouldn't have been above listening, if I'd had the chance. I'm not a particularly honorable customer in that respect I'm afraid—simply because I happen to be interested in my fellow creatures—objectively, you understand?"

"Yes," Donna agreed honestly. "You're very candid."

He shrugged. "My dear lady, having been an editor of a daily newspaper for most of my life I'm afraid that assessing people and situations has become something of a habit."

Her expression changed from friendliness to sudden wary defense as, with eyes turned away from him to the door, she started to rise, saying, "I think perhaps I'd better . . ."

He interrupted her quickly. "No. Don't go. You mustn't fear that I'm on to a story or even wanting one. I put all that behind me a year ago for a more peaceable existence in my retirement, and although anything you wish to tell me about yourself will be kept entirely confidential, believe me, I'm not really anxious to hear—unless of course it would help."

"Then why . . . ?"

"Why did I notice you? Well you're very different from the usual brand of guests here who are mostly commerical gentlemen, or people passing through like ships in the night as they say. You're young, unattended, beautiful, and at the moment quite clearly—forgive me saying so—under considerable strain."

"Oh dear," Donna sighed. "Is it so obvious?"

"Not to the majority I'd think," he answered. "You

bear your difficulties—whatever they are—with great dignity."

"That's not what my . . ." she broke off before the word husband left her lips, ". . . what my friends would say. Most would tell you that I'd managed my life very badly."

"But then your life so far has been comparatively short hasn't it?" he said, with the odd quizzical lift of one eyebrow that gave his plain face such appeal. "You've a considerable amount of it ahead, and wisdom's not generally characteristic of youth."

"No. I suppose not."

"Unless of course one happens to be a woman of no looks, no charm, and therefore has no temptation to lure one into wild and wayward channels."

Was he teasing her, she wondered? Or did he really know more of her circumstances than he pretended? He appeared not to. His face was solemn and uncommunicative when she glanced at him. Then he said suddenly, and quite unexpectedly, "Your name is Trevarvas, isn't it?"

She stared blankly. "How did you know? I only signed the book an hour or so ago. Have you been prying and . . . ?"

"No, no. I overheard the doorman address you when you came in. And I wasn't listening on purpose I assure you. But you—yes I noticed you, of course. What man wouldn't?"

She blushed.

"But I'm not seeking favors, or trying to force a relationship, which I know most men so easily might. I'm just doing my best to make you feel at home, and how trite that sounds doesn't it? The fact is, though, you are very young, and may need a friend. If you do, remember I'm here, that's all." He paused before continuing. "The fire must have been very distressing, and a great shock. I hope the change of scene will help."

"You mean you know about that too?"

"My dear young lady, it's been in all the newspapers. Such an event can't possibly escape attention—

340

especially in the press, which believe me is a very greedy animal, with an avaricious appetite on occasion. That's the reason—partly—I'm grateful for the chance of talking to you, before the others get in."

"Others?"

"Journalists? Even a busybody or two of the Fleet Street boys. They have a particular lust and nose— which happens also to be part of their job—for getting emotional domestic accounts, firsthand, from lovely ladies in distress.

"But a fire? That I've lost my home? That's not really news is it? Nothing to gloat over?"

"Well it has color. And there are other things aren't there?"

Looking away, Donna said, "I don't know what you mean."

"Your husband. Mr. Trevarvas. He's an adventurous character, well-known throughout Cornwall, and to the law I'm afraid, even though only a suspect. Women like him too, which adds color. Also . . ." he shrugged, "There's a strong rumor going around that I've a hunch may not be without foundation . . ."

"Rumor? What rumor?"

"Of a shipping combine which is very much more as well, in fact one vast business concern for smuggling certain goods illegally into the country from overseas."

"Ridiculous," Donna murmured, trying to sound convincing.

"The Revenue don't think so, and surely you must have an inkling?"

"I never pried into Nicholas's affairs," Donna said, in cold, firm tones, "and as I now have nothing to do with him—which you probably also know—" He inclined his head. "I don't see what any of this has to do with me."

"But you are still his wife," the kindly voice continued. "And alone here. News travels fast—even the most private news. Have no illusion on that score. Even tomorrow perhaps, the sleuths will be nosing around. Well, I want you to promise one thing."

"What is that?"

"Don't divulge your feelings to strangers. Don't answer any probing questions. And if anyone gets too persistent refer him to me. Hayley Grantham, late Editor of *The London Daily Mercury*."

At first she said nothing, just stared at him half uncomprehendingly, as though wondering whether to believe him or not. Then she got up, held out her hand, and replied impulsively, "Thank you. I'll remember. And now, if you don't mind, I think I'll go up to my room. I am rather tired."

"Of course." His fingers touched hers briefly before she turned and went toward the door. It opened before she got there, revealing a stout, elderly, balding man, with a cigar between his lips.

"I say, Grantham," he said, "What about our little expedition tomorrow . . . ?" He broke off on seeing Donna, gave a slight inclination of his head, and held the door for her to pass through.

She went upstairs in a kind of dream, with a queer sense of bemusement upon her, of living and breathing in a new sphere of existence that was suddenly too bewildering to comprehend properly.

All that talk about Nicholas and the revenue, of vast organizations and a smuggling concern . . . she had suspected something of the sort of course, for a considerable time. But to have it brought into the daylight, and the shipping myth so easily and factually dispelled by that puckish little man, the ex-editor of a daily newspaper! It was really almost too fantastic to accept.

But she knew it was true. Knew too, that Hayley Grantham did indeed wish to be her friend.

Why though? She wondered, as she brushed her long hair before the archaic mirror in the old-fashioned bedroom allotted to her. Was his interest purely philanthropic, or was he, as a man of advanced years, merely cleverer and more subtle than her more youthful admirers?

Later, recalling the direct glance and kindly smile, she dismissed the latter suggestion, and decided to accept him at face value, realizing that however hard she fought against it, loneliness was already engulfing her. There was no one in the world any more who really cared for her, except Sarah and Sam in a servile kind of way, and they would have their own lives to live now, far apart from hers.

She had a dream that night, of a sprightly, puckish figure, who led her, with a glittering light in his hand, across a waste of moonwashed bog and moor—on and on, past hovel and strange lurking beast-like shapes toward a rising mound of brightness where fantastic figures waited, arms outspread, to receive her. There was anticipation in her and a wish to surrender, until suddenly a black bank of cloud descended, as she stopped, transfixed by fear. The darkness curdled and resolved into a single shape, vast and watchful, standing impregnable against the green sky—the gigantic figure of a horseman whose magic was stronger than the magic of all other forces in that dream habitat and who, even in sleep, invaded her subconscious, waking her at last in torment.

Nicholas.

CHAPTER TWENTY-THREE

When Donna went down to breakfast the next day there was no one in the dining room but herself, no doubt due to the fact that it was already past nine thirty, and for the last few hours of the night she had slept heavily.

She had looked forward to a glimpse, and chat—however brief, with Hayley Grantham, but he had probably gone out, she thought, or was possibly in the smoking room.

As she toyed with her toast, following the bacon and egg, which she had eaten merely because of the waiter's watchful and critically intimidating air, she recalled Hayley Grantham's remarks the previous evening about Nicholas's involvement with the shady shipping concern. She had not been surprised, but was astonished that he had been careless enough to let anyone else know of it, especially an ex-newspaper editor. That such a wide and subtle grapevine could exist irritated and mildly worried her, although she couldn't have said why.

After breakfast she idled about the hall for a bit, went into the smoking and writing room where newspapers had been placed on a table for anyone requiring one. She picked up a copy of *The London Mercury*, thumbing it curiously, looking for any reference to smuggling in Cornwall or elsewhere. There seemed to be nothing. Just down to earth comments on political affairs—including the eternal Irish question, which though not so violently controversial as it had been before Disraeli's death in 1881, was being repeatedly raised by Gladstone, the staunch advocate of Home Rule.

Donna was bored. Politics and business did not really interest her, and had played no active part in her life at Trencobban or Polbreath. In fact, apart from her worries over the welfare of families like the Bordes, and Trevarvas's occasional comments on financial matters, world and home affairs made no impact on her at all. So she laid the paper down, went upstairs, and from her bedroom window looked out upon the street.

The weather was fine, but gray, with a few pedestrians walking sharply by, and the clip-clop of horses' hooves intermingling with the cries of newsboys and rattle of a vegetable cart over the cobbles. Two sailors, obviously still under the effect of some midnight orgy were zigzagging across the pavement with their arms around each other, and an old woman was crouched at the top of an alley with a basket of flowers, mostly bunched primroses, for sale.

A phaeton passed at a leisurely pace, followed by two cabs. The effect of the scene was of black and gray, lit by quivering light such as the Impressionists might have painted. This suggestion took her thoughts back to Lucien, and to his passion for painting her portrait, which had eventually resulted in such dire consequences for her marriage. She pulled herself together abruptly, saying to herself, it's over. I won't think of it any more. It's a good thing—a mercy—I found out in time the kind of man Nicholas Trevarvas is. Supposing I'd left it too late and had children. Supposing . . .

For a second or two, at this point, it seemed that her heart stopped beating. A wave of revulsion rose in her, and automatically her hand went to her breast as her pulse started up once more in a wild flutter of apprehension, and something else, something quite beyond her control.

She recalled Sarah's probing glance of dismay . . . "Surely 'ee bean't . . . ?" And her refusal even to consider such a thing.

345

But of course, it was possible. And if so, what would she do? Where live her life now that Trencobban was gone?

The future viewed from every angle, appeared, just then, as impossible as it was unpredictable. So, dismissing the unpleasant prospect temporarily from her mind, she decided on the spur of the moment to visit Janey and Zenobia Bray.

Hayley Grantham was in the hall by the time she arrived downstairs, apparently dressed for going out, but in surprisingly unconventional attire, wearing a squashed-down-looking hat, rather shabby velveteen jacket of indeterminate color, brown trousers, and carrying a flat box affair slung over his shoulder.

Seeing her, his face brightened. "Mrs. Trevarvas. And looking very fresh and fit. Did you sleep well?"

"So-so," she answered.

"I looked for you at breakfast which was stupid of me, as I had it early. I want to catch the light quickly, if the day does pick up."

"The light?"

"Down by the harbor," he answered, with a friendly grin. "Though an amateur, and a very bad one, I know what I want to get on to paper."

"Oh." Suddenly she understood. "You paint?"

"I dabble my dear. It was always my dream. And now having broken free from the shackles of journalism at last, and with no family ties, I'm indulging myself for the first time in following my bent—or perhaps I should say inclination, since I haven't really much knowledge of the craft."

Donna smiled. "I'd love to see some of your sketches. Could I, one day?"

He frowned impishly. "Are you teasing me? Or merely being polite?"

"Of course not. I'm not that kind of woman."

"Very well, yes. But I wager you'll not like them. Trash mostly I expect. My only virtue as far as painting's concerned is knowing exactly what I wish to depict, if at all possible. And that is the extraordinary

346

quality of the Cornish air and light. You wouldn't notice it so much probably, being born and bred here. That is true isn't it?"

"Oh yes. The north coast of course. Which is far more wild and rugged."

"And already becoming, so I've heard, the promised land for the most famous artists of our time, including Whistler. Sometime I shall change my headquarters from here to that part of Cornwall. At the moment though, I'm concentrating on impressions of ships reflected on water. Besides . . ." he paused whimsically, with his one rebellious eyebrow shooting up, ". . . the food here is so excellent."

Donna laughed.

"That's right," he said quickly. "If I can make you smile and look like that for a bit, I've probably accomplished more of worth than I ever shall with paints and brush. By the way . . ."

"Yes?"

"Are you going toward the harbor by any chance? If so we could walk together."

"I'm afraid not," Donna told him. "The opposite direction. I have a niece living there temporarily, with her governess, and thought I should look in to tell them I've arrived safe and sound."

"Ah. Yes. Of course. Very well then . . . we shall meet later. At lunch I hope."

"I expect so," Donna replied, with a warm feeling glowing and spreading inside her, in response to his courtesy and obvious admiration.

His hand automatically went to his hat as he took his leave and went into the street. She waited for a moment, glancing at herself in the oak-framed heavy hall mirror, adjusting her hat from which a gleaming dark strand of hair had fallen, and then, when his figure had disappeared round a corner of the porticoed, early Georgian entrance, she slipped out herself and was soon on her way up the hill leading to Miss Bray's cramped house.

She found both Zenobia and Janey in excellent spirits. Years seemed to have fallen from the prim spinster,

347

who even had a flush of faint color in her thin cheeks, and Janey, already wearing a new, if slightly over-elaborate, old-fashioned-style dress, was fully conscious of her appearance, and had learned in the short time with her governess more than a smattering of the good manners befitting a lady.

When Janey had been sent upstairs to wash her hands, comb her hair, and bring her new doll to show her Aunt Donna, Zenobia Bray said cautiously, "We're both very pleased to see you Mrs. Trevarvas, though we're extremely shocked, of course, to hear of your disaster."

Not knowing whether Zenobia was referring to her marriage, the fire, or both, Donna said calmly, "Yes. Since you left, several very unpleasant and tragic things have occurred. But you understand, I hope, that I don't wish to talk of them."

"Naturally." Miss Bray's voice assumed for a moment it's characteristic dry-as-dust quality. Then she said suddenly, "I hope you're pleased with Janey. She looks well, doesn't she?"

"Marvelously well," Donna agreed warmly. "She has a lot to thank you for. We both have. It's amazing in such a short time."

"That's what I wanted to discuss, Mrs. Trevarvas. I've thought the whole thing over, and was wondering—hoping—if you'd allow Janey to remain with me for good. Oh—not at your expense, of course. I'm not quite without capital; I have a few bonds I could sell, for her further education when the question arises. But the truth is that I'm very devoted to the child, and she is, I'm sure, to me—although I sometimes wonder why. I'm not a very . . . glamorous person . . . to wish to have for a mother. But I'm sure Janey looks on me already in this capacity. I don't like saying this, so few months after her . . . after Mrs. Penroze's death. But believe me, it would make a great difference to my life, and to hers, I think. Obviously she would have a more luxurious existence with you. But . . ."

Her voice wavered as she sniffed. She placed a handkerchief briefly to one eye, turned, and went to the window overlooking the street, where the conventional aspidistra still stood on the sill in its immense china pot.

Donna got up from her chair, and touched the other woman on the shoulder. "Miss Bray . . ."

"Yes?" Zenobia turned abruptly.

"If that's what Janey wants, and if you feel sure that you wouldn't find her an encumbrance—after all a young child is a responsibility—I really don't see any objection at all to her remaining indefinitely with you. But I would like to continue for the time anyway, with the financial arrangements. It's been a load off my mind having you to care for her. And you've earned the money. It would worry me to think you had to stint. It's not charity, quite the reverse."

She waited until Zenobia said cautiously, "If that's how you feel, of course I can't refuse. But I did want to be able to think of Janey as my child."

"She already is, from what I've seen," Donna said with a smile. "And there's no reason that I can see why you shouldn't adopt her—legally—if you want to and everything is well, after a normal period of time."

Zenobia's whole body and face seemed to relax, and it was as she was saying, "That's just what I hoped for," that Janey came back into the room, looking shiny from soap and water, her hair neatly combed and tied, and carrying a doll, exquisitely dressed, in her arms.

The interview did not last much longer, and when Donna left it was with mixed feelings—thankfulness to be away from such suburban, respectable, and conventionally colorless surroundings, mixed with pleasurable gratitude to have found Janey so content, and that this domestic problem was apparently settled for good.

During the days that followed, Donna and Hayley Grantham found their first mutual interest deepening into personal friendship. The weather turned mild, and most days were fine enough for Grantham to go sketching in the mornings or evenings. He was frequently accompanied by Donna, who, when he was actually working, went off by herself, wandering about the quaint alley ways or by the harbor, even taking an occasional trip to St. Mawes. Thanks to this new relationship with a man so completely unlike Nicholas, her bitterness began to abate a little, although she deliberately shut her mind and heart to Polbreath and all that it represented. Hayley's inherent courtesy combined with his humor and worldly knowledge quickened her interest in him, his life, and the various spheres of his journalistic experiences.

Occasionally she was mildly discomforted by a certain look in his eyes that suggested his feelings now went deeper than friendship, and she was just as illogically irritated by his refusal to commit himself.

Was she losing her charm? she wondered, on a late afternoon as they wandered back through the woods following one of Hayley's sketching sessions. No other man had been so completely content to keep his distance, while professing in words his admiration.

She did not want him to make sensational overtures. She simply needed at that point assurances that whatever else she had lost, she still retained her capacity to allure. It was all she had left, she thought, with an uncharacteristic stab of self-pity. Hayley's friendship at the beginning had been a comfort. But to have no argument, no challenge, no emotional situation to resolve, was becoming a trifle boring.

Perhaps he sensed her mood, for he said suddenly, "You're bothering about things again, aren't you? What's troubling you?"

She shrugged, pulling carelessly at a young frond of bracken as they passed.

"Nothing that hasn't been there all the time, at the back of my mind."

"Your husband?"

"Of course not. I detest him. We shall probably have a divorce."

"And then?"

"I really don't know," she answered. "Perhaps I'll travel."

"That's a very good idea," Hayley agreed. "Youth—life ahead, the whole world to see—what could anyone want more?"

"There are other things," Donna answered.

"Yes. I know that."

"But you're different aren't you?" she said, giving him a quick glance, "I mean you don't feel so desperately about anything that you think you'll die without it. You've had everything, I suppose."

"Most things. The important ones," he answered. "I lost my wife seven years ago. And until then I'd been as happy—more so maybe—than most men. Her death naturally left a tremendous vacuum. Oh there are always ways of filling a hole in one's life. But I've never been the type for second best. A one-woman man, you could say."

"I see."

"No. I don't think you do," he told her quietly. "I should have added, until now."

Donna felt the color rush to her face then fade again, leaving a sudden chill as he continued, "I'm an elderly man, Donna . . . I may call you that, mayn't I?"

"Of course."

"Not entirely in my dotage. Still—old enough to be your father. But that doesn't alter the fact that I could still love you—very dearly—if I thought there were a chance in the world of your wanting it. I'm not conventional. There are, as I've just said, many places in the world to visit. I would care, and look after you to the best of my ability. I'm not without means. But," he hesitated before continuing, "any step like that would have to mean something. Something very important. Do you understand?"

Donna hesitated for a moment, then said, with a catch of emotion in her voice. "Yes, I think so. And thank you."

If only he could be human, she thought—kiss her, even a gentle kiss—it would convey something, make her react either with revulsion or tenderness. But to be walking along under the trees with the pale sunlight

351

dappling the ferns, and the sleepy chortle of birds in the bushes—just as though they were acquaintances having a matter-of-fact discussion about a problematical future—was disconcerting to say the least. So she wandered on trying hard to think up a suitable remark, and presently, when he didn't speak, continued, "It's kind of you to . . . to think of me in that way. But I don't think it would work. Do you?"

They both paused suddenly, and then, with his hands on her shoulders, he did what she had hoped, kissed her full on her lips. There was no passion in it, just kindness, and a deep warmth. Tenderness, too.

When he released her, he said, "Unlike most newspapermen I'm not a very adept lover I'm afraid. But under different circumstances I assure you things would be different."

"You're very chivalrous," she said. "And I'm grateful for that. There's been so much in my life lately that's been quite . . . unspeakable."

He nodded. "I understand."

But of course he didn't, Donna told herself a moment later. How could he? He knew of Nicholas. His reputation. But the fire—the savagery—the passion with its alternating pain and peace . . . her heart contracted, as she remembered his hands on her body, her desire, and ultimate subjection to his will. So sweet, so terrifying, and ultimately humiliating. And yet—so wholly unforgettable.

If only she *could* forget. If only she could accept wholeheartedly and without reservation the undoubted affection this kindly and intelligent man offered, there'd be no need to worry or fret, or wonder what the next moment would bring, no torment or fear, or hungering any more for understanding that wasn't there. Her life would be on an even keel, and she might in the end learn to love him with the trust and patience he himself possessed.

But . . . such a small word, that but, yet how important.

She sighed involuntarily, and the whole wood, sud-

352

denly, to her heightened fancy seemed full of small sighs—as though spring were already mourning summer's decline into autumn.

Then she heard him saying gently, "My dear, don't think about it now. Give yourself time to get things into perspective. I can wait. I meant what I said though. Will you consider it, without any commitment on your part?"

"Of course I will," Donna answered, fully meaning it. "I'm . . . I'm really flattered. I don't know what . . ."

"Rubbish," he said quickly, to save her further embarrassment. "If you must know, I'm a very selfish individual, and certainly extremely arrogant, even to believe for one moment that so lovely a creature as yourself could spare an old fogey like me a serious thought."

"I didn't say that," Donna protested.

His hand touched hers lightly. "You didn't have to. As I told you before, I know people. You would never love me, Donna. In time you could possibly grow fond of me. But that's what you've got to decide for yourself—whether fondness could ever compensate for what you'd lose—a chance to reconciliation with Trevarvas."

"There's no chance," Donna said, with her chin out-thrust.

"My dear girl, there's every chance in the world, when the mere mention of his name sets your eyes blazing and your whole body trembling."

Donna realized that the last part of his statement was true. She was shaking, shaking so much inwardly that it sickened her, and made her feel faint.

She caught the trunk of a young tree quickly to steady herself.

"It's all right," she heard herself saying to her companion. "I shall be quite all right in a minute. It's ever since the fire . . ."

But her explanation did not really fool him.

"Why don't you return?" he said quickly. "I think you should Donna—because it's your place too. And you really want him don't you? Especially now."

"No, no! I don't, I don't!" she cried, with a sudden

desperate longing that she could hardly bear. "I've told you haven't I? He's hateful. I loathe him, as he loathes me. And I'm never going back. Never. *Never!*"

But three days later when she and Hayley were glancing though the papers in the writing room after breakfast, he happened to say, "It seems to me—though I'm breaking a confidence—that Nicholas Trevarvas is in for a pretty bad shock if events move in the way they are at present."

"Why?" Her voice was sharp. "What do you mean?"

"The Revenue," Hayley said briefly, "I happen to have a friend in the department who confided to me only this morning a pretty plot to catch him out."

Donna's heart missed a beat, then bounded on again. Trying to sound uninterested, she said, "Pretty plot? It sounds rather—melodramatic."

"Hm! Life is sometimes. Especially in some quarters."

Not wishing to press the matter too urgently, Donna controlled herself enough to study a news photograph before asking over-casually, "You mean smuggling? That sort of thing?"

"Yes. You've hit the nail right on the head. Apparently a merchant vessel with a French name, *La Belle Julie* will, tomorrow night at roughly eleven forty-five, unload several small boats bound for the north Cornish coast where they will deposit cargoes of spirits and lace in specific coves marked for the purpose. Unfortunately for your husband, officers of the Revenue will be conveniently placed to receive them." He paused before adding, "It was bound to happen sometime, my dear. I'm sorry for you. But not particularly for him. He's teased the authorities for far too long. Oh believe me, it will make a pretty scandal for some time to come. And that husband of yours will no doubt have ample opportunity in prison to consider his misdeeds and repent."

Donna was aghast. "*Nicholas*? *Prison*?"

"Cerainly, if he's found guilty, which I've no doubt at all he will be, and for a very long sentence indeed."

Donna was silent, unable to accept at first the full

implication of Grantham's flat statement. Prison! For Nicholas. It was unthinkable. And for a moment she hated Hayley for suggesting it, more even than she hated her husband. He would die, she told herself, cooped up as a convict behind high cold walls and in a cell where he'd chafe like some wild thing—an eagle, or a fiery stallion unable to race the skies or high moors. And she'd thought him so clever, never doubted his capacity to get his way or outwit anyone who threatened him.

"I don't believe it," she said at last. "You're trying to frighten me, aren't you?"

"Why should I, when I've such regard for you? What would be the point?"

"No. I suppose not."

"When—when did you say this French boat's due?"

"*La Belle Julie*? Tomorrow night. The conditions will be admirable. No moon. Only the vessel with its rich cargo to unload, and the Revenue waiting."

Donna shivered. "Why have you told me this?"

He shrugged. "Heaven knows, my dear. Sometimes even hardened newspapermen like me can act irrationally. I suppose I don't want the outcome to be too much of a shock to you."

"Thank you."

Although he pretended no further interest in the matter and devoted himself to his newspaper once more, Donna had the instinctive feeling that he was aware of her every movement, waiting for some reaction which at that point she was determined not to show.

After flipping the pages of a magazine vaguely, she said with apparent unconcern, "I think I shall take a walk now to the shops. It's fine, and I want to find a hairdresser's."

He looked up quizzically. "Good. I shan't do much sketching today, just wander presently to the harbor and take a few notes. After that I've an appointment at the bank. So if we both have a free morning to get our business over we can perhaps be together this afternoon?"

She smiled brightly. "That would be nice."

She left the room and went upstairs, filled with an excitement and urgency she hadn't experienced for weeks; not since the fire. One thought dominated all others in her head. Somehow she had to get news of the incriminating plot to Trevarvas. He didn't deserve her help, she told herself, as she dressed hurriedly in her outdoor winter attire. But just to be able to give it, would somehow make him subtly indebted to her, wiping away a little of the indignity she'd suffered from him.

So when she had seen Grantham, from her window, presently take off down the street with his box slung over his shoulder, she went down to the hall and asked the porter to hire a cab.

"I have to be out for the day," she explained. "Unexpected business. So would you please also inform the waiter that I will not be in for lunch."

"Certainly madam."

"And if Mr. . . . if Mr. Grantham inquires about me I would be grateful if you'd tell him that I'll expect to see him at dinner."

"I'll see that he gets the message," the man told her.

A little later, Donna, by then tensed up with excitement and nerves, was seated in a hackney cab jolting on the route northwest toward Polbreath. How would Nicholas greet her when she arrived? she wondered. And what would he say when she told him the news? Supposing he was away? The thought flooded her with a wave of depression. But then, with so much going on that concerned him, he would surely be around in the vicinity. Or would he? Would he, with his disconcerting habit of avoiding business trouble, somehow manage to be elsewhere—in possession of an alibi strong enough to protect him from suspicion?

She herself knew nothing of such matters. William, her father, would never have dreamed of being concerned in such shady affairs. "Be honest," he would always said, "and true to yourself. Then nothing can really hurt you."

How unlike Nicholas.

Herself too. She realized during the miles of travel that day, that honor and truth did not really count so much in the face of the other conflicting emotions within her—her deepening, wild desire to see Nicholas and watch him flinch, shamed a little perhaps, by her unexpectedly generous impulse. Yes. She watched him in her debt for once, instead of her forever having to be in his.

A sense of triumph and personal achievement had already overcome much of her fear and anxiety, when the cab drew up at Polbreath. She got out, told the driver to wait, as she would probably need him in a short time to take her back, then walked up the steps with her head high, back stiffened and erect, her heart beating more heavily than was comfortable, lips set coldly beneath the blazing eyes.

She pushed the door open, thankful that it wasn't locked, because she had forgotten her key, and walked into the hall.

How silent everything was.

At first she thought no one was in; no echo even came from the kitchens. But then of course the midday meal could be over. The journey from Falmouth had taken longer than she had thought.

And then she heard it. A high pitched trill of laughter, followed by a woman's voice: Rosina Penverrys saying, "I've enjoyed it so much, Nicholas. It's been *wonderful* seeing you . . . and all your precious plants. Of course I *do* know a little about botany . . ."

There was a sudden pause as Rosina Penverrys emerged with Nicholas beside her from the small room leading into the conservatory.

Donna felt her temper rising in a rush of hot jealousy and indignation as she stood quite still, watching and waiting. Rosina's hand went to her mouth automatically. "Oh dear," she gasped. "We didn't . . . I didn't . . ."

"You didn't expect me," Donna finished coldly. "Well, here I am. So . . ." She gulped before adding, "do you mind leaving us?"

Rosina drew herself up haughtily. "I'm here at the

invitation of Mr. Trevarvas. He is my host. I shall do exactly what he says."

Enraged by the highly-bred condescending voice, the lofty large countenance looking down on her so superciliously, Donna's fury got the better of her, and she did an outrageous thing. She stepped forward and brought her hand smartly and as hard as she could, flat across one of the odious pink cheeks.

Rosina stumbled back, white, shocked, trembling from head to toe with fury and shock.

"How dare you," she half gasped, half shrieked.

Nicholas then spoke for the first time. "I'm afraid that my headstrong wife is capable of daring to do much that most women wouldn't," he said wryly. "So perhaps after all, it would be better if you did leave. I apologize for such an unseemly show of temper, and promise you that it will certainly not happen again. The chaise is at the back. I'll inform Sarne. Meanwhile . . ." turning at the door to fling a hard glance at Donna, "I'll talk to you presently, when I hope you'll have recovered your equilibrium."

He turned sharply. The door closed behind them, and Donna, seething with anger and misery, was alone.

CHAPTER TWENTY-FOUR

The minutes ticked by slowly as Donna waited, stiff-backed for Nicholas's return. She realized that she had broken all codes of good behavior by her rash act, but in spite of a niggling regret there was pleasure in recalling Rosina Penverry's shocked face, the amazement in the prominent eyes, and stupid attempt at dignity as the large figure swept out of the room. What a farce it had been. And how aggravating to find the pompous creature once again installed at Polbreath, on good terms apparently with her husband. Why, of all people, had Rosina Penverrys always appeared at the most unpropitious moment? Even at the Coaching House she had had to sail in, drawing attention to matters that should never have been aired in public.

Still, Nicholas wouldn't understand that. He didn't even know. He would be angry, naturally. She didn't care though, not any more. Since their marriage was over all she had to do was to inform him about the *Belle Julie* business, and take her leave. He would be glad to see the back of her, and she would be more than thankful to get away. Any contact with Nicholas—even the mere thought of him—seemed to draw out the worst in her. With people like Miss Bray and Hayley Grantham she could act and talk in the civilized manner expected of William Penroze's daughter. But where Nicholas Trevarvas was concerned, her wild temper mostly got the better of her, leaving her at a disastrous disadvantage.

She simply couldn't help it, and she wasn't going to try any more.

But why didn't he come back? she wondered impatiently. If what Hayley had suggested was true—and she didn't doubt it—there might not be much time to get a warning to *La Belle Julie*. Even now the ship could be lying off the French coast ready to sail the next day. And Grantham hadn't actually referred to France. The vessel could be much further away, meaning that it would take longer to get to it.

Glancing at the clock intermittently, she wandered to the window, stared out briefly, but saw nothing clearly. Her thoughts were only on one thing—the danger Nicholas was in.

At last, thankfully, she heard the sounds of horse's hooves cantering down the drive and dying gradually into the distance. The chaise, then, had gone.

What a relief. Steeling herself for the confrontation, she waited stiffly, watching the door near the conservatory. He came in a moment later, and stood facing her, not moving at first, his dark eyes smoldering, lips compressed and stern.

Then he said in deadly cold tones, "What did you think you were doing?"

She hesitated before answering, her handkerchief a tight ball in one hand. "I . . . I . . . you mean Rosina?"

"Exactly. Not very sociable, were you? In fact you seem to have lost what vestige of manners you ever had. What have you to say for yourself, blundering in and attacking a guest of mine in such an unspeakable way?"

"Nothing," Donna answered promptly. "And if you expect me to apologize, I've no intention of doing it. That odious woman has been on my trail ever since I left here. She even came to The Bear and made me look ridiculous in front of everyone there, with her snide remarks and airs. I never liked her. Now I detest her. And I'm glad I slapped her face. I've been wanting to do it for a long time. Still . . ." She forced herself to smile brightly. "You'll be able to put things right there soon enough, won't you? And when we're divorced you can do the honorable thing and take her to the altar.

I'm sure she'll make a most dignified bride. Pompous, of course. All large women look pompous in white. But I expect her wealth and family will make up for it."

"Are you trying to be insulting?"

"Oh no, no, *no*," Donna retorted airily. "Why would I bother?"

"Why the devil did you come here then? And what do you mean by divorce?"

Looking deliberately away, she said, trying to sound calm though her heart was pounding, "Divorce is surely what we both want, and obviously the most sensible thing. As for why I came . . ." she turned quickly, head lifted, the warm color rich in her cheeks, eyes brilliantly orange-gold under the shadowed veiling of her velvet hat. "I came because I heard something. You're in danger."

Nicholas laughed. A curt, unbelieving sound that had no humor in it. "What the hell are you talking about? Danger? For heaven's sake stop your stupid games."

"It's not a game," she interrupted. "A friend of mine, Hayley Grantham, told me all about the *Belle Julie*. It's going to unload cargo, illegal cargo, around the coast here tomorrow night. Don't say it's not true, Nicholas. Mr. Grantham wouldn't lie, and he says . . . he says the Revenue will be waiting. You'll be caught, do you understand?"

He shook his head. "I can't say that I do. What has the *Belle Julie* to do with me?"

"You know," she cried passionately. "It's your cargo, isn't it? And don't pretend. I'm not a child any more. I told you that once before, lots of times. I've known for ages what you were up to. But you wouldn't admit it or listen. Now it could be too late unless—unless you act quickly. Hayley says . . ."

"For heaven's sake leave your precious Hayley out of it," he told her with a flash of sudden temper. "I don't wish to hear about your new admirer and his paltry gossip. Understand?"

"Yes. It's just like you to go into a rage because things don't please you."

"And it's just like you, madam, to return upsetting a pleasurable afternoon and evening with your moods and tantrums simply to get your own back."

"It's not that. I came because of you. To help."

"Dear me. Did you now! It seems to me you had quite another idea in your head—to steal back with any convenient lie that suited you, through sheer devilment. You don't want me, no! But on the other hand you're determined no other woman will. Well—let me tell you, you're wrong. If I want Rosina Penverrys I'll have her, and you, my love, can go your own sweet way to hell."

She gasped. "You're even worse than I thought. You're . . . you're . . ."

"I'm quite capable of looking after my own affairs as you should know, by now. So shall we end this unpleasant scene before we have a repetition of what happened before?"

"Certainly," she answered, her cheeks flaming. "And it's you, Nicholas Trevarvas, who'll find yourself in hell. I warned you because it was my duty. But don't think I care a jot any more what happens to you. I'm going."

He held the door open for her, a speculative, ironic gleam in his eye, as he said, "I hope you enjoy your walk."

"Walk?" She stared up at him blankly. "I have a cab waiting."

"The cab, madam, was dismissed a quarter of an hour ago."

"Do you mean you . . . ?"

"I mean that now you're back, you'll stay," he answered. "The rose room is prepared, the bed already aired. As Rosina Penverrys isn't here . . . you may as well take her place. But have no fear, I shan't intrude."

Donna stared at him, speechless for seconds, outraged by his nerve, though the odd thrill of being near him was already stirring her blood and heart. Then she said very clearly and coldly, "You mentioned a walk. I think I prefer to take that suggestion."

She walked very erectly into the hall, and to the front

362

door. But when she tried it, it was locked. She turned with her eyes blazing.

"Kindly let me out."

"Oh no. I think not."

She struggled with the knob, pushing her knee against it wildly, knowing all the time that she was being childish. Without the key she couldn't possibly leave.

She opened her mouth to shout. But before any sound could come, Trevarvas had her kicking, in his arms, one hand across her mouth. "Be quiet," he said, in a vibrant, low voice as the toes of her shoes caught his knees and shins sharply. "Shut up, Donna, or I won't answer for myself. Supposing Mrs. Thornton comes, or Beth?"

He held her for a few seconds more, until her struggles had stopped.

"Now," he said, "are you going to behave? Or shall I call on Sarne to assist me?"

Suddenly all resistance left her. Her body went limp, relaxed.

"All right. As you're so determined, I'll . . . I'll stay. Not because I want to. The whole place is odious to me. You too. Still . . ."

"You have no choice. That's true." He put her down, though hesitating briefly, as though grudging her freedom.

She sighed, made an attempt to straighten her hat and hair, then with a supreme effort of will and an assumption of dignity that she did not feel, went slowly to the foot of the stairs. Once there she paused and turned.

"I'll never forgive you for this," she said. "Never!"

He shrugged. "There are so many things that you seem to hold against me, one more won't make any difference I think. I suppose you won't wish to come down again, so I'll see that food is sent up to you. And for heaven's sake, don't look like that. It's—confoundedly irritating."

He watched her as she mounted the stairs, following

363

a moment later to see her open the bedroom door and go in. He heard the sound of a key being turned, and then silence.

With his shoulders sunk a trifle dejectedly, Nicholas made his way back to the hall and into the smoking room. From the expression on his face no one could have guessed what his thoughts were.

Donna flung herself on the lacy pink bed and lay there for a time, without even bothering to remove her outdoor things. Then, when the feeling of exhaustion and nausea had passed, she got up, and went to the door again to make sure that it was really secure.

Finding the key safely turned, she took off her jacket, hat, and removed her shoes, realizing how the brief interim with Nicholas had drained her. At the same time she felt a tiny pulse fluttering her stomach near the womb, and her hand instinctively went there, lingering protectively over the first frail beat of a life not entirely her own.

She knew then that Sarah had been right. Deep, deep down an embryo was already struggling and forming its own pattern within her—a pattern that she had not visualized but only dimly apprehended on the day of her father's death, when the dark horseman had watched her from the moors. She had known then, instinctively, but not consciously, that she would never belong to Jos, or have his child—something stronger and more primitive had been already awoken in her—something Trevarvas had which Jos would never possess, the power to claim and chain her, as he was chaining her at this moment against all her will and reason. And with a right more strong than any other now! The right of potential fatherhood.

An hour must have passed before the housekeeper came up carrying a light meal on a tray, with a glass of white wine. "It's me ma'am," she called, after knocking, "I've brought something for you to eat."

Donna went to the door, took the tray from her and when asked if she would also like coffee answered,

364

"No," thanked the woman, and as soon as she had gone, turned the key again in the lock.

Evening was already closing in, filling the shadows of the room with a muted, deep rose glow that once again flooded her with a heady sweetness and oppression as though another mocking presence still lingered there, reveling in her discomfiture. Everything was so soft, so luxurious, so exquisite in its refinement. The portrait, she noticed, was hanging in its original place once more, with the glass replaced. The ornate small clock ticking musically away, and the firelight flickering against the walls, as though the passing of time had made no impact at all. This was the domain of another woman—the woman who had been Nicholas's wife and lived at Polbreath before her. She had not sold herself, as Trevarvas appeared to think Donna had, for money or power, but had brought kudos to him, instead. Whatever he had thought of her, however dreary and unresponsive a marriage partner she had proved to be, her dignity must have remained intact, being a Vencarne and both socially and financially secure herself. Donna could have hated her, if it had been possible to hate a dead person. But it wasn't. All she could do was despise her own physical need of him which lingered despite her resolve to deny it.

And she was worried. However hard she tried, she couldn't rid her mind of Hayley Grantham's warning, and the dark picture of *La Belle Julie* drawing ever nearer with its disastrous and dangerous cargo.

If only Trevarvas had listened, taken her hasty actions at their face value for once, and believed in her. But obviously he would never do so. He simply did not trust her. The episode with Lucien had soured him beyond reason, increasing his determination to outwit the law. But how could he? If the Revenue really was on his track? And surely he must recognize the danger after what she'd told him about Grantham.

With the thoughts racing so wildly from one angle to another it seemed impossible to get things into perspective. She had a wild notion, at one point, of somehow

365

getting out to the stables—perhaps with Beth's help—
and saddling Saladin for a mad ride back to Falmouth.
If she pleaded pathetically, and made herself beguiling
enough, perhaps Hayley would intercede on her behalf
with this friend of his—the Revenue official.

It would be asking a great deal. But he was a kind
man. Surely there was something he could do?

The suggestion disintegrated as soon as it had occurred to her. Grantham had gone as far as he dared in
revealing even a hint of the business, and he was certainly not the kind of person to be bribed by feminine
wiles. Neither was it likely that she would be able to
leave Polbreath without Nicholas or his servants finding
out.

There was only one answer. In the morning she
would try again to make him see sense. There might still
be time to put an end to the illegal operation before it
penetrated Cornish waters.

At last, with matters resolved in this way, and too
tired to think any further, she undressed wearily, having
found one of her newly washed nightgowns and a thin
wrap lying in a drawer of the chest.

Out of habit rather than any conscious vanity, she
lingered naked before the mirror for a few minutes before getting into bed. In the reflection from the fire, her
body gleamed rosy-pink, subtle still, and beautifully
proportioned, showing no signs at all of the frail new
life struggling within. Her breasts, firm and tilted, gave
no indication of sagging—only a slight ripening to further plumpness. Her flanks were still lithe and slender,
her stomach flat. In such moments Trevarvas should
have been with her, she thought irrationally, not in anger or battle, or the wish to humiliate and subject, but
to give her peace and pride, with his strong hands gentle
about her body, his heart entirely hers for once, bound
by the miracle of this thing that had happened between
them—the begetting of a new life.

Perhaps if he had knocked and wished to see her
then, she would have complied and all would have been
well.

But he did not. And there was no sound of him from the landing or below. Everything was hauntingly and uncannily quiet. Even Beth did not come up to see her.

Presently she slipped on gown and wrap, took a match from a box lying nearby, and lit the lamp. Its mellow, incandescent glow shone comfortingly from the immense bulb-shade, like a miniature pale sun, dispelling the shadows. She seated herself on the elegant chair facing the dressing table, and lifted a brush to her tumbled hair. How soft it felt, like thick silk under the rhythmic strokes of firm fine bristles. And yet she was alone, with none to appreciate her beauty, and no one to care that in spite of her wayward and spirited bravado, she was so inwardly frightened, and desperately in need of assurance.

After a time she got up and went to bed, but sleep was long in coming, and when she woke daylight was already streaking the sky through the rose-colored curtains.

She got up, dressed quickly, and went downstairs.

Breakfast was already waiting for her on the table. Beth was hovering nearby to greet her and ask if she wanted coffee or tea.

"Tea, I think, Beth," Donna said, not really caring, adding as casually as possible, "Has my husband already had his?"

"Oh yes, and left, Mrs. Trevarvas," Beth answered, "quite an hour ago."

"Did he leave any message?"

"No. Except that he didn't expect to be long, although he couldn't say exactly."

"Oh."

"I think he had an appointment at the bank or something," Beth continued, "Anyway . . ." her voice faltered.

Donna looked up. "Yes?"

"We're all glad to see you back."

"Thank you."

"I hope it's permanent? Without wishing to sound impertinent ma'am. You must forgive me. I don't want

367

to pry, but things aren't the same with you away."

"Things are never the same for long," Donna answered ambiguously. "Each day's a bit different to the last. We'll have to see, won't we?"

Thinking she might have sounded a little unkind, she added more warmly, "It's nice to have you here anyway. And thank you—for wanting me."

Beth flung her a shrewd glance before she left, and just for an instant Donna wondered if she knew, or had at least guessed the root of her conflicting emotions and erratic behavior.

It didn't matter. Speculation, in a few weeks or months, would become proof, and everyone at Polbreath would know, provided that she was still here.

CHAPTER TWENTY-FIVE

For most of the morning Donna wandered about the house aimlessly from room to room, library, drawing room, conservatory and kitchens, chatting with servants to ease her tension, or making her way to the back where Sarne and a boy were busy with the horses. Ballard, the other Polbreath man, appeared on the scene when she was there, but seeing her, moved away disapprovingly. He had never shown much liking for the new young mistress, and it was obvious to Donna by the primping of his small mouth in his large face, and narrowed glance of his eyes, that he had absorbed his earful of the tasty gossip going around. And no doubt relished every bit of it, Donna thought, as his portly figure disappeared again.

Donna crossed to Saladin's stall. The lift of the head, fiery gleam of the velvet eyes, and whinny of joy as her hand touched the satin-black nose filled her with an overwhelming desire to be astride and riding him over the moors. But wisdom and the knowledge that Nicholas might return any moment restrained her.

"Have you any idea when Mr. Trevarvas will be back?" Donna asked Sarne. "I forgot to give him a message last night. It's very important."

Sarne shook his head. "No mistress. He doesn't tell much these days. Quiet he is, not always his usual self as you could say, except when someone calls to see him."

She went back to the house presently, hoping that Nicholas would have arrived, but he hadn't. Neither had anyone received a message of any kind.

369

"I shouldn't worry ma'am," Beth said once, meeting her in the hall. "Mr. Trevarvas hasn't been very punctual lately. A bit—unpredictable, as they say. But then that's only to be expected isn't it, with you so much away, and the fire and everything."

Her thoughts turned again to the wretched Revenue business, her restlessness increased again to unbearable anxiety. Why didn't he come? Where on earth was he? The bank could be a mere excuse to keep the servants satisfied. In any case a bank appointment was generally a very brief affair. Far more likely that he was off to comfort Rosina Penverrys. Well, good luck to her. If she had managed effectively to ensnare his affections in his wife's absence, it would serve her right to find that she had netted a convict for a lover.

For a short time Donna's anger dispelled a little of her anxiety, but it returned threefold as the day passed from morning to afternoon with still no sign of her husband. She ate hardly anything, sending her food away practically untouched, or else secretly dividing it between the dogs and the two cats who wandered into the dining room whenever possible.

By five o'clock Donna was feeling desperate, her mind a seething vortex of wild plans and conjectures that she knew now she had little time to resolve. The minutes and hours were closing in. If Nicholas didn't return soon everything would be too late; and it would serve him right . . . oh God! It would serve him right, she told herself with rising panic. But she couldn't let it happen. Not that. Not even to spite Rosina.

So presently she returned to the stables, where the boy, luckily, was alone. "Look Joe," she said, "I want you to leave Saladin's stall unbolted tonight and let me have the keys."

"But mistress . . . Mr. Sarne, he'd have the hide off me for sure. I couldn't do that."

"You can, and you will," Donna told him firmly. "I take it no one will be back here again this evening?"

"They shouldn't be, mistress. It's my job, see, to have

the animals fed and the stables safely shut, except when . . ."

"All right then. Give me the keys."

"But the master, mistress. Any time he could be here, on that Pluto of his. He'd see—oh I couldn', mistress. 'Tes all my job's worth."

"Nonsense," Donna told him. "If the master, my husband arrives? I'll see to it you're in no way blamed. I promise you. Don't you believe me?"

He scratched his ear thoughtfully, hesitated for a time, humming and hawing, until, under the pleading smile and softening luminous gaze of her strange glowing eyes, he capitulated.

"All right, mistress. If you be sure there'll not be trouble."

"None for you anyway, Joe," Donna promised.

So the keys were reluctantly handed over, Donna went back to the house, and the waiting started again. A restless, almost unbearable procedure that continued through the whole of the evening, until at last, at ten o'clock, the servants retired to bed.

Donna was already in her room by then, listening with ears alert for any sound or small sign that Nicholas had come back. There was none.

By eleven o'clock she could no longer remain confined in that pink shell of a bedroom. By great good luck she had found Luke's old breeches in a gardener's shed during the day, and secreted them already upstairs under the bed. They would help a good deal in the dark; riding astride was so much simpler than having to swish a leg confined by restricting skirts over the horned right side-saddle. And it would be dark that night. Very dark indeed.

She dressed quickly, her heart beating a wild tattoo against her ribs, as she pulled her dark winter jacket over the breeches. She had no boots there, but hoped to find a pair lying about somewhere, in the stables perhaps, or the woodshed. But if not she would have to ride as she was, calves bare, feet in the one pair of flat slippers she had at Polbreath.

371

What a sight, she thought briefly, catching a glimpse of herself in the mirror. Pale, set face, shadowed eyes, and darkened haggard lines of cheekbones, so emphasized from strain and determination in the wan candle flame. Her hair too . . . no longer a glory of burnished ebony, but scrimped back from her face with a red ribbon that gave her the appearance of some wild gypsy-boy rather than the young woman Nicholas Trevarvas had married. But that was all for the best. If she should be glimpsed making her get away following— which was what she meant to do—no one could conceivably guess her identity. If they did, if any canny Revenue official had an inkling, he would certainly not make any blundering accusations until he had proof, and this she would make sure he did not get, because by then every clue would be destroyed.

The very excitement of her plan—the risk even then—that she might be thwarted, gave impetus to her decision, and presently she was creeping downstairs quietly, pausing for a moment every time a stair faintly creaked, or any other slight sound disturbed the deadly silence of the house.

Once in the hall she felt more secure, hurrying to the kitchens and the adjoining butler's pantry, where she knew, under a shelf at the far end, the oil was kept. She lit a candle, and saw to her relief that a small can had already been filled for any lamp needed in the morning. It would do, without the trouble of having to fill a lidded jar or some other receptacle and could be comfortably pushed away into one of Luke's ample side-pockets. She picked it up gingerly, with matches and a sheet or two of newspaper in case it was needed, then returned to the kitchen, letting herself out by the side door, which she locked, slipping the key into the other pocket so that she could get in again without anyone knowing.

Only a few minutes later she was in Saladin's stall, whispering, soothing, trying in vain to check his first joyous whinny when he heard her voice. There was still no sign of Pluto or Nicholas. She waited anxiously, wondering if anyone had been roused, but apparently no one had, and in the shortest possible time she had saddled the colt and was leading him through a gate at the back, and across a field to the lane.

Once there, she quickly mounted, and was away through the darkness, cutting along the track skirting the northern hump of Rosebuzzan, a route that Saladin knew well and was quick to sense and scent, with the soft west wind blowing at their backs. She held him at a steady pace, wary of the dark, and taking no chance of a stumble or sudden rising squawk of birds that could scare the sensitive creature.

"Good boy," she kept reiterating softly. "It's all right, Saladin boy, we're together . . . you and me, Saladin . . . good boy . . . good boy . . ."

He seemed to respond and understand. The journey round rock and through thick furze passed without mishap—over miniature hillocks where gorse bushes crouched, and loose stones occasionally showered into heather and stunted bramble . . . until eventually they reached the high road overlooking the distant sea.

From there she cut down, turning sharply westward, passing above and beyond Trencobban's tumbled walls, on and on leaving the derelict mine behind, a ghost shape against the black sky, with only a few pinpointed stars glimmering intermittently.

Except for the scurry, once, of a fox ahead, there was no sound or sign of life other than their own; only the wind and the sea breaking below, and the rhythmic thud of Saladin's hooves on the soft earth.

Before taking a sharp line down to the cliffs, Donna drew the colt to a halt, and waited cautiously to get her bearings. Through the extreme dark it was difficult to see any form or shape except as mere muted blobs against the deeper tones of sky, but she knew that there was a track quite close by which had once led to a long derelict mine-house. It was barren and fairly wide— more of a rough, narrow truckway, which cut between massed boulders of rock, to the left of a ravine in the cliff where the building had once stood. As a child she had wandered there sometimes, feeling a queer kind of

373

awe about the dead-looking reddened soil, where no plants grew, no wild flowers, or even the pink thrift which was usually so abundant around the coast. A lonely, desolate place, but hidden from the high road, and if one went around a finger of rock, she remembered the undergrowth had encroached again in tangled masses of heather, gorse, and ugly bent bramble. This was what she wanted for her purpose. For this she had brought the oil and paper, to set a blaze from the cliff that would surely warn any lurking small boats and *La Belle Julie* herself, that there was danger for unloading in any nearby coves that night.

Her hands tautened on the reins as she located the track, urging Saladin on again, cautiously, and as soundlessly as she could, for fear that the Revenue might be lurking in the neighborhood. It was hardly likely though. At the bottom of the narrow ravine was only a flat stretch of sand, with no caves or inlets, and above, a little further to the west, a dank dangerous stretch of bog, where no one with any sense would venture. She would have to be careful herself, but she was thankful for the mire, because it would mean no risk of a moorland blaze or the fire spreading.

So she went ahead and down, taking the rough truck road steadily, keeping her head fairly low over Saladin's neck, so that they would both be shielded between the boulders, if the clouds suddenly lifted.

But they didn't, and when they reached the steepest cut down to the beach, Donna dismounted and tethered Saladin loosely by the reins to a stark, dead branch of a wind-blown tree, saying, "Wait here, boy. Steady. I won't be long."

Making sure that the can and paper were still secure in a pocket of Luke's breeches, with the matches in the other, she made her way half down the tortuous incline. Then she turned to her left, groping toward the thickening undergrowth, stepping cautiously and slowly, clutching at any available ledge, until at last she'd reached what was almost a thicket—a massed shape of briars and twisted nut-trees, bracken, and gorse. She looked once toward the inky sea before pushing the dried paper into a gap. No ship was visible, no sight or sound of any small boat. But she knew that if they were coming at all they must be already out there.

Her hands were trembling when she opened the can and swung it, spattering its contents over the paper and furze. Then, lighting several matches at a time, she threw them into the undergrowth, followed by the rest of the box.

There was a sudden crackling, followed by a roar and leap of flame that curdled and blew in a widening crimson streak toward the sky. As the wind was from the west it spread seaward away from the cliff, so that Donna, with the sting of smoke in her eyes and throat, was able to extricate herself without harm except for a cut hand grazed by rock, and a temporary constriction of the lungs due to shock and the acrid air.

She was pulling herself up the ravine when a terrified whinny of fear from above, accompanied by the pounding and stamping of horse's hooves, rose briefly above the spitting and crackling of the fire.

"Saladin! . . ." Donna tried to call soothingly, "Saladin boy, it's all right, Wait . . ."

But by the time she had reached the top of the cliff the colt had broken free and was galloping away wildly. His neighs intermingled weirdly with the screaming of gulls. Now and again she glimpsed him—a brief black shape against the lurid sky, then he was gone again into the dark night.

Donna slumped down by a rock, wet now from perspiration and shock. Her head swam and her stomach lurched. She propelled herself up, and tried to stand, gasping for air. But the air seemed not there—only a vast choking emptiness, a sense of the world slipping from under her, and then nothingness, as she fell.

The legendary horseman of Carn Kenidzek, the hooting Carn, was there, with his fiery company of devils, flying across moor and sky from the dreaded Gump. The insane chatter of birds and demons was around her, and there was no place to ride, hide in, or run to any more, only a haunted wilderness of groping rocks and clutching hands clawing her hair and flesh with macabre skeleton figures, while the wind moaned and the lowering sky enclosed her in a thickened carpet of smoke and flame. She tried to scream, but her lips were dumb, and her eyes were blind: blind to everything but the greedy swarm of batlike creatures on every side, grimacing, jeering, filling the universe with their inane chattering laughter. This was the end then—the final end of life and love and her passionate desire to have and to hold. Just nothing but darkness and ultimate defeat.

Did she really open her eyes for a moment before the last desperate effort for consciousness? She never knew. But presently all sound and sight of vision or dream faded, leaving her alone and lost there—a pale slip of a girl in boy's attire, with a bird twittering by her, and torn hair streaking her face with a tangle of wind-blown heather.

CHAPTER TWENTY-SIX

It was almost midnight when Trevarvas reached the outskirts of St. Inta after an irritating jaunt to Falmouth where he had stayed at The Boar most of the time, idling the moments away waiting for Hayley Grantham.

Mr. Grantham, he had been told at the desk when he arrived, was out painting somewhere. He would probably be back for lunch, but no one could possibly say.

Nicholas, having stabled Pluto temporarily in the yard, chafed at the waste of time. Grantham had a good deal to explain for himself, including why the devil he'd been putting such plaguey notions into his wife's head. The fellow, like most newspapermen, he'd thought testily, was probably an insufferable busybody with an eye for women into the bargain, and no compunction at all in putting a spoke in others' concerns if it furthered his interests.

Jealousy gnawed him when he recalled Donna's obvious admiration and faith in her new friend. He could so easily picture her capitulation to studied flattery, especially now, suffering as she was from the loss of her home, and from injured dignity. He didn't much hope that confrontation with Grantham would help matters. But he meant to get to the root of his allegations, find out for himself just how much he *really* knew of business deals that had nothing to do with him at all, blast the man.

Grantham had not returned until six, and the meeting, from Trevarvas's point of view, had proved highly unsatisfactory.

"My dear fellow," Hayley had said, as they took

drinks in the smoking room, "if I embroidered the truth a little that's surely a journalist's—forgive me, ex-journalist's—prerogative. And you must admit that far from dragging your lovely wife from your arms, I sent her headlong into them. Isn't that so?"

"No," Nicholas had answered coldly, but with the skin hot under his collar. "As a matter of fact, through your unwarranted lies you created an extremely unpleasant scene."

"Oh dear."

"Which involved not only an argument with my wife, but provoked an unseemly attack on a mutual friend, Miss Penverrys."

There was a pause during which Grantham's lips twitched and his eyes twinkled. "I know. A rather *large* young woman who will become distinctly larger and more formidable with the years, no doubt. Good heavens man!" his voice altered suddenly, snapping with impatience and a flash of anger. "Do you know how lucky you are? Have you the first idea of what you mean to that adorable creature you married? Do you think there isn't a single man around here or anywhere else for that matter, who wouldn't give his eyes to be in your shoes? If I'd thought I had a ghost of a chance with her, sending her hot on your trail again is the last thing I would have done. But some women never learn. As for the rest—don't pretend, that like Brutus, Trevarvas is so honorable a man. I know your shady deals and little affairs, just as I know your uncanny ability to steer clear of the law. But if you take my advice, you'll draw in your horns a little and spend less time on your adventures, and more in your home."

"And if you were a larger man I'd . . ."

"I know. I know, sir. But I happen to be exceedingly small, with no liking at all for either pistols or fists. I came here for peace and quiet, and I hope very much that you don't intend to bother me further."

Nicholas had been about to reply heatedly when the door opened for two men to enter, obviously the type of flourishing business gentlemen for which The Boar catered so efficiently.

Grantham had presently left the room with a curt nod to Trevarvas, and Nicholas, with the interview over, found to his surprise that he was astonishingly hungry.

He had eaten a satisfactory dinner of roast beef with the usual Yorkshire pudding, two vegetables and horseradish sauce, followed by apple tart liberally topped by thick cream and with two glasses of white wine. Afterward he'd had a double brandy, and was feeling almost optimistic when he set off again astride Pluto for Polbreath.

Unfortunately the horse had shed a shoe only half a mile or so out of Falmouth and he'd had to walk him back to the nearest blacksmith's, only to find that the man had taken off for a pint at a local kiddleywink. The journey back therefore had been a tedious drawn-out affair, aggravated further by thoughts of Donna.

Would she be still at Polbreath or have taken off somewhere in his absence?

He could imagine her walking out again in a huff, though heaven alone knew where. Most of her belongings, as far as he knew, were still at The Boar, but as she had not arrived before he left, it was hardly likely that she'd do so now. The uncertainty troubled him. As he took the corner at last to the high road that wound to the turn and valley-lane leading to Polbreath, her image rose to torment him with a hunger not only physical but of the heart and spirit also.

He ached and longed for her. Had he gone too far, he wondered? But what could she expect, throwing her tantrums about the way she did, taunting and playing him up—landing herself in compromising situations that no full-blooded man in his senses would tolerate?

Before their marriage he had hoped against hope that the security of being his wife would tame and bring her lovingly to his arms. He knew now it hadn't, and never would. Either he would have to accept her as she was—

379

wayward, willful, and utterly intriguing—or put an end to everything. In that case she could have a hefty settlement and live where she chose, that was—provided he agreed. And he didn't see why the devil he should. She'd married him. She was his. Or should be. Why couldn't she at least give a little, and call it quits? That cold, set look of her face—the blazing, wildcat eyes and stubborn little chin—her contempt and derision! The sudden sweet abandon of her when she turned to laughter and passion. Was there ever so maddening a creature, loving one moment, cold the next, so unpredictable that he didn't know how on earth to deal with her?

Maybe she should have taken young Jos Craze, after all, he thought, as he drove Pluto furiously on: gone with him, as he'd wanted, to America and had a chance to start life anew, freed of responsibilities and that load of a mine which had driven her into his own arms. But he rejected the notion instantly. He was not generally a believer in pre-ordination or fate, but he could not believe that Donna Penroze hadn't been destined to be his wife from his first clear glimpse of her when she was little more than a child.

He remembered the moment distinctly, even after so many years. Selina had been alive then, and he had been riding over his own fields after a particularly frustrating discussion of their marital problems. Donna had been wearing a blue dress, her dark hair alive with russet glints in the sunlight, her face hidden as she stooped to gather cowslips. He had been tempted to shout and drive her away, but the simplicity of her pose, the graceful slope of her young neck, and the brief glimpse of white petticoat above the slim ankles, had caught and held him transfixed.

Then she'd looked up, and it had seemed to him that all the colors of sun and water and changing spring light, had flooded her eyes. She had stared at him for a second or two, then turned quickly and run to the far lane leading northward toward Trencobban.

After that he'd seen her from time to time, but those first moments had remained unconsciously symbolic in his mind. He had thought, after Selina's death, that the bad blood between the two families could be resolved, but it hadn't happened. William Penroze, though always formally polite, had seemed to him a cold-blooded, austere man, overconscious of his lineage. In Trevarvas's opinion Penroze's professed democracy had merely been an inverted form of snobbery.

So there had been no meeting point, and Nicholas had seen to it that the poverty-stricken, proud Penrozes hadn't benefited by so much as a penny from his pocket. Now he saw that this was a mistake. If he had invested earlier in William Penroze's failing conern, Donna's grudge against him would almost certainly never have taken root.

The chaos of his thoughts so preoccupied him that he didn't notice the red glow over the cliffs until he neared the point where the high road cut down towards the ruined shell of Trencobban.

He drew Pluto to a halt, and waited for a minute trying to get his bearings accurately. Quite obviously there was—or had been—a fire on the cliff, and as accurately as he could judge some considerable distance to the west, beyond Wheal Faith or any other distinctive landmark. Odd, he thought; it hadn't been dry enough lately for a fire to start naturally, and that point in the coast wasn't one to encourage lovers or stray visitors.

Then what, in the name of old Harry, was it all about?

He kicked Pluto on again, deciding to go straight ahead, instead of turning at the crossroads for Polbreath. He cut westward and from there turned back slightly toward the coast down the old truck road. But when he reached the turn a dark figure sprang from the corner, waving a lantern crazily, causing the horse to whinny and rear, until Trevarvas pulled him viciously to a halt.

"Sarne!" he exclaimed. "What the . . ."

The exclamation died on his lips, as the man gibbered half coherently, "It's the mistress, sir . . . she's out there somewhere . . . she must be, master. There's

381

bin a fire, and her colt's back, saddle and all, but no mistress, sir—and no sign of her in her room!"

He broke off, waiting for the spate of words. Instead Nicholas paused, speechless, and rigid until the horse had quieted. Then he said in deadly tones, "Someone will answer for this. If she's come to harm, someone will pay . . . by God they will."

Without another word he started off again, taking the truck road wildly, bearing always slightly to the right, a dark figure on a dark horse, black against the smoldering crimson of the sky, skirting the edge of the inky bog until he reached the clifftop just beyond the ravine. The smell of oil still clung to the air. The stunted undergrowth still smoldered above the sea where the breaking waves rose and fell rhythmically with a froth of silvered milky pink. The wind had died. There was no sight or sound of a living thing. Not even the shape of a distant ship on the far horizon. Empty, and somehow curiously lonely and forbidding.

Nicholas jumped from the saddle, and leading Pluto quietly by the reins, started his search. The light was still bad, despite the remaining glow and drift of starlight below the passing clouds. "Donna!" he called, and then again, "Donna . . . Donna . . ." but there was no response. No answering cry save the sudden shriek of a gull from nearby. Desperation gave impetus to the quest. By every tump or boulder he stopped, disturbing undergrowth gently where he thought she might be lying, then kicking savagely at the blackened soil and wood when it revealed nothing. Fear was growing in him, although he wouldn't acknowlege it. She could easily have fallen to the sea, if indeed she had been there at all. The idea, only a vague half-formed suggestion at first, suddenly flared into frightening significance. If she'd been there! If. But why? *Why*?

Before the question had properly formulated, he knew the answer.

Grantham. His stupid suggestion that the Revenue were waiting. Donna's plea and assertion that he, Nicholas, was in danger.

Oh God, he thought, struggling with his emotion, with the desperate longing and love for her that he had not fully admitted until then. Pray heaven she's safe. And aloud . . . "Donna, Donna . . ."

He stumbled around, leaving Pluto to wander at will, tearing his hands on the clawing bramble, kicking stones, with the sweat damp on clothes and flesh, crying, shouting, until it seemed there was no breath left in his body.

And then, suddenly, he saw her. A pale, small face with closed eyes, her form hidden, except for the tips of fingers sticking awkwardly through a tump of heather.

He knelt down, lifting her head against his breast, cradling the scratched face close, whispering brokenly, "Donna . . . oh Donna, my wild one . . . my love."

He caught her into his arms and struggled to his feet, thinking at first that she must be dead. Then, as he stood there gnawed by torment and uncertainty, she slowly, miraculously, opened her eyes.

"It's all right, Nicholas," she whispered. "I've warned them. They won't get you now."

As she drifted off into sleep again he fancied that she edged a little closer. Very gently then, he somehow pulled her onto Pluto with him, and they started the slow trek back to Polbreath.

CHAPTER TWENTY-SEVEN

For three days after her return to Polbreath, Donna lay inert in her pink bedroom, apparently careless of what went on around her. She ate automatically, getting up from time to time to stare out of the window, or to search aimlessly through what belongings she had there.

Nicholas had been informed by the doctor that she was with child, and that apparently no physical harm had been done. At first he was delighted, then distressed by her attitude.

"Go away," she said, the first time he went in to see her, "I don't want to talk." And when he put out a hand to touch her, "Leave me alone."

"But Donna . . ."

"Go away."

With compressed lips he'd turned and left her.

As he went downstairs he met the doctor in the hall.

"Well?" he said in his habitual bright voice, "How is she?"

"I'm waiting for you to tell me," Nicholas retorted shortly. "Obviously I'm no use. She won't talk, or even look at me."

"My dear sir, she's still very shocked. And on top of other worries . . . losing her father's home, her sister-in-law's tragic death, and now this . . . this other business . . ." His voice wavered. There was a short silence until he resumed more practically, "How did it start, the fire? Was it chance or intent?"

"I'm sure I don't know," Nicholas replied "As it's on my own land and no real harm has been done I'm not

384

bothering about it. For the moment anyway. What concerns me is my wife."

"Naturally. Naturally."

"You're sure there's no concussion or anything?"

"I'm convinced in my own mind that there's nothing wrong with her but reaction combined with pregnancy. But if you want a second opinion I'll get one." His voice was tart.

Nicholas turned away. "I'm not doubting your opinion. If you're satisfied, I accept it."

"Good. I think you're wise. Mrs. Trevarvas has a strong constitution, in fact in a week she should be her old self again. There'll be no need for her to languish and lie about—the sooner you can get her out of doors taking healthy but careful exercise, the better it will be for both of you."

"Yes."

The doctor patted his arm. "Cheer up. Women often have strange moods at these times. Try and remember that."

Nicholas did try. The trouble was that Donna obviously had no intention of doing so. As the doctor had predicted, she quickly recovered physically, but emotionally she remained aloof and frigid, insisting on keeping to herself in the small pink room, refusing to allow the slightest intimacy between them, and when he protested as gently as possible, she merely faced him with cold eyes and tightened lips telling him to leave her alone and not bother her. Once she even added, "If you touch me I'll scream."

He nearly said, "Then scream away, darling. Let the whole house know," but controlled himself in time. If she'd been ill he'd have understood. But the fact was, she had never appeared healthier, and the doctor had assured him that for a month or two there was no reason at all why their married life shouldn't continue its normal pattern.

How delicately put, Nicholas had thought ironically. As if anything about Donna could conceivably be called normal. Whether the servants noticed the continuing

385

constraint between them he didn't know. In their company she was outwardly and formally polite, but he guessed that Beth and the shrewd button eyes of Mrs. Prowse missed nothing. Even Ianthe must have been aware that something was wrong, for one day when she and Donna were alone in the conservatory, the child said bluntly, with her large dark eyes full on her stepmother's face, "Why don't you and my father sleep together? Don't you like him any more?"

After a moment's hesitation Donna said, with the color mounting her face, "What a stupid question. I've not been well. Anyway, it's not your business."

"Why? Aunty Rosina says . . ."

Donna turned on her furiously. "What has she got to do with it? And how dare you pry into my . . . my private affairs?"

Ianthe shrugged. "She's nice. Father thinks so too. They had tea in Penzance yesterday, and Aunty Rosina bought me a game to play. I'll show you if you like . . . shall I fetch it?"

From crimson, Donna's cheeks had turned to ivory-white. Her whole body was trembling when she said, "No, no thank you. I'm sorry, I don't feel like games Ianthe. I'm going up to my room."

As she went to the door, closing it behind her, she could feel the little girl's eyes boring into her back, confused and unhappy, not understanding the upsurge of anger that her innocent remark had caused.

Rosina! Rosina! Donna thought, when she reached her bedroom. Always Rosina. So they'd been meeting again, she and Nicholas. In spite of all that he'd said—how she'd bored and wearied him, how thankful he'd been to get her out of the way, he had contrived an assignation in the full light of day, and with his own child into the bargain.

Well, that just showed. It was the final proof that she needed. In spite of all she had done for him—risking her life for him over that stupid Revenue affair—he didn't really care for her at all. After humiliating her physically in the privacy of their own home, he was now humiliating her publicly by running after the obnoxious Miss Penverrys. Probably they had both laughed at her together on numerous occasions; quite probably she was already his mistress, as others had been before her, and when an opportunity came for release from his frustrating marriage, he would take her legally and more than willingly to his bed.

So be it, Donna thought, surveying her cold image in the mirror. She was done with Nicholas Trevarvas. And at the first opportunity she would tell him so again in no uncertain terms.

The opportunity came earlier than expected. Just two minutes later, after a brief tap, Nicholas entered the room. He was carrying a bunch of roses, with a warm, almost supplicating look in his eyes.

She turned quickly, and her face chilled him.

"Donna . . ."

"This is my room now," she said. "Please go."

The flowers dropped from his hand to the carpet, and for a moment it seemed that he would comply. Then he changed his mind, strode across the floor, and took her by the shoulders.

"Look Donna, there's no point in this. It's ridiculous. We can't forever be under one roof spitting and scratching. Won't you meet me, now, and put the past behind?"

"I can't," she said. "Why should I?"

"Because you're my wife, and carrying my child."

"Oh!" She laughed contemptuously. "Your child. Yes, I understand. I suppose you'd like another son—one you can bully and bend and mold to your own image. That's generally what men of your type want, I believe. Well—if it's so important to you, you can have him—when he's born. If it is a boy of course. But I shan't be here Nicholas. As soon as the baby is old enough I shall leave you. Do you understand?" His arms fell away.

He actually winced, and from the look on his face—dumbfounded, and stricken—she knew how she'd hurt him. He appeared much older suddenly, defeated, as though all hope for the future had been swept away. Then, with his features hardening into the set mold she knew so well he said, "We'll see about that. But if you go, it will be alone, Donna. No son or daughter of mine will go with you. In any case aren't such plans a little precipitate?"

"You forced them."

"In what way?"

"By reminding me that I'm your wife. That's something I'd rather forget, and you, too, I should think—for both our sakes."

"What the devil do you mean?"

She turned her back on him and went to the mirror with a pretense of tidying her hair. Through the glass she could see him standing watching her, mouth grim, eyes dark and smoldering from the shadows.

"I think you know," she said calmly—far more calmly than she felt. "Rosina—or is it Regan? No, I'm sure it's Rosina. Regan's hardly the type to marry. But Rosina would be, wouldn't she? She'd bring you so much—and don't tell me you haven't been seeing her, Nicholas. I know you have." She wheeled round suddenly, breathing quickly, her eyes blazing pools of fire in her white face. "Don't think I care, though. Once I did, but I don't any more. Lie and lust with her as much as you like, so long as you don't dare to touch me."

There was a highly charged, long-drawn-out silence between them, until Nicholas said coldly and very clearly, "I don't need your permission, madam. I shall sleep with any woman I wish to, on any occasion I choose. And I shall never again lay a finger on you. After what you've just said I would as soon bed a cobra."

He turned sharply, and went out, closing the door with a slam that shook the floor.

Donna stood motionless as the color slowly returned to her face. Down the corridor she could hear his steps receding gradually, until at last all was quiet.

Deadly quiet. No sound but the clock ticking, and the frail tap of a twig against the window.

She moved presently and sat down on the bed. It was over at last. There'd be no more demands and refusals of reconciliation. He had meant what he said. For those few seconds she'd glimpsed more than annoyance or even dislike on his face. Hatred or contempt—but it didn't matter. The breach now was final between them.

As for the child—she wished irrationally and desperately that it had never been conceived. To be born of hate not love—what chance would it have?

At that moment she longed for her father as she had never done before. But her father was dead, and her home destroyed. In all the world there was no one of her own to turn to. In those first throes of self-pity, the tears rushed to her eyes. She got up from the bed and turned the key in the lock.

Then she cried, not with the impetuous abandonment of youth, but hopelessly and silently into her pillow, wondering how she would get through the days and years ahead.

When at length she had recovered sufficiently to wash and powder her face, she noticed the red roses lying where they'd dropped near her feet. One by one she picked them up and placed them in water, thinking how dark they were—velvety rich, with a lingering perfume about them that somehow contrived to express the deepest pain.

She pushed the vase from her, went to the window and opened it, waiting for the wild scent of heather and sea to flood the warm air.

It did not come. It wouldn't of course. Trencobban land was miles away. Here was only verdant closeness, with the thick earthy scent of evergreen and foliage hovering over the lush gardens and fields.

She had an overwhelming desire to be away by the cromlech overlooking Gwynvoor, to rest her face against the cold standing stones as she had done as a child, believing them to be wise and ancient creatures born of the Lordly Ones.

So she dressed herself in a green frock and plaid cape, and presently went downstairs. Nicholas she found, to her relief, had already gone, although no one seemed to know where.

"He didn't say," Mrs. Prowse said curtly in answer to her inquiry. "So it's not for long I'd think. You're going out are you madam?"

Donna nodded.

"Hm." The short comment was expressive of extreme disapproval. "There's a mist coming up, and you as you are, you're surely not riding?"

"Oh no," Donna replied briefly. "Just a stroll."

So they all knew, she thought, with grudging distaste. You as you are . . . how the grapevine worked. And who had spread the news? For certainly nothing really showed yet under the draped full skirts she wore.

Still it was unimportant. Let them say, think, guess what they liked. She didn't care a fig for a single one at Polbreath. Not even Beth. Her life was her own, and no one in the future was going to order or tell her what to do.

In this rebellious mood she walked sharply away from Polbreath crossing the lane near the turn and taking the track she had ridden so often on Saladin that skirted Rosebuzzan to the moors. The mist thickened as she climbed, jeweling her eyes and hair, brushing her lips with the faint faraway tang of sea. The furze and the twisted gorse were cobwebbed. Through the curdling air the large boulders had the crouched, brooding quality of immense primeval beasts come to greet her. She had the strangest sensation of walking through some dream-world to her own—her rightful—home. And as she neared the cromlech, the spirits of those who had gone before—who'd met and fashioned the pattern of her existence—seemed to converge and receive her, until nothing was real any more but the thickening milk-white mist, the bittersweet tang of earth and heather, and the one inside of her, the one she rejected yet still claimed life.

"Forgive me," her heart cried, as she eased herself to a rock, clutching her stomach. "You are mine . . . mine . . ." knowing in a moment of awareness that this

390

one thing was true, and would remain so. Nothing in the world would take him from her, the son to be born of her flesh and of the dark horseman. However much she might disclaim or resent, he would survive.

A tremendous sensation of awe filled her. She crouched there waiting, though what she waited for she didn't know. But the standing stones . . . born of the Lordly Ones . . . seemed to gather closer, filling her spirit and strange tawny eyes with a knowledge beyond all earthly things. And she remembered the day Nicholas had taken her in the heather, the wildness and sweetness of it, the teasing and laughter—the peace that followed. It seemed so long since she had laughed that way with the sheer joy of living. Nicholas . . . Nicholas . . . did the wild birds cry his name as they rose suddenly squawking to the sky? Did the whole hillside whisper it, trembling through the bracken as the small breeze rose and died again fitfully? Or was it merely in her own mind . . . a Celtic inner sense of what should be, her need and deepest heart's desire? Here, in this ancient place if anywhere, the truth must lie. She traced the cold granite with her hand, notched and ancient, symbolic of the earth's first eruption into life. And it seemed momentarily that something responded beneath her fingers.

Then it passed. The vision of the Lordly Ones had gone. Only the stones remained, with the mist thickening and spreading into deeper fog. She felt suddenly chilled, yet strangely at peace, her mind clear for the first time for many weeks. Like a ballet of conflicting forces, past events came into focus. She saw herself for what she was—jealous, proud, and unprepared to give an inch, taking what she had a mind to, and denying the rest. Co-operation, her father had said—without co-operation nothing was any use. He had understood her so well. Known from earliest youth the rebellious streak in her. Like a boy she had fought to keep her own, but the mine had failed, and Trencobban was but a shell. Tom, her one real friend, had died through loyalty to her. He had never *really* believed in that wealth of tin, she could see it now, looking back, but had done his best, simply because she demanded it, she, Donna Penroze, William's daughter. So many people had shaped their lives on her account. Even Hayley Grantham had been prepared to. But he had known that it was no use—sent her instead back to Nicholas by his tales of *La Belle Julie*.

There *was* no *Belle Julie*. She knew it suddenly, with a flash of clarity that piqued and at the same time humbled her. How clever he'd been; or was it that she'd merely been so obvious and gauche in handling her own emotions? Hayley was a nice man, but of course he didn't matter. She'd used him, and in return he had offered her the one thing in the world she wanted— contact with Nicholas again. She'd *tried* then, started the fire, done all she could to keep him out of trouble, but then the next day . . . remembering had started, and the old bitterness had risen, creating once more a wall of hatred and misunderstanding.

How simple it appeared now, here in the loneliness, where she could think for herself, her mind clear like a sheet of paper on which events could be clarified into words. As for Rosina . . . Rosina was nothing; or would be nothing if she, Donna, handled her properly.

Without realizing it, she got to her feet laboriously, and found to her dismay that her limbs would hardly move, chilled as they were by fog and waiting. How long had it been? Minutes or hours? She couldn't judge. Time hadn't registered. She drew her cape round her, huddling her arms against the woollen tartan. It was wet. Everything was wet and dripping, and clammily cold. So dark too. The evening must be falling, behind the fog and cloud, and except for the stones—her ancient companions—and one immense rounded boulder on her left, she had no clue to guide her. The rough path, overhung and dripping, was lost.

Nature had retreated into uniformity, and now, balanced and rational, she knew no stones or figments of imagination could aid her. Dreams were dreams and facts were facts. She had to cling to the latter, using all her senses and practical ability, or she could be lost on the moor for the night. And there were old shafts about too. Dark wells of nothingness concealed only by a film of bramble and weeds into which one could fall and lie at the dank bottom for hours or days, screaming for help until at last death replaced the screams when no one heard. By day and in a proper light she knew exactly the localities of such sinister relics, as riders and all local people did. But now, with the furred air thick in her eyes and lungs she realized that every step would be hazardous unless she kept reasonable bearings.

She turned and made her way cautiously past the great boulder that legend called Witch Stone, taking a direction to her left, which she knew with luck should eventually bring her down to the valley skirting the base of Rosebuzzan. No path was discernible. And from the tearing claws of gorse and bramble, she then knew she had lost it. Several times she paused, peering helplessly through the gray light, trying to discern some familiar landmark looming a little ahead. There was none.

She stopped presently, and cupping her hands, called, "Hallo . . . hallo . . ." but there was no response, and she started on again, her limbs growing heavier and more tired with every moment.

Was Nicholas back? she wondered, as she moved ahead, crouching instead of upright, and if so, would he care about her, or bother to go looking? She couldn't blame him if he didn't. What was it he'd said at their last encounter? . . . He'd as soon sleep with a cobra, or something of the sort. Well, she was like a cobra now, or some frightened adder, slithering and creeping through the furze, body icy and dripping, senses, though tired, strained, tense, and alert.

The journey seemed interminable. But at last, quite suddenly, she was there, with the mist lifting briefly to show her the glimmer of a lane winding fitfully, ribbon-like into the billowing fog. She rested for a moment, then continued, judging that she had still a mile to go before reaching Polbreath. And as she forced her legs mechanically onward she remembered the gypsies and

Chicknee, who had given her help on her flight from Nicholas.

How ridiculous it all seemed now. And yet she'd had to show him. Dispel once and for all the notion that he could use her like any primitive squaw. She wondered where they were now . . . what lanes they traveled, and to what strange destination? And was that a brown face rounding the corner? Hand outspread as though to dispel the encroaching elements?

"Chicknee . . ." she cried with a sudden warm glow enfolding her, "Chicknee . . . Chicknee . . ."

But it was not Chicknee.

Chicknee had been a small, lithe sapling of a youth; this man was broad and strong, and seemed as he approached, to fill the sky, blotting out the fog and all the menace of the evening.

Nicholas!

She waited for a moment, and then as he strode quickly toward her, ran a few breathless steps ahead, and was caught up into his arms, with her wet body crushed hard against his, so hard that she thought her ribs must break, and the breath die out of her. This time, though, she didn't kick or struggle. But the tears—though he didn't know it—were wet on her cheeks, mingling with the dampness of the dripping air, her heart, in spite of the cold, warm for the first time since their parting so many weeks ago.

And all the way back he was alternately scolding and muttering endearments. "You little tramp you . . . to take off like that . . . oh Donna, how could you? . . . And in the fog too. It's been an hour of hell . . . did you know that? I took Pluto first . . . but it was no use in all this. Why did you do it? Why, why? To drive me mad, was that it? I didn't mean what I said. You must have known, didn't you? Was it just—d'you want me to suffer? Haven't you done enough? Oh Donna it's not fair. I love you so. Understand? Love . . . love . . . *love!*"

His lips touched her cheek for a moment as she glanced up at him, pressing closer, closer, wanting to curl into him forever and be one, deep and secure as the kernel of a nut in its shell.

"Yes," she said. "I do. That's why . . ."

"Shsh! don't tire yourself. We'll soon be back."

She reached up suddenly and unpredictably tweaked his ear with a cold hand. "I'm not tired, not any more. I'm strong you know, and I . . . I love you, Nicholas. I do really.

He grunted, and stood still, staring down at her.

"Just for that, Mrs. Trevarvas, I've a mind to put you down and let you walk, to prove it."

But he didn't, and by the time they reached Pol-breath she was already asleep, curled up in his arms like a child.

CHAPTER TWENTY-EIGHT

All night Donna lay close in the curve of Nicholas's body, one of his arms loosely over her, the other beneath her, encircling a breast. Once or twice she stirred and half woke. His leg then stretched out automatically and he eased himself over while desire flowed from one to the other, and their flesh fused warmly and gently until they were one. Passion, in a deep tide, mounted rhythmically until the ultimate throb of mutual climax. Then there was peace for a time. They lay at rest bemused and still with each other, until at last he withdrew himself quietly, and glancing down through the darkness on the soft curve of cheeks and breasts, let his fingers and then his lips trace each gentle outline.

Sleep was fitful, but full of tranquility till one or the other stirred again, inciting love.

When morning came Nicholas was the first to wake. He lay for some time watching her, the deep even rise and fall of her breasts, and flushed rosy glow of her skin against the pillows, where the soft hair spread its ebony flood. Desire swelled in him with the urge to take her once more. But love and a queer kind of pity for her youth and vulnerability proved stronger than his need, and he swung out of bed lightly, and went to the bathroom where he had a cold wash and stringent rubdown.

He was already dressed when Donna woke.

"Nicholas," she said.

He went to the bed, lifted her up, and held her briefly to his chest. Then he chucked her under the chin. "You're a fine one and no mistake. Keeping me awake half the night, and expecting me to be ready for a hard morning's work, full of manly drive and purpose."

"What work?" she queried, her eyes wide and luminous on his own. "I thought you were a man of leisure." She paused before adding, "Come here, please, close. Don't leave me."

"Donna darling, if I once got between those sheets again, I'd be lost, as you well know. And it so happens that today I've quite a lot to do."

"Such as?"

"Sending Beth and Sarne to collect your things from The Boar, and a little visit to your doctor."

"There's no need."

"There's every need, sweet. You had a long spell on the moors and I'm taking no risks. Just as soon as I can get him he'll be here, and so will you, all warm and obedient in bed. And that's an order. Then I have a letter to write—a very important letter to a certain young lady called Rosina Penverrys . . ."

"*No!*"

"Telling her that under the circumstances, as my wife and I are curtailing all social commitments for a time it would be better for us to have no contact in the immediate future, and we would be grateful therefore if she refrained from calling until specifically requested. Nevertheless with grateful thanks for the interest shown in Ianthe's well being—I remain, Yours sincerely . . . et cetera . . . et cetera . . ."

He broke off, watching the impish gleam in Donna's eyes, the lurking triumph around her lips when she said, "She won't like that will she?" giggling, "especially the bit about Ianthe?"

"No. She won't. And you should be ashamed, forcing me into such an obnoxious situation."

"Oh I don't know. I think you deserve it, Nicholas, I really do. Besides you've never told me yet how far you went with the scheming creature."

"And I never will, my love," Nicholas replied maddeningly. "So that's something to ponder about isn't it?

Remember . . ." after kissing her hard, "no man decries one woman to another . . . especially his own wife, unless he happens to be a particularly nasty sort of individual."

"A sort of code you mean?"

He nodded. "Exactly."

"Pooh! a fig for codes," Donna said coquettishly. "Men are such cowards really. They simply have to have a code or something to hide under. And all an excuse."

He grinned. "You won't get me that way either. So for heaven's sake forget Rosina. She isn't worth it."

Donna looked smug. "That's all I wanted to know."

The morning passed uneventfully, although after the doctor's visit, which confirmed Donna's assertions that she was as fit as a fiddle, she *did* fancy Nicholas had a speculative gleam in his eye, an air of concealing something that had her immediately on tenterhooks.

When she was dressed and had come downstairs again a little later, she couldn't resist asking, "What are you thinking about, Nicholas?"

They were in the library where Trevarvas had been glancing through a book on minerology.

"Why?"

"I don't know. I can sense something. A sort of problem . . . is it?"

He put the book down quickly. "No, not exactly. It could be I suppose, if I cared to consider it properly."

"Do tell me," she begged.

"Well . . . I suppose you've got a right. It's about Trencobban."

"Trencobban?"

"This morning on the way back from the doctor, I skirted the land there. Sometime soon I suggest that the old wall's knocked down and flattened. It's really an eyesore, and we don't want that on our—on your land—do we?"

"Perhaps not," she agreed reluctantly.

"It was then, thinking about it, that I noticed something."

398

In an instant her attention was roused. "What? What did you notice?"

"On one side, where the old wing was, the soil looks odd."

"How do you mean odd?"

"A different color from the rest," he told her. "Not entirely black like the other, but reddish gray, yes, distinctly red, especially on the fringe."

"Go on."

"Now that was the oldest part of the house, wasn't it?"

"Oh yes. Centuries and centuries older. I believe there was a building there of some sort even before Trencobban itself was properly built as a manor. But what's so important in that?"

"I'm not an expert," Nicholas continued, "but I do know enough about mineral deposits to think—just *think,* mind you—that tin or maybe copper could be there. Could have been lying at the far side for God knows how long—maybe before the early streamers even started. And if so, if I'm right, a level could run from there in the opposite direction to Wheal Faith, either down or up toward Gwynvoor; machinery could be sunk from the surface in that case, but of course I don't know. It's all guesswork. Still, worth investigating, don't you think?"

Donna was silent for some moments, trying hard to assess the full meaning of Nicholas's suggestion. When at last she got the import she said with a touch of awe in her voice, "You mean that Wheal Faith could start up again?"

"I don't know. The old mine-house might not be a commercial proposition. In any case I may be onto a pipe dream. We'd have to get expert opinion on that one first. I'm not an engineer, Donna. But that color— and so clearly marked from the rest—it seemed odd. There could be a damp patch of course, near the surface. But where there's damp there's generally some sort of current below. That's logic."

"I'd like to go and see," Donna said presently. "Will you come with me?"

"All right," Nicholas agreed, "tomorrow. In the morning if it's fine. But promise me one thing."

"Yes?"

"Don't go setting your heart on things until we're sure. And don't be shocked when you get there. It isn't a pretty sight, and will probably revive a lot in your mind you ought to forget."

"Oh no. Nothing will be revived that isn't there already," Donna said firmly. "I've no illusions about Trencobban, Nicholas. That's one of the things I won't forget—ever. The way it burned that night. It may even help me, facing it again. It's so easy to think back and see something you loved as it once was, instead of what it's become. A hard glance at the present—you know what I mean, don't you? Like a woman, I suppose, a woman who's once been young and beautiful, and refuses to admit that she's old and past it. Then one day in a clear light she suddenly sees herself as she really is, in her mirror." She shivered involuntarily. "It must be awful. But I suppose, one day it'll happen to me and then I'll learn not to care."

He put his arm round her, sensing the sudden chill risen like a cloud to sadden her.

"Nonsense. You'll never be old or plain. Different perhaps, but that's life. And anyway . . ."—his voice faltered—". . . you'll always be the loveliest woman in the world to me—and the most maddening I've no doubt. So watch yourself, my love."

He turned away, suddenly embarrassed, adding more practically, "Maybe it isn't such a good idea after all taking you to Trencobban. To make you morbid would be the worst possible thing for both of us."

"I won't be morbid, I promise," she told him quickly. "And if you won't take me, I shall sneak off on my own one day, and be so shocked I'll probably throw myself off the cliff and drown."

Although she joked, he knew that she meant the first part, and gave in.

400

But before that, when Sarne and Beth returned after tea from Falmouth, with Donna's clothes and belongings in their various cases, she had a surprise, in the form of an accompanying letter from Hayley Grantham.

"Dear Donna," it ran, "I'm so glad that things have worked out in the way I intended, and you must forgive my phantom *Belle Julie*'s non-appearance. I didn't like lying to you, but if I hadn't concocted something, you could easily have been still with me at The Boar, and it obviously wouldn't have worked. Your swift action in going to your husband proved indisputably where your heart lay. I envy him very much, and wish I were in his shoes.

"A word of advice though—get him, if you can, to temper his adventurous inclinations with wisdom, and may I suggest—within the law. Initiative can be a worthy virtue when properly applied, but the very devil when it isn't. One wrong step and the balloon goes up. I wouldn't want that to happen, for your sake. I don't know how long I shall be here, a few months anyway, and if you both like to come and join me for a meal any evening, I'll be pleased to see you.

"Give my regards to your husband, and to yourself the very best of everything, my dear.

Take care of yourself,
    Yours ever in friendship,
    Hayley Grantham."

There was a postscript which ran: "If you should ever need a godfather and think an aging ex-editor would fit the role, I'd be delighted to oblige. Letters will be forwarded from here to any part of the globe where I may be. Adieu. H.G."

When Donna had read the letter she handed it to Nicholas. "He really is a very nice man," she commented. "And we do owe him something, Nicholas. Having him as a godfather might be a very good idea."

"Hm. I don't know about that. You might have died thanks to his crazy idea, and . . ."

"But I didn't, did I?" Donna interrupted smugly. "I came back."

"Did you? I rather thought I carried you. And anyway I prefer to think that you would have returned on your own in good time."

"Then think it, Nicholas." Donna said sweetly. "You keep your little secrets: about Rosina, I mean, and I'll keep mine."

"Are you asking to be spanked again, Mrs. Trevarvas?"

She flung herself against him. "I don't really mind, as long as you love me."

He strained her to him. "You really are a most beguiling creature. Too beguiling by half for your own good—and mine. I never realized before I knew you what peace of mind was. And now I've a notion I never will again."

She didn't say anything, realizing that all words between them just then were superfluous—a bantering façade to hide their deepest feelings.

The next morning, which was fine and filled with the thrusting promise and blossoming of young summer, Donna and Nicholas rode over to Trencobban. Donna on Bess, under strict injunctions from Nicholas to take no more jaunts on Saladin until after the baby's arrival.

"In fact this is the last time you'll go riding at all until then," Nicholas told her before setting off. "Walking's a different matter altogether. Do you understand?"

She slipped her hand into his. "Of course I understand. Oh Nicholas, you really are absurd. Such an old granny all of a sudden. And I'm strong as a horse. Doctor Maddern said so."

"Doctors don't know everything, although I've a hunch he may be right in your case. Come along then. No more arguing."

He gave Bess a slap on the flanks, jumped onto Saladin himself, and a minute later they were off, going at a steady pace, by the easiest route along the valley road then up to the high wide track stretching toward Trencobban.

As they approached the ruin, a flood of nostalgia, almost anguish, filled her. The view appeared so bleak without the familiar gray chimneys and square-fronted house. Cutting down from the moor Donna noticed how few of the trees remained bordering what used to be the drive, and how withered and stark they appeared, with gaunt singed arms only flecked with green. The ground and undergrowth around the single charred wall was still a wilderness of blackened soil and tangled burned masonry. Jagged splintered wood stuck up in places like the skeleton arms of something taken and destroyed under torture. Broken, charred bricks lay everywhere.

For a moment, seeing it at close range, a sense of sickness rose in her. With a lump in her throat, Donna put a hand to her eyes, trying to dispel the sudden surge of memories rising like ghosts from the dead to torment her.

"Here . . . steady on now," she heard Nicholas saying, as he took her arm. "I know it's awful. But it will pass. Look . . ."

She glanced up at him, and he urged her forward to a blackened stone, where a pale oasis of green was already spearing the dark earth nearby, and blossoming buds of purple and blue were beginning to show their heads.

"Bluebells," Donna said. "How strange, already."

"You can't beat nature, sweetheart," Nicholas remarked. "The bulbs must have been waiting somewhere ready to burst out—in the garden possibly, or by a path. The old earth doesn't waste much time."

Donna shivered. "But all this—the waste."

"We'll have it cleared away. I'll see to that this week. But at the moment try to forget the destruction. Come on, take my hand; it's over here. That patch we came for. Remember?" When she didn't speak his voice sharpened. "Donna, don't brood."

She pulled herself together and went along with him to the far side of the derelict property, where once windows had looked out toward the slope leading to Gwynvoor.

"There," Nicholas said. "That's what I mean."

What he had said was quite true. Although most of

the immediate surrounding terrain was still scorched, the dark grayish-red stain had been caused by tin. Or copper. And if it was so, it had lain all the time unsuspected under the foundations of Trencobban itself.

It took some time for the knowledge properly to penetrate Donna's confused mind. When it did she said, "And you mean—you really mean it could all be true? My father's hope—all he'd lived for?" Her words died, swallowed by an impatient whinny from Saladin.

"It just could be," Nicholas told her cautiously. "As I've said, we'll have to find out, and then decide what to do. It'll take a deal of thinking about. You must realize that."

"Yes of course." Donna's eyes strayed instinctively back over the tumbled house, prompting her to ask for the first time a question that had bothered her intermittently since the fire. "Do you think anyone started it, Nicholas? Anyone with a grudge?"

Nicholas shook her gently by the arm. "No. If there were slightest proof or suggestion of it, the police and insurance would have soon cottoned on to it. We shall never know the truth, Donna. The house was old and filled with ancient timber. Any chance spark—a lighted match thrown by some tramp or traveler could have ignited and started the whole blaze. An itinerant might easily have made his own fire there for comfort and taken off as soon as the thing got going. But there's no sign of deliberate arson, and it's best to let that side of the thing die now." He paused before asking, "Why though? What made you ask? Had you anyone in mind?"

"Not really," Donna replied. "I did wonder at first about Jed. He had a reason. It was through Jessica, and she was a Penroze, that he lost his arm; he had a grudge against the mine—or blamed my father for its failure if you like—then that night you beat him up, it was Jed you know. He always had his eye on me, and after that he couldn't miss a chance of insulting me. Then the Lucien business—he thought he had a claim there. But when we got married he guessed it would be no use any more."

"I always thought it was Jed," Nicholas said, though without emotion. "And you should have told me in the beginning. But no. You had to protect him. Why?"

"Because he was an excellent miner and a skilled engineer," Donna answered. "Tom thought that if I'd dismissed him there'd have been trouble. And he was probably right. Tom knew men."

"He may have done," Nicholas said grimly. "But being a pacifier, and a gentleman like your father was, doesn't always pay off. Sometimes brutality needs brutal action. Still, that man is to be pitied in a way."

"Pitied?"

"Oh yes. I'll grant him that. He's already lost a limb, and he saved your life. For that alone it seems to me I'll forever be in his debt."

"I can't understand you. Really I can't."

"You're a woman, my sweet. And I'm a man. So's Jed. Only he happens to be on the losing side."

Little more was said between them, until Donna remarked suddenly, "Let's go, Nicholas. I've seen all I want, the—the destruction, and the tin—if it really is. I'd like to get away."

"Not quite yet, Donna," Nicholas told her, with a new, rather strange note in his voice. "First of all I want you to take me to that place."

"What place?"

"The exact spot, my dear, where that infamous young half-brother of mine tried to ravish you."

"Oh but . . ." Donna winced, "No, no! It's all over. He explained. Lucien told you, and it was true . . . please Nicholas, not that. I thought . . ."

"You thought I was going to go through my life—our life—together, knowing there was any patch of ground in Cornwall or elsewhere that my wife couldn't visit without meeting a ghost?" He shook his head. "That's not my way, love. You're going with me now, even if I have to carry you, and we're going to stand there together, you and me, and do a little exorcism of our own."

There was a silence in which the gentle Cornish wind seemed to chill suddenly, filling her with dread.

"I wish you wouldn't," she whispered. "I wish you could believe me."

"Oh but I do. It's nothing to do with belief or not trusting you. It's just what I said. No other man's image is going to haunt our territory. This land is ours, Donna, and ours alone."

So presently, having tethered the two horses safely to a sturdy sycamore at the top of the cliff track, he went cautiously ahead of her for safety, stopping now and again to ease her over stones and jagged clefts, insisting on giving a hand although she could have managed better on her own, knowing the way so well.

Once she said, with a hint of impatience, "Oh Nicholas I'm not an idiot or an invalid. I've gone this way hundreds of times."

"Ah. So you have," he said, turning to look into her eyes. "What's the matter? Frightened?"

"Why should I be?"

"Ghosts? The past?"

Her lips tightened. "Don't be stupid. But I do think it's rather silly trying to resurrect everything. I don't understand you."

"Don't try," he replied abruptly. "Just concentrate on keeping your foothold and getting safely to the bottom."

When they reached the cove the tide was quiet and some way out, leaving the sand pale and even with only a few shining pools glistening between huddled rocks. A few seagulls were pecking about in a drift of seaweed, and two shags stood slim and dark on the tip of a small islet beyond the tide's rim.

"Pleasant," Nicholas said, drawing the salty air into his lungs. "Very picturesque."

"Don't speak as though you've never set eyes on it before," Donna said quickly. "I remember more than once looking up and seeing you on the cliff with Pluto."

406

"And the day you climbed up with your mine manager's son. Remember that too?"

Donna frowned. As though she could ever forget.

"What are you trying to do?" she demanded with a hint of temper.

His arm was around her waist suddenly, tightening before he released her, "No questions, my love. Just show me where he laid you."

"He didn't, though. This is unfair of you."

"Maybe. But I'm that sort of man, Donna. I've got to see for myself. Go on—take me. And remember, much as I love you, *because* of it—I'll know if you're telling the truth or not."

"All right, if that's how you feel, follow me. And if you stub your toe I shall laugh my head off."

She went before him, lifting her riding skirt delicately, showing an edge of cream underwear, stepping lightly as a young goat over the projecting tongue of rock, while jealous desire mounted in him with a hot longing to have her then and there—forever dispelling the distasteful memory of his brother's blundering intrusion.

She jumped down easily on the other side of the cove. The rocky inlet was shadowed and dark; a narrow aperture where only pale beams of sunlight penetrated at that hour, giving a dramatic effect as though designed by nature for theatrical enterprise. Nicholas could well understand how Lucien's artistic sense had been fired into something else: something more primitive and far more dangerous.

"Well?" he said, looking meaningfully at his wife.

The color of her skin, radiant through the fitful light, deepened to rose, as she queried, with the suggestion of a quiver in her voice, "What do you mean, 'well'?"

"Which was it? Which rock, or stone, or sandy niche?"

"You really are the limit. How can I remember such a stupid thing?"

"Don't prevaricate, Donna. You remember all

407

right—as any girl would who'd been seduced—well, as good as—by a handsome young man."

She sighed, and looked around, shrugging as she pointed to a boulder immediately under a receding point of cliff. Nicholas glanced at it then looked up. "So that's where he was . . . that cad Jed."

"Yes. Unspeakable, wasn't it?"

"So were you."

"But I . . ."

He picked her up and carried her with a minimum of resistance to the very spot where Lucien, so many months ago, had tried to ravish her. He sat down, pulling her onto his knee, holding her firmly, his dark eyes on her face reflectively.

"Poor boy," he said. "I can almost pity him."

"Pity? Lucien?"

"Of course. He hadn't an earthly chance, had he? And you knew it."

"Oh no I didn't."

"Then why did you ever bring him here?"

"Because I—because I suppose I like . . ."

"Danger? Temptation? A bit of flirting?"

She dimpled. "Yes. I'm afraid I did want him to admire me and feel romantic—at first, though. Only at first."

"And you succeeded, didn't you? Donna, my love. I should have given you a far sounder beating than I did that night, and if I ever catch . . ."

Her hand went to his lips silencing the threat before it was out. "Don't say it. Don't scold any more. I'm a woman, Nicholas."

"Are you? I'm not sure. Still . . ." his mouth came down on hers; her arms reached to his neck, as slowly and purposefully he loosened her clothes and his own, taking her once more to him.

"You're awful," she protested weakly. "Simply awful, Nicholas. To think that . . ."

"Hush. Be quiet, love. No words. We've talked such a lot in the past. Oh Donna . . . Donna . . ."

A gull wheeled overhead screaming mournfully as it flew upward to the west. But they did not hear.

Union was perfect, and complete.

Presently he got up, and pulled her to her feet. "Tidy yourself, darling," he said. "You look a real gypsy."

"Maybe I am one," she said, and looking around, "Nicholas, this really is a place for loving, isn't it?"

He waited before telling her. "That's what I wanted you to say. That was the whole idea. To have it *ours* . . . and no one else's."

"And we have now. You were right after all," she said dreamily.

"Yes."

They sat there for a time quietly and at peace, until he took her hand, leading her at a leisurely pace over the rocks to the cliff path. When they reached the top a few clouds had risen, temporarily dimming the sun.

"Funny," she said retrospectively, "when I saw you that day with Jos, staring from the moor, I had a strange feeling that something—queer was going to happen. A sort of foreboding. And it did. My father died."

"Oh, Donna."

"For a long time I connected you with it. Took you as a sort of symbol, like the dark horseman—that other dark horseman of Carn Kenidzeck, the Hooting Carn. I know now it was silly, and it's only a legend anyway—a Cornish legend."

"Hm! well make sure you remember that I'm real and tough enough to manage you; and that's saying quite a lot."

"Yes." Her hand clutched his tightly. "Keep me that way Nicholas. I'm wild and strange, and my temper's awful sometimes. But I will try to be good, and the kind of wife you should have. I suppose I was only jealous of Rosina because of things she could give you, material things I haven't got."

As they untethered their horses and mounted, a fox quickly darted from the undergrowth, speeding across the path toward the moor below Gwynvoor.

409

Somewhere a lark sang.

Then with a glow of spreading peace and fulfillment about them, they turned and started off at a leisurely pace for Polbreath.

During the next month Nicholas had two confrontations which would have surprised Donna had she known at the time. The first was with Rosina Penverrys, from whom he extracted the promise of a visit to make her peace with his wife. The second was with Jed Andrewartha. Nicholas had the enormous satisfaction of informing the man that he now knew all about the blackmailing, and then surprised himself by offering him a few shillings extra to support his sick wife and keep himself out of trouble.

Henry Harvey, a mining engineer from Derby, had spent a few days with them, then visited Trencobban and confirmed that there was tin to be mined there. Nicholas knew that if they decided to exploit it, they would need all the skilled men they could find, and with this in mind, he told Andrewartha that there might even be a job for him in the future.

Jed shrugged. "Just so long as you doan' want bowin' an' scrapin' to, an' yes surr, no surr, an' thank'ee surr every time we meet et'll suit me, an' I'm not ungrateful. A bit more in my pocket could be a deal of help just now."

"Very well. I'll see about it."

Discomfited and inwardly taken aback by his own philanthropy, Nicholas walked away, wondering what the deuce had prompted him to go throwing more money about on a rascal like Jed, and came to the conclusion that Donna's influence was softening him.

When she heard about it, though, she was annoyed.

"Jed? But *why*, after the despicable way he acted? His wife, yes. I'm sorry for her; everyone is. But do you suppose for one moment that she'll see a penny of the extra, once it goes into his pocket?"

"We shall just have to find some way to ensure she benefits," Nicholas told her with a certainty he didn't feel.

"I don't see how, unless I go around myself shopping for her and delivering."

"Which you certainly won't, my love. Now leave things to me, please. It's my business and I'm quite capable of seeing to it. Anyway—you didn't object to compensation for the accident."

"No. But I didn't expect you to continue forever, and more at that."

"He's had nothing for some time. And he'll never grow another limb."

"There are other miners . . . decent_men and their families far more deserving," Donna persisted.

Nicholas sighed. "Leave it, will you," he said with a hint of irritation, "There are more important things to discuss than Andrewartha. Tin."

"Trencobban you mean? Opening it up?"

He was surprised at the uninterested inflection of her voice. "Of course. It's what you want, isn't it? The one thing in life you've set your heart on—Wheal Faith? A thriving mine?"

She hesitated before saying, "It was. Once."

"What do you mean, once?"

They were in the sitting room. She got up and walked to the window, staring out over the garden where the afternoon light was already beginning to fade behind the trees. He could sense a reluctance in her that puzzled him; a subtle fear quite uncharacteristic of her usual buoyant self.

After a long pause she turned and said, "Just how certain are you that any fresh project would succeed?"

"There's no absolute certainty until you get the thing going," Nicholas answered. "But both Harvey and I feel pretty confident."

"In the meantime many of our own miners—Wheal Faith's—have gone away," Donna pointed out. "The others know the worst and have faced it, in one way or another. I can't forget what it was like seeing hopes raised and fade again, or having to stave off riots and watch women like Mrs. Borde bear the brunt." She broke off, sighed and went on, "We'd have to take on

411

new workers. And that isn't what my father wanted. It wouldn't be the same." Her lip quivered.

Nicholas put his arm around her. "Donna—I thought you'd be so pleased. You were so excited when I first suggested it."

"I know. At the beginning. Then when I remembered I wasn't sure. The house stood there so long, Nicholas. Machinery and shafts and things—disturbing the land—oh, I may be silly, but it seems desecration somehow, especially where there's no guarantee at all that it'll pay off."

Nicholas let her go and stood some feet away regarding her speculatively. "Did you feel this way when Harvey came?"

"I didn't know what I felt. It was nice meeting him, and stimulating, I suppose, feeling that we could begin all over again. But afterward—I started seeing it all in a new light. Besides, it would take a lot of capital, wouldn't it?"

"That's my affair."

"No, no. Not entirely." She went toward him quickly, took his hand and said, "Look at me, Nicholas."

He bent his head warily, sensing that she had something up her sleeve, and although his instinct was to smile and brush her mouth with his own, he remained serious and aloof, for once refusing to be intimidated by the searching, deep glow of her eyes.

"Well?"

"Will you do something for me? Something rather big, for you, I mean?"

"It depends," he answered guardedly.

"You won't like it," she told him. "But now—now there's going to be a child, a boy probably, couldn't you give up your—your sidelines, those risky adventures you go in for? Why have you to do it, Nicholas? We're not poor, are we? It's not necessary. I mean . . ." She broke off helplessly, and when he didn't answer continued recklessly, "You owe it to us, to the child and me. What do you think it's going to be like in the future if every time you go out at night I wonder if you'll be back or taken away by the Revenue or something? Don't you see, for God's sake?"

"I see that wretched Grantham man put a load of tomfool notions into your head," Nicholas answered curtly.

"Did he? I don't think so. I think he knew quite a bit. *La Belle Julie* was a fairy tale I know. But the rest wasn't. And one day you may be caught—you or your business, your phony shipping concern."

Nicholas studied her thoughtfully; then he said, "Henry Harvey was right when he suggested that you had me by the nose and would soon be running my life."

"Did he say *that*?"

"He did, and I'm not having it. In the first place, where and how I make my income is my concern alone. And believe me, keeping you in all your finery makes quite a hole in my pocket to begin with. In the second, dropping any remunerative project at this moment would mean a considerable cut in expenditure. Think of it that way. Fewer servants and fine clothes. Probably no jaunts at all to London. No expensive Nanny for the baby . . ."

"I don't want a nanny," Donna interrupted fiercely. "And I've got more clothes than I need. As for London—one taste of it's enough where I'm concerned. And if Polbreath's my home I want a share in running it. Not just the stupid hostessy wife role—but to know what's going on in the kitchen and—and everything. Probably I'd have to learn a good bit. But Beth would teach me. And remember, before we married I'd been used to stinting and scraping for quite a long time."

"It's not a matter of stinting," Nicholas said.

"Then what? Just your stupid pride? Is that more important to you than my peace of mind?"

"Donna . . . *Donna!*" She pulled herself away quickly.

"No. I mean it Nicholas. And I want your promise. You owe it to me."

"My dear love, I owe you nothing. Except this." He

413

caught her back to him and kissed her hard. Then he said abruptly, "All right, if that's what you want. I capitulate. No mine either, no extravagance, no showing off to admiring males in new dresses you don't need, with fine jewelry I can't afford. In fact, my girl, I'll expect you to keep your nose well and truly to the domestic grindstone, or else!"

"Agreed. And no more little adventures, promise? Say it, *say* it, Nicholas."

He eventually did so, though not entirely with a good grace. But afterward he relented.

"Maybe you're right, love. The first importance is our life together. But about that land . . ."

"I've been thinking and wondering about it ever since Henry Harvey left," Donna admitted, "and thought that perhaps we could have a monument there—near the spot where the tin is."

"A monument?"

"Oh yes. Couldn't we? To my father and Tom, and all the miners who worked, and lost their lives through their services to Wheal Faith? Something like that . . ." She broke off, misty-eyed, with a sudden lump in her throat. "It could be near the cliff edge, overlooking the sea, a monument so everyone who passed there, in the future, would know a little bit more about Cornwall."

"And just how did you picture it, Donna?"

"A simple square slab of polished Cornish granite with my father's name and Tom's on it. I'd like that. Could we, do you think?"

Nicholas's arm tightened around her. "Of course."

"And you think it's a good idea?"

"The best idea possible," he told her.

Donna's baby, a boy, William Nicholas, was born on a wild autumn night when high gales lashed the coast, and the wind drove its fury against the gaunt cliffs.

He was a strong healthy child with Nicholas's features and Donna's eyes, the first of three sons and a daughter which she would bear in the next seven years.

In the morning the seas were calm and the wind had

dropped, leaving the cliffs quiet in the pale winter light.

As the sun climbed, its lifting rays lit the stone briefly to silvered splendor, cutting clearly and decisively across the simple lettering.

IN MEMORY OF WILLIAM PENROZE,
AND HIS LOYAL WORKERS, INCLUDING
THOMAS CRAZE, MINING MANAGER,
WHO LOST HIS LIFE LIKE OTHERS
BEFORE HIM THROUGH UNREMITTING
AND DEVOTED SERVICE TO WHEAL
FAITH.
ERECTED THROUGH
DONNA TREVARVAS,

DAUGHTER OF WILLIAM.

1883.

The passionate sequel to
the scorching novel of
fierce pride and forbidden love

THE PROUD HUNTER

by Marianne Harvey

Author of *The Dark Horseman*
and *The Wild One*

Trefyn Connor—he demanded all that was his—and
more—with the arrogance of a man who fought to
win . . . with the passion of a man who meant to possess his enemy's daughter and make her pay the
price!

Juliet Trevarvas—the beautiful daughter of The Dark
Horseman. She would make Trefyn come to her. She
would taunt him, shock him, claim him body and soul
before she would surrender to THE PROUD HUNTER.

A Dell Book $3.25   (17098-2)

At your local bookstore or use this handy coupon for ordering:

Dell	**DELL BOOKS** THE PROUD HUNTER $3.25 (17098-2)
	P.O. BOX 1000, PINEBROOK, N.J. 07058

Please send me the above title. I am enclosing $ _____
(please add 75¢ per copy to cover postage and handling). Send check or money
order—no cash or C.O.D.'s. Please allow up to 8 weeks for shipment.

Mr/Mrs/Miss_____

Address_____

City_____ State/Zip_____